THE
LEFT HAND
OF DARKNESS

THE
LEFT HAND
OF DARKNESS

URSULA K. LE GUIN

ACE
New York

ACE
Published by Berkley
An imprint of Penguin Random House LLC
1745 Broadway, New York, NY 10019

ISBN: 9780441478125

Ace mass-market edition / March 1969
Walker & Co. hardcover edition / 1969
Ace trade paperback edition / July 2000
Ace premium edition / December 2010

Printed in the United States of America
108   107   106   105   104   103   102   101   100   99

Cover design by Jim Tierney

DEDICATION:

For Charles,
sine qua non

CONTENTS

INTRODUCTION

BY DAVID MITCHELL

Of Ursula Le Guin's trio of masterpieces—The Earthsea series (1968–2001), *The Dispossessed* (1974) and *The Left Hand of Darkness* (1969)—it is the latter which guards its secrets most jealously and which, perhaps, asks the most of its reader. Not that it's a difficult novel by any stretch, but *The Left Hand of Darkness* stays faithful to its varied form: a report submitted by an anthropologist from Earth and "first contact" envoy, Genly Ai, to his superiors; interspersed with myths and legends from the planet Gethen (known to its extra-planetary visitors as Winter); observations by one of Genly's predecessors who studied the planet and its people undercover; and journal extracts written by Estraven, a Gethenian statesman. This patchwork architecture and its tonal shifts give *The Left Hand of Darkness* a staccato quality—an effect heightened by the dreamlike, stranger-in-a-strange-land quality of Genly's wanderings in the cities and countries of Karhide and Orgoreyn. (At one point a febrile nightmare about a nighttime raid turns almost imperceptibly into a real nighttime raid.) Certainly, the colors, textures, and echoes that the "interruptions" lend to Genly's primary narrative can be subtle, covert, and disorienting. But they are also rich and strange, and repay attention at a high rate of interest. To write this introduction I read the novel for the fifth time and I'm still finding new rooms behind new doors I never noticed before. The novel displays its author's rare combination of talents pretty much to perfection, and it's these talents that I'd like to discuss in brief here.

Ursula Le Guin is ("is" because her best work will long outlast her death) a thought experimenter. This is a common denominator of many science-fiction writers, but Le Guin is more ambitious in her choice of experiments than most of her peers, and more assiduous in tracking the consequences of those choices. In *The Dispossessed* the experiment is "What if a society evolved where nobody owned anything?" In *The Left Hand of Darkness* it is "What if gender was not fixed but serially mutable?" For most of their twenty-six-day month and cycle, Gethenians are androgynous and celibate, but for two or three days of kemmer they become sexually active as either male or female, with no say in which. Any individual, then, can be both a mother and father, and can bear and sire children. (This physiology gives rise to the novel's most memorable line, "The king was pregnant.") Genly—like most of the book's readers—possesses a single one unchanging gender, making him, from a Gethenian perspective, a biological anomaly to be pitied—or, less kindly, mistrusted as a "pervert." True to the greatest science fiction, Gethen is the thumb-print whose thumb is our own world, and the gender fluidity of Gethenians poses questions for the Homo sapiens of Earth. Le Guin is unafraid to take her time examining these questions. Does violence have a gender? Rape does not exist on Gethen, and seduction "would have to be awfully well timed," but what of marriage, sexism, misogyny, and feminism? Is gender at the core of the self, or is there a deep-down "Gethenian layer" where we, too, are neither male nor female? Is gender as immutable as most cultures on Earth still insist? Like a benign relative struggling with his own transphobia, Estraven struggles to understand Genly, and through Estraven's eyes, we witness the limits upon Genly's worldview that his single unchanging gender imposes. *The Left Hand of Darkness* was published in 1969, the year of the Stonewall Riots, and this was audacious territory for a little-known genre writer to explore. In many countries of our still-benighted world, this is dangerous territory. It's not difficult to see why, for many activists in the LGBTQ circles, *The Left Hand of Darkness* has accrued the status of an early seminal text.

* * *

Ursula le Guin is a creator of vivid worlds. Earthsea is one of the most fully realized worlds in fantasy, to my mind, and the Hainish Cycle, to which *The Left Hand of Darkness* belongs, is one of the most evocative series in science fiction. What Earthsea and the Hainish Cycle have in common is maximal impact with minimal page count. Both feel vast, as if the novels are only glimpses of worlds, not full delineations of them; as if worlds continue to follow their histories even when no reader is watching. Just as the Ekumen, the body that sent Genly Ai to announce its existence to Gethen, is a far-flung and sparse union of isolated planets, so the cycle of books that depict the Ekumen is far-flung (through Le Guin's writing life) and sparse. Le Guin's space opera exists not on sprawling canvasses but in a handful of not-very-long novels, and it's not even operatic. Its influences are more Taoist and animist than they are Roman or Asimovian. Most articles about Le Guin mention her father, a respected anthropologist, at the University of California, Berkeley—for the valid reason that Le Guin created her worlds with an anthropologist's eye not only for language, but for rituals, myths, and influence of geography on culture. Gethen feels too replete with persuasive details to be made up. Cliche withers away. Le Guin does not resort to evil masterminds or dystopian states needing to be overthrown by a plucky band of misfits. A mentally unstable king and a quasi-totalitarian state threaten Genly Ai's safety, but the true antagonists of *The Left Hand of Darkness* are very human bigotry, politicking and the harshness of the Gethenian climate. What action sequences there are occur offstage, or are handled with undramatic brevity. They serve as location shifters, not as adrenaline tweakers. Future tech plays a minimal role in Le Guin's science fiction, and there is no exotic alien megafauna. The biggest animals walking Gethen are human beings. Similarly, Genly Ai is no Luke Skywalker, no *Star Trek* captain, no Doctor Who. He is an unarmed man in his late twenties from a distant planet, a self-exile out of his political and cultural depth, at the mercy of events he rarely, or barely, grasps. For most of the novel he fails to notice that he'd be dead without Estraven's discreet interventions. What heroism he possesses is about surviving failure and failing better.

Ursula Le Guin is a chemist of the heart. She constructs her characters with the same eye for detail that she uses to build her worlds. On Gethen we encounter tyrants, lovers, traitors, climbers of politics' greasy pole, refugees, convicts, children, landladies, bureaucrats, and prison guards, all depicted with the ease and dignity of an old master, even those who exist only for a sentence or two. Le Guin's major characters are as flawed, fickle, contradictory, and as prone to doubt and muddle as we are. Perhaps this is why they are so compelling and believable. Running parallel to the geographic journeys in *The Left Hand of Darkness* (notably an epic Shackleton-esque trek across polar ice) is the inner journey of the two main characters, Genly and Estraven, toward each other. Only as they cross the ice, when their codependence is total, does Genly understand what Estraven has sacrificed for him; that Estraven has always been his one faithful ally. Only as they cross the ice, when Estraven dispenses with his shifgrethor code of manners and face-saving, does he understand why Genly failed so dismally to understand the shadow plays of the novel's first two-thirds. The polar journey is both a metaphor for, and an act of, mutual understanding. A lesser chemist of the heart would emphasize the common ground of their joint humanity. Le Guin recognizes that it's the difference that is the point, that no bridge between two people—no friendship, no love—can exist without difference. There is no difficulty or achievement in understanding someone who is already very like you. Genly realizes ". . . it was from the difference between us, not from the affinities and likenesses, but from the difference, that that love came: and it was itself the bridge, the only bridge, across what divided us."

Finally, Ursula Le Guin is a planter of signposts to Utopia. Gethen is as full of self-serving arsonists posing as patriots and realists as our own embattled twenty-first century so far. Integrity and idealism are as apparently fragile in the cities of Karhide and Mishnory as they are in the capitals of Earth. Le Guin's 1960s analyses of bigotry, xenophobia, and dog-whistle politics have not dated one whit. I think they never shall. But

Le Guin's writing—in *The Left Hand of Darkness* as powerfully as anywhere—also dares to posit how society could be better and fairer and wiser than the one we have. Le Guin's fiction about others dreams seditious dreams for this one. It asserts that dysfunctions and injustices perpetrated by human beings can be amended and redeemed by those same human beings. It is a quiet, insistent call to arms by and for the better angels of our nature. Utopia may exist only in signposts to Utopia, but that's enough; it'll do; it'll have to. Just as long as we have those signposts.

AUTHOR'S NOTE

Science fiction is often described, and even defined, as extrapolative. The science fiction writer is supposed to take a trend or phenomenon of the here-and-now, purify and intensify it for dramatic effect, and extend it into the future. "If this goes on, this is what will happen." A prediction is made. Method and results much resemble those of a scientist who feeds large doses of a purified and concentrated food additive to mice, in order to predict what may happen to people who eat it in small quantities for a long time. The outcome seems almost inevitably to be cancer. So does the outcome of extrapolation. Strictly extrapolative works of science fiction generally arrive about where the Club of Rome arrives: somewhere between the gradual extinction of human liberty and the total extinction of terrestrial life.

This may explain why many people who do not read science fiction describe it as "escapist," but when questioned further, admit they do not read it because "it's so depressing."

Almost anything carried to its logical extreme becomes depressing, if not carcinogenic.

Fortunately, though extrapolation is an element in science fiction, it isn't the name of the game by any means. It is far too rationalist and simplistic to satisfy the imaginative mind, whether the writer's or the reader's. Variables are the spice of life.

This book is not extrapolative. If you like you can read it, and a lot of other science fiction, as a thought-experiment. Let's say (says Mary Shelley) that a young doctor creates a human being in his laboratory; let's say (says Philip K. Dick) that the Allies lost the Second World War; let's say this or that is such and so, and see what happens. . . . In a story so conceived, the moral complexity proper to the modern novel need not be sacrificed, nor is there any built-in dead end; thought and intuition can move freely within bounds set only by the terms of the experiment, which may be very large indeed.

The purpose of a thought-experiment, as the term was used by Schrödinger and other physicists, is not to predict the future—indeed Schrödinger's most famous thought-experiment goes to show that the "future," on the quantum level, *cannot* be predicted—but to describe reality, the present world.

Science fiction is not predictive; it is descriptive.

Predictions are uttered by prophets (free of charge),

by clairvoyants (who usually charge a fee, and are therefore more honored in their day than prophets), and by futurologists (salaried). Prediction is the business of prophets, clairvoyants, and futurologists. It is not the business of novelists. A novelist's business is lying.

The weather bureau will tell you what next Tuesday will be like, and the Rand Corporation will tell you what the twenty-first century will be like. I don't recommend that you turn to the writers of fiction for such information. It's none of their business. All they're trying to do is tell you what they're like, and what you're like—what's going on—what the weather is now, today, this moment, the rain, the sunlight, look! Open your eyes; listen, listen. That is what the novelists say. But they don't tell you what you will see and hear. All they can tell you is what they have seen and heard, in their time in this world, a third of it spent in sleep and dreaming, another third of it spent in telling lies.

"The truth against the world!"—Yes. Certainly. Fiction writers, at least in their braver moments, do desire the truth: to know it, speak it, serve it. But they go about it in a peculiar and devious way, which consists in inventing persons, places, and events which never did and never will exist or occur, and telling about these fictions in detail and at length and with a great deal of emotion, and then when they are done writing down this pack of lies, they say, There! That's the truth!

They may use all kinds of facts to support their tissue of lies. They may describe the Marshalsea Prison, which was a real place, or the battle of Borodino, which really was fought, or the process of cloning, which really takes place in laboratories, or the deterioration of a personality, which is described in real textbooks of psychology, and so on. This weight of verifiable place-event-phenomenon-behavior makes the reader forget that he is reading a pure invention, a history that never took place anywhere but in that unlocalizable region, the author's mind. In fact, while we read a novel, we are insane—bonkers. We believe in the existence of people who aren't there, we hear their voices, we watch the battle of Borodino with them, we may even become Napoleon. Sanity returns (in most cases) when the book is closed.

Is it any wonder that no truly respectable society has ever trusted its artists?

But our society, being troubled and bewildered, seeking guidance, sometimes puts an entirely mistaken trust in its artists, using them as prophets and futurologists.

I do not say that artists cannot be seers, inspired: that the *awen* cannot come upon them, and the god speak through them. Who would be an artist if they did not believe that that happens? If they did not *know* it happens, because they have felt the god within them use their tongue, their hands? Maybe only once, once in their lives. But once is enough.

Nor would I say that the artist alone is so burdened and so privileged. The scientist is another who prepares, who makes ready, working day and night, sleeping and awake, for inspiration. As Pythagoras knew, the god may speak in the forms of geometry as well as in the shapes of dreams; in the harmony of pure thought as well as in the harmony of sounds; in numbers as well as in words.

But it is words that make the trouble and confusion. We are asked now to consider words as useful in only one way: as signs. Our philosophers, some of them, would have us agree that a word (sentence, statement) has value only in so far as it has one single meaning, points to one fact that is comprehensible to the rational intellect, logically sound, and—ideally—quantifiable.

Apollo, the god of light, of reason, of proportion, harmony, number—Apollo blinds those who press too close in worship. Don't look straight at the sun. Go into a dark bar for a bit and have a beer with Dionysios, every now and then.

I talk about the gods; I am an atheist. But I am an artist too, and therefore a liar. Distrust everything I say. I am telling the truth.

The only truth I can understand or express is, logically defined, a lie. Psychologically defined, a symbol. Aesthetically defined, a metaphor.

Oh, it's lovely to be invited to participate in Futurological Congresses where Systems Science displays its grand apocalyptic graphs, to be asked to tell the newspapers what America will be like in 2001, and all that, but it's a terrible mistake. I write science fiction, and science fiction isn't about the future. I don't know any more about the future than you do, and very likely less.

This book is not about the future. Yes, it begins by announcing that it's set in the "Ekumenical Year 1490-97," but surely you don't *believe* that?

Yes, indeed the people in it are androgynous, but that doesn't mean that I'm predicting that in a millennium or so we will all be androgynous, or announcing that I think we damned well ought to be androgynous. I'm merely observing, in the peculiar, devious, and thought-experimental manner proper to science fiction, that if you look at us at certain odd times of day in certain weathers, we already are. I am not predicting, or pre-scribing. I am describing. I am describing certain aspects of psychological reality in the novelist's way, which is by inventing elaborately circumstantial lies.

In reading a novel, any novel, we have to know per-fectly well that the whole thing is nonsense, and then, while reading, believe every word of it. Finally, when we're done with it, we may find—if it's a good novel—that we're a bit different from what we were before we read it, that we have been changed a little, as if by having met a new face, crossed a street we never crossed before. But it's very hard to *say* just what we learned, how we were changed.

The artist deals with what cannot be said in words.

The artist whose medium is fiction does this *in words*. The novelist says in words what cannot be said in words.

Words can be used thus paradoxically because they have, along with a semiotic usage, a symbolic or meta-phoric usage. (They also have a sound—a fact the linguis-tic positivists take no interest in. A sentence or paragraph is like a chord or harmonic sequence in music: its mean-ing may be more clearly understood by the attentive ear, even though it is read in silence, than by the attentive intellect.)

All fiction is metaphor. Science fiction is metaphor.

What sets it apart from older forms of fiction seems to be its use of new metaphors, drawn from certain great dominants of our contemporary life—science, all the sciences, and technology, and the relativistic and the historical outlook, among them. Space travel is one of these metaphors; so is an alternative society, an alternative biology; the future is another. The future, in fiction, is a metaphor.

A metaphor for what?

If I could have said it non-metaphorically, I would not have written all these words, this novel; and Genly Ai would never have sat down at my desk and used up my ink and typewriter ribbon in informing me, and you, rather solemnly, that the truth is a matter of the imagination.

Ursula K. Le Guin

THE
LEFT HAND
OF DARKNESS

A PARADE IN ERHENRANG

From the Archives of Hain. Transcript of Ansible Document 01-01101-934-2-Gethen: To the Stabile on Ollul: Report from Genly Ai, First Mobile on Gethen/Winter, Hainish Cycle 93, Ekumenical Year 1490-97.

I'll make my report as if I told a story, for I was taught as a child on my homeworld that Truth is a matter of the imagination. The soundest fact may fail or prevail in the style of its telling: like that singular organic jewel of our seas, which grows brighter as one woman wears it and, worn by another, dulls and goes to dust. Facts are no more solid, coherent, round, and real than pearls are. But both are sensitive.

The story is not all mine, nor told by me alone. Indeed I am not sure whose story it is; you can judge better. But it is all one, and if at moments the facts seem to alter with an altered voice, why then you can choose the fact you like best; yet none of them is false, and it is all one story.

It starts on the 44th diurnal of the Year 1491, which on the planet Winter in the nation Karhide was Odhar-hahad Tuwa or the twenty-second day of the third month of spring in the Year One. It is always the Year One here. Only the dating of every past and future year changes each New Year's Day, as one counts backwards or forwards from the unitary Now. So it was spring of the Year One in Erhenrang, capital city of Karhide, and I was in peril of my life, and did not know it.

I was in a parade. I walked just behind the gossiwors and just before the king. It was raining.

Rainclouds over dark towers, rain falling in deep streets, a dark storm-beaten city of stone, through which one vein of gold winds slowly. First come merchants, potentates, and artisans of the City Erhenrang, rank after rank, magnificently clothed, advancing through the rain as comfortably as fish through the sea. Their faces are keen and calm. They do not march in step. This is a parade with no soldiers, not even imitation soldiers.

Next come the lords and mayors and representatives, one person, or five, or forty-five, or four hundred, from each Domain and Co-Domain of Karhide, a vast ornate procession that moves to the music of metal horns and hollow blocks of bone and wood and the dry, pure lilting of electric flutes. The various banners of the great Domains tangle in a rain-beaten confusion of color with the yellow pennants that bedeck the way, and the various musics of each group clash and interweave in many rhythms echoing in the deep stone street.

Next, a troop of jugglers with polished spheres of gold, which they hurl up high in flashing flights, and catch, and hurl again, making fountain-jets of bright jugglery. All at once, as if they had literally caught the light, the gold spheres blaze bright as glass: the sun is breaking through.

Next, forty men in yellow, playing gossiwors. The gossiwor, played only in the king's presence, produces a preposterous disconsolate bellow. Forty of them played together shake one's reason, shake the towers of Erhenrang, shake down a last spatter of rain from the windy clouds. If this is the Royal Music no wonder the kings of Karhide are all mad.

Next, the royal party, guards and functionaries and dignitaries of the city and the court, deputies, senators, chancellors, ambassadors, lords of the Kingdom, none of them keeping step or rank yet walking with great dignity; and among them is King Argaven XV, in white tunic and shirt and breeches, with leggings of saffron leather and a peaked yellow cap. A gold finger-ring is his only adornment and sign of office. Behind this group eight sturdy fellows bear the royal litter, rough with yellow sapphires, in which no king has ridden for centuries, a ceremonial relic of the very-long-ago. By the litter walk eight guards armed with "foray guns," also relics of a more barbaric past but not empty ones, being loaded with pellets of soft iron. Death walks behind the king. Behind death come the students of the Artisan Schools, the Colleges, the Trades, and the King's Hearths, long lines of children and young people in white and red and gold and green; and finally a number of soft-running, slow, dark cars end the parade.

The royal party, myself among them, gather on a platform of new timbers beside the unfinished Arch of the

River Gate. The occasion of the parade is the comple-
tion of that arch, which completes the new Road and
River Port of Erhenrang, a great operation of dredging
and building and roadmaking that has taken five years,
and will distinguish Argaven XV's reign in the annals
of Karhide. We are all squeezed rather tight on the platform in our damp and massive finery. The rain is gone,
the sun shines on us, the splendid, radiant, traitorous
sun of Winter. I remark to the person on my left, "It's
hot. It's really hot."

The person on my left—a stocky dark Karhider with
sleek and heavy hair, wearing a heavy overtunic of green
leather worked with gold, and a heavy white shirt, and
heavy breeches, and a neck-chain of heavy silver links a
hand broad—this person, sweating heavily, replies, "So
it is."

All about us as we stand jammed on our platform lie
the faces of the people of the city, upturned like a shoal
of brown, round pebbles, mica-glittering with thousands of watching eyes.

Now the king ascends a gangplank of raw timbers
that leads from the platform up to the top of the arch
whose unjoined piers tower over crown and wharves
and river. As he mounts the crowd stirs and speaks in a
vast murmur: "Argaven!" He makes no response. They
expect none. Gossiwors blow a thunderous discordant
blast, cease. Silence. The sun shines on city, river, crowd,
and king. Masons below have set an electric winch
going, and as the king mounts higher the keystone of
the arch goes up past him in its sling, is raised, settled,

and fitted almost soundlessly, great ton-weight block though it is, into the gap between the two piers, making them one, one thing, an arch. A mason with trowel and bucket awaits the king, up on the scaffolding; all the other workmen descend by rope ladders, like a swarm of fleas. The king and the mason kneel, high between the river and the sun, on their bit of planking. Taking the trowel the king begins to mortar the long joints of the keystone. He does not dab at it and give the trowel back to the mason, but sets to work methodically. The cement he uses is a pinkish color different from the rest of the mortarwork and after five or ten minutes of watching the king-bee work I ask the person on my left, "Are your keystones always set in a red cement?" For the same color is plain around the keystone of each arch of the Old Bridge, which soars beautifully over the river upstream from the arch.

Wiping sweat from his dark forehead the man—*man* I must say, having said *he* and *his*—the man answers, "Very-long-ago a keystone was always set in with a mortar of ground bones mixed with blood. Human bones, human blood. Without the blood bond the arch would fall, you see. We use the blood of animals, these days."

So he often speaks, frank yet cautious, ironic, as if always aware that I see and judge as an alien: a singular awareness in one of so isolate a race and so high a rank. He is one of the most powerful men in the country; I am not sure of the proper historical equivalent of his position, vizier or prime minister or councillor; the Karhidish word for it means the King's Ear. He is lord of a Domain and lord of the Kingdom, a mover of great events. His name is Therem Harth rem ir Estraven.

The king seems to be finished with his masonry work, and I rejoice; but crossing under the rise of the arch on his spiderweb of planks he starts in on the other side of the keystone, which after all has two sides. It doesn't do to be impatient in Karhide. They are anything but a phlegmatic people, yet they are obdurate, they are pertinacious, they finish plastering joints. The crowds on the Sess Embankment are content to watch the king work, but I am bored, and hot. I have never before been hot, on Winter; I never will be again; yet I fail to appreciate the event. I am dressed for the Ice Age and not for the sunshine, in layers and layers of clothing, woven plant-fiber, artificial fiber, fur, leather, a massive armor against the cold, within which I now wilt like a radish leaf. For distraction I look at the crowds and the other paraders drawn up around the platform, their Domain and Clan banners hanging still and bright in sunlight, and idly I ask Estraven what this banner is and that one and the other. He knows each one I ask about, though there are hundreds, some from remote Domains, Hearths and Tribelets of the Pering Stormborder and Kerm Land.

"I'm from Kerm Land myself," he says when I admire his knowledge. "Anyhow it's my business to know the Domains. They are Karhide. To govern this land is to govern its lords. Not that it's ever been done. Do you know the saying, *Karhide is not a nation but a family quarrel?*" I haven't, and I suspect that Estraven made it up; it has his stamp.

At this point another member of the *kyorremy*, the upper chamber or parliament that Estraven heads, pushes and squeezes a way up close to him and begins talking to him. This is the king's cousin Pemmer Harge rem ir Tibe. His voice is very low as he speaks to Estraven, his posture faintly insolent, his smile frequent. Estraven, sweating like ice in the sun, stays slick and cold as ice, answering Tibe's murmurs aloud in a tone whose commonplace politeness makes the other look rather a fool. I listen, as I watch the king grouting away, but understand nothing except the animosity between Tibe and Estraven. It's nothing to do with me, in any case, and I am simply interested in the behavior of these people who rule a nation, in the old-fashioned sense, who govern the fortunes of twenty million other people. Power has become so subtle and complex a thing in the ways taken by the Ekumen that only a subtle mind can watch it work; here it is still limited, still visible. In Estraven, for instance, one feels the man's power as an augmentation of his character; he cannot make an empty gesture or say a word that is not listened to. He knows it, and the knowledge gives him more reality than most people own: a solidness of being, a substantiality, a human grandeur. Nothing succeeds like success. I don't trust Estraven, whose motives are forever obscure; I don't like him; yet I feel and respond to his authority as surely as I do to the warmth of the sun.

Even as I think this the world's sun dims between clouds regathering, and soon a flaw of rain runs sparse and hard upriver, spattering the crowds on the Embankment, darkening the sky. As the king comes down the gangplank the light breaks through a last time, and his white figure and the great arch stand out a moment vivid and splendid against the storm-darkened south. The clouds close. A cold wind comes tearing up Port-and-Palace Street, the river goes gray, the trees on the Embankment shudder. The parade is over. Half an hour later it is snowing.

As the king's car drove off up Port-and-Palace Street and the crowds began to move like a rocky shingle rolled by a slow tide, Estraven turned to me again and said, "Will you have supper with me tonight, Mr. Ai?" I accepted, with more surprise than pleasure. Estraven had done a great deal for me in the last six or eight months, but I did not expect or desire such a show of personal favor as an invitation to his house. Harge rem ir Tibe was still close to us, overhearing, and I felt that he was meant to overhear. Annoyed by this sense of effeminate intrigue I got off the platform and lost myself in the mob, crouching and slouching somewhat to do so. I'm not much taller than the Gethenian norm, but the difference is most noticeable in a crowd. *That's him, look, there's the Envoy.* Of course that was part of my job, but it was a part that got harder not easier as time went on; more and more often I longed for anonymity, for sameness. I craved to be like everybody else.

A couple of blocks up Breweries Street I turned off towards my lodgings and suddenly, there where the crowd thinned out, found Tibe walking beside me.

"A flawless event," said the king's cousin, smiling at me. His long, clean, yellow teeth appeared and disappeared in a yellow face all webbed, though he was not an old man, with fine, soft wrinkles.

"A good augury for the success of the new Port," I said.

"Yes indeed." More teeth.

"The ceremony of the keystone is most impressive—"

"Yes indeed. That ceremony descends to us from very-long-ago. But no doubt Lord Estraven explained all that to you."

"Lord Estraven is most obliging."

I was trying to speak insipidly, yet everything I said to Tibe seemed to take on a double meaning.

"Oh very much indeed," said Tibe. "Indeed Lord Estraven is famous for his kindness to foreigners." He smiled again, and every tooth seemed to have a meaning, double, multiple, thirty-two different meanings.

"Few foreigners are so foreign as I, Lord Tibe. I am very grateful for kindnesses."

"Yes indeed, yes indeed! And gratitude's a noble, rare emotion, much praised by the poets. Rare above all here in Erhenrang, no doubt because it's impracticable. This is a hard age we live in, an ungrateful age. Things aren't as they were in our grandparents' days, are they?"

"I scarcely know, sir, but I've heard the same lament on other worlds."

Tibe stared at me for some while as if establishing lunacy. Then he brought out the long yellow teeth. "Ah yes! Yes indeed! I keep forgetting that you come from another planet. But of course that's not a matter you ever forget. Though no doubt life would be much sounder and simpler and safer for you here in Erhenrang if you could forget it, eh? Yes indeed! Here's my car, I had it wait here out of the way. I'd like to offer to drive you to your island, but must forgo the privilege, as I'm due at the King's House very shortly and poor relations must be in good time, as the saying is, eh? Yes indeed!" said the king's cousin, climbing into his little black electric car, teeth bared across his shoulder at me, eyes veiled by a net of wrinkles.

I walked on home to my island.* Its front garden was revealed now that the last of the winter's snow had melted and the winter-doors, ten feet aboveground, were sealed off for a few months, till the autumn and the deep snow should return. Around at the side of the building in the mud and the ice and the quick, soft, rank spring growth of the garden, a young couple stood talking. Their right hands were clasped. They were in the first phase of kemmer. The large, soft snow danced about them as they stood barefoot in the icy mud, hands clasped, eyes all for each other. Spring on Winter.

I had dinner at my island and at Fourth Hour striking on the gongs of Remmy Tower I was at the Palace ready for supper. Karhiders eat four solid meals a day, breakfast, lunch, dinner, supper, along with a lot of

---

* Karhosh, island, the usual word for the apartment-boardinghouse buildings that house the greatest part of the urban populations of Karhide. Islands contain 20 to 200 private rooms; meals are communal; some are run as hotels, others as cooperative communes, others combine these types. They are certainly an urban adaptation of the fundamental Karhidish institution of the Hearth, though lacking, of course, the topical and genealogical stability of the Hearth.

adventitious nibbling and gobbling in between. There are no large meat-animals on Winter, and no mammalian products, milk, butter or cheese; the only high-protein, high-carbohydrate foods are the various kinds of eggs, fish, nuts, and the Hainish grains. A low-grade diet for a bitter climate, and one must refuel often. I had got used to eating, as it seemed, every few minutes. It wasn't until later in that year that I discovered the Gethenians have perfected the technique not only of perpetually stuffing, but also of indefinitely starving.

The snow still fell, a mild spring blizzard, much pleasanter than the relentless rain of the Thaw just past. I made my way to and through the Palace in the quiet and pale darkness of snowfall, losing my way only once. The Palace of Erhenrang is an inner city, a walled wilderness of palaces, towers, gardens, courtyards, cloisters, roofed bridgeways, roofless tunnel-walks, small forests and dungeon-keeps, the product of centuries of paranoia on a grand scale. Over it all rise the grim, red, elaborate walls of the Royal House, which though in perpetual use is inhabited by no one beside the king himself. Everyone else, servants, staff, lords, ministers, parliamentarians, guards or whatever, sleeps in another palace or fort or keep or barracks or house inside the walls. Estraven's house, sign of the king's high favor, was the Corner Red Dwelling, built 440 years ago for Harmes, beloved kemmering of Emran III, whose beauty is still celebrated, and who was abducted, mutilated, and rendered imbecile by hirelings of the Innerland Faction. Emran III died forty years after, still wreaking vengeance on his unhappy country: Emran the Illfated. The tragedy is so old that its horror has leached away and only a certain air of faithlessness and melancholy clings to the stones and shadows of the house. The garden was small and walled; serem-trees leaned over a rocky pool. In dim shafts of light from the windows of the house I saw snowflakes and the threadlike white sporecases of the trees falling softly together onto the dark water. Estraven stood waiting for me, bare-headed and coatless in the cold, watching that small secret ceaseless descent of snow and seeds in the night. He greeted me quietly and brought me into the house. There were no other guests.

I wondered at this, but we went to table at once, and one does not talk business while eating; besides, my wonder was diverted to the meal, which was superb, even the eternal breadapples transmuted by a cook whose art I heartily praised. After supper, by the fire, we drank hot beer. On a world where a common table implement is a little device with which you crack the ice that has formed on your drink between drafts, hot beer is a thing you come to appreciate.

Estraven had conversed amiably at table; now, sitting across the hearth from me, he was quiet. Though I had been nearly two years on Winter I was still far from being able to see the people of the planet through their own eyes. I tried to, but my efforts took the form of self-consciously seeing a Gethenian first as a man, then as a woman, forcing him into those categories so irrelevant to his nature and so essential to my own. Thus as I sipped my smoking sour beer I thought that at table Estraven's performance had been womanly, all charm and tact and lack of substance, specious and adroit. Was it in fact perhaps this soft supple femininity that I disliked and distrusted in him? For it was impossible to think of him as a woman, that dark, ironic, powerful presence near me in the firelit darkness, and yet whenever I thought of him as a man I felt a sense of falseness, of imposture: in him, or in my own attitude towards him? His voice was soft and rather resonant but not deep, scarcely a man's voice, but scarcely a woman's voice either . . . but what was it saying?

"I'm sorry," he was saying, "that I've had to forestall for so long this pleasure of having you in my house; and to that extent at least I'm glad there is no longer any question of patronage between us."

I puzzled at this awhile. He had certainly been my patron in court until now. Did he mean that the audience he had arranged for me with the king tomorrow had raised me to an equality with himself? "I don't think I follow you," I said.

At that, he was silent, evidently also puzzled. "Well, you understand," he said at last, "being here . . . you understand that I am no longer acting on your behalf with the king of course."

He spoke as if ashamed of me, not of himself. Clearly there was a significance in his invitation and my acceptance of it that I had missed. But my blunder was in manners, his in morals. All I thought at first was that I had been right all along not to trust Estraven. He was not merely adroit and not merely powerful, he was

faithless. All these months in Ehrenrang it had been he
who listened to me, who answered my questions, sent
physicians and engineers to verify the alienness of my
physique and my ship, introduced me to people I needed
to know, and gradually elevated me from my first year's
status as a highly imaginative monster to my present recognition as the mysterious Envoy, about to be received
by the king. Now, having got me up on that dangerous
eminence, he suddenly and coolly announced he was
withdrawing his support.

"You've led me to rely on you—"

"It was ill done."

"Do you mean that, having arranged this audience,
you haven't spoken in favor of my mission to the king,
as you—" I had the sense to stop short of "promised."

"I can't."

I was very angry, but I met neither anger nor apology
in him.

"Will you tell me why?"

After a while he said, "Yes," and then paused again.
During the pause I began to think that an inept and
undefended alien should not demand reasons from the
prime minister of a kingdom, above all when he does not
and perhaps never will understand the foundations of
power and the workings of government in that kingdom.
No doubt this was all a matter of *shifgrethor*—prestige,
face, place, the pride-relationship, the untranslatable and
all-important principle of social authority in Karhide
and all civilizations of Gethen. And if it was I would not
understand it.

"Did you hear what the king said to me at the ceremony today?"

"No."

Estraven leaned forward across the hearth, lifted the beer-jug out of the hot ashes, and refilled my tankard. He said nothing more, so I amplified, "The king didn't speak to you in my hearing."

"Nor in mine," said he.

I saw at last that I was missing another signal. Damning his effeminate deviousness, I said, "Are you trying to tell me, Lord Estraven, that you're out of favor with the king?"

I think he was angry then, but he said nothing that showed it, only, "I'm not trying to tell you anything, Mr. Ai."

"By God, I wish you would!"

He looked at me curiously. "Well, then, put it this way. There are some persons in court who are, in your phrase, in favor with the king, but who do not favor your presence or your mission here."

And so you're hurrying to join them, selling me out to save your skin, I thought, but there was no point in saying it. Estraven was a courtier, a politician, and I a fool to have trusted him. Even in a bisexual society the politician is very often something less than an integral man. His inviting me to dinner showed that he thought I would accept his betrayal as easily as he committed it. Clearly face-saving was more important than honesty. So I brought myself to say, "I'm sorry that your kindness to me has made trouble for you." Coals of fire. I enjoyed a flitting sense of moral superiority, but not for long; he was too incalculable.

He sat back so that the firelight lay ruddy on his knees and his fine, strong, small hands and the silver tankard he held, but left his face in shadow: a dark face always shadowed by the thick low growing hair and heavy brows and lashes, and by a somber blandness of expression. Can one read a cat's face, a seal's, an otter's? Some Gethenians, I thought, are like such animals, with deep bright eyes that do not change expression when you speak.

"I've made trouble for myself," he answered, "by an act that had nothing to do with you, Mr. Ai. You know that Karhide and Orgoreyn have a dispute concerning a stretch of our border in the high North Fall near Sassinoth. Argaven's grandfather claimed the Sinoth Valley for Karhide, and the Commensals have never recognized the claim. A lot of snow out of one cloud, and it grows thicker. I've been helping some Karhidish farmers who live in the Valley to move back east across the old border, thinking the argument might settle itself if the Valley were simply left to the Orgota, who have lived there for several thousand years. I was in the Administration of the North Fall some years ago, and got to know some of those farmers. I dislike the thought of their being killed in forays, or sent to Voluntary Farms in Orgoreyn. Why not obviate the subject of dispute? . . . But that's not a patriotic idea. In fact it's a cowardly one, and impugns the shifgrethor of the king himself."

His ironies, and these ins and outs of a border-dispute

with Orgoreyn, were of no interest to me. I returned to the matter that lay between us. Trust him or not, I might still get some use out of him. "I'm sorry," I said, "but it seems a pity that this question of a few farmers may be allowed to spoil the chances of my mission with the king. There's more at stake than a few miles of national boundary."

"Yes. Much more. But perhaps the Ekumen, which is a hundred light-years from border to border, will be patient with us awhile."

"The Stabiles of the Ekumen are very patient men, sir. They'll wait a hundred years or five hundred for Karhide and the rest of Gethen to deliberate and consider whether or not to join the rest of mankind. I speak merely out of personal hope. And personal disappointment. I own that I thought that with your support—"

"I too. Well, the Glaciers didn't freeze overnight. . . ." Cliché came ready to his lips, but his mind was elsewhere. He brooded. I imagined him moving me around with the other pawns in his power game. "You came to my country," he said at last, "at a strange time. Things are changing; we are taking a new turning. No, not so much that, as following too far on the way we've been going. I thought that your presence, your mission, might prevent our going wrong, give us a new option entirely. But at the right moment—in the right place. It is all exceedingly chancy, Mr. Ai."

Impatient with his generalities, I said, "You imply that this isn't the right moment. Would you advise me to cancel my audience?"

My gaffe was even worse in Karhidish, but Estraven did not smile, or wince. "I'm afraid only the king has that privilege," he said mildly.

"Oh God, yes. I didn't mean that." I put my head in my hands a moment. Brought up in the wide-open, free-wheeling society of Earth, I would never master the protocol, or the impassivity, so valued by Karhiders. I know what a king was, Earth's own history is full of them, but I had no experiential feel for privilege—no tact. I picked up my tankard and drank a hot and violent draft. "Well, I'll say less to the king than I intended to say, when I could count on you."

"Good."

"Why good?" I demanded.

"Well, Mr. Ai, you're not insane. I'm not insane. But then neither of us is a king, you see . . . I suppose that you intended to tell Argaven, rationally, that your mission here is to attempt to bring about an alliance between Gethen and the Ekumen. And, rationally, he knows that already; because, as you know, I told him. I urged your case with him, tried to interest him in you. It was ill done, ill timed. I forgot, being too interested myself, that he's a king, and does not see things rationally, but as a king. All I've told him means to him simply that his power is threatened, his kingdom is a dust mote in space, his kingship is a joke to men who rule a hundred worlds."

"But the Ekumen doesn't rule, it co-ordinates. Its power is precisely the power of its member states and worlds. In alliance with the Ekumen, Karhide will become infinitely less threatened and more important than it's ever been."

Estraven did not answer for a while. He sat gazing at the fire, whose flames winked, reflected, from his tankard and from the broad bright silver chain of office over his shoulders. The old house was silent around us. There had been a servant to attend our meal, but Karhiders, having no institutions of slavery or personal bondage, hire services not people, and the servants had all gone off to their own homes by now. Such a man as Estraven must have guards about him somewhere, for assassination is a lively institution in Karhide, but I had seen no guard, heard none. We were alone.

I was alone, with a stranger, inside the walls of a dark palace, in a strange snow-changed city, in the heart of the Ice Age of an alien world.

Everything I had said, tonight and ever since I came to Winter, suddenly appeared to me as both stupid and incredible. How could I expect this man or any other to believe my tales about other worlds, other races, a vague benevolent government somewhere off in outer space? It was all nonsense. I had appeared in Karhide in a queer kind of ship, and I differed physically from Gethenians in some respects; that wanted explaining. But my own explanations were preposterous. I did not, in that moment, believe them myself.

"I believe you," said the stranger, the alien alone with me, and so strong had my access of self-alienation been that I looked up at him bewildered. "I'm afraid that Argaven also believes you. But he does not trust you. In part because he no longer trusts me. I have made mistakes, been careless. I cannot ask for your trust any longer, either, having put you in jeopardy. I forgot what a king is, forgot that the king in his own eyes *is* Karhide, forgot what patriotism is and that he is, of necessity, the perfect patriot. Let me ask you this, Mr. Ai: do you know, by your own experience, what patriotism is?"

"No," I said, shaken by the force of that intense personality suddenly turning itself wholly upon me. "I don't think I do. If by patriotism you don't mean the love of one's homeland, for that I do know."

"No, I don't mean love, when I say patriotism. I mean fear. The fear of the other. And its expressions are political, not poetical: hate, rivalry, aggression. It grows in us, that fear. It grows in us year by year. We've followed our road too far. And you, who come from a world that outgrew nations centuries ago, who hardly know what I'm talking about, who show us the new road—" He broke off. After a while he went on, in control again, cool and polite: "It's because of fear that I refuse to urge your cause with the king, now. But not fear for myself, Mr. Ai. I'm not acting patriotically. There are, after all, other nations on Gethen."

I had no idea what he was driving at, but was sure that he did not mean what he seemed to mean. Of all the dark, obstructive, enigmatic souls I had met in this bleak city, his was the darkest. I would not play his labyrinthine game. I made no reply. After a while he went on, rather cautiously, "If I've understood you, your Ekumen is devoted essentially to the general interest of mankind. Now, for instance, the Orgota have experience in subordinating local interests to a general interest, while Karhide has almost none. And the Commensals of Orgoreyn are mostly sane men, if unintelligent, while the king of Karhide is not only insane but rather stupid."

It was clear that Estraven had no loyalties at all. I said in faint disgust, "It must be difficult to serve him, if that's the case."

"I'm not sure I've ever served the king," said the king's prime minister. "Or ever intended to. I'm not anyone's servant. A man must cast his own shadow. . . ."

The gongs in Remny Tower were striking Sixth Hour, midnight, and I took them as my excuse to go. As I was putting on my coat in the hallway he said, "I've lost my chance for the present, for I suppose you'll be leaving Ehrenrang"—why did he suppose so?—"but I trust a day will come when I can ask you questions again. There's so much I want to know. About your mindspeech, in particular; you'd scarcely begun to try to explain it to me."

His curiosity seemed perfectly genuine. He had the effrontery of the powerful. His promises to help me had seemed genuine, too. I said yes, of course, whenever he liked, and that was the evening's end. He showed me out through the garden, where snow lay thin in the light of Gethen's big, dull, rufous moon. I shivered as we went out, for it was well below freezing, and he said with polite surprise, "You're cold?" To him of course it was a mild spring night.

I was tired and downcast. I said, "I've been cold ever since I came to this world."

"What do you call it, this world, in your language?"

"Gethen."

"You gave it no name of your own?"

"Yes, the First Investigators did. They called it Winter."

We had stopped in the gateway of the walled garden. Outside, the Palace grounds and roofs loomed in a dark snowy jumble lit here and there at various heights by the faint gold slits of windows. Standing under the narrow arch I glanced up, wondering if that keystone too was mortared with bone and blood. Estraven took leave of me and turned away; he was never fulsome in his greetings and farewells. I went off through the silent courts and alleys of the Palace, my boots crunching on the thin moonlit snow, and homeward through the deep streets of the city. I was cold, unconfident, obsessed by perfidy, and solitude, and fear.

2

THE PLACE INSIDE THE BLIZZARD

From a sound-tape collection of North Karhidish "hearth-tales" in the archives of the College of Historians in Erhenrang, narrator unknown, recorded during the reign of Argaven VIII.

About two hundred years ago in the Hearth of Shath in the Pering Storm-border there were two brothers who vowed kemmering to each other. In those days, as now, full brothers were permitted to keep kemmer until one of them should bear a child, but after that they must separate; so it was never permitted them to vow kemmering for life. Yet this they had done. When a child was conceived the Lord of Shath commanded them to break their vow and never meet in kemmer again. On hearing this command one of the two, the one who bore the child, despaired and would hear no comfort or counsel, and procuring poison, committed suicide. Then the people of the Hearth rose up against the other brother and drove him out of Hearth and Domain, laying the shame of the suicide upon him. And since his own lord had exiled him and his story went before him, none would take him in, but after the three days' guesting all sent him from their doors as an outlaw. So from place to place he went until he saw that there was no kindness left for him in his own land, and his crime would not be forgiven.* He had not believed this would be so, being a young man and unhardened. When he saw that it was so indeed, he returned over the land to Shath and as an exile stood in the doorway of the Outer Hearth. This he said to his hearthfellows there: "I am without a face among men. I am not seen. I speak and am not heard. I come and am not welcomed. There is no place by the fire for me, nor food on the table for me, nor a bed made for me to lie in. Yet I still have my name: Getheren is my name. That name I lay on this Hearth as a curse, and with it my shame. Keep that for me. Now nameless I will go seek my death." Then some of the hearthmen jumped up with shouts and tumult, intending to kill him, for murder is a lighter shadow on a house than suicide. He escaped them and ran northward over the land towards the Ice, outrunning all who pursued him. They came back all chapfallen to Shath. But Getheren went on, and after two days' journey came to the Pering Ice.**

For two days he walked northward on the Ice. He had no food with him, nor shelter but his coat. On the Ice noth-

* His transgression of the cole controlling incest became a crime when seen as the cause of his brother's suicide. (G.A.)
** The Pering Ice is the glacial sheet that covers the northernmost portion of Karhide, and is (in winter when the Guthen Bay is frozen) contiguous with the Gobrin Ice of Orgoreyn.

ing grows and no beasts run. It was the month of Susmy and the first great snows were falling those days and nights. He went alone through the storm. On the second day he knew he was growing weaker. On the second night he must lie down and sleep awhile. On the third morning waking he saw that his hands were frostbitten, and found that his feet were too, though he could not unfasten his boots to look at them, having no use left of his hands. He began to crawl forward on knees and elbows. He had no reason to do so, as it did not matter whether he died in one place on the Ice or another, but he felt that he should go northward.

After a long while the snow ceased to fall around him, and the wind to blow. The sun shone out. He could not see far ahead as he crawled, for the fur of his hood came forward over his eyes. No longer feeling any cold in his legs and arms nor on his face, he thought that the frost had benumbed him. Yet he could still move. The snow that lay over the glacier looked strange to him, as if it were a white grass growing up out of the ice. It bent to his touch and straightened again, like grass-blades. He ceased to crawl and sat up, pushing back his hood so he could see around him. As far as he could see lay fields of the snowgrass, white and shining. There were groves of white trees, with white leaves growing on them. The sun shone, and it was windless, and everything was white.

Getheren took off his gloves and looked at his hands. They were white as the snow. Yet the frostbite was gone out of them, and he could use his fingers, and stand upon his feet. He felt no pain, and no cold, and no hunger.

He saw away over the ice to the north a white tower

like the tower of a Domain, and from this place far away one came walking towards him. After a while Getheren could see that the person was naked, his skin was all white, and his hair was all white. He came nearer, and near enough to speak. Getheren said, "Who are you?"

The white man said, "I am your brother and kemmering, Hode."

Hode was the name of his brother who had killed himself. And Getheren saw that the white man was his brother in body and feature. But there was no longer any life in his belly, and his voice sounded thin like the creaking of ice.

Getheren asked, "What place is this?"

Hode answered, "This is the place inside the blizzard. We who kill ourselves dwell here. Here you and I shall keep our vow."

Getheren was frightened, and he said, "I will not stay here. If you had come away with me from our Hearth into the southern lands we might have stayed together and kept our vow lifelong, no man knowing our transgression. But you broke your vow, throwing it away with your life. And now you cannot say my name."

This was true. Hode moved his white lips, but could not say his brother's name.

He came quickly to Getheren, reaching out his arms to hold him, and seized him by the left hand. Getheren broke free and ran from him. He ran to the southward, and running saw rise up before him a white wall of falling snow, and when he entered into it he fell again on his knees, and could not run, but crawled.

On the ninth day after he had gone up on the Ice he was found in their Domain by people of Orhoch Hearth, which lies northeast of Shath. They did not know who he was nor where he came from, for they found him crawling in the snow, starving, snowblind, his face blackened by sun and frost, and at first he could not speak. Yet he took no lasting harm except in his left hand, which was frozen and must be amputated. Some of the people there said this was Getheren of Shath, of whom they had heard talk; others said it could not be, for that Getheren had gone up on the Ice in the first blizzard of autumn, and was certainly dead. He himself denied that his name was Getheren. When he was well he left Orhoch and the Storm-border and went into the southern lands, calling himself Ennoch.

When Ennoch was an old man dwelling in the plains of Rer he met a man from his own country, and asked him, "How fares Shath Domain?" The other told him that Shath fared ill. Nothing prospered there in Hearth or tilth, all being blighted with illness, the spring seed frozen in the ground or the ripe grain rotten, and so it had been for many years. Then Ennoch told him, "I am Getheren of Shath," and told him how he had gone up on the Ice and what he had met with there. At the end of his tale he said, "Tell them at Shath that I take back my name and my shadow." Not many days after this Getheren took sick and died. The traveler carried his words back to Shath, and they say that from that time on the Domain prospered again, and all went as it should go in field and house and Hearth.

3

THE MAD KING

I slept late and spent the tail of the morning reading over my own notes on Palace etiquette and the observations on Gethenian psychology and manners made by my predecessors, the Investigators. I didn't take in what I read, which didn't matter since I knew it by heart and was reading merely to shut up the interior voice that kept telling me, *It has all gone wrong.* When it would not be shut up I argued with it, asserting that I could get on without Estraven—perhaps better than with him. After all, my job here was a one-man job. There is only one First Mobile. The first news from the Ekumen on any world is spoken by one voice, one man present in the flesh, present and alone. He may be killed, as Pellelge was on Four-Taurus, or locked up with madmen, as were the first three Mobiles on Gao, one after the other; yet the practice is kept, because it works. One voice speaking truth is a greater force than fleets and armies, given time; plenty of time; but time is the thing that the Ekumen has plenty of . . . *You don't,* said the interior voice, but I reasoned it into silence, and arrived at the Palace for my audience with the king at Second Hour full of calm and resolution. It was all knocked right out of me in the anteroom, before I ever saw the king.

Palace guards and attendants had showed me to the anteroom, through the long halls and corridors of the King's House. An aide asked me to wait and left me alone in the high windowless room. There I stood, all decked out for a visit with royalty. I had sold my fourth ruby (the Investigators having reported that Gethenians value the carbon jewels much as Terrans do, I came to Winter with a pocketful of gems to pay my way), and spent a third of the proceeds on clothes for the parade yesterday and the audience today: everything new, very heavy and well-made as clothing is in Karhide—a white knitfur; shirt, gray breeches; the long tabardlike over-tunic, *hieb,* of bluegreen leather; new cap; new gloves tucked at the proper angle under the loose belt of the hieb; new boots. . . . The assurance of being well dressed augmented my feeling of calm and resolution. I looked calmly and resolutely about me.

Like all the King's House this room was high, red, old, bare, with a musty chill on the air as if the drafts blew in not from other rooms but from other centuries. A fire roared in the fireplace, but did no good. Fires in Karhide are to warm the spirit not the flesh. The mechanical-industrial Age of Invention in Karhide is at least three thousand years old, and during these thirty centuries they have developed excellent and economical central-heating devices using steam, electricity, and other principles, but they do not install them in their houses. Perhaps if they did they would lose their physiological weatherproofing, like Arctic birds kept in warm tents, who being released get frostbitten feet. I, however, a tropical bird, was cold—cold one way outdoors and cold another way indoors, ceaselessly and more or less thoroughly cold. I walked up and down to warm myself. There was little besides myself and the fire in the long anteroom: a stool and a table on which stood a bowl of fingerstones and an ancient radio of carved wood inlaid with silver and bone, a noble piece of workmanship. It was playing at a whisper, and I turned it a touch louder, hearing the Palace Bulletin replace the droning Chant or Lay that was being broadcast. Karhiders do not read much as a rule, and prefer their news and literature heard not seen; books and televising devices are less common than radios, and newspapers don't exist. I had missed the morning Bulletin on my set at home, and half-listened now, my mind elsewhere, until the repetition of the name several times caught my ear at last and stopped my pacing. What was it about Estraven? A proclamation was being reread.

"Therem Harth rem ir Estraven, Lord of Estre in Kerm, by this order forfeits title of the Kingdom and seat in the Assemblies of the Kingdom, and is commanded to quit the Kingdom and all Domains of Karhide. If he be not gone out of the Kingdom and all Domains in three days' time, or if in his life he return into the Kingdom, he shall be put to death by any man without further judgment. No countryman of Karhide shall suffer Harth rem ir Estraven to speak to him or stay within his house or on his lands, on pain of imprisonment, nor shall any countryman of Karhide give or lend Harth rem ir Estraven money or goods, nor repay any debt owing him, on pain of imprisonment and fine. Let all countrymen of Karhide know and say that the crime for which Harth rem ir Estraven is exiled is the crime of Treason: he having urged privily and openly in Assembly and Palace, under pretense of loyal service to the king, that the Nation-Dominion of Karhide cast away its sovereignty and surrender up its power in order to become an inferior and subject nation in a certain Union of Peoples, concerning which let all men know and say that no such Union does exist, being a device and baseless fiction of certain conspiring traitors who seek to weaken the Authority of Karhide in the king, to the profit of the real and present enemies of the land. Odguyrny Tuwa, Eighth Hour, in the Palace in Erhenrang: ARGAVEN HARGE."

The order was printed and posted on several gates and road-posts about the city, and the above is verbatim from one such copy.

My first impulse was simple. I cut off the radio as if to stop it from giving evidence against me, and scuttled to the door. There of course I stopped. I went back to the table by the fireplace, and stood. I was no longer calm or resolute. I wanted to open my case, get out the ansible,

and send an Advise/Urgent! through to Hain. I sup-
pressed this impulse also, as it was even sillier than the
first. Fortunately I had no time for more impulses. The
double door at the far end of the anteroom was opened
and the aide stood aside for me to pass, announcing me,
"Genry Ai"—my name is Genly, but Karhiders can't say
l—and left me in the Red Hall with King Argaven XV.

An immense, high, long room, that Red Hall of the
King's House. Half a mile down to the fireplaces. Half
a mile up to the raftered ceiling hung with red, dusty
drapes or banners all ragged with the years. The windows are only slits or slots in the thick walls, the lights
few, high, and dim. My new boots go *eck, eck, eck, eck*
as I walk down the hall towards the king, a six months'
journey.

Argaven was standing in front of the central and largest fireplace of three, on a low, large dais or platform:
a short figure in the reddish gloom, rather potbellied,
very erect, dark and featureless in silhouette except for
the glint of the big seal-ring on his thumb.

I stopped at the edge of the dais and, as I had been
instructed, did and said nothing.

"Come up, Mr. Ai. Sit down."

I obeyed, taking the right-hand chair by the central
hearth. In all this I had been drilled. Argaven did not
sit down; he stood ten feet from me with the roaring
bright flames behind him, and presently said, "Tell me
what you have to tell me, Mr. Ai. You bear a message,
they say."

The face that turned towards me, reddened and cratered by firelight and shadow, was as flat and cruel as the moon, Winter's dull rufous moon. Argaven was less kingly, less manly, than he looked at a distance among his courtiers. His voice was thin, and he held his fierce lunatic head at an angle of bizarre arrogance.

"My lord, what I have to say is gone out of my head. I only just now learned of Lord Estraven's disgrace."

Argaven smiled at that, a stretched, staring grin. He laughed shrilly like an angry woman pretending to be amused. "Damn him," he said, "the proud, posturing, perjuring traitor! You dined with him last night, eh? And he told you what a powerful fellow he is, and how he runs the king, and how easy you'll find me to deal with since he's been talking to me about you—eh? Is that what he told you, Mr. Ai?"

I hesitated.

"I'll tell you what he's been saying to me about you, if you've an interest in knowing. He's been advising me to refuse you audience, keep you hanging about waiting, maybe pack you off to Orgoreyn or the Islands. All this halfmonth he's been telling me, damn his insolence! It's he that got packed off to Orgoreyn, ha ha ha—!" Again the shrill false laugh, and he clapped his hands together as he laughed. A silent immediate guard appeared between curtains at the end of the dais. Argaven snarled at him and he vanished. Still laughing and still snarling Argaven came up close and stared straight at me. The dark irises of his eyes glowed slightly orange. I was a good deal more afraid of him than I had expected to be.

I could see no course to follow among these

incoherencies but that of candor. I said, "I can only ask you, sir, whether I'm considered to be implicated in Estraven's crime."

"You? No." He stared even more closely at me. "I don't know what the devil you are, Mr. Ai, a sexual freak or an artificial monster or a visitor from the Domains of the Void, but you're not a traitor, you've merely been the tool of one. I don't punish tools. They do harm only in the hands of a bad workman. Let me give you some advice." Argaven said this with curious emphasis and satisfaction, and even then it occurred to me that nobody else, in two years, had ever given me advice. They answered questions, but they never openly gave advice, not even Estraven at his most helpful. It must have to do with shifgrethor. "Let no one else use you, Mr. Ai," the king was saying. "Keep clear of factions. Tell your own lies, do your own deeds. And trust no one. D'you know that? Trust no one. Damn that lying cold-blooded traitor, I trusted him. I put the silver chain around his damned neck. I wish I'd hanged him with it. I never trusted him. Never. Don't trust anybody. Let him starve in the cesspits of Mishnory hunting garbage, let his bowels rot, never—" King Argaven shook, choked, caught his breath with a retching sound, and turned his back on me. He kicked at the logs of the great fire till sparks whirled up thick in his face and fell on his hair and his black tunic, and he caught at them with open hands.

Not turning around he spoke in a shrill painful voice: "Say what you've got to say, Mr. Ai."

"May I ask you a question, sir?"

"Yes." He swayed from foot to foot as he stood facing the fire. I had to address his back.

"Do you believe that I am what I say I am?"

"Estraven had the physicians send me endless tapes about you, and more from the engineers at the Workshops who have your vehicle, and so on. They can't all be liars, and they all say you're not human. What then?"

"Then, sir, there are others like me. That is, I'm a representative . . ."

"Of this union, this Authority, yes, very well. What did they send you here for, is that what you want me to ask?"

Though Argaven might be neither sane nor shrewd, he had had long practice in the evasions and challenges and rhetorical subtleties used in conversation by those whose main aim in life was the achievement and maintenance of the shifgrethor relationship on a high level. Whole areas of that relationship were still blank to me, but I knew something about the competitive, prestige-seeking aspect of it, and about the perpetual conversational duel that can result from it. That I was not dueling with Argaven, but trying to communicate with him, was itself an incommunicable fact.

"I've made no secret of it, sir. The Ekumen wants an alliance with the nations of Gethen."

"What for?"

"Material profit. Increase of knowledge. The augmentation of the complexity and intensity of the field of intelligent life. The enrichment of harmony and the greater glory of God. Curiosity. Adventure. Delight."

I was not speaking the tongue spoken by those who rule men, the kings, conquerors, dictators, generals; in that language there was no answer to his question. Sullen and unheeding, Argaven stared at the fire, shifting from foot to foot.

"How big is this kingdom out in Nowhere, this Ekumen?"

"There are eighty-three habitable planets in the Ekumenical Scope, and on them about three thousand nations or anthrotypic groups—"

"Three thousand? I see. Now tell me why we, one against three thousand, should have anything to do with all these nations of monsters living out in the Void?" He turned around now to look at me, for he was still dueling, posing a rhetorical question, almost a joke. But the joke did not go deep. He was—as Estraven had warned me—uneasy, alarmed.

"Three thousand nations on eighty-three worlds, sir; but the nearest to Gethen is seventeen year's journey in ships that go at near lightspeed. If you've thought that Gethen might be involved in forays and harassments from such neighbors, consider the distance at which they live. Forays are worth no one's trouble, across space." I did not speak of war, for a good reason; there's no word for it in Karhidish. "Trade, however, is worthwhile. In ideas and techniques, communicated by ansible; in goods and artifacts, sent by manned or unmanned ships. Ambassadors, scholars, and merchants, some of them might come here; some of yours might go offworld. The Ekumen is not a kingdom, but a co-ordinator, a clearinghouse for trade and knowledge; without it communication between the worlds of men would be haphazard, and trade very risky, as you can see. Men's lives are too short to cope with the time-jumps between worlds, if there's no network and centrality, no control, no continuity to work through; therefore they become members of the Ekumen. . . . We are all men, you know, sir. All of us. All the worlds of men were settled, eons ago, from one world, Hain. We vary, but we're all sons of the same Hearth. . . ."

None of this caught the king's curiosity or gave him any reassurance. I went on a bit, trying to suggest that his shifgrethor, or Karhide's, would be enhanced, not threatened by the presence of the Ekumen, but it was no good. Argaven stood there sullen as an old she-otter in a cage, swinging back and forth, from foot to foot, back and forth, baring his teeth in a grin of pain. I stopped talking.

"Are they all black as you?"

Gethenians are yellow-brown or red-brown, generally, but I had seen a good many as dark as myself. "Some are blacker," I said; "we come all colors," and I opened the case (politely examined by the guards of the Palace at four stages of my approach to the Red Hall) that held my ansible and some pictures. The pictures—films, photos, paintings, actives, and some cubes—were a little gallery of Man: people of Hain, Chiffewar, and the Cetians, of S and Terra and Alterra, of the Uttermosts, Kapetyn, Ollul, Four-Taurus, Rokanan, Ensbo, Cime, Gde and Sheashel Haven. . . . The king glanced at a couple without interest. "What's this?"

"A person from Cime, a female." I had to use the word that Gethenians would apply only to a person in the culminant phase of kemmer, the alternative being their word for a female animal.

"Permanently?"

"Yes."

He dropped the cube and stood swinging from foot to foot, staring at me or a little past me, the firelight shifting on his face. "They're all like that—like you?"

This was the hurdle I could not lower for them. They must, in the end, learn to take it in their stride.

"Yes. Gethenian sexual physiology, so far as we yet know, is unique among human beings."

"So all of them, out on these other planets, are in permanent kemmer? A society of perverts? So Lord Tibe put it; I thought he was joking. Well, it may be the fact, but it's a disgusting idea, Mr. Ai, and I don't see why human beings here on earth should want or tolerate any dealings with creatures so monstrously different. But then, perhaps you're here to tell me I have no choice in the matter."

"The choice, for Karhide, is yours, sir."

"And if I send you packing too?"

"Why, I'll go. I might try again, with another generation. . . ."

That hit him. He snapped, "Are you immortal?"

"No, not at all, sir. But the time-jumps have their uses. If I left Gethen now for the nearest world, Ollul, I'd spend seventeen years of planetary time getting there. Timejumping is a function of traveling nearly as fast as light. If I simply turned around and came back, my few hours spent on the ship would, here, amount to thirty-four years; and I could start all over." But the idea of timejumping, which with its false hint of immortality had fascinated everyone who listened to me, from the Horden Island fisherman on up to the prime minister, left him cold. He said in his shrill harsh voice, "What's that?"—pointing to the ansible.

"The ansible communicator, sir."

"A radio?"

"It doesn't involve radio waves, or any form of energy. The principle it works, on the constant of simultaneity, is analogous in some ways to gravity—" I had forgotten again that I wasn't talking to Estraven, who had read every report on me and who listened intently and intelligently to all my explanations, but instead to a bored king. "What it does, sir, is produce a message at any two points simultaneously. Anywhere. One point has to be fixed, on a planet of a certain mass, but the other end is portable. That's this end. I've set the coordinates for the Prime World, Hain. A NAFAL ship takes 67 years to go between Gethen and Hain, but if I write a message on that keyboard it will be received on Hain at the same moment as I write it. Is there any communication you'd care to make with the Stabiles on Hain, sir?"

"I don't speak Voidish," said the king with his dull, malign grin.

"They'll have an aide standing ready—I alerted them—who can handle Karhidish."

"What d'you mean? How?"

"Well, as you know, sir, I'm not the first alien to come to Gethen. I was preceded by a team of Investigators, who didn't announce their presence, but passed as well as they could for Gethenians, and traveled about in Karhide and Orgoreyn and the Archipelago for a year. They left, and reported to the Councils of the Ekumen, over forty years ago, during your grandfather's reign. Their report was extremely favorable. And so I studied the information they'd gathered, and the languages they'd recorded, and came. Would you like to see the device working, sir?"

"I don't like tricks, Mr. Ai."

"It's not a trick, sir. Some of your own scientists have examined—"

"I'm not a scientist."

"You're a sovereign, my lord. Your peers on the Prime World of the Ekumen wait for a word from you."

He looked at me savagely. In trying to flatter and interest him I had cornered him in a prestige-trap. It was all going wrong.

"Very well. Ask your machine there what makes a man a traitor."

I typed out slowly on the keys, which were set to Karhidish characters, "King Argaven of Karhide asks the Stabiles on Hain what makes a man a traitor." The letters burned across the small screen and faded. Argaven watched, his restless shifting stilled for a minute.

There was a pause, a long pause. Somebody seventy-two light-years away was no doubt feverishly punching demands on the language computer for Karhidish, if not

on a philosophy-storage computer. At last the bright letters burned up out of the screen, hung awhile, and faded
slowly away: "To King Argaven of Karhide on Gethen,
greetings. I do not know what makes a man a traitor.
No man considers himself a traitor: this makes it hard to
find out. Respectfully, Spimolle G. F., for the Stabiles, in
Saire on Hain, 93/1491/45."

When the tape was recorded I pulled it out and gave
it to Argaven. He dropped it on the table, walked again
to the central fireplace, almost into it, and kicked the
flaming logs and beat down the sparks with his hands.
"As useful an answer as I might get from any Foreteller.
Answers aren't enough, Mr. Ai. Nor is your box, your
machine there. Nor your vehicle, your ship. A bag of
tricks and a trickster. You want me to believe you, your
tales and messages. But why need I believe, or listen? If
there are eighty thousand worlds full of monsters out
there among the stars, what of it? We want nothing from
them. We've chosen our way of life and have followed it
for a long time. Karhide's on the brink of a new epoch,
a great new age. We'll go our own way." He hesitated
as if he had lost the thread of his argument—not his
own argument, perhaps, in the first place. If Estraven
was no longer the King's Ear, somebody else was. "And
if there were anything these Ekumens wanted from us,
they wouldn't have sent you alone. It's a joke, a hoax.
Aliens would be here by the thousand."

"But it doesn't take a thousand men to open a door,
my lord."

"It might to keep it open."

"The Ekumen will wait till you open it, sir. It will force nothing on you. I was sent alone, and remain here alone, in order to make it impossible for you to fear me."

"Fear you?" said the king, turning his shadow-scarred face, grinning, speaking loud and high. "But I do fear you, Envoy. I fear those who sent you. I fear liars, and I fear tricksters, and worst I fear the bitter truth. And so I rule my country well. Because only fear rules men. Nothing else works. Nothing else lasts long enough. You are what you say you are, yet you're a joke, a hoax. There's nothing in between the stars but void and terror and darkness, and you come out of that all alone trying to frighten me. But I am already afraid, and I am the king. Fear is king! Now take your traps and tricks and go, there's no more needs saying. I have ordered that you be given the freedom of Karhide."

So I departed from the royal presence—*eck, eck, eck* all down the long red floor in the red gloom of the hall, until at last the double doors shut me off from him.

I had failed. Failed all around. What worried me as I left the King's House and walked through the Palace grounds, however, was not my failure, but Estraven's part in it. Why had the king exiled him for advocating the Ekumen's cause (which seemed to be the meaning of the proclamation) if (according to the king himself) he had been doing the opposite? When had he started advising the king to steer clear of me, and why? Why was he exiled, and I let go free? Which of them had lied more, and what the devil were they lying for?

Estraven to save his skin, I decided, and the king to

save his face. The explanation was neat. But had Estraven, in fact, ever lied to me? I discovered that I did not know.

I was passing the Corner Red Dwelling. The gates of the garden stood open. I glanced in at the serem-trees leaning white above the dark pool, the paths of pink brick lying deserted in the serene gray light of afternoon. A little snow still lay in the shadow of the rocks by the pool. I thought of Estraven waiting for me there as the snow fell last night, and felt a pang of pure pity for the man whom I had seen in yesterday's parade sweating and superb under the weight of his panoply and power, a man at the prime of his career, potent and magnificent—gone now, down, done. Running for the border with his death three days behind him, and no man speaking to him. The death-sentence is rare in Karhide. Life on Winter is hard to live, and people there generally leave death to nature or to anger, not to law. I wondered how Estraven, with that sentence driving him, would go. Not in a car, for they were all Palace property here; would a ship or landboat give him passage? Or was he afoot on the road, carrying what he could carry with him? Karhides go afoot, mostly; they have no beasts of burden, no flying vehicles, the weather makes slow going for powered traffic most of the year, and they are not a people who hurry. I imagined the proud man going into exile step by step, a small trudging figure on the long road west to the Gulf. All this went through my mind and out of it as I passed the gate of the Corner Red Dwelling, and with it went my confused speculations concerning the acts and motives of Estraven and the king. I was done with them. I had failed. What next?

I should go to Orgoreyn, Karhide's neighbor and rival. But once I went there I might find it hard to return to Karhide, and I had unfinished business here. I had to keep in mind that my entire life could be, and might well be, used in achieving my mission for the Ekumen. No hurry. No need to rush off to Orgoreyn before I had learned more about Karhide, particularly about the Fastnesses. For two years I had been answering questions, now I would ask some. But not in Erhenrang. I had finally understood that Estraven had been warning me, and though I might distrust his warning I could not disregard it. He had been saying, however indirectly, that I should get away from the city and the court. For some reason I thought of Lord Tibe's teeth. . . . The king had given me the freedom of the country; I would avail myself of it. As they say in Ekumenical School, when action grows unprofitable, gather information; when information grows unprofitable, sleep. I was not sleepy, yet. I would go east to the Fastnesses, and gather information from the Foretellers, perhaps.

4

THE NINETEENTH DAY

An East Karhidish story, as told in Gorinhering Hearth by Tobord Chorhawa, and recorded by G. A., 93/1492.

Lord Berosty rem ir Ipe came to Thangering Fastness and offered forty beryls and half the year's yield from his orchards as the price of a Foretelling, and the price was acceptable. He set his question to the Weaver Odren, and the question was, *On what day shall I die?*

The Foretellers gathered and went together into the darkness. At the end of darkness Odren spoke the answer: *You will die on Odstreth* (the 19th day of any month).

"In what month? in how many years?" cried Berosty, but the bond was broken, and there was no answer. He ran into the circle and took the Weaver Odren by the throat, choking him, and shouted that if he got no further answer he would break the Weaver's neck. Others pulled him off and held him, though he was a strong

man. He strained against their hands and cried out,
"Give me the answer!"

Odren said, "It is given, and the price paid. Go."

Raging then Berosty rem ir Ipe returned to Charuthe,
the third Domain of his family, a poor place in northern Osnoriner, which he had made poorer in getting
together the price of a Foretelling. He shut himself up
in the strong-place, in the highest rooms of the Hearth-
Tower, and would not come out for friend or foe, for
seedtime or harvest, for kemmer or foray, all that month
and the next and the next, and six months went by and
ten months went by, and he still kept like a prisoner to
his room, waiting. On Onnetherhad and Odstreth (the
18th and 19th days of the month) he would not eat any
food, nor would he drink, nor would he sleep.

His kemmering by love and vow was Herbor of the
Geganner clan. This Herbor came in the month of
Grende to Thangering Fastness and said to the Weaver,
"I seek a Foretelling."

"What have you to pay?" Odren asked, for he saw
that the man was poorly dressed and badly shod, and
his sledge was old, and everything about him wanted
mending.

"I will give my life," said Herbor.

"Have you nothing else, my lord?" Odren asked him,
speaking now as to a great nobleman, "nothing else to
give?"

"I have nothing else," said Herbor. "But I do not
know if my life is of any value to you here."

"No," said Odren, "it is of no value to us."

Then Herbor fell on his knees, struck down by shame and love, and cried to Odren, "I beg you to answer my question. It is not for myself!"

"For whom, then?" asked the Weaver.

"For my lord and kemmering Ashe Berosty," said the man, and he wept. "He has no love nor joy nor lordship since he came here and got that answer which was no answer. He will die of it."

"That he will: what does a man die of but his death?" said the Weaver Odren. But Herbor's passion moved him, and at length he said, "I will seek the answer of the question you ask, Herbor, and I will ask no price. But bethink you, there is always a price. The asker pays what he has to pay."

Then Herbor set Odren's hands against his own eyes in sign of gratitude, and so the Foretelling went forward. The Foretellers gathered and went into the darkness. Herbor went among them and asked his question, and the question was, *How long will Ashe Berosty rem ir Ipe live?* For Herbor thought thus to get the count of days or years, and so set his love's heart at rest with certain knowledge. Then the Foretellers moved in the darkness and at last Odren cried in great pain, as if he burned in a fire, *Longer than Herbor of Geganner!*

It was not the answer Herbor had hoped, but it was the answer he got, and having a patient heart he went home to Charuthe with it, through the snows of Grende. He came into the Domain and into the strong-place and climbed the tower, and there found his kemmering Berosty sitting as ever blank and bleak by an ash-smothered fire, his arms lying on a table of red stone, his head sunk between his shoulders.

"Ashe," said Herbor, "I have been to Thangering Fastness, and have been answered by the Foretellers. I asked them how long you would live and their answer was, Berosty will live longer than Herbor."

Berosty looked up at him as slow as if the hinge in his neck had rusted, and said, "Did you ask them when I would die, then?"

"I asked how long you would live."

"How long? You fool! You had a question of the Fore-tellers, and did not ask them when I am to die, what day, month, year, how many days are left to me—you asked *how long?* Oh you fool, you staring fool, longer than you, yes, longer than you!" Berosty took up the great table of red stone as if it had been a sheet of tin and brought it down on Herbor's head. Herbor fell, and the stone lay on him. Berosty stood awhile demented. Then he raised up the stone, and saw that it had crushed Herbor's skull. He set the stone back on its pedestal. He lay down beside the dead man and put his arms about him, as if they were in kemmer and all was well. So the people of Charuthe found them when they broke into the tower-room at last. Berosty was mad thereafter and had to be kept under lock, for he would always go looking for Herbor, who he thought was somewhere about the Domain. He lived a month thus, and then hanged himself, on Odstreth, the nineteenth day of the month of Thern.

5

THE DOMESTICATION OF HUNCH

My landlady, a voluble man, arranged my journey into the East. "If a person wants to visit Fastnesses he's got to cross the Kargav. Over the mountains, into Old Karhide, to Rer, the old King's City. Now I'll tell you, a hearthfellow of mine runs a landboat caravan over the Eskar Pass and yesterday he was telling me over a cup of orsh that they're going to make their first trip this summer on Getheny Osme, it having been such a warm spring and the road already clear up to Engohar and the plows will have the pass clear in another couple of days. Now you won't catch me crossing the Kargav, Erhenrang for me and a roof over my head. But I'm a Yomeshta, praise to the nine hundred Throne-Upholders and blest be the Milk of Meshe, and one can be a Yomeshta anywhere. We're a lot of newcomers, see, for my Lord Meshe was born 2,202 years ago, but the Old Way of the Handdara goes back ten thousand years before that. You have to go back to the Old Land if you're after the Old Way. Now look here, Mr. Ai, I'll have a room in this island for you whenever you come back, but I believe you're a wise man to be going out of Erhenrang for a while, for everybody knows that the Traitor made a great show of befriending you at the Palace. Now with old Tibe as the King's Ear things will go smooth again. Now if you go down to the New Port you'll find my hearthfellow there, and if you tell him I sent you . . ."

And so on. He was, as I said, voluble, and having discovered that I had no shifgrethor took every chance to give me advice, though even he disguised it with ifs and as-ifs. He was the superintendent of my island; I thought of him as my landlady, for he had fat buttocks that wagged as he walked, and a soft fat face, and a prying, spying, ignoble, kindly nature. He was good to me, and also showed my room while I was out to thrill-seekers for a small fee: See the Mysterious Envoy's room! He was so feminine in looks and manner that I once asked him how many children he had. He looked glum. He had never borne any. He had, however, sired four. It was one of the little jolts I was always getting. Cultural shock was nothing much compared to the biological shock I suffered as a human male among human beings who were, five-sixths of the time, hermaphroditic neuters.

The radio bulletins were full of the doings of the new prime minister, Pemmer Harge rem ir Tibe. Much of the news concerned affairs up north in the Sinoth Valley. Tibe evidently was going to press Karhide's claim to that region: precisely the kind of action which, on any other world at this stage of civilization, would lead to war. But on Gethen nothing led to war. Quarrels, murders, feuds, forays, vendettas, assassinations, tortures and abominations, all these were in their repertory of human accomplishments; but they did not go to war. They lacked, it seemed, the capacity to *mobilize*. They behaved like animals, in that respect; or like women. They did not behave like men, or ants. At any rate they never yet had done so. What I knew of Orgoreyn indicated that it had become, over the last five or six centuries, an increasingly mobilizable society, a real nation-state. The prestige-competition, heretofore mostly economic, might force Karhide to emulate its larger neighbor, to become a nation instead of a family quarrel, as Estraven had said; to become, as Estraven had also said, patriotic. If this occurred the Gethenians might have an excellent chance of achieving the condition of war.

I wanted to go to Orgoreyn and see if my guesses concerning it were sound, but I wanted to finish up with Karhide first; so I sold another ruby to the scarfaced jeweler in Eng Street, and with no baggage but my money, my ansible, a few instruments and a change of clothes, set off as a passenger on a trade-caravan on the first day of the first month of summer.

The landboats left at daybreak from the windswept loading-yards of the New Port. They drove under the Arch and turned east, twenty bulky, quiet-running, barge-like trucks on caterpillar treads, going single file down the deep streets of Erhenrang through the shadows of morning. They carried boxes of lenses, reels of soundtapes, spools of copper and platinum wire, bolts of plant-fiber cloth raised and woven in the West Fall, chests of dried fish-flakes from the Gulf, crates of ballbearings and other small machine parts, and ten truckloads of Orgota kardik-grain: all bound for the Pering Stormborder, the northeast corner of the land. All shipping on the Great Continent is by these electric-powered trucks, which go on barges on the rivers and canals where possible. During the deep-snow months, slow tractor-plows, power-sledges, and the erratic ice-ships on frozen rivers are the only transport beside skis and manhauled sledges; during the Thaw no form of transport is reliable; so most freight traffic goes with a rush, come summer. The roads then are thick with caravans. Traffic is controlled, each vehicle or caravan being required to keep in constant radio touch with checkpoints along the way. It all moves along, however crowded, quite steadily at the rate of 25 miles per hour (Terran). Gethenians could make their vehicles go faster, but they do not. If asked why not, they answer "Why?" Like asking Terrans why all our vehicles must go so fast; we answer "Why not?" No disputing tastes. Terrans tend to feel they've got to get ahead, make progress. The people of Winter, who always live in the Year One, feel that progress is less important than presence. My tastes were Terran, and leaving Erhenrang I was impatient with the methodical pace of the caravan; I wanted to get out and run. I was glad to get clear of those long stone streets overhung with black, steep roofs and innumerable towers, that sunless city where all my chances had turned to fear and betrayal.

Climbing the Kargav foothills the caravan halted briefly but often for meals at roadside inns. Along in the afternoon we got our first full view of the range from a foothill summit. We saw Kostor, which is four miles high, from foot to crest; the huge slant of its western slope hid the peaks north of it, some of which go up to thirty thousand feet. South from Kostor one peak after another stood out white against a colorless sky; I counted thirteen, the last an undefined glimmer in the mist of distance in the south. The driver named the thirteen for me, and told me stories of avalanches, and landboats blown off the road by mountain winds, and snowplow crews marooned for weeks in inaccessible heights, and so on, in a friendly effort to terrify me. He described having seen the truck ahead of his skid and go over a thousand-foot precipice; what was remarkable, he said, was the slowness with which it fell. It seemed to take all afternoon floating down into the abyss, and he had been very glad to see it at last vanish, with no sound at all, into a forty-foot snowdrift at the bottom.

At Third Hour we stopped for dinner at a large inn, a grand place with vast roaring fireplaces and vast beam-roofed rooms full of tables loaded with good food; but we did not stay the night. Ours was a sleeper-caravan, hurrying (in its Karhidish fashion) to be the first of the season into the Pering Storm country, to skim the cream of the market for its merchant-entrepreneurs. The truck-batteries were recharged, a new shift of drivers took over, and we went on. One truck of the caravan served as sleeper, for drivers only. No beds for passengers. I spent the night in the cold cab on the hard seat, with one break along near midnight for supper at a little inn high in the hills. Karhide is no country for comfort. At dawn I was awake and saw that we had left everything behind except rock, and ice, and light, and the narrow road always going up and up under our treads. I thought, shivering, that there are things that outweigh comfort, unless one is an old woman or a cat.

No more inns now, among these appalling slopes of snow and granite. At mealtimes the landboats came silently to a halt one after the other on some thirty-degree, snow-encroached grade, and everybody climbed down from the cabs and gathered about the sleeper, from which bowls of hot soup were served, slabs of dried bread-apple, and sour beer in mugs. We stood about stamping in the snow, gobbling up food and drink, backs to the bitter wind that was filled with a glittering dust of dry snow. Then back into the landboats, and on, and up. At noon in the passes of Wehoth, at about 14,000 feet, it was 82°F in the sun and 13° in the shade. The electric engines were so quiet that one could hear avalanches grumble down immense blue slopes on the far side of chasms twenty miles across.

Late that afternoon we passed the summit, at Eskar, 15,200 feet. Looking up the slope of the southern face of Kostor, on which we had been infinitesimally crawling all day, I saw a queer rock-formation a quarter mile or so above the road, a castle-like outcropping. "See the Fast-ness up there?" said the driver.

"That's a building?"

"That's Arikostor Fastness."

"But no one could live up here."

"Oh, the Old Men can. I used to drive in a caravan that brought up their food from Erhenrang, late in sum-mer. Of course they can't get in or out for ten or eleven months of the year, but they don't care. There's seven or eight Indwellers up there."

I stared up at the buttresses of rough rock, solitary in the huge solitude of the heights, and I did not believe the driver; but I suspended my disbelief. If any people could survive in such a frozen aerie, they would be Karhiders.

The road descending swung far north and far south, edging along precipices, for the east slope of the Kar-gav is harsher than the west, falling to the plains in great stairsteps, the raw fault-blocks of the mountains' making. At sunset we saw a tiny string of dots creep-ing through a huge white shadow seven thousand feet below: a landboat caravan that had left Erhenrang a day ahead of us. Late the next day we had got down there and were creeping along that same snow-slope, very softly, not sneezing, lest we bring down the avalanche. From there we saw for a while, away below and beyond us eastward, vague vast lands blurred with clouds and shadows of clouds and streaked with silver of rivers, the Plains of Rer.

At dusk of the fourth day out from Erhenrang we came to Rer. Between the two cities lie eleven hundred miles, and a wall several miles high, and two or three thousand years. The caravan halted outside the Western Gate, where it would be shifted onto canal-barges. No landboat or car can enter Rer. It was built before Karhiders used powered vehicles, and they have been using them for over twenty centuries. There are no streets in Rer. There are covered walks, tunnel-like, which in summer one may walk through or on top of as one pleases. The houses and islands and Hearths sit every which way, chaotic, in a profuse prodigious confusion that suddenly culminates (as anarchy will do in Karhide) in splendor: the great Towers of the Un-Palace, bloodred, windowless. Built seventeen centuries ago, those towers housed the kings of Karhide for a thousand years, until Argaven Harge, first of his dynasty, crossed the Kargav and settled the great valley of the West Fall. All the buildings of Rer are fantastically massive, deep-founded, weatherproof and waterproof. In winter the wind of the plains may keep the city clear of snow, but when it blizzards and piles up they do not clear the streets, having no streets to clear. They use the stone tunnels, or burrow temporary ones in the snow. Nothing of the houses but the roof sticks out above the snow, and the winter-doors may be set under the eaves or in the roof itself, like dormers. The Thaw is the bad time on that plain of many rivers. The tunnels then are storm-sewers, and the spaces between buildings become canals or lakes, on which the people of Rer boat to their business, fending off small ice-floes with the oars. And always, over the dust of summer, the snowy roof-jumble of winter, or the floods of spring, the red Towers loom, the empty heart of the city, indestructible.

I lodged in a dreary overpriced inn crouching in the lee of the Towers. I got up at dawn after many bad dreams, and paid the extortioner for bed and breakfast and inaccurate directions as to the way I should take, and set forth afoot to find Otherhord, an ancient Fastness not far from Rer. I was lost within fifty yards of the inn. By keeping the Towers behind me and the huge white loom of the Kargav on my right, I got out of the city headed south, and a farmer's child met on the road told me where to turn off for Otherhord.

I came there at noon. That is, I came somewhere at noon, but I wasn't sure where. It was mainly a forest or a thick wood; but the woods were even more carefully tended than is usual in that country of careful foresters, and the path led along the hillside right in among the trees. After a while I became aware that there was a wooden hut just off the path to my right, and then I noticed a quite large wooden building a little farther off to my left; and from somewhere there came a delicious smell of fresh frying fish.

I went slowly along the path, a little uneasy. I didn't know how the Handdarata felt about tourists. I knew very little about them in fact. The Handdara is a religion without institution, without priests, without hierarchy, without vows, without creed; I am still unable to say whether it has a God or not. It is elusive. It is always somewhere else. Its only fixed manifestation is in the Fastnesses, retreats to which people may retire and spend the night or a lifetime. I wouldn't have been pursuing this curiously intangible cult into its secret places at all, if I hadn't wanted to answer the question left unanswered by the Investigators: What are the Foretellers, and what do they actually do?

I had been longer in Karhide now than the Investigators had, and I doubted that there was anything to the stories of Foretellers and their prophecies. Legends of prediction are common throughout the whole Household of Man. God speaks, spirits speak, computers speak. Oracular ambiguity or statistical probability provides loopholes, and discrepancies are expunged by Faith. However, the legends were worth investigating. I hadn't yet convinced any Karhider of the existence of telephathic communication; they wouldn't believe it till they "saw" it: my position exactly, regarding the Foretellers of the Handdara.

As I went on along the path I realized that a whole village or town was scattered about in the shadow of that slanting forest, all as random as Rer was, but secretive, peaceful, rural. Over every roof and path hung the boughs of the hemmens, the commonest tree of Winter, a stout conifer with thick pale-scarlet needles. Hemmen-cones littered the branching paths, the wind was scented with hemmen-pollen, and all the houses were built of the dark hemmen-wood. I stopped at last wondering which door to knock at, when a person came sauntering out of the trees and greeted me courteously. "Will you be looking for a dwelling-place?" he asked.

"I've come with a question for the Foretellers." I

had decided to let them take me, at first anyhow, for a Karhider. Like the Investigators I had never had any trouble passing as a native, if I wanted to; among all the Karhidish dialects my accent went unnoticed, and my sexual anomalies were hidden by the heavy clothing. I lacked the fine thick hair-thatch and the downward eye-slant of the typical Gethenian, and was blacker and taller than most, but not beyond the range of normal variation. My beard had been permanently depilated before I left Ollul (at that time we didn't yet know about the "pelted" tribes of Perunter, who are not only bearded but hairy all over, like White Terrans). Occasionally I was asked how my nose got broken. I have a flat nose; Gethenian noses are prominent and narrow, with constricted passages, well adapted to breathing subfreezing air. The person on the path at Otherhord looked with mild curiosity at my nose, and answered, "Then perhaps you'll want to speak to the Weaver? He's down in the glade now, unless he went out with the woodsledge. Or would you rather talk first to one of the Celibates?"

"I'm not sure. I'm exceedingly ignorant—"

The young man laughed and bowed. "I am honored!" he said. "I've lived here three years, but haven't yet acquired enough ignorance to be worth mentioning." He was highly amused, but his manner was gentle, and I managed to recollect enough scraps of Handdara lore to realize that I had been boasting, very much as if I'd come up to him and said, "I'm exceedingly handsome . . ."

"I meant, I don't know anything about the Fore-tellers—"

"Enviable!" said the young Indweller. "Behold, we must sully the plain snow with footprints, in order to get anywhere. May I show you the way to the glade? My name is Goss."

It was a first name. "Genry," I said, abandoning my "l." I followed Goss farther into the chill shade of the forest. The narrow path changed direction often, winding up the slope and down again; here and there, near it or away off among the massive trunks of the hemmens, stood the small, forest-colored houses. Everything was red and brown, dank, still, fragrant, gloomy. From one of the houses drifted the faint whistling sweetness of a Karhidish flute. Goss went light and quick, graceful as a girl, some yards ahead of me. All at once his white shirt blazed out, and I came out after him from shadow into full sunlight on a wide green meadow.

Twenty feet from us stood a figure, straight, motionless, profiled, the scarlet hieb and white shirt an inlay of bright enamel against the green of the high grass. A hundred yards beyond him stood another statue, in blue and white; this one never moved or glanced our way all the time we talked with the first one. They were practicing the Handdara discipline of Presence, which is a kind of trance—the Handdarata, given to negatives, call it an untrance—involving self-loss (self-augmentation?) through extreme sensual receptiveness and awareness. Though the technique is the exact opposite of most techniques of mysticism it probably is a mystical discipline, tending towards the experience of Immanence; but I can't categorize any practice of the Handdarata with certainty. Goss spoke to the person in scarlet. As he broke from his intense movelessness and looked at us and came slowly towards us, I felt an awe of him. In that noon sunlight he shone of his own light.

He was as tall as I, and slender, with a clear, open, and beautiful face. As his eyes met mine I was suddenly moved to bespeak him, to try to reach him with the mindspeech I had never used since I landed on Winter, and should not use, yet. The impulse was stronger than the restraint. I bespoke him. There was no response. No contact was made. He continued to look straight at me. After a moment he smiled and said in a soft, rather high voice, "You're the Envoy, aren't you?"

I stammered and said, "Yes."

"My name is Faxe. We're honored to receive you. Will you stay with us in Otherhord awhile?"

"Willingly. I am seeking to learn about your practice of Foretelling. And if there's anything I can tell you in return about what I am, where I come from—"

"Whatever you like," said Faxe with a serene smile. "This is a pleasant thing, that you should cross the Ocean of Space, and then add another thousand miles and a crossing of the Karga to your journey to come to us here."

"I wanted to come to Otherhord because of the fame of its predictions."

"You want to watch us foretelling, then, perhaps. Or have you a question of your own?"

His clear eyes compelled truth. "I don't know," I said.

"Nusuth," said he, "it doesn't matter. Perhaps if you

stay awhile you'll find if you have a question, or no question. . . . There are only certain times, you know, when the Foretellers are able to meet together, so in any case you'd dwell with us some days."

I did, and they were pleasant days. Time was unorganized except for the communal work, field labor, gardening, woodcutting, maintenance, for which transients such as myself were called on by whatever group most needed a hand. Aside from the work, a day might pass without a word spoken; those I talked with most often were young Goss, and Faxe the Weaver, whose extraordinary character, as limpid and unfathomable as a well of very clear water, was a quintessence of the character of the place. In the evenings there might be a gathering in the hearth-room of one or another of the low, tree-surrounded houses; there was conversation, and beer, and there might be music, the vigorous music of Karhide, melodically simple but rhythmically complex, always played extempore. One night two Indwellers danced, men so old that their hair had whitened, and their limbs were skinny, and the downward folds at the outer eye-corners half hid their dark eyes. Their dancing was slow, precise, controlled; it fascinated eye and mind. They began dancing during Third Hour after dinner. Musicians joined in and dropped out at will, all but the drummer who never stopped his subtle changing beat. The two old dancers were still dancing at Sixth Hour, midnight, after five Terran hours. This was the first time I had seen the phenomenon of *dothe*—the voluntary, controlled use of what we call "hysterical strength"—

and thereafter I was readier to believe tales concerning the Old Men of the Handdara.

It was an introverted life, self-sufficient, stagnant, steeped in that singular "ignorance" prized by the Handdarata and obedient to their rule of inactivity or non-interference. That rule (expressed in the word *nusuth*, which I have to translate as "no matter") is the heart of the cult, and I don't pretend to understand it. But I began to understand Karhide better, after a halfmonth in Otherhord. Under that nation's politics and parades and passions runs an old darkness, passive, anarchic, silent, the fecund darkness of the Handdara.

And out of that silence inexplicably rises the Foreteller's voice.

Young Goss, who enjoyed acting as my guide, told me that my question to the Foretellers could concern anything and be phrased as I liked. "The more qualified and limited the question, the more exact the answer," he said. "Vagueness breeds vagueness. And some questions of course are not answerable."

"What if I ask one of those?" I inquired. This hedging seemed sophisticated, but not unfamiliar. But I did not expect his answer: "The Weaver will refuse it. Unanswerable questions have wrecked Foretelling groups."

"Wrecked them?"

"Do you know the story of the Lord of Shorth, who forced the Foretellers of Asen Fastness to answer the question *What is the meaning of life?* Well, it was a couple of thousand years ago. The Foretellers stayed in the darkness for six days and nights. At the end, all the Celibates were catatonic, the Zanies were dead, the Pervert clubbed the Lord of Shorth to death with a stone, and the Weaver . . . He was a man named Meshe."

"The founder of the Yomesh cult?"

"Yes," said Goss, and laughed as if the story was very funny, but I didn't know whether the joke was on the Yomeshta or on me.

I had decided to ask a yes-or-no question, which might at least make plain the extent and kind of obscurity or ambiguity in the answer. Faxe confirmed what Goss had said, that the matter of the question could be one of which the Foretellers were perfectly ignorant. I could ask if the hoolm crops would be good this year in the northern hemisphere of S, and they would answer, having no previous knowledge even of the existence of a planet called S. This seemed to put the business on the plane of pure chance divination, along with yarrow stalks and flipped coins. No, said Faxe, not at all, chance was not involved. The whole process was in fact precisely the reverse of chance.

"Then you mind read."

"No," said Faxe, with his serene and candid smile.

"You mind read without knowing you're doing it, perhaps."

"What good would that be? If the asker knew the answer he wouldn't pay our price for it."

I chose a question to which I certainly lacked the answer. Only time could prove the Foretelling right or wrong, unless it was, as I expected, one of those admirable professional prophecies applicable to any outcome.

It was not a trivial question; I had given up the notion of asking when it would stop raining, or some such trifle, when I learned that the undertaking was a hard and dangerous one for the nine Foretellers of Otherhord. The cost was high for the asker—two of my rubies went to the coffers of the Fastness—but higher for the answerers. And as I got to know Faxe, if it became difficult to believe that he was a professional faker it became still more difficult to believe that he was an honest, self-deluded faker; his intelligence was as hard, clear, and polished as my rubies. I dared set no trap for him. I asked what I most wanted to know.

On Onnetherhad, the 18th of the month, the nine met together in a big building usually kept locked: one high hall, stone-floored and cold, dimly lighted by a couple of slit-windows and a fire in the deep hearth at one end. They sat on the bare stone in a circle, all of them cloaked and hooded, rough still shapes like a circle of dolmens in the faint glow of the fire yards away. Goss, and a couple of other young Indwellers, and a physician from the nearest Domain, watched in silence from seats by the hearth while I crossed the hall and entered the circle. It was all very informal, and very tense. One of the hooded figures looked up as I came amongst them, and I saw a strange face, coarse-featured, heavy, with insolent eyes watching me.

Faxe sat cross-legged, not moving, but charged, full of a gathering force that made his light, soft voice crack like an electric bolt. "Ask," he said.

I stood within the circle and asked my question.

"Will this world Gethen be a member of the Ekumen of Known Worlds, five years from now?"

Silence. I stood there; I hung in the center of a spider-web woven of silence.

"It is answerable," the Weaver said quietly.

There was a relaxation. The hooded stones seemed to soften into movement; the one who had looked so strangely at me began to whisper to his neighbor. I left the circle and joined the watchers by the hearth.

Two of the Foretellers remained withdrawn, unspeaking. One of them lifted his left hand from time to time and patted the floor lightly and swiftly ten or twenty times, then sat motionless again. I had seen neither of them before; they were the Zanies, Goss said. They were insane. Goss called them "time-dividers," which may mean schizophrenics. Karhidish psychologists, though lacking mindspeech and thus like blind surgeons, were ingenious with drugs, hypnosis, spotshock, cryonic touch, and various mental therapies; I asked if these two psychopaths could not be cured. "Cured?" Goss said. "Would you cure a singer of his voice?"

Five others of the circle were Indwellers of Otherhord, adepts in the Handdara disciplines of Presence and also, said Goss, so long as they remained Foretellers, celibate, taking no mate during their periods of sexual potency. One of these Celibates must be in kemmer during the Foretelling. I could pick him out, having learned to notice the subtle physical intensification, a kind of brightness, that signalizes the first phase of kemmer.

Beside the kemmerer sat the Pervert.

"He came up from Spreve with the physician," Goss told me. "Some Foretelling groups artificially arouse perversion in a normal person—injecting female or male hormones during the days before a session. It's better to have a natural one. He's willing to come; likes the notoriety."

Goss used the pronoun that designates a male animal, not the pronoun for a human being in the masculine role of kemmer. He looked a little embarrassed. Karhiders discuss sexual matters freely, and talk about kemmer with both reverence and gusto, but they are reticent about discussing perversion—at least, they were with me. Excessive prolongation of the kemmer period, with permanent hormonal imbalance towards the male or the female, causes what they call perversion; it is not rare; three or four percent of adults may be physiological perverts or abnormals—normals, by our standard. They are not excluded from society, but they are tolerated with some disdain, as homosexuals are in many bisexual societies. The Karhidish slang for them is *halfdeads*. They are sterile.

The Pervert of the group, after that first long strange stare at me, paid no heed to anyone but the one next to him, the kemmerer, whose increasingly active sexuality would be further roused and finally stimulated into full, female sexual capacity by the insistent, exaggerated maleness of the Pervert. The Pervert kept talking softly, leaning towards the kemmerer, who answered little and seemed to recoil. None of the others had spoken for a long time now, there was no sound but the whisper, whisper of the Pervert's voice. Faxe was steadily watching one of the Zanies. The Pervert laid his hand quickly and softly on the kemmerer's hand. The kemmerer avoided the touch hastily, with fear or disgust, and looked across at Faxe as if for help. Faxe did not move. The kemmerer kept his place, and kept still when the Pervert touched him again. One of the Zanies lifted up his face and laughed a long false crooning laugh, "Ah-ah-ah-ah. . . ."

Faxe raised his hand. At once each face in the circle turned to him as if he had gathered up their gazes into a sheaf, a skein.

It had been afternoon and raining when we entered the hall. The gray light had soon died out of the slit-windows under the eaves. Now whitish strips of light stretched like slanting phantasmal sails, long triangles and oblongs, from wall to floor, over the faces of the nine; dull scraps and shreds of light from the moon rising over the forest, outside. The fire had burned down long since and there was no light but those strips and slants of dimness creeping across the circle, sketching out a face, a hand, a moveless back. For a while I saw Faxe's profile rigid as pale stone in a diffuse dust of light. The diagonal of moonlight crept on and came to a black hump, the kemmerer, head bowed on his knees, hands clenched on the floor, body shaken by a regular tremor repeated by the *slutter-pat-pat* of the Zany's hands on stone in darkness across the circle. They were all connected, all of them, as if they were the suspension-points of a spider-web. I felt, whether I wished or not, the connection, the communication that ran, wordless, inarticulate, through Faxe, and which Faxe was trying to pattern and control, for he was the center, the Weaver. The dim light fragmented and died away creeping up the eastern wall. The web of force, of tension, of silence, grew.

I tried to keep out of contact with the minds of the Foretellers. I was made very uneasy by that silent electric tension, by the sense of being drawn in, of becoming a point or figure in the pattern, in the web. But when I set up a barrier, it was worse: I felt cut off and cowered inside my own mind obsessed by hallucinations of sight and touch, a stew of wild images and notions, abrupt visions and sensations all sexually charged and grotesquely violent, a red-and-black seething of erotic rage. I was surrounded by great gaping pits with ragged lips, vaginas, wounds, hellmouths, I lost my balance, I was falling. . . . If I could not shut out this chaos I would fall indeed, I would go mad, and there was no shutting it out. The emphatic and paraverbal forces at work, immensely powerful and confused, rising out of the perversion and frustration of sex, out of an insanity that distorts time, and out of an appalling discipline of total concentration and apprehension of immediate reality, were far beyond my restraint or control. And yet they were controlled: the center was still Faxe. Hours and seconds passed, the moonlight shone on the wrong wall, there was no moonlight only darkness, and in the center of all darkness Faxe: the Weaver: a woman, a woman dressed in light. The light was silver, the silver was armor, an armored woman with a sword. The light burned sudden and intolerable, the light along her limbs, the fire, and she screamed aloud in terror and pain, "Yes, yes, yes!"

The crooning laugh of the Zany began, "Ah-ah-ah-ah," and rose higher and higher into a wavering yell that went on and on, much longer than any voice could go on yelling, right across time. There was movement in the darkness, scuffling and shuffling, a redistribution of ancient centuries, an evasion of foreshadows. "Light, light," said an immense voice in vast syllables once or innumerable times. "Light. Log on the fire, there. Some light." It was the physician from Spreve. He had entered the circle. It was all broken. He was kneeling by the Zanies, the frailest ones, the fuse-points; both of them lay huddled up on the floor. The kemmerer lay with his head on Faxe's knees, breathing in gasps, still trembling; Faxe's hand, with absent gentleness, stroked his hair. The Pervert was off by himself in a corner, sullen and dejected. The session was over, time passed as usual, the web of power had fallen apart into indignity and weariness. Where was my answer, the riddle of the oracle, the ambiguous utterance of prophecy?

I knelt down beside Faxe. He looked at me with his clear eyes. For that instant I saw him as I had seen him in the dark, as a woman armed in light and burning in a fire, crying out, "Yes—"

Faxe's soft speaking-voice broke the vision. "Are you answered, Asker?"

"I am answered, Weaver."

Indeed I was answered. Five years from now Gethen would be a member of the Ekumen: yes. No riddles, no hedging. Even then I was aware of the quality of that answer, not so much a prophecy as an observation. I could not evade my own certainty that the answer was right. It had the imperative clarity of a hunch.

We have NAFAL ships and instantaneous transmission and mindspeech, but we haven't yet tamed hunch to run in harness; for that trick we must go to Gethen.

"I serve as the filament," Faxe said to me a day or two after the Foretelling. "The energy builds up and builds up in us, always sent back and back, redoubling the impulse every time, until it breaks through and the light is in me, around me, I am the light. . . . The Old Man of Arbin Fastness once said that if the Weaver could be put in a vacuum at the moment of the answer, he'd go on burning for years. That's what the Yomeshta believe of Meshe: that he saw past and future clear, not for a moment, but all during his life after the Question of Shorth. It's hard to believe. I doubt a man could endure it. But no matter. . . ."

Nusuth, the ubiquitous and ambiguous negative of the Handdara.

We were strolling side by side, and Faxe looked at me. His face, one of the most beautiful human faces I ever saw, seemed hard and delicate as carved stone. "In the darkness," he said, "there were ten; not nine. There was a stranger."

"Yes, there was. I had no barrier against you. You are a Listener, Faxe, a natural empath; and probably a powerful natural telepath as well. That's why you're the Weaver, the one who can keep the tensions and responses of the group running in a self-augmenting pattern until the strain breaks the pattern itself and you reach through for your answer."

He listened with grave interest. "It is strange to see the mysteries of my discipline from outside, through your eyes. I've only seen them from within, as a disciple."

"If you permit—if you wish, Faxe, I should like to communicate with you in mindspeech." I was sure now that he was a natural Communicant; his consent and a little practice should serve to lower his unwitting barrier.

"Once you did that, I would hear what others think?"

"No, no. No more than you do already as an empath. Mindspeech is communication, voluntarily sent and received."

"Then why not speak aloud?"

"Well, one can lie, speaking."

"Not mindspeaking?"

"Not intentionally."

Faxe considered awhile. "That's a discipline that must arouse the interest of kings, politicians, men of business."

"Men of business fought against the use of mindspeech when it first was found to be a teachable skill; they outlawed it for decades."

Faxe smiled. "And kings?"

"We have no more kings."

"Yes. I see that. . . . Well, I thank you, Genry. But my business is unlearning, not learning. And I'd rather not yet learn an art that would change the world entirely."

"By your own foretelling this world will change, and within five years."

"And I'll change with it, Genry. But I have no wish to change it."

It was raining, the long, fine rain of Gethenian summer. We walked under the hemmen-trees on the slopes above the Fastness, where there were no paths. Light fell gray among dark branches, clear water dropped from the scarlet needles. The air was chill yet mild, and full of the sound of rain.

"Faxe, tell me this. You Handdarata have a gift that men on every world have craved. You have it. You can predict the future. And yet you live like the rest of us—it doesn't seem to *matter*—"

"How should it matter, Genry?"

"Well, look. For instance, this rivalry between Karhide and Orgoreyn, this quarrel about the Sinoth Valley. Karhide has lost face badly these last weeks, I gather. Now why didn't King Argaven consult his Foretellers, asking which course to take, or which member of the kyorremy to choose as prime minister, or something of that sort?"

"The questions are hard to ask."

"I don't see why. He might simply ask, Who'll serve me best as prime minister?—and leave it at that."

"He might. But he doesn't know what *serving him best* may mean. It might mean the man chosen would surrender the valley to Orgoreyn, or go into exile, or assassinate the king; it might mean many things he wouldn't expect or accept."

"He'd have to make his question very precise."

"Yes. Then there'd be many questions, you see. Even the king must pay the price."

"You'd charge him high?"

"Very high," said Faxe tranquilly. "The Asker pays

what he can afford, as you know. Kings have in fact come
to the Foretellers; but not very often. . . ."

"What if one of the Foretellers is himself a powerful
man?"

"Indwellers of the Fastness have no rank or status. I
may be sent to Erhenrang to the kyorremy; well, if I go,
I take back my status and my shadow, but my foretelling's at an end. If I had a question while I served in the
kyorremy, I'd go to Orgny Fastness there, pay my price,
and get my answer. But we in the Handdara don't want
answers. It's hard to avoid them, but we try to."

"Faxe, I don't think I understand."

"Well, we come here to the Fastnesses mostly to learn
what questions not to ask."

"But you're the Answerers!"

"You don't see yet, Genry, why we perfected and
practice Foretelling?"

"No—"

"To exhibit the perfect uselessness of knowing the
answer to the wrong question."

I pondered that a good while, as we walked side by
side through the rain, under the dark branches of the
Forest of Otherhord. Within the white hood Faxe's
face was tired and quiet, its light quenched. Yet he still
awed me a little. When he looked at me with his clear,
kind, candid eyes, he looked at me out of a tradition
thirteen thousand years old: a way of thought and way
of life so old, so well established, so integral and coherent as to give a human being the unself-consciousness,
the authority, the completeness of a wild animal, a great

strange creature who looks straight at you out of his
eternal present. . . .

"The unknown," said Faxe's soft voice in the forest,
"the unforetold, the unproven, that is what life is based
on. Ignorance is the ground of thought. Unproof is the
ground of action. If it were proven that there is no God
there would be no religion. No Handdara, no Yomesh,
no hearthgods, nothing. But also if it were proven that
there is a God, there would be no religion. . . . Tell me,
Genry, what is known? What is sure, predictable, inevi-
table—the one certain thing you know concerning your
future, and mine?"

"That we shall die."

"Yes. There's really only one question that can be
answered, Genry, and we already know the answer. . . .
The only thing that makes life possible is permanent,
intolerable uncertainty: not knowing what comes next."

6

ONE WAY INTO ORGOREYN

The cook, who was always at the house very early, woke me up; I sleep sound, and he had to shake me and say in my ear, "Wake up, wake up, Lord Estraven, there's a runner come from the King's House!" At last I understood him, and confused by sleep and urgency got up in haste and went to the door of my room, where the messenger waited, and so I entered stark naked and stupid as a newborn child into my exile.

Reading the paper the runner gave me I said in my mind that I had looked for this, though not so soon. But when I must watch the man nail that damn paper on the door of the house, then I felt as if he might as well be driving the nails into my eyes, and I turned from him and stood blank and bereft, undone with pain, which I had not looked for.

That fit past, I saw to what must be done, and by

Ninth Hour striking on the gongs was gone from the Palace. There was nothing to keep me long. I took what I could take. As for properties and banked monies, I could not raise cash from them without endangering the men I dealt with, and the better friends they were to me the worse their danger. I wrote to my old kemmering Ashe how he might get the profit of certain valuable things to keep for our sons' use, but told him not to try to send me money, for Tibe would have the border watched. I could not sign the letter. To call anyone by telephone would be to send them to jail, and I hurried to be gone before some friend should come in innocence to see me, and lose his money and his freedom as a reward for his friendship.

I set off west through the city. I stopped at a street-crossing and thought, Why should I not go east, across the mountains and the plains back to Kerm Land, a poor man afoot, and so come home to Estre where I was born, that stone house on a bitter mountainside: why not go home? Three times or four I stopped thus and looked back. Each time I saw among the indifferent street-faces one that might be the spy sent to see me out of Erhenrang, and each time I thought of the folly of trying to go home. As well kill myself. I was born to live in exile, it appeared, and my one way home was by way of dying. So I went on westward and turned back no more.

The three days' grace I had would see me, given no mishap, at farthest to Kuseben on the Gulf, eighty-five miles. Most exiles have had a night's warning of the Order of their Exile and so a chance to take passage on a ship down the Sess before the shipmasters are liable to punishment for giving aid. Such courtesy was not in Tibe's vein. No shipmaster would dare take me now; they all knew me at the Port, I having built it for Argaven. No landboat would let me ride, and to the land border from Erhenrang is four hundred miles. I had no choice but Kuseben afoot.

The cook had seen that. I had sent him off at once, but leaving, he had set out all the ready food he could find done up in a packet as fuel for my three days' run. That kindness saved me, and also saved my courage, for whenever on the road I ate of that fruit and bread I thought, "There's one man thinks me no traitor; for he gave me this."

It is hard, I found, to be called traitor. Strange how hard it is, for it's an easy name to call another man; a name that sticks, that fits, that convinces. I was half convinced myself.

I came to Kuseben at dusk of the third day, anxious and footsore, for these last years in Erhenrang I had gone all to grease and luxury and had lost my wind for walking; and there waiting for me at the gate of the little town was Ashe.

Seven years we were kemmerings, and had two sons. Being of his flesh born they had his name Foreth rem ir Osborth, and were reared in that Clanhearth. Three years ago he had gone to Orgny Fastness and he wore now the gold chain of a Celibate of the Foretellers. We had not seen each other those three years, yet seeing his face in the twilight under the arch of stone I felt the old habit of our love as if it had been broken yesterday, and knew the faithfulness in him that had sent him to share my ruin. And feeling that unavailing bond close on me anew, I was angry; for Ashe's love had always forced me to act against my heart.

I went on past him. If I must be cruel no need to hide it, pretending kindness. "Therem," he called after me, and followed. I went fast down the steep streets of Kuseben towards the wharves. A south wind was blowing up from the sea, rustling the black trees of the gardens, and through that warm stormy summer dusk I hastened from him as from a murderer. He caught up with me, for I was too footsore to keep up my pace. He said, "Therem, I'll go with you."

I made no answer.

"Ten years ago in this month of Tuwa we took oath—"

"And three years ago you broke it, leaving me, which was a wise choice."

"I never broke the vow we swore, Therem."

"True. There was none to break. It was a false vow, a second vow. You know it; you knew it then. The only true vow of faithfulness I ever swore was not spoken, nor could it be spoken, and the man I swore it to is dead and the promise broken, long ago. You owe me nothing, nor I you. Let me go."

As I spoke my anger and bitterness turned from Ashe against myself and my own life, which lay behind me like a broken promise. But Ashe did not know this, and the tears stood in his eyes. He said, "Will you take this, Therem? I owe you nothing, but I love you well." He held a little packet out to me.

"No. I have money, Ashe. Let me go. I must go alone."

I went on, and he did not follow me. But my brother's shadow followed me. I had done ill to speak of him. I had done ill in all things.

I found no luck waiting for me at the harbor. No ship from Orgoreyn lay in port that I might board and so be off Karhide's ground by midnight, as I was bound to be. Few men were on the wharves and those few all hurrying homeward; the one I found to speak to, a fisherman mending the engine of his boat, looked once at me and turned his back unspeaking. At that I was afraid. The man knew me; he would not have known unwarned. Tibe had sent his hirelings to forestall me and keep me in Karhide till my time ran out. I had been busy with pain and rage, but not with fear, till now; I had not thought that the Order of Exile might be mere pretext for my execution. Once Sixth Hour struck I was fair game for Tibe's men, and none could cry Murder, but only Justice done.

I sat down on a ballast-sack of sand there in the windy glare and darkness of the port. The sea slapped and sucked at the pilings, and fishing-boats jogged at their moorings, and out at the end of the long pier burned a lamp. I sat and stared at the light and past it at darkness over the sea. Some rise to present danger, not I. My gift is forethought. Threatened closely I grow stupid, and sit on a bag of sand wondering if a man could swim to Orgoreyn. The ice has been out of Charisune Gulf for a month or two, one might stay alive awhile in the water.

It is a hundred and fifty miles to the Orgota shore. I do not know how to swim. When I looked away from the sea and back up the streets of Kuseben I found myself looking for Ashe in hopes he still was following me. Having come to that, shame pushed me out of stupor, and I was able to think.

Bribery or violence was my choice if I dealt with that fisherman still at work in his boat in the inner dock: a faulty engine seemed not worth either. Theft, then. But the engines of fishing craft are locked. To bypass the locked circuit, start the engine, steer the boat out of dock under the pier-lamps and so off to Orgoreyn, having never run a motorboat, seemed a silly desperate venture. I had not run a boat but rowed one on Ice-foot Lake in Kerm; and there was a rowboat tied up in the outer dock between two launches. No sooner seen than stolen. I ran out the pier under the staring lamps, hopped into the boat, untied the painter, shipped the oars, and rowed out onto the swelling harbor-water where the lights slipped and dazzled on black waves. When I was pretty well away I stopped rowing to reset the thole of one oar, for it was not working smoothly and I had, though I hoped to be picked up next day by an Orgota patrol or fisherman, a good bit of rowing to do. As I bent to the oarlock a weakness ran all through my body. I thought I would faint, and crouched back in a heap on the thwart. It was the sickness of cowardice overcoming me. But I had not known my cowardice lay so heavy in my belly. I lifted my eyes and saw two figures on the pier's end like two jumping black twigs in the distant electric glare across the water, and then I began to think that my paralysis was not an effect of terror, but of a gun at extreme range.

I could see that one of them held a foray gun, and had it been past midnight I suppose he would have fired it and killed me; but the foray gun makes a loud noise and that would want explaining. So they had used a sonic gun. At stun setting a sonic gun can locate its resonance-field only within a hundred feet or so. I do not know its range at lethal setting, but I had not been far out of it, for I was doubled up like a baby with colic. I found it hard to breathe, the weakened field having caught me in the chest. As they would soon have a powered boat out to come finish me off, I could not spend any more time hunched over my oars gasping. Darkness lay behind my back, before the boat, and into darkness I must row. I rowed with weak arms, watching my hands to make sure I kept hold of the oars, for I could not feel my grip. I came thus into rough water and the dark, out on the open Gulf. There I had to stop. With each oarstroke the numbness of my arms increased. My heart kept bad time, and my lungs had forgotten how to get air. I tried to row but I was not sure my arms were moving. I tried to pull the oars into the boat then, but could not. When the sweeplight of a harbor patrol ship picked me out of the night like a snowflake on soot, I could not even turn my eyes away from the glare.

They unclenched my hands from the oars, hauled me up out of the boat, and laid me out like a gutted blackfish on the deck of the patrol ship. I felt them look down at me but could not well understand what they said, except for one, the ship's master by his tone; he said, "It's not Sixth Hour yet," and again, answering another, "What affair of mine is that? The king exiled him, I'll follow the king's order, no lesser man's."

So against radio commands from Tibe's men ashore and against the arguments of his mate, who feared retribution, that officer of the Kuseben Patrol took me across the Gulf of Charisune and set me ashore safe in Shelt Port in Orgoreyn. Whether he did this in shifgrethor against Tibe's men who would kill an unarmed man, or in kindness, I do not know. *Nusuth.* "The admirable is inexplicable."

I got up on my feet when the Orgota coast came gray out of the morning fog, and I made my legs move, and walked from the ship into the waterfront streets of Shelt, but somewhere there I fell down again. When I woke I was in the Commensal Hospital of Charisune Coastal Area Four, Twenty-fourth Commensality, Sennethny. I made sure of this, for it was engraved or embroidered in Orgota script on the headpiece of the bed, the lampstand by the bed, the metal cup on the bedtable, the bedtable, the nurses' hiebs, the bedcovers and the bedshirt I wore. A physician came and said to me, "Why did you resist dothe?"

"I was not in dothe," I said, "I was in a sonic field."

"Your symptoms were those of a person who has resisted the relaxation phase of dothe." He was a domineering old physician, and made me admit at last that I might have used dothe-strength to counter the paralysis while I rowed, not clearly knowing that I did so; then this morning, during the *thangen* phase when one must keep still, I had got up and walked and so near killed myself. When all that was settled to his satisfaction he told me I could leave in a day or two, and went on to the next bed. Behind him came the Inspector.

Behind every man in Orgoreyn comes the Inspector.

"Name?"

I did not ask him his. I must learn to live without shadows as they do in Orgoreyn; not to take offense; not to offend uselessly. But I did not give him my land-name, which is no business of any man in Orgoreyn.

"Therem Harth? That is not an Orgota name. What Commensality?"

"Karhide."

"That is not a Commensality of Orgoreyn. Where are your papers of entry and identification?"

Where were my papers?

I had been considerably rolled about in the streets of Shelt before someone had me carted off to the hospital, where I had arrived without papers, belongings, coat, shoes, or cash. When I heard this I let go of anger and laughed; at the pit's bottom is no anger. The Inspector was offended by my laughter. "Do you not understand that you are an indigent and unregistered alien? How do you intend to return to Karhide?"

"By coffin."

"You are not to give inappropriate answers to official questions. If you have no intention to return to your own country you will be sent to the Voluntary Farm, where there is a place for criminal riffraff, aliens, and unregistered persons. There is no other place for indigents and subversives in Orgoreyn. You had better declare your intention to return to Karhide within three days, or I shall be—"

"I'm proscribed from Karhide."

The physician, who had turned around from the next bed at the sound of my name, drew the Inspector aside and muttered at him awhile. The Inspector got to looking sour as bad beer, and when he came back to me he said, taking long to say it and grudging me each word, "Then I assume you will declare your intention to me to enter application for permission to obtain permanent residence in the Great Commensality of Orgoreyn pending your obtaining and retaining useful employment as a digit of a Commensality or Township?"

I said, "Yes." The joke was gone out of it with that word *permanent*, a skull-word if there ever was one.

After five days I was granted permanent residence pending my registry as a digit in the Township of Mishnory (which I had requested), and was issued temporary papers of identification for the journey to that city. I would have been hungry those five days, if the old physician had not kept me in the hospital. He liked having a prime minister of Karhide in his ward, and the prime minister was grateful.

I worked my way to Mishnory as a landboat loader on a fresh-fish caravan from Shelt. A fast smelly trip, ending in the great Markets of South Mishnory, where I soon found work in the ice-houses. There is always work in such places in summer, with the loading and packing and storing and shipping of perishable stuff. I handled mostly fish, and lodged in an island by the Markets with my fellows from the ice-house; Fish Island they called it; it stank of us. But I liked the job for keeping me most of the day in the refrigerated warehouse. Mishnory in summer is a steam-bath. The doors of the hills are shut; the river boils; men sweat. In the month of Ockre there were ten days and nights when the temperature never went below sixty degrees, and one day the heat rose to 88°. Driven out into that smelting-furnace from my cold fishy refuge at day's end, I would walk a couple of miles to the Kunderer Embankment, where there are trees and one may see the great river, though not get down to it. There I would roam late and go back at last to Fish Island through the fierce, close night. In my part of Mishnory they broke the streetlamps, to keep their doings in the dark. But the Inspectors' cars were forever snooping and spotlighting those dark streets, taking from poor men their one privacy, the night.

The new Alien Registry Law enacted in the month of Kus as a move in the shadow-fight with Karhide invalidated my registration and lost me my job, and I spent a halfmonth waiting in the anterooms of infinite Inspectors. My mates at work lent me money and stole fish for my dinner, so that I got re-registered before I starved; but I had heard the lesson. I liked those hard loyal men, but they lived in a trap there was no getting out of, and I had work to do among people I liked less. I made the calls I had put off for three months.

Next day I was washing out my shirt in the wash-house in the courtyard of Fish Island along with several others, all of us naked or half naked, when through the steam and stink of grime and fish and the clatter of water I heard someone call me by my land-name: and there was Commensal Yegey in the wash-house, looking just as he had looked at the Reception of the Archipela-gan Ambassador in the Ceremonial Hall of the Palace in Erhenrang seven months before. "Come along out of this, Estraven," he said in the high, loud, nasal voice of the Mishnory rich. "Oh, leave the dammed shirt."

"I haven't got another."

"Fish it out of that soup then and come on. It's hot in here."

The others stared at him with dour curiosity, knowing him a rich man, but they did not know him for a Commensal. I did not like his being there; he should have sent someone after me. Very few Orgota have any feeling for decency. I wanted to get him out of there. The shirt was no good to me wet, so I told a hearthless lad that hung about the courtyard to keep it on his back for me till I returned. My debts and rent were paid and my papers in my hieb-pocket; shirtless I left the island in the Markets, and went with Yegey back among the houses of the powerful.

As his "secretary" I was again reregistered in the rolls of Orgoreyn, not as a digit but as a dependent. Names won't do, they must have labels, and say the kind before they can see the thing. But this time their label fit, I was dependent, and soon was brought to curse the purpose that brought me here to eat another man's bread. For they gave me no sign for a month yet that I was any nearer achieving that purpose than I had been at Fish Island.

On the rainy evening of the last day of summer Yegey sent for me to his study, where I found him talking with the Commensal of the Sekeve District, Obsle, whom I had known when he headed the Orgota Naval Trade Commission in Erhenrang. Short and swaybacked, with little triangular eyes in a fat, flat face, he was an odd match with Yegey, all delicacy and bone. The frump and the fop, they looked, but they were something more than that. They were two of the Thirty-Three who rule Orgoreyn; yet again, they were something more than that.

Politenesses exchanged and a dram of Sithish lifewater drunk, Obsle sighed and said to me, "Now tell me why you did what you did in Sassinoth, Estraven, for if there was ever a man I thought unable to err in the timing of an act or the weighing of shifgrethor, that man was you."

"Fear outweighed caution in me, Commensal."

"Fear of what, the devil? What are you afraid of, Estraven?"

"Of what's happening now. The continuation of the prestige-struggle in the Sinoth Valley; the humiliation of Karhide, the anger that rises from humiliation; the use of the anger by the Karhidish Government."

"Use? To what end?"

Obsle has no manners; Yegey, delicate and prickly, broke in, "Commensal, Lord Estraven is my guest and need not suffer questioning—"

"Lord Estraven will answer questions when and as he sees fit, as he ever did," said Obsle grinning, a needle hidden in a heap of grease. "He knows himself between friends, here."

"I take my friends where I find them, Commensal, but I no longer look to keep them long."

"I can see that. Yet we can pull a sledge together without being kemmerings, as we say in Eskeve—eh? What the devil, I know what you were exiled for my dear: for liking Karhide better than its king."

"Rather for liking the king better than his cousin, perhaps."

"Or for liking Karhide better than Orgoreyn," said Yegey. "Am I wrong, Lord Estraven?"

"No, Commensal."

"You think, then," said Obsle, "that Tibe wants to run Karhide as we run Orgoreyn—efficiently?"

"I do. I think that Tibe, using the Sinoth Valley dispute as a goad, and sharpening it at need, may within a year work a greater change in Karhide than the last thousand years have seen. He has a model to work from, the Sarf. And he knows how to play on Argaven's fears. That's easier than trying to arouse Argaven's courage, as I did. If Tibe succeeds, you gentlemen will find you have an enemy worthy of you."

Obsle nodded. "I waive shifgrethor," said Yegey, "what are you getting at, Estraven?"

"This: Will the Great Continent hold two Orgoreyns?"

"Aye, aye, aye, the same thought," said Obsle, "the same thought: you planted it in my head a long time ago,

Estraven, and I never can uproot it. Our shadow grows too long. It will cover Karhide too. A feud between two Clans, yes; a foray between two towns, yes; a border-dispute and a few barn-burnings and murders, yes; but a feud between two nations? a foray involving fifty million souls? O by Meshe's sweet milk, that's a picture that has set fire to my sleep, some nights, and made me get up sweating. . . . We are not safe, we are not safe. You know it, Yegey; you've said it in your own way, many times."

"I've voted thirteen times now against pressing the Sinoth Valley dispute. But what good? The Domination faction holds twenty votes ready at command, and every move of Tibe's strengthens the Sarf's control over those twenty. He builds a fence across the valley, puts guards along the fence armed with foray guns—foray guns! I thought they kept them in museums. He feeds the Domination faction a challenge whenever they need one."

"And so strengthens Orgoreyn. But also Karhide. Every response you make to his provocations, every humiliation you inflict upon Karhide, every gain in your prestige, will serve to make Karhide stronger, until it is your equal—controlled all from one center as Orgoreyn is. And in Karhide they don't keep foray guns in muse-ums. The King's Guard carry them."

Yegey poured out another dram around of lifewater. Orgota noblemen drink that precious fire, brought five thousand miles over the foggy seas from Sith, as if it were beer. Obsle wiped his mouth and blinked his eyes.

"Well," he said, "all that is much as I thought, and

much as I think. And I think we have a sledge to pull together. But I have a question before we get in harness, Estraven. You have my hood down over my eyes entirely. Now tell me: what was all this obscuration, obfuscation and fiddlefaddle concerning an Envoy from the far side of the moon?"

Genly Ai, then, had requested permission to enter Orgoreyn.

"The Envoy? He is what he says he is."

"And that is—"

"An envoy from another world."

"None of your damned shadowy Karhidish metaphors, now, Estraven. I waive shifgrethor; I discard it. Will you answer me?"

"I have done so."

"He is an alien being?" Obsle said, and Yegey, "And he has had audience with King Argaven?"

I answered yes to both. They were silent a minute and then both started to speak at once, neither trying to mask his interest. Yegey was for circumambulating, but Obsle went to the point. "What was he in your plans, then? You staked yourself on him, it seems, and fell. Why?"

"Because Tibe tripped me. I had my eyes on the stars, and didn't watch the mud I walked in."

"You've taken up astronomy, my dear?"

"We'd better all take up astronomy, Obsle."

"Is he a threat to us, this Envoy?"

"I think not. He brings from his people offers of communication, trade, treaty, and alliance, nothing else. He came alone, without arms or defense, with nothing but a communicating device, and his ship, which he allowed us to examine completely. He is not to be feared, I think. Yet he brings the end of Kingdom and Commensalities with him in his empty hands."

"Why?"

"How shall we deal with strangers, except as brothers? How shall Gethen treat with a union of eighty worlds, except as a world?"

"Eighty worlds?" said Yegey, and laughed uneasily. Obsle stared at me athwart and said, "I'd like to think that you've been too long with the madman in his palace and had gone mad yourself. . . . Name of Meshe! What's this babble of alliances with the suns and treaties with the moon? How did the fellow come here, riding on a comet? Astride a meteor? A ship, what sort of ship floats on air? On void space? Yet you're no madder than you ever were, Estraven, which is to say shrewdly mad, wisely mad. All Karhiders are insane. Lead on, my lord, I follow. Go on!"

"I go nowhere, Obsle. Where have I to go? You, however, may get somewhere. If you should follow the Envoy a little way, he might show you a way out of the Sinoth Valley, out of the evil course we're caught in."

"Very good. I'll take up astronomy in my old age. Where will it lead me?"

"Towards greatness, if you go more wisely than I went. Gentlemen, I've been with the Envoy, I've seen his ship that crossed the Void, and I know that he is truly and exactly a messenger from elsewhere than this earth.

As to the honesty of his message and the truth of his descriptions of that elsewhere, there is no knowing; one can only judge as one would judge any man; if he were one of us I should call him an honest man. That you'll judge for yourselves, perhaps. But this is certain: in his presence, lines drawn on the earth make no boundaries, and no defense. There is a greater challenger than Karhide at the doors of Orgoreyn. The men who meet that challenge, who first open the doors of earth, will be the leaders of us all. All: the Three Continents: all the earth. Our border now is no line between two hills, but the line our planet makes in circling the Sun. To stake shifgrethor on any lesser chance is a fool's doing, now."

I had Yegey, but Obsle sat sunk in his fat, watching me from his small eyes. "This will take a month's believing," he said. "And if it came from anyone's mouth but yours, Estraven, I'd believe it to be pure hoax, a net for our pride woven out of starshine. But I know your stiff neck. Too stiff to stoop to an assumed disgrace in order to fool us. I can't believe you're speaking truth and yet I know a lie would choke you. . . . Well, well. Will he speak to us, as it seems he spoke to you?"

"That is what he seeks: to speak, to be heard. There or here. Tibe will silence him if he tries to be heard again in Karhide. I am afraid for him; he seems not to understand his danger."

"Will you tell us what you know?"

"I will; but is there a reason why he can't come here and tell you himself?"

Yegey said, biting his fingernail delicately, "I think not. He has requested permission to enter the Commensality. Karhide makes no objection. His request is under consideration. . . ."

7

THE QUESTION
OF SEX

From field notes of Ong Tot Oppong, Investigator, of the first Ekumenical landing party on Gethen/Winter, Cycle 93 E.Y. 1448.

1448 day 81. It seems likely that they were an experiment. The thought is unpleasant. But now that there is evidence to indicate that the Terran Colony was an experiment, the planting of one Hainish Normal group on a world with its own proto-hominid autochthones, the possibility cannot be ignored. Human genetic manipulation was certainly practiced by the Colonizers; nothing else explains the hilfs of S or the degenerate winged hominids of Rokanan; will anything else explain Gethenian sexual physiology? Accident, possibly; natural selection, hardly. Their ambisexuality has little or no adaptive value.

Why pick so harsh a world for an experiment? No answer. Tinibossol thinks the Colony was introduced during a major Interglacial. Conditions may have been fairly mild for their first 40 or 50,000 years here. By the time the ice was advancing again, the Hainish Withdrawal was complete and the Colonists were on their own, an experiment abandoned.

I theorize about the origins of Gethenian sexual physiology. What do I actually know about it? Otie Nim's communication from the Orgoreyn region has cleared up some of my earlier misconceptions. Let me set down all I know, and after that my theories; first things first.

The sexual cycle averages 26 to 28 days (they tend to speak of it as 26 days, approximating it to the lunar cycle). For 21 or 22 days the individual is *somer,* sexually inactive, latent. On about the 18th day hormonal changes are initiated by the pituitary control and on the 22nd or 23rd day the individual enters *kemmer,* estrus. In this first phase of kemmer (Karh, *secher*) he remains completely androgynous. Gender, and potency, are not attained in isolation. A Gethenian in first-phase kemmer, if kept alone or with others not in kemmer, remains incapable of coitus. Yet the sexual impulse is tremendously strong in this phase, controlling the entire personality, subjecting all other drives to its imperative. When the individual finds a partner in kemmer, hormonal secretion is further stimulated (most importantly by touch—secretion? scent?) until in one partner either a male or female hormonal dominance is established. The genitals engorge or shrink accordingly, foreplay intensifies, and the partner, triggered by the change, takes on the other sexual role (? without exception? If there are exceptions, resulting in kemmer-partners of the same sex, they are so rare as to be ignored). This second phase of kemmer (Karh. *thorharmen*), the mutual process of establishing sexuality and potency, apparently occurs within a time-span of two to twenty hours. If one of the partners is already in full kemmer, the phase for the newer partner is liable to be quite short; if the two are entering kemmer together, it is likely to take longer. Normal individuals have no predisposition to either sexual role in kemmer; they do not know whether they will be the male or the female, and have no choice in the matter. (Otie Nim wrote that in the Orgoreyn region the use of hormone derivatives to establish a preferred sexuality is quite common; I haven't seen this done in rural Karhide.) Once the sex is determined it cannot change during the kemmer-period. The culminant phase of kemmer (Karh. *thokemmer*) lasts from two to five days, during which sexual drive and capacity are at maximum. It ends fairly abruptly, and if conception has not taken place, the individual returns to the somer phase within a few hours (note: Otie Nim thinks this "fourth phase" is the equivalent of the menstrual cycle) and the cycle begins anew. If the individual was in the female role and was impregnated, hormonal activity of course continues, and for the 8.4-month gestation period and the 6- to 8-month lactation period this individual remains female. The male sexual organs remain retracted (as they are in somer), the breasts enlarge somewhat, and the pelvic girdle widens. With the cessation of lactation the female reenters somer and becomes once more a perfect androgyne. No physiological habit is established, and the mother of several children may be the father of several more.

Social observations: very superficial as yet; I have

been moving about too much to make coherent social observations.

Kemmer is not always played by pairs. Pairing seems to be the commonest custom, but in the kemmerhouses of towns and cities, groups may form and intercourse take place promiscuously among the males and females of the group. The furthest extreme from this practice is the custom of *vowing kemmering* (Karh. *oskyommer*), which is to all intents and purposes monogamous marriage. It has no legal status, but socially and ethically is an ancient and vigorous institution. The whole structure of the Karhidish Clan-Hearths and Domains is indubitably based upon the institution of monogamous marriage. I am not sure of divorce rules in general; here in Osnoriner there is divorce, but no remarriage after either divorce or the partner's death: one can only vow kemmering once.

Descent of course is reckoned, all over Gethen, from the mother, the "parent in the flesh" (Karh. *amha*).

Incest is permitted, with various restrictions, between siblings, even the full siblings of a vowed-kemmering pair. Siblings are not however allowed to vow kemmering, nor keep kemmering after the birth of a child to one of the pair. Incest between generations is strictly forbidden (In Karhide/Orgoreyn; but is said to be permitted among the tribesmen of Perunter, the Antarctic Continent. This may be slander.).

What else have I learned for certain? That seems to sum it up.

There is one feature of this anomalous arrangement that might have adaptive value. Since coitus takes place only during the period of fertility, the chance of conception is high, as with all mammals that have an estrous cycle. In harsh conditions where infant mortality is great, a race survival value may be indicated. At present neither infant mortality nor the birthrate runs high in the civilized areas of Gethen. Tinibossol estimates a population of not over 100 million on the Three Continents, and considers it to have been stable for at least a millennium. Ritual and ethical abstention and the use of contraceptive drugs seem to have played the major part in maintaining this stability.

There are aspects of ambisexuality that we have only glimpsed or guessed at, and which we may never grasp entirely. The kemmer phenomenon fascinates all of us Investigators, of course. It fascinates us, but it rules the Gethenians, dominates them. The structure of their societies, the management of their industry, agriculture, commerce, the size of their settlements, the subjects of their stories, everything is shaped to fit the somer-kemmer cycle. Everybody has his holiday once a month; no one, whatever his position, is obliged or forced to work when in kemmer. No one is barred from the kemmerhouse, however poor or strange. Everything gives way before the recurring torment and festivity of passion. This is easy for us to understand. What is very hard for us to understand is that, four-fifths of the time, these people are not sexually motivated at all. Room is made for sex, plenty of room; but a room, as it were, apart. The society of Gethen, in its daily functioning and in its continuity, is without sex.

Consider: Anyone can turn his hand to anything. This sounds very simple, but its psychological effects are incalculable. The fact that everyone between seventeen and thirty-five or so is liable to be (as Nim put it) "tied down to childbearing," implies that no one is quite so thoroughly "tied down" here as women, elsewhere, are likely to be—psychologically or physically. Burden and privilege are shared out pretty equally; everybody has the same risk to run or choice to make. Therefore nobody here is quite so free as a free male anywhere else.

Consider: A child has no psycho-sexual relationship to his mother and father. There is no myth of Oedipus on Winter.

Consider: There is no unconsenting sex, no rape. As with most mammals other than man, coitus can be performed only by mutual invitation and consent; otherwise it is not possible. Seduction certainly is possible, but it must have to be awfully well timed.

Consider: There is no division of humanity into strong and weak halves, protective/protected, dominant/submissive, owner/chattel, active/passive. In fact the whole tendency to dualism that pervades human thinking may be found to be lessened, or changed, on Winter.

The following must go into my finished Directives: when you meet a Gethenian you cannot and must not do what a bisexual naturally does, which is to cast him in the role of Man or Woman, while adopting towards him a corresponding role dependent on your expectations of the patterned or possible interactions between persons of the same or the opposite sex. Our entire pattern of socio-sexual interaction is nonexistent here. They cannot play the game. They do not see one another as men or women. This is almost impossible for our imagination to accept. What is the first question we ask about a newborn baby?

Yet you cannot think of a Gethenian as "it." They are not neuters. They are potentials, or integrals. Lacking the Karhidish "human pronoun" used for persons in somer, I must say "he," for the same reasons as we used the masculine pronoun in referring to a transcendent god: it is less defined, less specific, than the neuter or the feminine. But the very use of the pronoun in my thoughts leads me continually to forget that the Karhider I am with is not a man, but a manwoman.

The First Mobile, if one is sent, must be warned that unless he is very self-assured, or senile, his pride will suffer. A man wants his virility regarded, a woman wants her femininity appreciated, however indirect and subtle the indications of regard and appreciation. On Winter they will not exist. One is respected and judged only as a human being. It is an appalling experience.

Back to my theory. Contemplating the motives for such an experiment, if such it was, and trying perhaps to exculpate our Hainish ancestors from the guilt of barbarism, of treating lives as things, I have made some guesses as to what they might have been after.

The somer-kemmer cycle strikes us as degrading, a return to the estrous cycle of the lower mammals, a subjection of human beings to the mechanical imperative of rut. It is possible that the experimenters wished to see

whether human beings lacking continuous sexual potentiality would remain intelligent and capable of culture.

On the other hand, the limitation of the sexual drive
to a discontinuous time-segment, and the "equalizing"
of it in androgyny, must prevent, to a large extent, both
the exploitation and frustration of the drive. There must
be sexual frustration (though society provides as well as
it can against it; so long as the social unit is large enough
that more than one person will be in kemmer at one
time, sexual fulfillment is fairly certain), but at least it
cannot build up; it is over when kemmer is over. Fine;
thus they are spared much waste and madness; but what
is left, in somer? What is there to sublimate? What would
a society of eunuchs achieve?—But of course they are not
eunuchs, in somer, but rather more comparable to pre-
adolescents: not castrate, but latent.

Another guess concerning the hypothetical experiment's object: the elimination of war. Did the Ancient
Hainish postulate that continuous sexual capacity and
organized social aggression, neither of which are attri-
butes of any mammal but man, are cause and effect? Or,
like Tumass Song Angot, did they consider war to be a
purely masculine displacement-activity, a vast Rape, and
therefore in their experiment eliminate the masculinity
that rapes and the femininity that is raped? God knows.
The fact is that Gethenians, though highly competitive (as proved by the elaborate social channels provided
for competition for prestige, etc.) seem not to be very
aggressive; at least they apparently have never yet had
what one could call a war. They kill one another readily

by ones and twos; seldom by tens or twenties; never by hundreds or thousands. Why?

It may turn out to have nothing to do with their androgyne psychology. There are not very many of them, after all. And there is the climate. The weather of Winter is so relentless, so near the limit of tolerability even to them with all their cold-adaptations, that perhaps they use up their fighting spirit fighting the cold. The marginal peoples, the races that just get by, are rarely the warriors. And in the end, the dominant factor in Gethenian life is not sex or any other human thing: it is their environment, their cold world. Here man has a crueler enemy even than himself.

I am a woman of peaceful Chiffewar, and no expert on the attractions of violence or the nature of war. Someone else will have to think this out. But I really don't see how anyone could put much stock in victory or glory after he had spent a winter on Winter, and seen the face of the Ice.

8

ANOTHER WAY
INTO ORGOREYN

I spent the summer more as an Investigator than a Mobile, going about the land of Karhide from town to town, from Domain to Domain, watching and listening—things a Mobile cannot do at first, while he is still a marvel and monstrosity, and must be forever on show and ready to perform. I would tell my hosts in those rural Hearths and villages who I was; most of them had heard a little about me over the radio and had a vague idea what I was. They were curious, some more, some less. Few were frightened of me personally, or showed the xenophobic revulsion. An enemy, in Karhide, is not a stranger, an invader. The stranger who comes unknown is a guest. Your enemy is your neighbor.

During the month of Kus I lived on the Eastern coast in a Clan-Hearth called Gorinhering, a house-town-fort-farm built up on a hill above the eternal fogs of the

Hodomin Ocean. Some five hundred people lived there. Four thousand years ago I should have found their ancestors living in the same place, in the same kind of house. Along in those four millennia the electric engine was developed, radios and power loom and power vehicles and farm machinery and all the rest began to be used, and a Machine Age got going, gradually, without any industrial revolution, without any revolution at all. Winter hasn't achieved in thirty centuries what Terra once achieved in thirty decades. Neither has Winter ever paid the price that Terra paid.

Winter is an inimical world; its punishment for doing things wrong is sure and prompt: death from cold or death from hunger. No margin, no reprieve. A man can trust his luck, but a society can't; and cultural change, like random mutation, may make things chancier. So they have gone very slowly. At any one point in their history a hasty observer would say that all technological progress and diffusion had ceased. Yet it never has. Compare the torrent and the glacier. Both get where they are going.

I talked a lot with the old people of Gorinhering, and also with the children. It was my first chance to see much of Gethenian children, for in Erhenrang they are all in the private or public Hearths and Schools. A quarter to a third of the adult urban population is engaged full-time in the nurture and education of the children. Here the clan looked after its own; nobody and everybody was responsible for them. They were a wild lot, chasing about over those fog-hidden hills and beaches. When I could round one up long enough to talk, I found them shy, proud, and immensely trustful.

The parental instinct varies as widely on Gethen as anywhere. One can't generalize. I never saw a Karhider hit a child. I have seen one speak very angrily to a child. Their tenderness towards their children struck me as being profound, effective, and almost wholly unpossessive. Only in that unpossessiveness does it perhaps differ from what we call the "maternal" instinct. I suspect that the distinction between a maternal and a paternal instinct is scarcely worth making; the parental instinct, the wish to protect, to further, is not a sex-linked characteristic. . . .

Early in Hakanna we heard in Gorinhering on the static-fuzzed Palace Bulletin that King Argaven had announced his expectation of an heir. Not another kemmering-son, of which he already had seven, but an heir of the body, king-son. The king was pregnant.

I found this funny, and so did the clansmen of Gorinhering, but for different reasons. They said he was too old to be bearing children, and they got hilarious and obscene on the subject. The old men went about cackling over it for days. They laughed at the king, but were not otherwise much interested in him. "The Domains are Karhide," Estraven had said, and like so much Estraven had said it kept recurring to me as I learned more. The seeming nation, unified for centuries, was a stew of uncoordinated principalities, towns, villages, "pseudo-feudal tribal economic units," a sprawl and splatter of vigorous, competent, quarrelsome individualities over which a grid of authority was insecurely and lightly laid. Nothing, I thought, could ever unite Karhide as a nation. Total diffusion of rapid communication devices, which is supposed to bring about nationalism almost inevitably, had not done so. The Ekumen could not appeal to these people as a social unit, a mobilizable entity: rather it must speak to their strong though undeveloped sense of humanity, of human unity. I got quite excited thinking about this. I was, of course, wrong; yet I had learned something about Gethenians which in the long run proved to be useful knowledge.

Unless I was to spend all year in Old Karhide I must return to the West Fall before the passes of the Kargav closed. Even here on the coast there had been two light snowfalls in the last month of summer. Rather reluctantly I set off west again, and came to Erhenrang early in Gor, the first month of autumn. Argaven was now in seclusion in the summer-palace at Warrever, and had named Pemmer Harge rem ir Tibe as Regent during his confinement. Tibe was already making the most of his term of power. Within a couple of hours of my arrival I began to see the flaw in my analysis of Karhide—it was already out of date—and also began to feel uncomfortable, perhaps unsafe, in Erhenrang.

Argaven was not sane; the sinister incoherence of his mind darkened the mood of his capital; he fed on fear. All the good of his reign had been done by his ministers and the kyorremy. But he had not done much harm. His wrestles with his own nightmares had not damaged the Kingdom. His cousin Tibe was another kind of fish, for his insanity had logic. Tibe knew when to act, and how to act. Only he did not know when to stop.

Tibe spoke on the radio a good deal. Estraven when in power had never done so, and it was not in the Karhidish vein: their government was not a public performance, normally; it was covert and indirect. Tibe, however, orated. Hearing his voice on the air I saw again the long-toothed smile and the face masked with a net of fine wrinkles. His speeches were long and loud: praises of Karhide, disparagements of Orgoreyn, vilifications of "disloyal factions," discussions of the "integrity of the Kingdom's borders," lectures in history and ethics and economics, all in a ranting, canting, emotional tone that went shrill with vituperation or adulation. He talked much about pride of country and love of the parentland, but little about shifgrethor, personal pride or prestige. Had Karhide lost so much prestige in the Sinoth Valley business that the subject could not be brought up? No; for he often talked about the Sinoth Valley. I decided that he was deliberately avoiding talk of shifgrethor because he wished to rouse emotions of a more elemental, uncontrollable kind. He wanted to stir up something that the whole shifgrethor-pattern was a refinement upon, a sublimation of. He wanted his hearers to be frightened and angry. His themes were not pride and love at all, though he used the words perpetually; as he used them they meant self-praise and hate. He talked a great deal about Truth also, for he was, he said, "cutting down beneath the veneer of civilization."

It is a durable, ubiquitous, specious metaphor, that

one about veneer (or paint, or pliofilm, or whatever) hiding the nobler reality beneath. It can conceal a dozen fallacies at once. One of the most dangerous is the implication that civilization, being artificial, is unnatural: that it is the opposite of primitiveness. . . . Of course there is no veneer, the process is one of growth, and primitiveness and civilization are degrees of the same thing. If civilization has an opposite, it is war. Of those two things, you have either one, or the other. Not both. It seemed to me as I listened to Tibe's dull fierce speeches that what he sought to do by fear and by persuasion was to force his people to change a choice they had made before their history began, the choice between those opposites.

The time was ripe, perhaps. Slow as their material and technological advance had been, little as they valued "progress" in itself, they had finally, in the last five or ten or fifteen centuries, got a little ahead of Nature. They weren't absolutely at the mercy of their merciless climate any longer; a bad harvest would not starve a whole province, or a bad winter isolate every city. On this basis of material stability Orgoreyn had gradually built up a unified and increasingly efficient centralized state. Now Karhide was to pull herself together and do the same; and the way to make her do it was not by sparking her pride, or building up her trade, or improving her roads, farms, colleges, and so on; none of that; that's all civilization, veneer, and Tibe dismissed it with scorn. He was after something surer, the sure, quick, and lasting way to make people into a nation: war. His ideas concerning it could not have been too precise, but they were quite sound. The only other means of mobilizing people rapidly and entirely is with a new religion; none was handy; he would make do with war.

I sent the Regent a note in which I quoted to him the question I had put to the Foretellers of Otherhord and the answer I had got. Tibe made no response. I then went to the Orgota Embassy and requested permission to enter Orgoreyn.

There are fewer people running the offices of the Stabiles of the Ekumen in Hain than there were running that embassy of one small country to another, and all of them were armed with yards of soundtapes and records. They were slow, they were thorough; none of the slapdash arrogance and sudden deviousness that marked Karhidish officialdom. I waited, while they filled out their forms.

The waiting got rather uneasy. The number of Palace Guards and city police on the streets of Erhenrang seemed to multiply every day; they were armed, and they were even developing a sort of uniform. The mood of the city was bleak, although business was good, prosperity general, and the weather fair. Nobody wanted much to do with me. My "landlady" no longer showed people my room, but rather complained about being badgered by "people from the Palace," and treated me less as an honored sideshow than as a political suspect. Tibe made a speech about a foray in the Sinoth Valley: "brave Karhidish farmers, true patriots," had dashed across the border south of Sassinoth, had attacked an Orgota village, burned it, and killed nine villagers, and then dragging the bodies back had dumped them into the Ey River, "such a grave," said the Regent, "as all the enemies of our nation will find!" I heard this broadcast in the eating-hall of my island. Some people looked grim as they listened, others uninterested, others satisfied, but in these various expressions there was one common element, a little tic or facial cramp that had not used to be there, a look of anxiety.

That evening a man came to my room, my first visitor since I had returned to Erhenrang. He was slight, smooth-skinned, shy-mannered, and wore the gold chain of a Foreteller, one of the Celibates. "I'm a friend of one who befriended you," he said, with the brusqueness of the timid. "I've come to ask you a favor, for his sake."

"You mean Faxe—?"

"No. Estraven."

My helpful expression must have changed. There was a little pause, after which the stranger said, "Estraven, the traitor. You remember him, perhaps?"

Anger had displaced timidity, and he was going to play shifgrethor with me. If I wanted to play, my move was to say something like, "I'm not sure; tell me something about him." But I didn't want to play, and was used to volcanic Karhidish tempers by now. I faced his anger deprecatingly and said, "Of course I do."

"But not with friendship." His dark, down-slanted eyes were direct and keen.

"Well, rather with gratitude, and disappointment. Did he send you to me?"

"He did not."

I waited for him to explain himself.

He said, "Excuse me. I presumed; I accept what presumption has earned me."

I stopped the stiff little fellow as he made for the door. "Please: I don't know who you are, or what you want. I haven't refused, I simply haven't consented. You must allow me the right to a reasonable caution. Estraven was exiled for supporting my mission here—"

"Do you consider yourself to be in his debt for that?"

"Well, in a sense. However, the mission I am on overrides all personal debts and loyalties."

"If so," said the stranger with fierce certainty, "it is an immoral mission."

That stopped me. He sounded like an Advocate of the Ekumen, and I had no answer. "I don't think it is," I said finally; "the shortcomings are in the messenger, not the message. But please tell me what it is you want me to do."

"I have certain monies, rents and debts, which I was able to collect from the wreck of my friend's fortune. Hearing that you were about to go to Orgoreyn, I thought to ask you to take the money to him, if you find him. As you know, it would be a punishable offense to do so. It may also be useless. He may be in Mishnory, or on one of their damnable Farms, or dead. I have no way of finding out. I have no friends in Orgoreyn, and none here I dared ask this of. I thought of you as one above politics, free to come and go. I did not stop to think that you have, of course, your own politics. I apologize for my stupidity."

"Well, I'll take the money for him. But if he's dead or can't be found, to whom shall I return it?"

He stared at me. His face worked and changed, and he caught his breath in a sob. Most Karhiders cry easily, being no more ashamed of tears than of laughter. He said, "Thank you. My name is Foreth. I'm an Indweller at Orgny Fastness."

"You're of Estraven's clan?"

"No. Foreth rem ir Osboth: I was his kemmering."

Estraven had had no kemmering when I knew him, but I could rouse no suspicion of this fellow in myself. He might be unwittingly serving someone else's purpose, but he was genuine. And he had just taught me a lesson: that shifgrethor can be played on the level of ethics, and that the expert player will win. He had cornered me in about two moves. —He had the money with him and gave it to me, a solid sum in Royal Karhidish Merchants' notes of credit, nothing to incriminate me, and consequently nothing to prevent me from simply spending it.

"If you find him . . ." He stuck.

"A message?"

"No. Only if I knew . . ."

"If I do find him, I'll try to send news of him to you."

"Thank you," he said, and he held out both his hands

to me, a gesture of friendship that in Karhide is not lightly made. "I wish success to your mission, Mr. Ai. He—Estraven—he believed you came here to do good, I know. He believed it very strongly."

There was nothing in the world for this man outside Estraven. He was one of those who are damned to love once. I said again, "Is there no word from you that I might take him?"

"To tell him the children are well," he said, then hesitated, and said quietly, "*Nusuth,* no matter," and left me.

Two days later I took the road out of Erhenrang, the northwest road this time, afoot. My permission to enter Orgoreyn had arrived much sooner than the clerks and officials of the Orgota Embassy had led me to expect or had themselves expected; when I went to get the papers they treated me with a sort of poisonous respect, resentful that protocol and regulations had, on somebody's authority, been pushed aside for me. As Karhide had no regulations at all about leaving the country, I set straight off. Over the summer I had learned what a pleasant land Karhide was for walking in. Roads and inns are set for foot-traffic as well as for powered vehicles, and where inns are wanting one may count infallibly on the code of hospitality. Townsfolk of Co-Domains and the villagers, farmers, or lord of any Domain will give a traveler food and lodging, for three days by the code, and in practice for much longer than that; and what's best is that you are always received without fuss, welcomed, as if they had been expecting you to come.

I meandered across the splendid slanting land between the Sess and the Ey, taking my time, working out my keep a couple of mornings in the fields of the great Domains, where they were getting the harvest in, every hand and tool and machine at work to get the golden fields cut before the weather turned. It was all golden, all benign, that week of walking; and at night before I slept I would step out of the dark farmhouse or firelit Hearth-Hall where I was lodged and walk a way into the dry stubble to look up at the stars, flaring like far cities in the windy autumn dark.

In fact I was reluctant to leave this land, which I had found, though so indifferent to the Envoy, so gentle to the stranger. I dreaded starting all over, trying to repeat my news in a new language to new hearers, failing again perhaps. I wandered more north than west, justifying my course by a curiosity to see the Sinoth Valley region, the locus of the rivalry between Karhide and Orgoreyn. Though the weather held clear it began to grow colder, and at last I turned west before I got to Sassinoth, remembering that there was a fence across that stretch of border, and I might not be so easily let out of Karhide there. Here the border was the Ey, a narrow river but fierce, glacier-fed like all rivers of the Great Continent. I doubled back a few miles south to find a bridge, and came on one linking two little villages, Passerer on the Karhide side and Siuwensin in Orgoreyn, staring sleepily at each other across the noisy Ey.

The Karhidish bridge-keeper asked me only if I planned to return that night, and waved me on across. On the Orgota side an Inspector was called out to inspect my passport and papers, which he did for about an hour, a Karhidish hour at that. He kept the passport, telling me I must call for it next morning, and gave me in place of it a permiso for meals and lodging at the Commensal Transient-House of Siuwensin. I spent another hour in the office of the superintendent of the Transient-House, while the superintendent read my papers and checked on the authenticity of my permiso by telephoning the Inspector at the Commensal Border-Station from which I had just come.

I can't properly define that Orgota word here translated as "commensal," "commensality." Its root is a word meaning "to eat together." Its usage includes all national/governmental institutions of Orgoreyn, from the State as a whole through its thirty-three component substates or Districts to the sub-substates, townships, communal farms, mines, factories, and so on, that compose these. As an adjective it is applied to all the above; in the form "the Commensals" it usually means the thirty-three Heads of Districts, who form the governing body, executive and legislative, of the Great Commensality of Orgoreyn, but it may also mean the citizens, the people themselves. In this curious lack of distinction between the general and specific applications of the word, in the use of it for both the whole and the part, the state and the individual, in this imprecision is its precisest meaning.

My papers and my presence were at last approved, and by Fourth Hour I got my first meal since early breakfast—

supper: kadik-porridge and cold sliced breadapple. For all its array of officials, Siuwensin was a very small, plain place, sunk deep in rural torpor. The Commensal Transient-House was shorter than its name. Its dining-room had one table, five chairs, and no fire; food was brought in from the village hot-shop. The other room was the dormitory: six beds, a lot of dust, a little mildew. I had it to myself. As everybody in Siuwensin appeared to have gone to bed directly after supper, I did the same. I fell asleep in that utter country silence that makes your ears ring. I slept an hour and woke in the grip of a nightmare about explosions, invasion, murder, and conflagration.

It was a particularly bad dream, the kind in which you run down a strange street in the dark with a lot of people who have no faces, while houses go up in flames behind you, and children scream.

I ended up in an open field, standing in dry stubble by a black hedge. The dull-red half-moon and some stars showed through clouds overhead. The wind was bitter cold. Near me a big barn or granary bulked up in the dark, and in the distance beyond it I saw little volleys of sparks going up on the wind.

I was bare-legged and barefoot, in my shirt, without breeches, hieb, or coat; but I had my pack. It held not only spare clothes but also my rubies, cash, documents, papers, and ansible, and I slept with it as a pillow when I traveled. Evidently I hung onto it even during bad dreams. I got out shoes and breeches and my fur lined winter hieb, and dressed, there in the cold, dark country silence, while Siuwensin smoldered half a mile behind me. Then I struck out looking for a road, and soon found one, and on it, other people. They were refugees like me, but they knew where they were going. I followed them, having no direction of my own, except away from Siuwensin; which, I gathered as we walked, had been raided by a foray from Passerer across the bridge.

They had struck, set fire, withdrawn; there had been no fight. But all at once lights glared down the dark at us, and scuttling to the roadside we watched a land-caravan, twenty trucks, come at top speed out of the west towards Siuwensin and pass us with a flash of light and a hiss of wheels twenty times repeated; then silence and the dark again.

We soon came to a communal farm-center, where we were halted and interrogated. I tried to attach myself to the group I had followed down the road, but no luck; no luck for them either, if they did not have their identification-papers with them. They, and I as a foreigner without passport, were cut out of the herd and given separate quarters for the night in a storage-barn, a vast stone semi-cellar with one door locked on us from outside, and no window. Now and then the door was unlocked and a new refugee thrust in by a farm-policeman armed with the Gethenian sonic "gun." The door shut, it was perfectly dark: no light. One's eyes, cheated of sight, sent starbursts and fiery blots whirling through the black. The air was cold, and heavy with the dust and odor of grain. No one had a hand light; these were people who had been routed out of their beds, like me; a couple of them were literally naked, and had been given blankets by others on the way. They had nothing. If they had had anything, it would have been their papers. Better to be naked than to lack papers, in Orgoreyn.

They sat dispersed in that hollow, huge, dusty blindness. Sometimes two conversed awhile, low-voiced. There was no fellowfeeling of being prisoners together. There was no complaint.

I heard one whisper to my left: "I saw him in the street, outside my door. His head was blown off."

"They use those guns that fire pieces of metal. Foray guns."

"Tiena said they weren't from Passerer, but from Ovord Domain, come down by truck."

"But there isn't any quarrel between Ovord and Siuwensin. . . ."

They did not understand; they did not complain. They did not protest being locked up in a cellar by their fellow-citizens after having been shot and burned out of their homes. They sought no reasons for what had happened to them. The whispers in the dark, random and soft, in the sinuous Orgota language that made Karhidish sound like rocks rattled in a can, ceased little by little. People slept. A baby fretted awhile, away off in the dark, crying at the echo of its own cries.

The door squealed open and it was broad day, sunlight like a knife in the eyes, bright and frightening. I stumbled out behind the rest and was mechanically following them when I heard my name. I had not recognized it; for one thing the Orgota could say *l*. Someone had been calling it at intervals ever since the door was unlocked.

"Please come this way, Mr. Ai," said a hurried person in red, and I was no longer a refugee. I was set apart from those nameless ones with whom I had fled down a dark road and whose lack of identity I had shared all night in a dark room. I was named, known, recognized; I existed. It was an intense relief. I followed my leader gladly.

The office of the Local Commensal Farm Centrality was hectic and upset, but they made time to look after me, and apologized to me for the discomforts of the night past. "If only you had not chosen to enter the Commensality at Siuwensin!" lamented one fat Inspector. "If only you had taken the customary roads!" They did not know who I was or why I was to be given particular treatment; their ignorance was evident, but made no difference. Genly Ai, the Envoy, was to be treated as a distinguished person. He was. By midafternoon I was on my way to Mishnory in a car put at my disposal by the Commensal Farm Centrality of East Homsvashom, District Eight. I had a new passport, and a free pass to all Transient-Houses on my road, and a telegraphed invitation to the Mishnory residence of the First Commensal District Commissioner of Entry-Roads and Ports, Mr. Uth Shusgis.

The radio of the little car came on with the engine and ran while the car did; so all afternoon as I drove through the great level grainlands of East Orgoreyn, fenceless (for there are no herd-beasts) and full of streams, I listened to the radio. It told me about the weather, the crops, road-conditions; it cautioned me to drive carefully; it gave me various kinds of news from all thirty-three Districts, the output of various factories, the shipping-information from various sea and river ports; it singsonged some Yomesh chants, and then told me about the weather again. It was all very mild, after the ranting I had heard on the radio in Erhenrang. No mention was made of the raid on Siuwensin; the Orgota government evidently meant to prevent, not rouse, excitement. A brief official bulletin repeated every so often said simply that order was being and would be maintained along the Eastern Border. I liked that; it was reassuring and unprovocative, and had the quiet toughness that I had always admired in Gethenians: order will be maintained. . . . I was glad, now, to be out of Karhide, an incoherent land driven towards violence by a paranoid, pregnant king and an egomaniac Regent. I was glad to be driving sedately at twenty-five miles an hour through vast, straight-furrowed grainlands, under an even gray sky, towards a capital whose government believed in Order.

The road was posted frequently (unlike the signless Karhidish roads on which you had to ask or guess your way) with directions to prepare to stop at the Inspection-Station of such-and-such Commensal Area or Region; at these internal customs-houses one's identification must be shown and one's passage recorded. My papers were valid to all examination, and I was politely waved on after minimal delay, and politely advised how far it was

to the next Transient-House if I wanted to eat or sleep.
At 25 mph it is a considerable journey from the North
Fall to Mishnory, and I spent two nights on the way.
Food at the Transient-Houses was dull but plentiful,
lodging decent, lacking only privacy. Even that was sup-
plied in some measure by the reticence of my fellow travelers. I did not strike up an acquaintance or have a real
conversation at any of these halts, though I tried several
times. The Orgota seemed not an unfriendly people, but
incurious; they were colorless, steady, subdued. I liked
them. I had had two years of color, choler, and passion
in Karhide. A change was welcome.

Following the east bank of the great River Kunderer
I came on my third morning in Orgoreyn to Mishnory,
the largest city on that world.

In the weak sunlight between autumn showers it was
a queer-looking city, all blank stone walls with a few
narrow windows set too high, wide streets that dwarfed
the crowds, streetlamps perched on ridiculous tall posts,
roofs pitched steep as praying hands, shed-roofs sticking out of housewalls eighteen feet aboveground like
big aimless bookshelves—an ill-proportioned, grotesque
city, in the sunlight. It was not built for sunlight. It was
built for winter. In winter, with those streets filled ten
feet up with packed, hard-rolled snow, the steep roofs
icicle-fringed, sleds parked under the shed-roofs, narrow
window-slits shining yellow through driving sleet, you
would see the fitness of that city, its economy, its beauty.

Mishnory was cleaner, larger, lighter than Erhenrang,
more open and imposing. Great buildings of yellowish-

white stone dominated it, simple stately blocks all built to a pattern, housing the offices and services of the Commensal Government and also the major temples of the Yomesh cult, which is promulgated by the Commensality. There was no clutter and contortion, no sense of always being under the shadow of something high and gloomy, as in Erhenrang; everything was simple, grandly conceived, and orderly. I felt as if I had come out of a dark age, and wished I had not wasted two years in Karhide. This, now, looked like a country ready to enter the Ekumenical Age.

I drove about the city awhile, then returned the car to the proper Regional Bureau and went on foot to the residence of the First Commensal District Commissioner of Entry-Roads and Ports. I had never made quite sure whether the invitation was a request or a polite command. *Nusuth*. I was in Orgoreyn to speak for the Ekumen, and might as well begin here as anywhere.

My notions of Orgota phlegm and self-control were spoiled by Commissioner Shusgis, who advanced on me smiling and shouting, grabbed both my hands in the gesture that Karhiders reserve for moments of intense personal emotion, pumped my arms up and down as if trying to start a spark in my engine, and bellowed a greeting to the Ambassador of the Ekumen of the Known Worlds to Gethen.

That was a surprise, for not one of the twelve or fourteen Inspectors who had studied my papers had shown any sign of recognizing my name or the terms Envoy or Ekumen—all of which had been at least vaguely familiar to all Karhiders I had met. I had decided that Karhide had never let any broadcasts concerning me be used on Orgota stations, but had tried to keep me a national secret.

"Not Ambassador, Mr. Shusgis. Only an envoy."

"Future Ambassador, then. Yes, by Meshe!" Shusgis, a solid, beaming man, looked me up and down and laughed again. "You're not what I expected, Mr. Ai! Nowhere near it. Tall as a streetlamp, they said, thin as a sledge-runner, soot-black and slant-eyed—an ice-ogre I expected, a monster! Nothing of the kind. Only you're darker than most of us."

"Earth-colored," I said.

"And you were in Siuwensin the night of the foray? By the breasts of Meshe! what a world we live in. You might have been killed crossing the bridge over the Ey, after crossing all space to get here. Well! Well! You're here. And a lot of people want to see you, and hear you, and make you welcome to Orgoreyn at last."

He installed me at once, no arguments, in an apartment of his house. A high official and wealthy man, he lived in a style that has no equivalent in Karhide, even among lords of a great Domain. Shusgis' house was a whole island, housing over a hundred employees, domestic servants, clerks, technical advisers, and so on, but no relatives, no kinfolk. The system of extended-family clans, of Hearths and Domains, though still vaguely discernible in the Commensal structure, was "nationalized" several hundred years ago in Orgoreyn. No child over a year old lives with its parent or parents; all are brought up in the Commensal Hearths. There is no rank by descent. Private wills are not legal: a man dying leaves his fortune to the state. All start equal. But obviously they don't go on so. Shusgis was rich, and liberal with his riches. There were luxuries in my rooms that I had not known existed on Winter—for instance, a shower. There was an electric heater as well as a well-stocked fireplace. Shusgis laughed: "They told me, keep the Envoy warm, he's from a hot world, an oven of a world, and can't stand our cold. Treat him as if he were pregnant, put furs on his bed and heaters in his room, heat his wash-water and keep his windows shut! Will it do? Will you be comfortable? Please tell me what else you'd like to have here."

Comfortable! Nobody in Karhide had ever asked me, under any circumstances, if I was comfortable.

"Mr. Shusgis," I said with emotion, "I feel perfectly at home."

He wasn't satisfied till he had got another pesthry-fur blanket on the bed, and more logs into the fireplace. "I know how it is," he said; "when I was pregnant I couldn't keep warm—my feet were like ice, I sat over the fire all that winter. Long ago of course, but I remember!"— Gethenians tend to have their children young; most of them, after the age of twenty-four or so, use contraceptives, and they cease to be fertile in the female phase at about forty. Shusgis was in his fifties, therefore his "long ago of course," and it certainly was difficult to imagine him as a young mother. He was a hard shrewd jovial politician, whose acts of kindness served his interest and whose interest was himself. His type is panhuman. I had met him on Earth, and on Hain, and on Ollul. I expect to meet him in Hell.

"You're well informed as to my looks and tastes, Mr. Shusgis. I'm flattered; I thought my reputation hadn't preceded me."

"No," he said, understanding me perfectly, "they'd just as soon have kept you buried under a snowdrift, there in Erhenrang, eh? But they let you go, they let you go; and that's when we realized, here, that you weren't just another Karhidish lunatic but the real thing."

"I don't follow you, I think."

"Why, Argaven and his crew were afraid of you, Mr. Ai—afraid of you and glad to see your back. Afraid if they mishandled you, or silenced you, there might be retribution. A foray from outer space, eh! So they didn't dare touch you. And they tried to hush you up. Because they're afraid of you and of what you bring to Gethen!"

It was exaggerated; I certainly hadn't been censored out of the Karhidish news, at least so long as Estraven was in power. But I already had the impression that for some reason news hadn't got around about me much in Orgoreyn, and Shusgis confirmed my suspicions.

"Then you aren't afraid of what I bring to Gethen?"

"No, we're not, sir!"

"Sometimes I am."

He chose to laugh jovially at that. I did not qualify my words. I'm not a salesman, I'm not selling Progress to the Abos. We have to meet as equals, with some mutual understanding and candor, before my mission can even begin.

"Mr. Ai, there are a lot of people waiting to meet you, bigwigs and little ones, and some of them are the ones you'll be wanting to talk to here, the people who get things done. I asked for the honor of receiving you because I've got a big house and because I'm well known as a neutral sort of fellow, not a Dominator and not an Open-Trader, just a plain Commissioner who does his job and won't lay you open to any talk about whose house you're staying in." He laughed. "But that means you'll be eating out a good deal, if you don't mind."

"I'm at your disposal, Mr. Shusgis."

"Then tonight it'll be a little supper with Vanake Slose."

"Commensal from Kuwera—Third District, is it?" Of course I had done some homework before I came. He fussed over my condescension in deigning to learn anything about his country. Manners here were certainly different from manners in Karhide; there, the fuss he was making would either have degraded his own shifgrethor or insulted mine; I wasn't sure which, but it would have done one or the other—practically everything did.

I needed clothes fit for a supper-party, having lost my good Erhenrang suit in the raid on Siuwensin, so that afternoon I took a government taxi downtown and bought myself an Orgota rig. Hieb and shirt were much as in Karhide, but instead of summer breeches they wore thigh-high leggings the year round, baggy and cumbrous;

the colors were loud blues or reds, and the cloth and cut and make were all a little shoddy. It was standardized work. The clothes showed me what it was that this impressive, massive city lacked: elegance. Elegance is a small price to pay for enlightenment, and I was glad to pay it. I went back to Shusgis' house and reveled in the hot showerbath, which came at one from all sides in a kind of prickly mist. I thought of the cold tin tubs of East Karhide that I had chattered and shuddered in last summer, the ice-ringed basin in my Erhenrang room. Was that elegance? Long live comfort! I put on my gaudy red finery, and was driven with Shusgis to the supper-party in his chauffeured private car. There are more servants, more services in Orgoreyn than in Karhide. This is because all Orgota are employees of the state; the state must find employment for all citizens, and does so. This, at least, is the accepted explanation, though like most economic explanations it seems, under certain lights, to omit the main point.

Commensal Slose's fiercely lighted, high, white reception room held twenty or thirty guests, three of them Commensals and all of them evidently notables of one kind or another. This was more than a group of Orgota curious to see "the alien." I was not a curiosity, as I had been for a whole year in Karhide; not a freak; not a puzzle. I was, it seemed, a key.

What door was I to unlock? Some of them had a notion, these statesmen and officials who greeted me effusively, but I had none.

I wouldn't find out during supper. All over Winter, even in frozen barbarian Perunter, it is considered execrably vulgar to talk business while eating. As supper was served promptly I postponed my questions and attended to a gummy fish soup and to my host and fellow guests. Slose was a frail, youngish person, with unusually light, bright eyes and a muted, intense voice; he looked like an idealist, a dedicated soul. I liked his manner, but I wondered what it was he was dedicated to. On my left sat another Commensal, a fat-faced fellow named Obsle. He was gross, genial, and inquisitive. By the third sip of soup he was asking me what the devil, was I really born on some other world—what was it like there—warmer than Gethen, everybody said—how warm?

"Well, in this same latitude on Terra, it never snows."

"It never snows. It never snows?" He laughed with real enjoyment, as a child laughs at a good lie, encouraging further flights.

"Our sub-arctic regions are rather like your habitable zone; we're farther out of our last Ice Age than you, but not out, you see. Fundamentally Terra and Gethen are very much alike. All the inhabited worlds are. Men can live only within a narrow range of environments; Gethen's at one extreme. . . ."

"Then there are worlds hotter than yours?"

"Most of them are warmer. Some are hot; Gde, for instance. It's mostly sand and rock desert. It was warm to start with, and an exploitive civilization wrecked its natural balances fifty or sixty thousand years ago, burned up the forests for kindling, as it were. There are still people there, but it resembles—if I understand the Text—the Yomesh idea of where thieves go after death."

That drew a grin from Obsle—a quiet, approving grin that made me suddenly revise my estimation of the man.

"Some subcultists hold that those Afterlife Interims are actually, physically situated on other worlds, other planets of the real universe. Have you met with that idea, Mr. Ai?"

"No; I've been variously described, but nobody's yet explained me away as a ghost." As I spoke I chanced to look to my right, and saying "ghost" saw one. Dark, in dark clothing, still and shadowy, he sat at my elbow, the specter at the feast.

Obsle's attention had been taken up by his other neighbor, and most people were listening to Slose at the head of the table. I said in a low voice, "I didn't expect to see you here, Lord Estraven."

"The unexpected is what makes life possible," he said.

"I was entrusted with a message for you."

He looked inquiring.

"It takes the form of money—some of your own— Foreth rem ir Osboth sends it. I have it with me, at Mr. Shusgis' house. I'll see that it comes to you."

"It's kind of you, Mr. Ai."

He was quiet, subdued, reduced—a banished man living off his wits in a foreign land. He seemed disinclined to talk with me, and I was glad not to talk with him. Yet now and then during that long, heavy, talkative supperparty, though all my attention was given to those complex and powerful Orgota who meant to befriend or use me, I was sharply aware of him: of his silence; of his dark averted face. And it crossed my mind, though I dismissed the idea as baseless, that I had not come to Mishnory to eat roast blackfish with the Commensals of my own free will; nor had they brought me here. He had.

9

ESTRAVEN THE TRAITOR

An East Karhidish tale, as told in Gorin-hering by Tobord Chorhawa and recorded by G.A. The story is well known in various versions, and a "habben" play based on it is in the repertory of traveling players east of the Kargav.

Long ago, before the days of King Argaven I, who made Karhide one kingdom, there was a blood feud between the Domain of Stok and the Domain of Estre in Kerm Land. The feud had been fought in forays and ambushes for three generations, and there was no settling it, for it was a dispute over land. Rich land is scarce in Kerm, and a Domain's pride is in the length of its borders, and the lords of Kerm Land are proud men and umbrageous men, casting black shadows.

It chanced that the heir of the flesh of the Lord of Estre, a young man, skiing across Icefoot Lake in the month of Irrem hunting pesthry, came onto rotten ice and fell into the lake. Though by using one ski as a lever on a firmer ice-edge he pulled himself up out of the water at last, he was in almost as bad case out of the

lake as in it, for he was drenched, the air was *kurem,**
and night was coming on. He saw no hope of reaching
Estre eight miles away uphill, and so set off towards the
village of Ebos on the north shore of the lake. As night
fell the fog flowed down off the glacier and spread out
all across the lake, so that he could not see his way, nor
where to set his skis. Slowly he went for fear of rotten
ice, yet in haste, because the cold was at his bones and
before long he would not be able to move. He saw at last
a light before him in the night and fog. He cast off his
skis, for the lakeshore was rough going and bare of snow
in places. His legs would not well hold him up anymore,
and he struggled as best he could to the light. He was
far astray from the way to Ebos. This was a small house
set by itself in a forest of the thore-trees that are all the
woods of Kerm Land, and they grew close all about the
house and no taller than its roof. He beat at the door
with his hands and called aloud, and one opened the
door and brought him into firelight.

There was no else there, only this one person alone.
He took Estraven's clothes off him that were like clothes
of iron with the ice, and put him naked between furs,
and with the warmth of his own body drove out the frost
from Estraven's feet and hands and face, and gave him
hot ale to drink. At last the young man was recovered,
and looked on the one who cared for him.

---

* *Kurem*, damp weather, 0° to -20°F.

This was a stranger, young as himself. They looked at each other. Each of them was comely, strong of frame and fine of feature, straight and dark. Estraven saw that the fire of kemmer was in the face of the other.

He said, "I am Arek of Estre."

The other said, "I am Therem of Stok."

Then Estraven laughed, for he was still weak, and said, "Did you warm me back to life in order to kill me, Stokven?"

The other said, "No."

He put out his hand and touched Estraven's hand, as if he were making certain that the frost was driven out. At the touch, though Estraven was a day or two from his kemmer, he felt the fire waken in himself. So for a while both held still, their hands touching.

"They are the same," said Stokven, and laying his palm against Estraven's showed it was so: their hands were the same in length and form, finger by finger, matching like the two hands of one man laid palm to palm.

"I have never seen you before," Stokven said. "We are mortal enemies." He rose, and built up the fire in the hearth, and returned to sit by Estraven.

"We are mortal enemies," said Estraven. "I would swear kemmering with you."

"And I with you," said the other. Then they vowed kemmering to each other, and in Kerm Land then as now that vow of faithfulness is not to be broken, not to be replaced. That night, and the day that followed, and the night that followed, they spent in the hut in the forest by the frozen lake. On the next morning a party of men from Stok came to the hut. One of them knew young Estraven by sight. He said no word and gave no warning but drew his knife, and there in Stokven's sight stabbed Estraven in the throat and chest, and the young man fell across the cold hearth in his blood, dead.

"He was the heir of Estre," the murderer said.

Stokven said, "Put him on your sledge, and take him to Estre for burial."

He went back to Stok. The men set off with Estraven's body on the sledge, but they left it far in the thore-forest for wild beasts to eat, and returned that night to Stok. Therem stood up before his parent in the flesh, Lord Harish rem ir Stokven, and said to the men, "Did you do as I bid you?" They answered, "Yes." Therem said, "You lie, for you would never have come back alive from Estre. These men have disobeyed my command and lied to hide their disobedience: I ask their banishment." Lord Harish granted it, and they were driven out of Hearth and law.

Soon after this Therem left his Domain, saying that he wished to indwell at Rotherer Fastness for a time, and he did not return to Stok until a year had passed.

Now in the Domain of Estre they sought for Arek in mountain and plain, and then mourned for him: bitter the mourning through summer and autumn, for he had been the lord's one child of the flesh. But in the end of the month Thern when winter lay heavy on the land, a man came up the mountainside on skis, and gave to the warder at Estre Gate a bundle wrapped in furs, saying, "This is Therem, the son's son of Estre." Then he was down the mountain on his skis like a rock skipping over water, gone before any thought to hold him.

In the bundle of furs lay a newborn child, weeping, They brought the child in to Lord Sorve and told him the stranger's words; and the old lord full of grief saw in the baby his lost son Arek. He ordered that the child be reared as a son of the Inner Hearth, and that he be called Therem, though that was not a name ever used by the clan of Estre.

The child grew comely, fine and strong; he was dark of nature and silent, yet all saw in him some likeness to the lost Arek. When he was grown Lord Sorve in the willfulness of old age named him heir of Estre. Then there were swollen hearts among Sorve's kemmering-sons, all strong men in their prime, who had waited long for lordship. They laid ambush against young Therem when he went out alone hunting pesthry in the month of Irrem. But he was armed, and not taken unawares. Two of his hearth-brothers he shot, in the fog that lay thick on Icefoot Lake in the thaw-weather, and a third he fought with, knife to knife, and killed at last, though he himself was wounded on the chest and neck with deep cuts. Then he stood above his brother's body in the mist over the ice, and saw that night was falling. He grew sick and weak as the blood ran from his wounds, and he thought to go to Ebos village for help; but in the gathering dark he went astray, and came to the thore-forest on the east shore of the lake. There seeing an abandoned hut he entered it, and too faint to light a fire he fell down on the cold stones of the hearth, and lay so with his wounds unstanched.

One came in out of the night, a man alone. He stopped in the doorway and was still, staring at the man who lay in his blood across the hearth. Then he entered in haste, and made a bed of furs that he took out of an old chest, and built up a fire, and cleaned Therem's wounds and bound them. When he saw the young man look at him he said, "I am Therem of Stok."

"I am Therem of Estre."

There was silence awhile between them. Then the young man smiled and said, "Did you bind up my wounds in order to kill me, Stokven?"

"No," said the older one.

Estraven asked, "How does it chance that you, the Lord of Stok, are here on disputed land alone?"

"I come here often," Stokven replied.

He felt the young man's pulse and hand for fever, and for an instant laid his palm flat to Estraven's palm, and finger by finger their two hands matched, like the two hands of one man.

"We are mortal enemies," said Stokven.

Estraven answered, "We are mortal enemies. Yet I have never seen you before."

Stokven turned aside his face. "Once I saw you, long ago," he said. "I wish there might be peace between our houses."

Estraven said, "I will vow peace with you."

So they made that vow, and then spoke no more,

and the hurt man slept. In the morning Stokven was gone, but a party of people from Ebos village came to the hut and carried Estraven home to Estre. There none dared longer oppose the old lord's will, the rightness of which was written plain in three men's blood on the lake-ice; and at Sorve's death Therem became Lord of Estre. Within the year he ended the old feud, giving up half the disputed lands to the Domain of Stok. For this, and for the murder of his hearth-brothers, he was called Estraven the Traitor. Yet his name, Therem, is still given to children of that Domain.

10

CONVERSATIONS IN MISHNORY

Next morning as I finished a late breakfast served to me in my suite in Shusgis' mansion the house-phone emitted a polite bleat. When I switched it on, the caller spoke in Karhidish: "Therem Harth here. May I come up?"

"Please do."

I was glad to get the confrontation over with at once. It was plain that no tolerable relationship could exist between Estraven and myself. Even though his disgrace and exile were at least nominally on my account, I could take no responsibility for them, feel no rational guilt; he had made neither his acts nor his motives clear to me in Erhenrang, and I could not trust the fellow. I wished that he was not mixed up with these Orgota who had, as it were, adopted me. His presence was a complication and an embarrassment.

He was shown into the room by one of the many house-employees. I had him sit down in one of the large padded chairs, and offered him breakfast-ale. He refused. His manner was not constrained—he had left shyness a long way behind him if he ever had any—but it was restrained: tentative, aloof.

"The first real snow," he said, and seeing my glance at the heavily curtained window, "You haven't looked out yet?"

I did so, and saw snow whirling thick on a light wind down the street, over the whitened roofs; two or three inches had fallen in the night. It was Odarhad Gor, the 17th of the first month of autumn. "It's early," I said, caught by the snow-spell for a moment.

"They predict a hard winter this year."

I left the curtains drawn back. The bleak even light from outside fell on his dark face. He looked older. He had known some hard times since I saw him last in the Corner Red Dwelling of the Palace in Erhenrang by his own fireside.

"I have here what I was asked to bring you," I said, and gave him the foilskin-wrapped packet of money, which I had set out on a table ready after his call. He took it and thanked me gravely. I had not sat down. After a moment, still holding the packet, he stood up.

My conscience itched a little, but I did not scratch it. I wanted to discourage him from coming to me. That this involved humiliating him was unfortunate.

He looked straight at me. He was shorter than I, of course, short-legged and compact, not as tall even as many women of my race. Yet when he looked at me he did not seem to be looking up at me. I did not meet his eyes. I examined the radio on the table with a show of abstracted interest.

"One can't believe everything one hears on that radio, here," he said pleasantly. "Yet it seems to me that here in Mishnory you are going to be in some need of information, and advice."

"There seem to be a number of people quite ready to supply it."

"And there's safety in numbers, eh? Ten are more trustworthy than one. Excuse me, I shouldn't use Karhidish, I forgot." He went on in Orgota, "Banished men should never speak their native tongue; it comes bitter from their mouths. And this language suits a traitor better, I think; drips off one's teeth like sugar-syrup. Mr. Ai, I have the right to thank you. You performed a service both for me and for my old friend and kemmering Ashe Foreth, and in his name and mine I claim my right. My thanks take the form of advice." He paused; I said nothing. I had never heard him use this sort of harsh, elaborate courtesy, and had no idea what it signified. He went on, "You are, in Mishnory, what you were not, in Erhenrang. There they said you were; here they'll say you're not. You are the tool of a faction. I advise you to be careful how you let them use you. I advise you to find out what the enemy faction is, and who they are, and never to let them use you, for they will not use you well."

He stopped. I was about to demand that he be more specific, but he said, "Good-bye, Mr. Ai," turned, and left. I stood benumbed. The man was like an electric shock—nothing to hold on to and you don't know what hit you.

He had certainly spoiled the mood of peaceful self-congratulation in which I had eaten breakfast. I went to the narrow window and looked out. The snow had thinned a little. It was beautiful, drifting in white clots and clusters like a fall of cherry-petals in the orchards of my home, when a spring wind blows down the green slopes of Borland, where I was born: on Earth, warm Earth, where trees bear flowers in spring. All at once I was utterly downcast and homesick. Two years I had spent on this damned planet, and the third winter had begun before autumn was underway—months and months of unrelenting cold, sleet, ice, wind, rain, snow, cold, cold inside, cold outside, cold to the bone and the marrow of the bone. And all that time on my own, alien and isolate, without a soul I could trust. Poor Genly, shall we cry? I saw Estraven come out of the house onto the street below me, a dark foreshortened figure in the even, vague gray-white of the snow. He looked about, adjusting the loose belt of his hieb—he wore no coat. He set off down the street, walking with a deft, definite grace, a quickness of being that made him seem in that minute the only thing alive in all Mishnory.

I turned back to the warm room. Its comforts were stuffy and cloddish, the heater, the padded chairs, the bed piled with furs, the rugs, drapes, wrappings, mufflings.

I put on my winter coat and went out for a walk, in a disagreeable mood, in a disagreeable world.

I was to lunch that day with Commensals Obsle and Yegey and others I had met the night before, and to be introduced to some I had not met. Lunch is usually served from a buffet and eaten standing up, perhaps so that one will not feel he has spent the entire day sitting at table. For this formal affair, however, places were set at table, and the buffet was enormous, eighteen or twenty hot and cold dishes, mostly variations on sube-eggs and breadapple. At the sideboard, before the taboo on conversation applied, Obsle remarked to me while loading up his plate with batter-fried sube-eggs, "The fellow named Mersen is a spy from Erhenrang, and Gaum there is an open agent of the Sarf, you know." He spoke conversationally, laughed as if I had made an amusing reply, and moved off to the pickled blackfish.

I had no idea what the Sarf was.

As people were beginning to sit down a young fellow came in and spoke to the host, Yegey, who then turned to us. "News from Karhide," he said. "King Argaven's child was born this morning, and died within the hour."

There was a pause, and a buzz, and then the handsome man called Gaum laughed and lifted up his beer-tankard. "May all the kings of Karhide live as long!" he cried. Some drank the toast with him, most did not. "Name of Meshe, to laugh at a child's death," said a fat old man in purple sitting heavily down beside me, his leggings bunched around his thighs like skirts, his face heavy with disgust.

Discussion arose as to which of his kemmering-sons Argaven might name as his heir—for he was well over forty and would now surely have no child of his flesh—and how long he might leave Tibe as Regent. Some thought the regency would be ended at once, others were dubious. "What do you think, Mr. Ai?" asked the man called Mersen, whom Obsle had identified as a Karhidish agent, and thus presumably one of Tibe's own men. "You've just come from Erhenrang; what are they saying there about these rumors that Argaven has in fact abdicated without announcement, handed the sledge over to his cousin?"

"Well, I've heard the rumor, yes."

"Do you think it's got any foundation?"

"I have no idea," I said, and at this point the host intervened with a mention of the weather, for people had begun to eat.

After servants had cleared away the plates and the mountainous wreckage of roasts and pickles from the buffet, we all sat on around the long table; small cups of a fierce liquor were served, lifewater they called it, as men often do, and they asked me questions.

Since my examination by the physicians and scientists of Erhenrang I had not been faced with a group of people who wanted me to answer their questions. Few Karhiders, even the fishermen and farmers with whom I had spent my first months, had been willing to satisfy their curiosity—which was often intense—by simply asking. They were involute, introvert, indirect; they did not like questions and answers. I thought of Otherhord

Fastness, of what Faxe the Weaver had said concerning answers. . . . Even the experts had limited their questions to strictly physiological subjects, such as the glandular and circulatory functions in which I differed most notably from the Gethenian norm. They had never gone on to ask, for example, how the continuous sexuality of my race influenced its social institutions, how we handled our "permanent kemmer." They listened, when I told them; the psychologists listened when I told them about mindspeech; but not one of them had brought himself to ask enough general questions to form any adequate picture of Terran or Ekumenical society—except, perhaps, Estraven.

Here they weren't quite so tied up by considerations of everybody's prestige and pride, and questions evidently were not insulting either to the asker or the one questioned. However I soon saw that some of the questioners were out to catch me, to prove me a fraud. That threw me off balance a minute. I had of course met with incredulity in Karhide, but seldom with a will to incredulity. Tibe had put on an elaborate show of going-along-with-the-hoax, the day of the parade in Erhenrang, but as I now knew that was part of the game he had played to discredit Estraven, and I guessed that Tibe did in fact believe me. He had seen my ship, after all, the little lander that had brought me down on planet; he had free access along with anyone else to the engineers' reports on the ship and the ansible. None of these Orgota had seen the ship. I could show them the ansible, but it didn't make a very convincing Alien Artifact, being so incomprehensible

as to fit in with hoax as well as with reality. The old Law
of Cultural Embargo stood against the importation of
analyzable, imitable artifacts at this stage, and so I had
nothing with me except the ship and ansible, my box of
pictures, the indubitable peculiarity of my body, and the
unprovable singularity of my mind. The pictures passed
around the table, and were examined with the noncom-
mittal expression you see on the faces of people looking
at pictures of somebody else's family. The questioning
continued. What, asked Obsle, was the Ekumen—a
world, a league of worlds, a place, a government?

"Well, all of those and none. Ekumen is our Terran
word; in the common tongue it's called the Household;
in Karhidish it would be the Hearth. In Orgota I'm not
sure, I don't know the language well enough yet. Not
the Commensality, I think, though there are undoubt-
edly similarities between the Commensal Government
and the Ekumen. But the Ekumen is not essentially a
government at all. It is an attempt to reunify the mystical with the political, and as such is of course mostly a
failure; but its failure has done more good for humanity
so far than the successes of its predecessors. It is a society
and it has, at least potentially, a culture. It is a form of
education; in one aspect, it's a sort of very large school—
very large indeed. The motives of communication and
cooperation are of its essence, and therefore in another
aspect it's a league or union of worlds, possessing some
degree of centralized conventional organization. It's this
aspect, the League, that I now represent. The Ekumen
as a political entity functions through coordination, not

by rule. It does not enforce laws; decisions are reached by council and consent, not by consensus or command. As an economic entity it is immensely active, looking after interworld communication, keeping the balance of trade among the Eighty Worlds. Eighty-four, to be precise, if Gethen enters the Ekumen. . . ."

"What do you mean, it doesn't enforce its laws?" said Slose.

"It hasn't any. Member states follow their own laws; when they clash the Ekumen mediates, attempts to make a legal or ethical adjustment or collation or choice. Now if the Ekumen, as an experiment in the superorganic, does eventually fail, it will have to become a peace-keeping force, develop a police, and so on. But at this point there's no need. All the central worlds are still recovering from a disastrous era a couple of centuries ago, reviving lost skills and lost ideas, learning how to talk again. . . ." How could I explain the Age of the Enemy, and its after-effects, to a people who had no word for war?

"This is absolutely fascinating, Mr. Ai," said the host, Commensal Yegey, a delicate, dapper, drawling fellow with keen eyes. "But I can't see what they'd want with us. I mean to say, what particular good is an eighty-fourth world to them? And not, I take it, a very clever world for we don't have Star Ships and so on, as they all do."

"None of us did, until the Hainish and the Cetians arrived. And some worlds still weren't allowed to, for centuries, until the Ekumen established the canons for what I think you here call Open Trade." That got a laugh all around, for it was the name of Yegey's party or faction within the Commensality. "Open trade is really what I'm here to try to set up. Trade not only in goods, of course, but in knowledge, technologies, ideas, philosophies, art, medicine, science, theory . . . I doubt that Gethen would ever do much physical coming-and-going to the other worlds. We are seventeen light-years here from the nearest Ekumenical World, Ollul, a planet of the star you call Asyomse; the farthest is two hundred and fifty light-years away and you cannot even see its star. With the ansible communicator, you could talk with that world as if by radio with the next town. But I doubt you'd ever meet any people from it. . . . The kind of trade I speak of can be highly profitable, but it consists largely of simple communication rather than of transportation. My job here is, really, to find out if you're willing to communicate with the rest of mankind."

"'You,'" Slose repeated, leaning forward intensely. "Does that mean Orgoreyn? Or does it mean Gethen as a whole?"

I hesitated a moment, for it was not the question I had expected.

"Here and now, it means Orgoreyn. But the contract cannot be exclusive. If Sith, or the Island Nations, or Karhide decide to enter the Ekumen, they may. It's a matter of individual choice each time. Then what generally happens, on a planet as highly developed as Gethen, is that the various anthrotypes or regions or nations end up by establishing a set of representatives to function as coordinator on the planet and with the other planets—a local Stability, in our terms. A lot of time is saved by beginning this way; and money, by sharing the expense. If you decided to set up a Star Ship of your own, for instance."

"By the milk of Meshe!" said fat Humery beside me. "You want *us* to go shooting off into the Void? Ugh!" He wheezed, like the high notes of an accordion, in disgust and amusement.

Gaum spoke: "Where is *your* ship, Mr. Ai?"

He put the question softly, half-smiling, as if it were extremely subtle and he wished the subtlety to be noticed. He was a most extraordinarily handsome human being, by any standards and as either sex, and I couldn't help staring at him as I answered, and also wondered again what the Sarf was. "Why, that's no secret; it was talked about a good bit on the Karhidish radio. The rocket that landed me on Horden Island is now in the Royal Workshop Foundry in the Artisan School; most of it, anyway; I think various experts went off with various bits of it after they'd examined it."

"Rocket?" inquired Humery, for I had used the Orgota word for firecracker.

"It succinctly describes the method of propulsion of the landingboat, sir."

Humery wheezed some more. Gaum merely smiled, saying, "Then you have no means of returning to . . . well, wherever you came from?"

"Oh, yes. I could speak to Ollul by ansible and ask them to send a NAFAL ship to pick me up. It would get here in seventeen years. Or I could radio to the Star Ship that brought me into your solar system. It's in orbit around your sun now. It would get here in a matter of days."

The sensation that caused was visible and audible, and even Gaum couldn't hide his surprise. There was some discrepancy here. This was the one major fact I had kept concealed in Karhide, even from Estraven. If, as I had been given to understand, the Orgota knew about me only what Karhide had chosen to tell them, then this should have been only one among many surprises. But it wasn't. It was the big one.

"Where is this ship, sir?" Yegey demanded.

"Orbiting the sun, somewhere between Gethen and Kuhurn."

"How did you get from it to here?"

"By the firecracker," said old Humery.

"Precisely. We don't land an interstellar ship on a populated planet until open communication or alliance is established. So I came in on a little rocket-boat, and landed on Horden Island."

"And you can get in touch with the—with the big ship by ordinary radio, Mr. Ai?" That was Obsle.

"Yes." I omitted mention for the present of my little relay satellite, set into orbit from the rocket; I did not want to give them the impression that their sky was full of my junk. "It would take a fairly powerful transmitter, but you have plenty of those."

"Then we could radio your ship?"

"Yes, if you had the proper signal. The people aboard are in a condition we call stasis, hibernation you might say, so that they won't lose out of their lives the years they spend waiting for me to get my business done down here. The proper signal on the proper wavelength will set machinery in motion that will bring them out of stasis; after which they'll consult with me by radio, or by ansible, using Ollul as relay-center."

Someone asked uneasily, "How many of them?"

"Eleven."

That brought a little sound of relief, a laugh. The tension relaxed a little.

"What if you never signaled?" Obsle asked.

"They'll come out of stasis automatically, about four years from now."

"Would they come here after you, then?"

"Not unless they'd heard from me. They'd consult with the Stabiles on Ollul and Hain, by ansible. Most likely they'd decide to try again—send down another person as Envoy. The Second Envoy often finds things easier than the First. He has less explaining to do, and people are likelier to believe him. . . ."

Obsle grinned. Most of the others still looked thoughtful and guarded. Gaum gave me an airy little nod, as if applauding my quickness to reply: a conspirator's nod. Slose was staring bright-eyed and tense at some inner vision, from which he turned abruptly to me. "Why," he said, "Mr. Envoy, did you never speak of this other ship, during your two years in Karhide?"

"How do we know that he didn't?" said Gaum, smiling.

"We know damned well that he didn't, Mr. Gaum," said Yegey, also smiling.

"I didn't," I said. "This is why. The idea of that ship, waiting out there, can be an alarming one. I think some of you find it so. In Karhide, I never advanced to a point of confidence with those I dealt with that allowed me to take the risk of speaking of the ship. Here, you've had longer to think about me; you're willing to listen to me out in the open, in public; you're not so much ruled by fear. I took the risk because I think the time has come to take it, and that Orgoreyn is the place."

"You are right, Mr. Ai, you are right!" Slose said violently. "Within a month you will send for that ship, and it will be made welcome in Orgoreyn as the visible sign and seal of the new epoch. Their eyes will be opened who will not see now!"

It went on, right on till dinner was served to us where we sat. We ate and drank and went home, I for one worn out, but pleased all in all with the way things had gone. There were warnings and obscurities, of course. Slose wanted to make a religion of me. Gaum wanted to make a sham of me. Mersen seemed to want to prove that he was not a Karhidish agent by proving that I was. But Obsle, Yegey, and some others were working on a higher level. They wanted to communicate with the Stabiles, and to bring the NAFAL ship down on Orgota ground, in order to persuade or coerce the Commensality of Orgoreyn to ally itself with the Ekumen. They believed that in doing so Orgoreyn would gain a large and lasting prestige-victory over Karhide, and that the Commensals who engineered this victory would gain according prestige and power in their government. Their Open Trade faction, a minority in the Thirty-Three, opposed the continuation of the Sinoth Valley dispute, and in general represented a conservative, unaggressive, non-nationalistic policy. They had been out of power for a long time and were calculating that their way back to power might, with some risks taken, lie on the road I pointed out. That they saw no farther than that, that my mission was a means to them and not an end, was no great harm. Once they were on the road, they might begin to get some sense of where it could take them. Meanwhile, if shortsighted, they were at least realistic.

Obsle, speaking to persuade others, had said, "Either Karhide will fear the strength this alliance will give us— and Karhide is always afraid of new ways and new ideas, remember—and so will hang back and be left behind. Or else the Erhenrang Government will get up their courage and come and ask to join, after us, in second place. In either case the shifgrethor of Karhide will be diminished; and in either case, we drive the sledge. If we have the wits to take this advantage now, it will be a permanent advantage and a certain one!" Then turning to me, "But the Ekumen must be willing to help us, Mr. Ai. We have got to have more to show our people than you alone, one man, already known in Erhenrang."

"I see that, Commensal. You'd like a good, showy proof, and I'd like to offer one. But I cannot bring down the ship until its safety and your integrity are reasonably secure. I need the consent and the guarantee of your government, which I take it would mean the whole board of Commensals—publicly announced."

Obsle looked dour, but said, "Fair enough."

Driving home with Shusgis, who had contributed nothing but his jovial laugh to the afternoon's business, I asked, "Mr. Shusgis, what is the Sarf?"

"One of the Permanent Bureaus of the Internal Administration. Looks out after false registries, unauthorized travel, job-substitutions, forgeries, that sort of thing—trash. That's what *sarf* means in gutter-Orgota, trash, it's a nickname."

"Then the Inspectors are agents of the Sarf?"

"Well, some are."

"And the police, I suppose they come under its authority to some extent?" I put the question cautiously and was answered in kind. "I suppose so. I'm in the External Administration, of course, and I can't keep all the offices straight, over in Internal."

"They certainly are confusing; now what's the Waters Office, for instance?" So I backed off as best I could from the subject of the Sarf. What Shusgis had not said on the subject might have meant nothing at all to a man from Hain, say, or lucky Chiffewar; but I was born on Earth. It is not altogether a bad thing to have criminal ancestors. An arsonist grandfather may bequeath one a nose for smelling smoke.

It had been entertaining and fascinating to find here on Gethen governments so similar to those in the ancient histories of Terra: a monarchy, and a genuine full-blown bureaucracy. This new development was also fascinating, but less entertaining. It was odd that in the less primitive society, the more sinister note was struck.

So Gaum, who wanted me to be a liar, was an agent of the secret police of Orgoreyn. Did he know that Obsle knew him as such? No doubt he did. Was he then the agent provocateur? Was he nominally working with, or against, Obsle's faction? Which of the factions within the Government of Thirty-Three controlled, or was controlled by, the Sarf? I had better get these matters straight, but it might not be easy to do so. My course, which for a while had looked so clear and hopeful, seemed likely to become as tortuous and beset with secrets as it had been in Ehrenrang. Everything had gone all right, I thought, until Estraven had appeared shadowlike at my side last night.

"What's Lord Estraven's position, here in Mishnory?" I asked Shusgis, who had settled back as if half-asleep in the corner of the smooth-running car.

"Estraven? Harth, he's called here, you know. We don't have titles in Orgoreyn, dropped all that with the New Epoch. Well, he's a dependent of Commensal Yegey's, I understand."

"He lives there?"

"I believe so."

I was about to say that it was odd that he had been at Slose's last night and not at Yegey's today, when I saw that in the light of our brief morning interview it wasn't very odd. Yet even the idea that he was intentionally keeping away made me uncomfortable.

"They found him," said Shusgis, resetting his broad hips on the cushioned seat, "over in the Southside in a glue factory or a fish cannery or some such place, and gave him a hand out of the gutter. Some of the Open Trade crowd, I mean. Of course he was useful to them when he was in the kyorremy and prime minister, so they stand by him now. Mainly they do it to annoy Mersen, I think. Ha, ha! Mersen's a spy for Tibe, and of course he thinks nobody knows it but everybody does, and he can't stand the sight of Harth—thinks he's either a traitor or a double agent and doesn't know which, and can't risk shifgrethor in finding out. Ha, ha!"

"Which do you think Harth is, Mr. Shusgis?"

"A traitor, Mr. Ai. Pure and simple. Sold out his country's claims in the Sinoth Valley in order to prevent Tibe's rise to power, but didn't manage it cleverly enough. He'd have met with worse punishment than exile, here. By Meshe's tits! If you play against your own side you'll lose the whole game. That's what these fellows with no patriotism, only self-love, can't see. Though I don't suppose Harth much cares where he is so long as he can keep on wriggling towards some kind of power. He hasn't done so badly here, in five months, as you see."

"Not so badly."

"You don't trust him either, eh?"

"No, I don't."

"I'm glad to hear it, Mr. Ai. I don't see why Yegey and Obsle hang on to the fellow. He's a proven traitor, out for his own profit, and trying to hang on to your sledge, Mr. Ai, until he can keep himself going. That's how I see it. Well, I don't know that I'd give him any free rides, if he came asking me for one!" Shusgis puffed and nodded vigorously in approval of his own opinion, and smiled at me, the smile of one virtuous man to another. The car ran softly through the wide, well-lit streets. The morning's snow was melted except for dingy heaps along the gutters; it was raining now, a cold, small rain.

The great buildings of central Mishnory, government offices, schools, Yomesh temples, were so blurred by rain in the liquid glare of the high streetlights that they looked as if they were melting. Their corners were vague, their façades streaked, dewed, smeared. There was something fluid, insubstantial, in the very heaviness of this city built of monoliths, this monolithic state that called the part and the whole by the same name. And Shusgis, my jovial host, a heavy man, a substantial man, he too was somehow, around the corners and edges, a little vague, a little, just a little bit unreal.

Ever since I had set off by car through the wide golden fields of Orgoreyn four days ago, beginning my successful progress towards the inner sanctums of Mishnory, I had been missing something. But what? I felt insulated. I had not felt the cold, lately. They kept rooms decently warm, here. I had not eaten with pleasure, lately. Orgota cooking was insipid; no harm in that. But why did the people I met, whether well or ill disposed towards me, also seem insipid? There were vivid personalities among them—Obsle, Slose, the handsome and detestable Gaum—and yet each of them lacked some quality, some dimension of being; and they failed to convince. They were not quite solid.

It was, I thought, as if they did not cast shadows.

This kind of rather highflown speculation is an

essential part of my job. Without some capacity for it I could not have qualified as a Mobile, and I received formal training in it on Hain, where they dignify it with the title of Farfetching. What one is after when farfetching might be described as the intuitive perception of a moral entirety; and thus it tends to find expression not in rational symbols, but in metaphor. I was never an outstanding farfetcher, and this night I distrusted my own intuitions, being very tired. When I was back in my apartment I took refuge in a hot shower. But even there I felt a vague unease, as if the hot water was not altogether real and reliable, and could not be counted on.

SOLILOQUIES
IN MISHNORY

Mishnory. Streth Susmy. I am not hopeful, yet all events show cause for hope. Obsle haggles and dickers with his fellow Commensals, Yegey employs blandishments, Slose proselytizes, and the strength of their following grows. They are astute men, and have their faction well in hand. Only seven of the Thirty-Three are reliable Open Traders; of the rest, Obsle thinks to gain the sure support of ten, giving a bare majority.

One of them seems to have a true interest in the Envoy: Csl. Ithepen of the Eynyen District, who has been curious about the Alien Mission since, while working for the Sarf, he was in charge of censoring the broadcasts we sent out from Erhenrang. He seems to carry the weight of those suppressions on his conscience. He proposed to Obsle that the Thirty-Three announce their invitation to the Star Ship not only to their countrymen, but at the same time to Karhide, asking Argaven to join Karhide's voice to the invitation. A noble plan, and it will not be followed. They will not ask Karhide to join them in anything.

The Sarf's men among the Thirty-Three of course oppose any consideration at all of the Envoy's presence and mission. As for those lukewarm and uncommitted whom Obsle hopes to enlist, I think they fear the Envoy, much as Argaven and most of the Court did; with this difference, that Argaven thought him mad, like himself, while they think him a liar, like themselves. They fear to swallow a great hoax in public, a hoax already refused by Karhide, a hoax perhaps even invented by Karhide. They make their invitation, they make it publicly; then where is their shifgrethor, when no Star Ship comes?

Indeed Genly Ai demands of us an inordinate trustfulness.

To him evidently it is not inordinate.

And Obsle and Yegey think that a majority of the Thirty-Three will be persuaded to trust him. I do not know why I am less hopeful than they; perhaps I do not really want Orgoreyn to prove more enlightened than Karhide, to take the risk and win the praise and leave Karhide in the shadow. If this envy be patriotic, it comes too late; as soon as I saw that Tibe would soon have me ousted, I did all I could to ensure that the Envoy would come to Orgoreyn, and in exile here I have done what I could to win them to him.

Thanks to the money he brought me from Ashe I now

live by myself again, as a "unit" not a "dependent." I go
to no more banquets, am not seen in public with Obsle
or other supporters of the Envoy, and have not seen the
Envoy himself for over a halfmonth, since his second day
in Mishnory.

He gave me Ashe's money as one would give a hired
assassin his fee. I have not often been so angry, and I
insulted him deliberately. He knew I was angry but I am
not sure he understood that he was insulted; he seemed
to *accept* my advice despite the manner of its giving; and
when my temper cooled I saw this, and was worried by it.
Is it possible that all along in Erhenrang he was seeking
my advice, not knowing how to tell me that he sought
it? If so, then he must have misunderstood half and not
understood the rest of what I told him by my fireside
in the Palace, the night after the Ceremony of the Keystone. His shifgrethor must be founded, and composed,
and sustained, altogether differently from ours; and
when I thought myself most blunt and frank with him
he may have found me most subtle and unclear.

His obtuseness is ignorance. His arrogance is ignorance. He is ignorant of us: we of him. He is infinitely a
stranger, and I a fool, to let my shadow cross the light
of the hope he brings us. I keep my mortal vanity down.
I keep out of his way: for clearly that is what he wants.
He is right. An exiled Karhidish traitor is no credit to
his cause.

Conformable to the Orgota law that each "unit" must
have employment, I work from Eighth Hour to noon in
a plastics factory. Easy work: I run a machine that fits

together and heatbonds pieces of plastic to form little transparent boxes. I do not know what the boxes are for. In the afternoon, finding myself dull, I have taken up the old disciplines I learned in Rotherer. I am glad to see I have lost no skill at summoning dothe-strength, or entering the untrance; but I get little good out of the untrance, and as for the skills of stillness and of fasting, I might as well never have learned them, and must start all over, like a child. I have fasted now one day, and my belly screams, A week! A month!

The nights freeze now; tonight a hard wind bears frozen rain. All evening I have thought continually of Estre and the sound of the wind seems the sound of the wind that blows there. I wrote to my son tonight, a long letter. While writing it I had again and again a sense of Arek's presence, as if I should see him if I turned. Why do I keep such notes as these? For my son to read? Little good they would do him. I write to be writing in my own language, perhaps.

Harhahad Susmy. Still no mention of the Envoy has been made on the radio, not a word. I wonder if Genly Ai sees that in Orgoreyn, despite the vast visible apparatus of government, nothing is done visibly, nothing is said aloud. The machine conceals the machinations.

Tibe wants to teach Karhide how to lie. He takes his lessons from Orgoreyn: a good school. But I think we shall have trouble learning how to lie, having for so long practiced the art of going round and round the truth without ever lying about it, or reaching it either.

A big Orgota foray yesterday across the Ey; they burned the granaries of Tekember. Precisely what the Sarf wants, and what Tibe wants. But where does it end?

Slose, having turned his Yomesh mysticism onto the Envoy's statements, interprets the coming of the Ekumen to Earth as the coming of the Reign of Meshe among men, and loses sight of our purpose. "We must halt this rivalry with Karhide *before* the New Men come," he says. "We must cleanse our spirits for their coming. We must forgo shifgrethor, forbid all acts of vengeance, and unite together without envy as brothers of one Hearth."

But how, until they come? How to break the circle?

Guyrny Susmy. Slose heads a committee that purposes to suppress the obscene plays performed in public kemmerhouses here; they must be like the Karhidish *huhuth.* Slose opposes them because they are trivial, vulgar, and blasphemous.

To oppose something is to maintain it.

They say here "all roads lead to Mishnory." To be sure, if you turn your back on Mishnory and walk away from it, you are still on the Mishnory road. To oppose vulgarity is inevitably to be vulgar. You must go somewhere else; you must have another goal; then you walk a different road.

Yegey in the Hall of the Thirty-Three today: "I unalterably oppose this blockade of grain-exports to Karhide, and the spirit of competition that motivates it." Right enough, but he will not get off the Mishnory road going that way. He must offer an alternative. Orgoreyn and Karhide both must stop following the road they're on, in either direction; they must go somewhere else, and break the circle. Yegey, I think, should be talking of the Envoy and of nothing else.

To be an atheist is to maintain God. His existence or his nonexistence, it amounts to much the same, on the plane of proof. Thus *proof* is a word not often used among the Handdarata, who have chosen not to treat God as a fact, subject either to proof or to belief: and they have broken the circle, and go free.

To learn which questions are unanswerable, and *not to answer them:* this skill is most needful in times of stress and darkness.

Tormenbod Susmy. My unease grows: still not one word about the Envoy has been spoken on the Central Bureau Radio. None of the news about him that we used to broadcast from Erhenrang was ever released here, and rumors rising out of illegal radio reception over the border, and traders' and travelers' stories, never seem to have spread far. The Sarf has more complete control over communications than I knew, or thought possible. The possibility is awesome. In Karhide king and kyorremy have a good deal of control over what people do, but very little over what they hear, and none over what they say. Here, the government can check not only act but thought. Surely no men should have such power over others.

Shusgis and others take Genly Ai about the city openly. I wonder if he sees that this openness hides the fact that he is hidden. No one knows he is here. I ask my fellow-workers at the factory; they know nothing and think I am talking of some crazy Yomesh sectarian. No information, no interest, nothing that might advance Ai's cause, or protect his life.

It is a pity he looks so like us. In Erhenrang people often pointed him out on the street, for they knew some truth or talk about him and knew he was there. Here where his presence is kept secret his person goes unremarked. They see him no doubt much as I first saw him: an unusually tall, husky, and dark youth just entering kemmer. I studied the physicians' reports on him last year. His differences from us are profound. They are not superficial. One must know him to know him alien.

Why do they hide him, then? Why does not one of the Commensals force the issue and speak of him in a public speech or on the radio? Why is even Obsle silent? Out of fear.

My king was afraid of the Envoy; these fellows are afraid of one another

I think that I, a foreigner, am the only person Obsle trusts. He has some pleasure in my company (as I in his), and several times has waived shifgrethor and frankly asked my advice. But when I urge him to speak out, to raise public interest as a defense against factional intrigue, he does not hear me.

"If the entire Commensality had their eyes on the Envoy, the Sarf would not dare touch him," I say, "or you, Obsle."

Obsle sighs. "Yes, yes, but we can't do it, Estraven. Radio, printed bulletins, scientific periodicals, they're all in the Sarf's hands. What am I to do, make speeches on a street-corner like some fanatic priest?"

"Well, one can talk to people, set rumors going; I had to do something of the same sort last year in Erhenrang. Get people asking questions to which you have the answer, that is, the Envoy himself."

"If only he'd bring that damned Ship of his down here, so that we had something to show people! But as it is—"

"He won't bring his Ship down until he knows that you're acting in good faith."

"Am I not?" cries Obsle, fattening out like a great hob-fish. "Haven't I spent every hour of the past month on this business? Good faith! He expects us to believe whatever he tells us, and then doesn't trust us in return!"

"Should he?"

Obsle puffs and does not reply.

He comes nearer honesty than any Orgota government official I know.

Odgetheny Susmy. To become a high officer in the Sarf one must have, it seems, a certain complex form of stupidity. Gaum exemplifies it. He sees me as a Karhidish agent attempting to lead Orgoreyn into a tremendous prestige-loss by persuading them to believe in the hoax of the Envoy from the Ekumen; he thinks that I spent my time as prime minister preparing this hoax. By God, I have better things to do than play shifgrethor with scum. But that is a simplicity he is unequipped to see. Now that Yegey has apparently cast me off Gaum thinks I must be purchasable, and so prepared to buy me out in his own curious fashion. He has watched me or had me watched close enough that he knew I would be due to enter kemmer on Posthe or Tormenbod; so he turned up last night in full kemmer, hormone-induced no doubt, ready to seduce me. An accidental meeting on Pyenefen Street. "Harth! I haven't seen you in a halfmonth; where have you been hiding yourself lately? Come have a cup of ale with me."

He chose an alehouse next door to one of the Commensal Public Kemmerhouses. He ordered us not ale, but lifewater. He meant to waste no time. After one glass he put his hand on mine and shoved his face up close, whispering, "We didn't meet by chance, I waited for you: I crave you for my kemmering tonight," and he called me by my given name. I did not cut his tongue out, because since I left Estre I don't carry a knife. I told him that I intended to abstain while in exile. He cooed and muttered and held on to my hands. He was going very rapidly into full phase as a woman. Gaum is very beautiful in kemmer, and he counted on his beauty and his sexual insistence, knowing, I suppose, that being of the Handdara I would be unlikely to use kemmer-reduction drugs, and would make a point of abstinence against the odds. He forgot that detestation is as good as any drug. I got free of his pawing, which of course was having some effect on me, and left him, suggesting that he try the public kemmerhouse next door. At that he looked at me with pitiable hatred: for he was, however false his purpose, truly in kemmer and deeply roused.

Did he really think I'd sell myself for his small change? He must think me very uneasy; which, indeed, makes me uneasy.

Damn them, these unclean men. There is not one clean man among them.

Odsordny Susmy. This afternoon Genly Ai spoke in the Hall of the Thirty-Three. No audience was permitted and no broadcast made, but Obsle later had me in and played me his own tape of the session. The Envoy spoke well, with moving candor and urgency. There is an innocence in him that I have found merely foreign and foolish; yet in another moment that seeming innocence reveals a discipline of knowledge and a largeness of purpose that awes me. Through him speaks a shrewd and magnanimous people, a people who have woven together into one wisdom a profound, old, terrible, and unimaginably various experience of life. But he himself is young: impatient, inexperienced. He stands higher than we stand, seeing wider, but he is himself only the height of a man.

He speaks better now than he did in Erhenrang, more simply and more subtly; he has learned his job in doing it, like us all.

His speech was often interrupted by members of the Domination faction demanding that the President stop this lunatic, turn him out, and get on with the order of business. Csl. Yemenbey was most obstreperous, and probably spontaneous. "You don't swallow this *gichy-michy*?" he kept roaring across to Obsle. Planned interruptions, which made part of the tape hard to follow, were led, Obsle says, by Kaharosile.—From memory:

Alshel (presiding): Mr. Envoy, we find this information, and the proposals made by Mr. Obsle, Mr. Slose, Mr. Ithepen, Mr. Yegey and others, most interesting—most stimulating. We need, however, a little more to go on. (Laughter) Since the King of Karhide has your . . . the vehicle you arrived on, locked up where we can't see it, would it be possible, as suggested, for you to bring down your . . . Star Ship? What do you call it?

Ai: Star Ship is a good name, sir.

Alshel: Oh? What do you call it?

Ai: Well, technically, it's a manned interstellar Cetian Design NAFAL-20.

Voice: You're sure it's not St. Pethethe's sledge? (Laughter)

Alshel: Please. Yes. Well, if you can get this ship down onto the ground here—solid ground you might say—so that we can, as it were, have some substantial—

Voice: Substantial fishguts!

Ai: I want very much to bring that ship down, Mr. Alshel, as proof and witness of our reciprocal good faith. I await only your preliminary public announcement of the event.

Kaharosile: Don't you see, Commensals, what all this is? It's not just a stupid joke. It is, in intention, a public mockery of our credulity, our gullibility, our stupidity—engineered, with incredible impudence, by this person who stands here before us today. You know he comes from Karhide. You know he is a Karhidish agent. You can see he is a sexual deviant of a type that in Karhide, due to the influence of the Dark Cult, is left uncured, and sometimes is even artificially created for the Fore-tellers' orgies. And yet when he says, "I am from outer space," some of you actually shut your eyes, abase your intellects, and *believe!* Never could I have thought it possible, etc., etc.

To judge by the tape, Ai withstood gibes and assaults with patience. Obsle says he handled himself well. I was hanging about outside the Hall to see them come out after the Session of the Thirty-Three. Ai had a grim pondering look. Well he might.

My helplessness is intolerable. I was one who set this machine running, and now cannot control its running. I slink in the streets with my hood pulled forward, to catch a glimpse of the Envoy. For this useless sneaking life I threw away my power, my money, and my friends. What a fool you are, Therem.

Why can I never set my heart on a possible thing?

Odeps Susmy. The transmitting device Genly Ai has now turned over to the Thirty-Three, in Obsle's care, is not going to change any minds. No doubt it does what he says it does, but if Royal Mathematician Shorst would say of it only, "I don't understand the principles," then no Orgota mathematician or engineer will do much better, and nothing is proved or disproved. An admirable outcome, were this world one Fastness of the Handdara, but alas we must walk forward troubling the new snow, proving and disproving, asking and answering.

Once more I pressed on Obsle the feasibility of having Ai radio his Star Ship, waken the people aboard, and ask them to converse with the Commensals by radio hookup to the Hall of the Thirty-Three. This time Obsle had a reason ready for not doing so. "Listen, Estraven my dear, the Sarf runs all our radio, you know that by now. I have no idea, even I, which of the men in Communications are the Sarf men; most of them, no doubt, for I know as a fact that they run the transmitters and receivers on every level right down to the technicians and repairmen. They could and would block—or falsify—any transmission we received, if we did receive one! Can you imagine that scene, in the Hall? We 'Outerspacers' victims of our own hoax, listening with bated breath to a clutter of static—and nothing else—no answer, no Message?"

"And you have no money to hire some loyal technicians, or buy off some of theirs?" I asked; but no use. He fears for his own prestige. His behavior towards me is already changed. If he calls off his reception for the Envoy tonight, things are in a bad way.

Odarhad Susmy. He called off the reception.

This morning I went to see the Envoy, in proper Orgota style. Not openly, at Shusgis' house, where the staff must be crawling with Sarf agents, Shusgis being one himself, but in the street, by chance, Gaum-fashion, sneaking and creeping. "Mr. Ai, will you hear me a moment?"

He looked around, startled, and recognizing me, alarmed. After a moment he broke out, "What good is it, Mr. Harth? You know that I can't rely on what you say—since Erhenrang—"

That was candid, if not perceptive; yet it was perceptive too: he knew that I wanted to advise him, not to ask something of him, and spoke to save my pride.

I said, "This is Mishnory, not Erhenrang, but the danger you are in is the same. If you cannot persuade Obsle or Yegey to let you make radio contact with your ship, so that the people aboard it can, while remaining safe, lend some support to your statements, then I think you should use your own instrument, the ansible, and call the ship down at once. The risk it will run is less than the risk you are now running, alone."

"The Commensals' debates concerning my messages have been kept secret. How do you know about my 'statements,' Mr. Harth?"

"Because I have made it my life's business to know—"

"But it is not your business here, sir. It is up to the Commensals of Orgoreyn."

"I tell you that you're in danger of your life, Mr. Ai," I said; to that he said nothing, and I left him.

I should have spoken to him days ago. It is too late. Fear undoes his mission and my hope, once more. Not fear of the alien, the unearthly, not here. These Orgota have not the wits nor size of spirit to fear what is truly and immensely strange. They cannot even see it. They look at the man from another world and see what? A spy from Karhide, a pervert, an agent, a sorry little political Unit like themselves.

If he does not send for the ship at once it will be too late; it may be already too late.

It is my fault. I have done nothing right.

12

ON TIME
AND DARKNESS

From The Sayings of Tuhulme the High Priest, a book of the Yomesh Canon, composed in North Orgoreyn about 900 years ago.

Meshe is the Center of Time. That moment of his life when he saw all things clearly came when he had lived on Earth thirty years, and after it he lived on Earth again thirty years, so that the Seeing befell in the center of his life. And all the ages up until the Seeing were as long as the ages will be after the Seeing, which befell in the Center of Time. And in the Center there is no time past and no time to come. In all time past it is. In all time to come it is. It has not been nor yet will it be. It is. It is all.

Nothing is unseen.

The poor man of Sheney came to Meshe lamenting that he had not food to give the child of his flesh, nor grain to sow, for the rains had rotted the seed in the ground and all the folk of his Hearth starved. Meshe said, "Dig in the stone-fields of Tuerresh, and you will find there a treasure of silver and precious stones; for I see a king bury it there, ten thousand years ago, when a neighboring king presses feud upon him."

The poor man of Sheney dug in the moraines of Tuerresh and unearthed where Meshe pointed a great hoard of ancient jewels, and at sight of it he shouted aloud for joy. But Meshe standing by wept at sight of it, saying, "I see a man kill his hearth-brother for one of those carven stones. That is ten thousand years from now, and the bones of the murdered man will lie in this grave where the treasure lies. O man of Sheney, I know too where your grave is: I see you lying in it."

The life of every man is in the Center of Time, for all were seen in the Seeing of Meshe, and are in his Eye. We are the pupils of his Eye. Our doing is his Seeing: our being his Knowing.

A hemmen-tree in the heart of Ornen Forest, which lies a hundred miles long and a hundred miles wide, was old and greatly grown, with a hundred branches and on every branch a thousand twigs and on every twig a hundred leaves. The tree said in its rooted being, "All my leaves are seen, but one, this one in the darkness cast by all the others. This one leaf I keep secret to myself. Who will see it in the darkness of my leaves? And who will count the number of them?"

Meshe passed through the Forest of Ornen in his wanderings, and from that one tree plucked that one leaf.

No raindrop falls in the storms of autumn that ever fell before, and the rain has fallen, and falls, and will fall throughout all the autumns of the years. Meshe saw each drop, where it fell, and falls, and will fall.

In the Eye of Meshe are all the stars, and the darknesses between the stars: and all are bright.

In the answering of the Question of the Lord of Shorth, in the moment of the Seeing, Meshe saw all the sky as if it were all one sun. Above the earth and under the earth all the sphere of sky was bright as the sun's surface, and there was no darkness. For he saw not what was, nor what will be, but what is. The stars that flee and take away their light all were present in his Eye, and all their light shone presently.*

Darkness is only in the mortal eye, that thinks it sees, but sees not. In the Sight of Meshe there is no darkness.

Therefore those that call upon the darkness** are made fools of and spat out from the mouth of Meshe, for they name what is not, calling it Source and End.

There is neither source nor end, for all things are in the Center of Time. As all the stars may be reflected in a round raindrop falling in the night: so too do all the stars reflect the raindrop. There is neither darkness nor death, for all things are, in the light of the Moment, and their end and their beginning are one.

One center, one seeing, one law, one light. Look now into the Eye of Meshe!

---

* This is a mystical expression of one of the theories used to support the expanding-universe hypothesis, first proposed by the Mathematical School of Sith over four thousand years ago and generally accepted by later cosmologists, even though meteorological conditions on Gethen prevent their gathering much observational support from astronomy. The rate of expansion (Hubble's constant; Rreherek's constant) can in fact be estimated from the observed amount of light in the night sky; the point here involved is that, if the universe were not expanding, the night sky would not appear to be dark.
** The Handdarata.

13

DOWN ON
THE FARM

Alarmed by Estraven's sudden reappearance, his familiarity with my affairs, and the fierce urgency of his warnings, I hailed a taxi and drove straight to Obsle's island, meaning to ask the Commensal how Estraven knew so much and why he had suddenly popped up from nowhere urging me to do precisely what Obsle yesterday had advised against doing. The Commensal was out, the doorkeeper did not know where he was or when he would be in. I went to Yegey's house with no better luck. A heavy snow, the heaviest of the autumn so far, was falling; my driver refused to take me farther than to Shusgis' house, as he did not have snow-cleats on his tires. That evening I failed to reach Obsle, Yegey, or Slose by telephone.

At dinner Shusgis explained: a Yomesh festival was going on, the Solemnity of the Saints and Throne-Upholders,

and high officials of the Commensality were expected
to be seen at the temples. He also explained Estraven's
behavior, shrewdly enough, as that of a man once powerful and now fallen, who grasps at any chance to influence
persons or events—always less rationally, more desperately, as time passes and he knows himself sinking into
powerless anonymity. I agreed that this would explain
Estraven's anxious, almost frantic manner. The anxiety
had however infected me. I was vaguely ill at ease all
through that long and heavy meal. Shusgis talked and
talked to me and to the many employees, aides, and
sycophants who sat down at his table nightly; I had
never known him so longwinded, so relentlessly jovial.
When dinner was over it was pretty late for going out
again, and in any case the Solemnity would keep all the
Commensals busy, Shusgis said, until after midnight. I
decided to pass up supper, and went to bed early. Some
time between midnight and dawn I was awakened by
strangers, informed that I was under arrest, and taken by
an armed guard to the Kundershaden Prison.

Kundershaden is old, one of the few very old buildings left in Mishnory. I had noticed it often as I went
about the city, a long grimy many-towered ill-looking
place, distinct among the pallid bulks and hulks of the
Commensal edifices. It is what it looks like and is called.
It is a jail. It is not a front for something else, not a
façade, not a pseudonym. It is real, the real thing, the
thing behind the words.

The guards, a sturdy, solid lot, hustled me through
the corridors and left me alone in a small room, very

dirty and very brightly lit. In a few minutes another lot of guards came crowding in as escort to a thin-faced man with an air of authority. He dismissed all but two. I asked him if I would be allowed to send word to Commensal Obsle.

"The Commensal knows of your arrest."

I said, "Knows of it?" very stupidly.

"My superiors act, of course, by order of the Thirty-Three.—You will now undergo interrogation."

The guards caught my arms. I resisted them, saying angrily, "I'm willing to answer what you ask, you can leave out the intimidation!" The thin-faced man paid no attention, but called back another guard. The three of them got me strapped on a pull-down table, stripped me, and injected me with, I suppose, one of the veridical drugs.

I don't know how long the questioning lasted or what it concerned, as I was drugged more or less heavily all the time and have no memory of it. When I came to myself again I had no idea how long I had been kept in Kundershaden: four or five days, judging by my physical condition, but I was not sure. For some while after that I did not know what day of the month it was, nor what month, and in fact I came only slowly to comprehend my surroundings at all.

I was in a caravan-truck, much like the truck that had carried me over the Kargav to Rer, but in the van; not the cab. There were twenty or thirty other people in with me, hard to tell how many, since there were no windows and light came only through a slit in the rear door,

screened with four thicknesses of steel mesh. We had evidently been traveling some while when I recovered con-
scious thought, as each person's place was more or less
defined, and the smell of excreta, vomit, and sweat had
already reached a point it neither surpassed nor declined
from. No one knew any of the others. No one knew
where we were being taken. There was little talking. It
was the second time I had been locked in the dark with
uncomplaining, unhopeful people of Orgoreyn. I knew
now the sign I had been given, my first night in this
country. I had ignored that black cellar and gone looking
for the substance of Orgoreyn aboveground, in daylight.
No wonder nothing had seemed real.

I felt that the truck was going east, and couldn't get
rid of this impression even when it became plain that
it was going west, farther and farther into Orgoreyn.
One's magnetic and directional subsenses are all wrong
on other planets; when the intellect won't or can't compensate for that wrongness, the result is a profound
bewilderment, a feeling that everything, literally, has
come loose.

One of the truckload died that night. He had been
clubbed or kicked in the abdomen, and died hemorrhag-
ing from anus and mouth. No one did anything for him;
there was nothing to be done. A plastic jug of water had
been shoved in amongst us some hours before, but it was
long since dry. The man happened to be next to me on
the right, and I took his head on my knees to give him
relief in breathing: so he died. We were all naked, but
thereafter I wore his blood for clothing, on my legs and

thighs and hands: a dry, stiff, brown garment with no warmth in it.

The night grew bitter, and we had to get close together for warmth. The corpse, having nothing to give, was pushed out of the group, excluded. The rest of us huddled together, swaying and jolting all in one motion, all night. Darkness was total inside our steel box. We were on some country road, and no truck followed us; even with face pressed up close to the mesh one could see nothing out the door-slit but darkness and the vague loom of fallen snow.

Falling snow; new-fallen snow; long-fallen snow; snow after rain has fallen on it; refrozen snow . . . Orgota and Karhidish have a word for each of these. In Karhidish (which I know better than Orgota) they have by my count sixty-two words for the various kinds, states, ages, and qualities of snow; fallen snow, that is. There is another set of words for the varieties of snowfall, another for ice, a set of twenty or more that define what the temperature range is, how strong a wind blows, and what kind of precipitation is occurring, all together. I sat and tried to draw up lists of these words in my head that night. Each time I recalled another one I would repeat the lists, inserting it in its alphabetical place.

Along after dawn the truck stopped. People screamed out the slit that there was a dead body in the truck: come and take it out. One after another of us screamed and shouted. We pounded together on the sides and door, making so hideous a pandemonium inside the steel box that we could not stand it ourselves. No one came.

The truck stood still for some hours. At last there was a sound of voices outside; the truck lurched, skidding on an ice-patch, and set off again. One could see through the slit that it was late on a sunny morning, and that we were going through wooded hills.

The truck continued thus for three more days and nights—four in all since my awakening. It made no stops at Inspection Points, and I think it never passed through a town of any size. Its journey was erratic, furtive. There were stops to change drivers and recharge batteries; there were other, longer stops for no reason that could be discerned from inside the van. Two of the days it sat still from noon till dark, as if deserted, then began its run again at night. Once a day, around noon, a big jug of water was passed in through a trap in the door.

Counting the corpse there were twenty-six of us, two thirteens. Gethenians often think in thirteens, twenty-sixes, fifty-twos, no doubt because of the 26-day lunar cycle that makes their unvarying month and approximates their sexual cycle. The corpse was shoved up tight against the steel doors that formed the rear wall of our box, where he would keep cold. The rest of us sat and lay crouched, each in his own place, his territory, his Domain, until night; when the cold grew so extreme that little by little we drew together and merged into one entity occupying one space, warm in the middle, cold at the periphery.

There was kindness. I and certain others, an old man and one with a bad cough, were recognized as being least resistant to the cold, and each night we were at the center of the group, the entity of twenty-five, where it was warmest. We did not struggle for the warm place, we simply were in it each night. It is a terrible thing, this kindness that human beings do not lose. Terrible, because when we are finally naked in the dark and cold, it is all we have. We who are so rich, so full of strength, we end up with that small change. We have nothing else to give.

Despite our crowdedness and our huddling together nights, we in the truck were remote from one another. Some were stupefied from drugging, some were probably mental or social defectives to start with, all were abused and scared; yet it may be strange that among twenty-five not one ever spoke to all the others together, not even to curse them. Kindness there was and endurance, but in silence, always in silence. Jammed together in the sour darkness of our shared mortality, we bumped one another continually, jolted together, fell over one another, breathed our breaths mingling, laid the heat of our bodies together as a fire is laid—but remained strangers. I never learned the name of any of them in the truck.

One day, the third day I think, when the truck stopped still for hours and I wondered if they had simply left us in some desert place to rot, one of them began to talk to me. He kept telling me a long story about a mill in South Orgoreyn where he had worked, and how he had got into trouble with an overseer. He talked and talked in his soft dull voice and kept putting his hand on mine as if to be sure he had my attention. The sun was getting west of us and as we stood slewed around on the shoulder of the road a shaft of light entered in the window-slit; suddenly, even back in the box, one could see. I saw a girl, a filthy, pretty, stupid, weary girl looking up into my face as she talked, smiling timidly, looking for solace. The young Orgota was in kemmer, and had been drawn to me. The one time any one of them asked anything of me, and I couldn't give it. I got up and went to the window-slit as if for air and a look out, and did not come back to my place for a long time.

That night the truck went up long grades, down, up again. From time to time it halted inexplicably. At each halt a frozen, unbroken silence lay outside the steel walls of our box, the silence of vast wastelands, of the heights. The one in kemmer still kept the place beside mine, and still sought to touch me. I stood up for a long time again with my face pressed to the steel mesh of the window, breathing clean air that cut my throat and lungs like a razor. My hands pressed against the metal door became numb. I realized at last that they were or soon would be frostbitten. My breath had made a little ice-bridge between my lips and the mesh. I had to break this bridge with my fingers before I could turn away. When I huddled down with the others I began to shake with cold, a kind of shaking I had not experienced, jumping, racking spasms like the convulsions of fever. The truck started up again. Noise and motion gave an illusion of warmth, dispelling that utter, glacial silence, but I was still too cold to sleep that night. I thought we were at a fairly high altitude most of the night, but it was hard to tell, one's breathing, heartbeat, and energy-level being unreliable indicators, given the circumstances.

As I knew later, we were crossing the Sembensyens that night, and must have gone up over nine thousand feet on the passes.

I was not much troubled by hunger. The last meal I remembered eating was that long and heavy dinner in Shusgis' house; they must have fed me in Kundershaden, but I had no recollection of it. Eating did not seem to be a part of this existence in the steel box, and I did not often think about it. Thirst, on the other hand, was one of the permanent conditions of life. Once daily at a stop the trap, evidently set into the rear-door for this purpose, was unbolted; one of us thrust out the plastic jug and it was soon thrust back in filled, along with a brief gust of icy air. There was no way to measure out the water among us. The jug was passed, and each got three or four good swallows before the next hand reached for it. No one person or group acted as dispensers or guardians; none saw to it that a drink was saved for the man who coughed, though he was now in a high fever. I suggested this once and those around me nodded, but it was not done. The water was shared more or less equally—no one ever tried to get much more than his share—and was gone within a few minutes. Once the last three, up against the forward wall of the box, got none, the jug being dry when it came to them. The next day two of them insisted on being first in line, and were. The third lay huddled in his front corner unstirring, and nobody saw to it that he got his share. Why didn't I try to? I don't know. That was the fourth day in the truck. If I had been passed over I'm not sure I would have made an effort to get my share. I was aware of his thirst and his suffering, and the sick man's, and the others', much as I was aware of my own. I was unable to do anything about any of this suffering, and therefore accepted it, as they did, placidly.

I know that people might behave very differently in the same circumstances. These were Orgota, people trained from birth in a discipline of cooperation, obedience, submission to a group purpose ordered from above. The qualities of independence and decision were weakened in them. They had not much capacity for anger. They formed a whole, I among them; each felt it, and it was a refuge and true comfort in the night, that wholeness of the huddled group each drawing life from the others. But there was no spokesman for the whole, it was headless, passive.

Men whose will was tempered to a sharper edge might have done much better: talked more, shared the water more justly, given more ease to the sick, and kept their courage higher. I don't know. I only know what it was like inside that truck.

On the fifth morning, if my count is right, from the day I wakened in the truck, it stopped. We heard talking outside and calling back and forth. The steel rear-doors were unbolted from the outside and flung wide open.

One by one we crept to that open end of the steel box, some on hands and knees, and jumped or crawled down onto the ground. Twenty-four of us did. Two dead men, the old corpse and a new one, the one who had not got his drink of water for two days, were dragged out.

It was cold outside, so cold and so glaring with white sunlight on white snow that to leave the fetid shelter of the truck was very hard, and some of us wept. We stood bunched up beside the great truck, all of us naked and stinking, our little whole, our night-entity exposed to the bright cruel daylight. They broke us up, made us form a line, and led us towards a building a few hundred yards away. The metal walls and snow-covered roof of the building, the plain of snow all around, the great range of mountains that lay under the rising sun, the vast sky, all seemed to shake and glitter with excess of light.

We were lined up to wash ourselves at a big trough in a frame hut; everybody began by drinking the washwater. After that we were led into the main building and given undershirts, gray felt shirts, breeches, leggings, and felt boots. A guard checked off our names on a list as we filed into the refectory, where with a hundred or more other people in gray we sat at bolted-down tables and were served breakfast: grain-porridge and beer. After that the whole lot of us, new prisoners and old, were divided up into squads of twelve. My squad was taken to a sawmill a few hundred yards behind the main building, inside the fence. Outside the fence and not far from it a forest began that covered the folded hills as far to northward as the eye could see. Under the direction of our guard we carried and stacked sawn boards from the mill to a huge shed where lumber was stored through the winter.

It was not easy to walk, stoop, and lift loads, after the days in the truck. They didn't let us stand idle, but they didn't force the pace either. In the middle of the day we were served a cupful of the unfermented grainbrew, orsh; before sunset we were taken back to the barracks and given dinner, porridge with some vegetables, and beer. By nightfall we were locked into the dormitory, which was kept fully lighted all night. We slept on five-foot-deep shelves all around the walls of the room in two tiers. Old prisoners scrambled for the upper tier, the more desirable, since heat rises. For bedding each man was issued a sleeping-bag at the door. They were coarse heavy bags, foul with other men's sweat, but well insulated and warm. Their drawback for me was their shortness. An average-sized Gethenian could get clear inside head and all, but I couldn't; nor could I ever stretch out fully on the sleeping-shelf.

The place was called Pulefen Commensality Third Voluntary Farm and Resettlement Agency. Pulefen, District Thirty, is in the extreme northwest of the habitable zone of Orgoreyn, bounded by the Sembensyen Mountains, the Esagel River, and the coast. The area is thinly settled, without big cities. The town nearest us was a place called Turuf, several miles to the southwest; I never saw it. The Farm was on the edge of a great unpopulated forest region, Tarrenpeth. Too far north for the larger trees, hemmen or serem or black vate, the forest was all of one kind of tree, a gnarled scrubby conifer ten or twelve feet high, gray-needled, called thore. Though the number of native species, plant or animal, on Winter is unusually small, the membership of each species is very large: there were thousands of square miles of thore-trees, and nothing much else, in that forest. Even

the wilderness is carefully husbanded there, and though
that forest had been logged for centuries there were no
waste places in it, no desolations of stumps, no eroded
slopes. It seemed that every tree in it was accounted for,
and that not one grain of sawdust from our mill went
unused. There was a small plant on the Farm, and when
the weather prevented parties from going out into the
forest we worked in the mill or in the plant, treating and
compressing chips, bark, and sawdust into various forms,
and extracting from the dried thore-needles a resin used
in plastics.

The work was genuine work, and we were not over-
driven. If they had allowed a little more food and better
clothing much of the work would have been pleasant, but
we were too hungry and cold most of the time for any
pleasure. The guards were seldom harsh and never cruel.
They tended to be stolid, slovenly, heavy, and to my eyes
effeminate—not in the sense of delicacy, etc., but in just
the opposite sense: a gross, bland fleshiness, a bovinity
without point or edge. Among my fellow-prisoners I had
also for the first time on Winter a certain feeling of being
a man among women, or among eunuchs. The prisoners
had that same flabbiness and coarseness. They were hard
to tell apart; their emotional tone seemed always low,
their talk trivial. I took this lifelessness and leveling at
first for the effect of the privation of food, warmth, and
liberty, but I soon found out that it was more specific an
effect than that: it was the result of the drugs given all
prisoners to keep them out of kemmer.

I knew that drugs existed that could reduce or virtually eliminate the potency phase of the Gethenian sexual cycle; they were used when convenience, medicine, or morality dictated abstinence. One kemmer, or several, could be skipped thus without ill effect. The voluntary use of such drugs was common and accepted. It had not occurred to me that they might be administered to unwilling persons.

There were good reasons. A prisoner in kemmer would be a disruptive element in his work-squad. If let off work, what was to be done with him?—especially if no other prisoner was in kemmer at the time, as was possible, there being only some 150 of us. To go through kemmer without a partner is pretty hard on a Gethenian; better, then, simply obviate the misery and wasted work-time, and not go through kemmer at all. So they prevented it.

Prisoners who had been there for several years were psychologically and I believe to some extent physically adapted to this chemical castration. They were as sexless as steers. They were without shame and without desire, like the angels. But it is not human to be without shame and without desire.

Being so strictly defined and limited by nature, the sexual urge of Gethenians is really not much interfered with by society: there is less coding, channeling, and repressing of sex there than in any bisexual society I know of. Abstinence is entirely voluntary; indulgence is entirely acceptable. Sexual fear and sexual frustration are both extremely rare. This was the first case I had seen of the social purpose running counter to the sexual drive.

Being a suppression, not merely a repression, it produced not frustration, but something more ominous, perhaps, in the long run: passivity.

There are no communal insects on Winter. Gethenians do not share their earth as Terrans do with those older societies, those innumerable cities of little sexless workers possessing no instinct but that of obedience to the group, the whole. If there were ants on Winter, Gethenians might have tried to imitate them long ago. The regime of the Voluntary Farms is a fairly recent thing, limited to one country of the planet and literally unknown elsewhere. But it is an ominous sign of the direction that a society of people so vulnerable to sexual control might take.

At Pulefen Farm we were, as I said, underfed for the work we did, and our clothing, particularly our footgear, was completely inadequate for that winter climate. The guards, most of them probationary prisoners, were not much better off. The intent of the place and its regime was punitive, but not destructive, and I think it might have been endurable, without the druggings and the examinations.

Some of the prisoners underwent the examination in groups of twelve; they merely recited a sort of confessional and catechism, got their anti-kemmer shot, and were released to work. Others, the political prisoners, were subjected every fifth day to questioning under drugs.

I don't know what drugs they used. I don't know the purpose of the questioning. I have no idea what questions they asked me. I would come to myself in the dormitory after a few hours, laid out on the sleeping-shelf with six or seven others, some waking like myself, some still slack and blank in the grip of the drug. When we were all afoot the guards would take us out to the plant to work; but after the third or fourth of these examinations I was unable to get up. They let me be, and next day I could go out with my squad, though I felt shaky. After the next examination I was helpless for two days. Either the anti-kemmer hormones or the veridicals evidently had a toxic effect on my non-Gethenian nervous system, and the effect was cumulative.

I remember planning how I would plead with the Inspector when the next examination came. I would start by promising to answer truthfully anything he asked, without drugs; and later I would say to him, "Sir, don't you see how useless it is to know the answer to the wrong question?" Then the Inspector would turn into Faxe, with the Foreteller's gold chain around his neck, and I would have long conversations with Faxe, very pleasantly, while I controlled the drip of acid from a tube into a vat of pulverized wood-chips. Of course when I came to the little room where they examined us, the Inspector's aide had pulled back my collar and given me the injection before I could speak, and all I remember from that session, or perhaps the memory is from an earlier one, is the Inspector, a tired-looking young Orgota with dirty fingernails, saying drearily, "You must answer my questions in Orgota, you must not speak any other language. You must speak in Orgota."

There was no infirmary. The principle of the Farm was work or die; but there were leniencies in practice—gaps between work and death, provided by the guards. As I said, they were not cruel; neither were they kind. They were slipshod and didn't much care, so long as they kept out of trouble themselves. They let me and another prisoner stay in the dormitory, simply left us there in our sleeping-bags as if by oversight, when it was plain that we could not stand up on our feet. I was extremely ill after the last examination; the other, a middle-aged fellow, had some disorder or disease of the kidney, and was dying. As he could not die all at once, he was allowed to spend some time at it, on the sleeping-shelf.

I remember him more clearly than anything else in Pulefen Farm. He was physically a typical Gethenian of the Great Continent, compactly made, short-legged and short-armed, with a solid layer of subcutaneous fat giving him even in illness a sleek roundness of body. He had small feet and hands, rather broad hips, and a deep chest, the breasts scarcely more developed than in a male of my race. His skin was dark ruddy-brown, his black hair fine and furlike. His face was broad, with small, strong features, the cheekbones pronounced. It is a type not unlike that of various isolated Terran groups living in very high altitudes or Arctic areas. His name was Asra; he had been a carpenter.

We talked.

Asra was not, I think, unwilling to die, but he was afraid of dying; he sought distraction from his fear.

We had little in common other than our nearness to

death, and that was not what we wanted to talk about; so, much of the time, we did not understand each other very well. It did not matter to him. I, younger and incredulous, would have liked understanding, comprehension, explanation. But there was no explanation. We talked.

At night the barracks dormitory was glaring, crowded, and noisy. During the day the lights were turned off and the big room was dusky, empty, still. We lay close together on the sleeping-shelf and talked softly. Asra liked best to tell long meandering tales about his young days on a Commensal farm in the Kunderer Valley, that broad splendid plain I had driven through coming from the border to Mishnory. His dialect was strong, and he used many names of people, places, customs, tools, that I did not know the meaning of, so I seldom caught more than the drift of his reminiscences. When he was feeling easiest, usually around noon, I would ask him for a myth or tale. Most Gethenians are well stuffed with these. Their literature, though it exists in written form, is a live oral tradition, and they are all in this sense literate. Asra knew the Orgota staples, the Short-Tales of Meshe, the tale of Parsid, parts of the great epics and the novel-like Sea-Traders saga. These, and bits of local lore recalled from his childhood, he would tell in his soft slurry dialect, and then growing tired would ask me for a story. "What do they tell in Karhide?" he would say, rubbing his legs, which tormented him with aches and shooting pains, and turning to me his face with its shy, sly, patient smile.

Once I said, "I know a story about people who live on another world."

"What kind of world would that be?"

"One like this one, all in all; but it doesn't go around the sun. It goes around the star you call Selemy. That's a yellow star like the sun, and on that world, under that sun, live other people."

"That's in the Sanovy teachings, that about the other worlds. There used to be an old Sanovy crazy-priest would come by my Hearth when I was little and tell us children all about that, where the liars go when they die, and where the suicides go, and where the thieves go— that's where we're going, me and you, eh, one of those places?"

"No, this I'm telling of isn't a spirit-world. A real one. The people that live on it are real people, alive, just like here. But very-long-ago they learned how to fly."

Asra grinned.

"Not by flapping their arms, you know. They flew in machines like cars." But it was hard to say in Orgota, which lacks a word meaning precisely "to fly"; the closest one can come has more the meaning of "glide." "Well, they learned how to make machines that went right over the air as a sledge goes over snow. And after a while they learned how to make them go farther and faster, till they went like the stone out of a sling off the earth and over the clouds and out of the air, clear to another world, going around another sun. And when they got to that world, what did they find there but men. . . ."

"Sliding in the air?"

"Maybe, maybe not. . . . When they got to my world, we already knew how to get about in the air. But they taught us how to get from world to world, we didn't yet have the machines for that."

Asra was puzzled by the injection of the teller into the tale. I was feverish, bothered by the sores that the drugs had brought out on my arms and chest, and I could not remember how I had meant to weave the story.

"Go on," he said, trying to make sense of it. "What did they do besides go in the air?"

"Oh, they did much as people do here. But they're all in kemmer all the time."

He chuckled. There was of course no chance of concealment in this life, and my nickname among prisoners and guards was, inevitably, "the Pervert." But where there is no desire and no shame no one, however anomalous, is singled out; and I think Asra made no connection of this notion with myself and my peculiarities. He saw it merely as a variation on an old theme, and so he chuckled a little and said, "In kemmer all the time. . . . Is it a place of reward, then? Or a place of punishment?"

"I don't know, Asra. Which is this world?"

"Neither, child. This here is just the world, it's how it is. You get born into it and . . . things are as they are. . . ."

"I wasn't born into it. I came to it. I chose it."

The silence and the shadow hung around us. Away off in the country silence beyond the barracks walls there was one tiny edge of sound, a handsaw keening: nothing else.

"Ah well. . . . Ah well," Asra murmured, and sighed, and rubbed his legs, making a little moaning sound that he was not aware of himself. "We none of us choose," he said.

A night or two after that he went into a coma, and presently died. I had not learned what he had been sent to the Voluntary Farm for, what crime or fault or irregularity in his identification papers, and knew only that he had been in Pulefen Farm less than a year.

The day after Asra's death they called me for examination; this time they had to carry me in, and I can't remember anything further than that.

14

THE ESCAPE

When Obsle and Yegey both left town, and Slose's doorkeeper refused me entrance, I knew it was time to turn to my enemies, for there was no more good in my friends. I went to Commissioner Shusgis, and blackmailed him. Lacking sufficient cash to buy him with, I had to spend my reputation. Among the perfidious, the name of traitor is capital in itself. I told him that I was in Orgoreyn as agent of the Nobles Faction in Karhide, which was planning the assassination of Tibe, and that he had been designated as my Sarf contact; if he refused to give me the information I needed I would tell my friends in Erhenrang that he was a double agent, serving the Open Trade Faction, and this word would of course get back to Mishnory and to the Sarf: and the damned fool believed me. He told me quick enough what I wanted to know; he even asked me if I approved.

I was not in immediate danger from my friends Obsle, Yegey, and the others. They had bought their safety by sacrificing the Envoy, and trusted me to make no trouble for them or myself. Until I went to Shusgis, no one in the Sarf but Gaum had considered me worthy of their notice, but now they would be hard at my heels. I must finish my business and drop out of sight. Having no way to get word directly to anyone in Karhide, as mail would be read and telephone or radio listened to, I went for the first time to the Royal Embassy. Sardon rem ir Chenewich, whom I had known well at court, was on the staff there. He agreed at once to convey to Argaven a message stating what had become of the Envoy and where he was to be imprisoned. I could trust Chenewich, a clever and honest person, to get the message through unintercepted, though what Argaven would make of it or do with it I could not guess. I wanted Argaven to have that information in case Ai's Star Ship did come suddenly falling down out of the clouds; for at that time I still kept some hope that he had signaled the Ship before the Sarf arrested him.

I was now in peril, and if I had been seen to enter the Embassy, in instant peril. I went straight from its door to the caravan port on the Southside and before noon of that day, Odstreth Susmy, I left Mishnory as I had entered it, as carry-loader on a truck. I had my old permits with me, a little altered to fit the new job. Forgery

of papers is risky in Orgoreyn where they are inspected
fifty-two times daily, but it is not rare for being risky,
and my old companions in Fish Island had shown me the
tricks of it. To wear a false name galls me, but nothing
else would save me, or get me clear across the width of
Orgoreyn to the coast of the Western Sea.

My thoughts were all there in the west as the caravan
went rumbling across the Kunderer Bridge and out of
Mishnory. Autumn was facing towards winter now, and
I must get to my destination before the roads closed to
fast traffic, and while there was still some good in getting there. I had seen a Voluntary Farm over in Koms-
vashom when I was in the Sinoth Administration, and
had talked with ex-prisoners of Farms. What I had seen
and heard lay heavy on me now. The Envoy, so vulnerable to cold that he wore a coat when the weather was in
the 30s, would not survive winter in Pulefen. Thus need
drove me fast, but the caravan took me slow, weaving
from town to town northward and southward of the way,
loading and unloading, so that it took me a halfmonth
to get to Ethwen, at the mouth of the River Esagel.

In Ethwen I had luck. Talking with men in the
Transient-House I heard of the fur trade up the river,
how licensed trappers went up and downriver by sledge
or iceboat through Tarrenpeth Forest almost to the Ice.
Out of their talk of traps came my plan of trap-springing.
There are white-fur pesthry in Kerm Land as in the
Gobrin Hinterlands; they like places that lie under the
breath of the glacier. I had hunted them when I was

young in the thore-forests of Kerm, why not go trapping them now in the thore-forests of Pulefen?

In that far west and north of Orgoreyn, in the great wild lands west of the Sembensyen, men come and go somewhat as they like, for there are not enough Inspectors to keep them all penned in. Something of the old freedom survives the New Epoch, there. Ethwen is a gray port built on the gray rocks of Esagel Bay; a rainy sea-wind blows in the streets, and the people are grim seamen, straight-spoken. I look back with praise to Ethwen, where my luck changed.

I bought skis, snowshoes, traps, and provisions, acquired my hunter's license and authorization and identification and so forth from the Commensal Bureau, and set out afoot up the Esagel with a party of hunters led by an old man called Mavriva. The river was not yet frozen, and wheels were on the roads still, for it rained more than it snowed on this coastal slope even now in the year's last month. Most hunters waited till full winter, and in the month of Thern went up the Esagel by iceboat, but Mavriva meant to get far north early and trap the pesthry as they first came down into the forests in their migration. Mavriva knew the Hinterlands, the North Sembensyen, and the Fire-Hills as well as any man knows them, and in those days going upriver I learned much from him that served me later.

At the town called Turuf I dropped out of the party feigning illness. They went on north, after which I struck out northeastward by myself into the high foothills of the Sembensyen. I spent some days learning the land and then, caching almost all I carried in a hidden valley twelve or thirteen miles from Turuf, I came back to the town, approaching it from the south again, and this time entered it and put up at the Transient-House. As if stocking up for a trapping run I bought skis, snowshoes, and provisions, a fur bag and winter clothing, all over again; also a Chabe stove, a polyskin tent, and a light sledge to load it all on. Then nothing to do but wait for the rain to turn to snow and the mud to ice; not long, for I had spent over a month on my way from Mishnory to Turuf. On Arhad Thern the winter was frozen in and the snow I had waited for was falling.

I passed the electric fences of Pulefin Farm in early afternoon, all track and trace behind me soon covered by the snowfall. I left the sledge in a stream-gully well into the forest east of the Farm and carrying only a backpack snowshoed back around to the road; along it I came openly to the Farm's front gate. There I showed the papers that I had reforged again while waiting in Turuf. They were "blue stamp" now, identifying me as Thener Benth, paroled convict, and attached to them was an order to report on or before Eps Thern to Pulefen Commensality Third Voluntary Farm for two years' guard duty. A sharp-eyed Inspector would have been suspicious of those battered papers, but there were few sharp eyes here.

Nothing easier than getting into prison. I was somewhat reassured as to the getting out.

The chief guard on duty berated me for arriving a day

later than my orders specified, and sent me to the barracks. Dinner was over, and luckily it was too late to issue me regulation boots and uniform and confiscate my own good clothing. They gave me no gun, but I found one handy while I scrounged around the kitchen coaxing the cook for a bite to eat. The cook kept his gun hung on a nail behind the bake-ovens. I stole it. It had no lethal setting: perhaps none of the guards' guns did. They do not kill people on their Farms: they let hunger and winter and despair do their murders for them.

There were thirty or forty jailkeepers and a hundred and fifty or sixty prisoners, none of them very well off, most of them sound asleep though it was not much past Fourth Hour. I got a young guard to take me around and show me the prisoners asleep. I saw them in the staring light of the great room they slept in, and all but gave up my hope of acting that first night before I had drawn suspicion on myself. They were all hidden away on the longbeds in their bags like babies in wombs, invisible, indistinguishable.—All but one, there, too long to hide, a dark face like a skull, eyes shut and sunken, a mat of long, fibrous hair.

The luck that had turned in Ethwen now turned the world with it under my hand. I never had a gift but one, to know when the great wheel gives to a touch, to know and act. I had thought that foresight lost, last year in Erhenrang, and never to be regained. A great delight it was to feel that certainty again, to know that I could steer my fortune and the world's chance like a bobsled down the steep, dangerous hour.

Since I still went roaming and prying about, in my part as a restless curious dimwitted fellow, they wrote me onto the late watch-shift; by midnight all but I and one other late watcher within doors slept. I kept up my shiftless poking about the place, wandering up and down from time to time by the longbeds. I settled my plans, and began to ready my will and body to enter dothe, for my own strength would never suffice unaided by the strength out of the Dark. Awhile before dawn I went into the sleeping-room once more and with the cook's gun gave Genly Ai a hundredth-second of stun to the brain, then hoisted him up bag and all and carried him out over my shoulder to the guardroom. "What's doing?" says the other guard half asleep. "Let him be!"

"He's dead."

"Another one dead? By Meshe's guts, and not hardly winter yet." He turned his head sideways to look into the Envoy's face as it hung down on my back. "That one, the Pervert, is it. By the Eye, I didn't believe all they say about Karhiders, till I took a look at him, the ugly freak he is. He spent all week on the longbed moaning and sighing, but I didn't think he'd die right off like that. Well, go dump him outside where he'll keep till daylight, don't stand there like a carry-loader with a sack of turds. . . ."

I stopped by the Inspection Office on my way down the corridor, and I being the guard none stopped me from entering and looking till I found the wall-panel that contained the alarms and switches. None was labeled, but guards had scratched letters beside the switches to jog their memory when haste was needed; taking F.f. for "fences" I turned that switch to cut the current to the outermost defenses of the Farm, and then went on, pulling Ai along now by the shoulders. I came by the guard on duty in the watchroom by the door. I made a show of laboring to haul the dead load, for the dothe-strength was full within me and I did not want it seen how easily, in fact, I could pull or carry the weight of a man heavier than myself. I said, "A dead prisoner, they said get him out of the sleeping-room. Where do I stow him?"

"I don't know. Get him outside. Under a roof, so he won't get snow-buried and float up stinking next spring in the thaws. It's snowing *peditia*." He meant that we call *sove*-snow, a thick, wet fall, the best of news to me. "All right, all right," I said, and lugged my load outside and around the corner of the barracks, out of his sight. I got Ai up over my shoulders again, went northeast a few hundred yards, clambered up over the dead fence and slung my burden down, jumped down free, took up Ai once more and made off as fast as I could towards the river. I was not far from the fence when a whistle began to shriek and the floodlights went on. It snowed hard enough to hide me, but not hard enough to hide my tracks within minutes. Yet when I got down to the river they were not yet on my trail. I went north on clear ground under the trees, or through the water when there was no clear ground; the river, a hasty little tributary of the Esagel, was still unfrozen. Things were growing plain now in the dawn and I went fast. In full dothe I found the Envoy, though a long awkward load, no heavy one. Following the stream into the forest I came to the ravine where my sledge was, and onto the sledge I strapped the Envoy, loading my stuff around and over him till he was well hidden, and a weather-sheet over all; then I changed clothes, and ate some food from my pack, for the great hunger one feels in long-sustained dothe was already gnawing at me. Then I set off north on the main Forest Road. Before long a pair of skiers came up with me.

I was now dressed and equipped as a trapper, and told them that I was trying to catch up with Mavriva's outfit, which had gone north in the last days of Grende. They knew Mavriva, and accepted my story after a glance at my trapper's license. They were not expecting to find the escaped men heading north, for nothing lies north of Pule-fen but the forest and the Ice; they were perhaps not very interested in finding the escaped men at all. Why should they be? They went on, and only an hour later passed me again on their way back to the Farm. One of them was the fellow I had stood late watch with. He had never seen my face, though he had had it before his eyes half the night.

When they were surely gone I turned off the road and all that day followed a long halfcircle back through the forest and the foothills east of the Farm, coming in at last from the east, from the wilderness, to the hidden dell above Turuf where I had cached all my spare equipment. It was hard sledging in that much-folded land, with more than my weight to pull, but the snow was thick and already growing firm, and I was in dothe. I had to maintain the condition, for once one lets the dothe-strength lapse one is good for nothing at all. I had never maintained dothe before for over an hour or so, but I knew that some of the Old Men can keep in the full strength for a day and a night or even longer, and my present need proved a good supplement to my training. In dothe one does not worry much, and what anxiety I had was for the Envoy, who should have waked long ago from the light dose of sonic I had given him. He never stirred, and I had no time to tend to him. Was his body so alien that what to us is mere paralysis was death to him? When the wheel turns under your hand, you must watch your words: and I had twice called him dead, and carried him as the dead are carried. The thought would come that this was then a dead man that I hauled across the hills, and that my luck and his life had gone to waste after all. At that I would sweat and swear, and the dothe-strength would seem to run out of me like water out of a broken jar. But I went on, and the strength did not fail me till I had reached the cache in the foothills, and set up the tent, and done what I could for Ai. I opened a box of hyperfood cubes, most of which I devoured, but some of which I got into him as a broth, for he looked near to starving. There were ulcers on his arms and breast, kept raw by the filthy sleeping-bag he lay in. When these sores were cleaned and he lay warm in the fur bag, as well hidden as winter and wilderness could hide him, there was no more I could do. Night had fallen and the greater darkness, the payment for the voluntary summoning of the body's full strength, was coming hard upon me; to darkness I must entrust myself, and him.

We slept. Snow fell. All the night and day and night on my *thangen*-sleep it must have snowed, no blizzard, but the first great snowfall of winter. When at last I roused and pulled myself up to look out, the tent was half buried. Sunlight and blue shadows lay vivid on the snow. Far and high in the east one drift of gray dimmed the sky's brightness: the smoke of Udenushreke, nearest to us of the Fire-Hills. Around the little peak of the tent lay the snow, mounds, hillocks, swells, slopes, all white, untrodden.

Being still in the recovery-period I was very weak and sleepy, but whenever I could rouse myself I gave Ai broth, a little at a time; and in the evening of that day he came to life, if not to his wits. He set up crying out as if in great terror. When I knelt by him he struggled to get away from me, and the effort being too much for him, fainted. That night he talked much, in no tongue I knew. It was strange, in that dark stillness of the wilds, to hear him mutter words of a language he had learned on another world than this. The next day was hard, for whenever I tried to look after him he took me, I think, for one of the guards at the Farm, and was in terror that I would give him some drug. He would break out into Orgota and Karhidish all babbled pitifully together, begging me "not to," and he fought me with a panic strength. This happened again and again, and as I was still in thangen and weak of limb and will, it seemed I could not care for him at all. That day I thought that they had not only drugged but mindchanged him, leaving him insane or imbecile. Then I wished that he had died on the sledge in the thore-forest, or that I had never had any luck at all, but had been arrested as I left Mishnory and sent to some Farm to work out my own damnation.

I woke from sleep and he was watching me.

"Estraven?" he said in a weak, amazed whisper.

Then my heart lifted up. I could reassure him, and see to his needs; and that night we both slept well.

The next day he was much improved, and sat up to eat. The sores on his body were healing. I asked him what they were.

"I don't know. I think the drugs caused them; they kept giving me injections. . . ."

"To prevent kemmer?" That was one report I had heard from men escaped or released from Voluntary Farms.

"Yes. And others, I don't know what they were, veridicals of some kind. They made me ill, and they kept giving them to me. What were they trying to find out, what could I tell them?"

"They may have not so much been questioning as domesticating you."

"Domesticating?"

"Rendering you docile by a forced addiction to one of the orgrevy derivatives. That practice is not unknown in Karhide. Or they may have been carrying out an experiment on you and the others. I have been told they test mindchanging drugs and techniques on prisoners, in the Farms. I doubted that, when I heard it; not now."

"You have these Farms in Karhide?"

"In Karhide?" I said. "No."

He rubbed his forehead fretfully. "They'd say in Mishnory that there are no such places in Orgoreyn, I suppose."

"On the contrary. They'd boast of them, and show you tapes and pictures of the Voluntary Farms, where deviates are rehabilitated and vestigial tribal groups are given refuge. They might show you around the First District Voluntary Farm just outside Mishnory, a fine showplace from all accounts. If you believe that we have Farms in Karhide, Mr. Ai, you overestimate us seriously. We are not a sophisticated people."

He lay a long time staring at the glowing Chabe stove, which I had turned up till it gave out suffocating heat. Then he looked at me.

"You told me this morning, I know, but my mind wasn't clear, I think. Where are we, how did we get here?"

I told him again.

"You simply . . . walked out with me?"

"Mr. Ai, any one of you prisoners, or all of you together, could have walked out of that place, any night. If you weren't starved, exhausted, demoralized, and drugged; and if you had winter clothing; and if you had somewhere to go. . . . There's the catch. Where would you go? To a town? No papers; you're done for. Into the wilderness? No shelter; you're done for. In summer, I expect they bring more guards into Pulefen Farm. In winter, they use winter itself to guard it."

He was scarcely listening. "You couldn't carry me a

hundred feet, Estraven. Let alone run, carrying me, a couple of miles cross-country in the dark—"

"I was in dothe."

He hesitated. "Voluntarily induced?"

"Yes."

"You are . . . one of the Handdarata?"

"I was brought up in the Handdara, and indwelt two years at Rotherer Fastness. In Kerm Land most people of the Inner Hearths are Handdarata."

"I thought that after the dothe period, the extreme drain on one's energy necessitated a sort of collapse—"

"Yes; thangen, it's called, the dark sleep. It lasts much longer than the dothe period, and once you enter the recovery period it's very dangerous to try to resist it. I slept straight through two nights. I'm still in thangen now; I couldn't walk over the hill. And hunger's part of it; I've eaten up most of the rations I'd planned to last me the week."

"All right," he said with peevish haste. "I see, I believe you—what can I do but believe you. Here I am, here you are. . . . But I don't understand. I don't understand what you did all this for."

At that my temper broke, and I must stare at the ice-knife which lay close by my hand, not looking at him and not replying until I had controlled my anger. Fortunately there was not yet much heat or quickness in my heart, and I said to myself that he was an ignorant man, a foreigner, ill-used and frightened. So I arrived at justice, and said finally, "I feel that it is in part my fault that you came to Orgoreyn and so to Pulefen Farm. I am trying to amend my fault."

"You had nothing to do with my coming to Orgoreyn."

"Mr. Ai, we've seen the same events with different eyes; I wrongly thought they'd seem the same to us. Let me go back to last spring. I began to encourage King Argaven to wait, to make no decision concerning you or your mission, about a halfmonth before the day of the Ceremony of the Keystone. The audience was already planned, and it seemed best to go through with it, though without looking for any results from it. All this I thought you understood, and in that I erred. I took too much for granted; I didn't wish to offend you, to advise you; I thought you understood the danger of Pemmer Harge rem ir Tibe's sudden ascendancy in the kyorremy. If Tibe had known any good reason to fear you, he would have accused you of serving a faction, and Argaven, who is very easily moved by fear, would likely have had you murdered. I wanted you down, and safe, while Tibe was up and powerful. As it chanced, I went down with you. I was bound to fall, though I didn't know it would be that very night we talked together; but no one is Argaven's prime minister for long. After I received the Order of Exile I could not communicate with you lest I contaminate you with my disgrace, and so increase your peril. I came here to Orgoreyn. I tried to suggest to you that you should also come to Orgoreyn. I urged the men I distrusted least among the Thirty-Three Commensals to grant you entry; you would not have got it without their favor. They saw, and I encouraged them to see, in you a way towards power, a way out of the increasing rivalry with Karhide and back towards the restoration of open trade, a chance perhaps to break the grip of the Sarf. But they are over-cautious men, afraid to act. Instead of proclaiming you, they hid you, and so lost their chance, and sold you to the Sarf to save their own pelts. I counted too much on them, and therefore the fault is mine."

"But for what purpose—all this intriguing, this hiding and power-seeking and plotting—what was it all for, Estraven? What were you after?"

"I was after what you're after: the alliance of my world with your worlds. What did you think?"

We were staring at each other across the glowing stove like a pair of wooden dolls.

"You mean, even if it was Orgoreyn that made the alliance—?"

"Even if it was Orgoreyn. Karhide would soon have followed. Do you think I would play shifgrethor when so much is at stake for all of us, all my fellow men? What does it matter which country wakens first, so long as we waken?"

"How the devil can I believe anything you say!" he burst out. Bodily weakness made his indignation sound aggrieved and whining. "If all this is true, you might have explained some of it earlier, last spring, and spared us both a trip to Pulefen. Your efforts on my behalf—"

"Have failed. And have put you in pain, and shame, and danger. I know it. But if I had tried to fight Tibe for your sake, you would not be here now, you'd be in a grave in Erhenrang. And there are now a few people in

Karhide, and a few in Orgoreyn, who believe your story, because they listened to me. They may yet serve you. My greatest error was, as you say, in making myself clear to you. I am not used to doing so. I am not used to giving, or accepting, either advice or blame."

"I don't mean to be unjust, Estraven—"

"Yet you are. It is strange. I am the only man in all Gethen that has trusted you entirely, and I am the only man in Gethen that you have refused to trust."

He put his head in his hands. He said at last, "I'm sorry, Estraven." It was both apology and admission.

"The fact is," I said, "that you're unable, or unwilling, to believe in the fact that I believe in you." I stood up, for my legs were cramped, and found I was trembling with anger and weariness. "Teach me your mindspeech," I said, trying to speak easily and with no rancor, "your language that has no lies in it. Teach me that, and then ask me why I did what I've done."

"I should like to do that, Estraven."

15

TO THE ICE

I woke. Until now it had been strange, unbelievable, to wake up inside a dim cone of warmth, and to hear my reason tell me that it was a tent, that I lay in it, alive, that I was not still in Pulefen Farm. This time there was no strangeness in my waking, but a grateful sense of peace. Sitting up I yawned and tried to comb back my matted hair with my fingers. I looked at Estraven, stretched out sound asleep on his sleeping-bag a couple of feet from me. He wore nothing but his breeches; he was hot. The dark secret face was laid bare to the light, to my gaze. Estraven asleep looked a little stupid, like everyone asleep: a round, strong face relaxed and remote, small drops of sweat on the upper lip and over the heavy eyebrows. I remembered how he had stood sweating on the parade-stand in Erhenhang in panoply of rank and sunlight. I saw him now defenseless and half-naked in a colder light, and for the first time saw him as he was.

He woke late, and was slow in waking. At last he staggered up yawning, pulled on his shirt, stuck his head out to judge the weather, and then asked me if I wanted a cup of orsh. When he found that I had crawled about and brewed up a pot of the stuff with the water he had left in a pan as ice on the stove last night, he accepted a cup, thanked me stiffly, and sat down to drink it.

"Where do we go from here, Estraven?"

"It depends on where you want to go, Mr. Ai. And on what kind of travel you can manage."

"What's the quickest way out of Orgoreyn?"

"West. To the coast. Thirty miles or so."

"What then?"

"The harbors will be freezing or already frozen, here. In any case no ships go out far in winter. It would be a matter of waiting in hiding somewhere until next spring, when the great traders go out to Sith and Perunter. None will be going to Karhide, if the trade-embargoes continue. We might work our passage on a trader. I am out of money, unfortunately."

"Is there any alternative?"

"Karhide. Overland."

"How far is it—a thousand miles?"

"Yes, by road. But we couldn't go on the roads. We wouldn't get past the first Inspector. Our only way would be north through the mountains, east across the Gobrin, and down to the border at Guthen Bay."

"Across the Gobrin—the ice-sheet, you mean?"

He nodded.

"It's not possible in winter, is it?"

"I think so; with luck, as in all winter journeys. In one respect a glacier crossing is better in winter. The good weather, you know, tends to stay over the great glaciers, where the ice reflects the heat of the sun; the storms are pushed out to the periphery. Therefore the legends about the Place inside the Blizzard. That might be in our favor. Little else."

"Then you seriously think—"

"There would have been no point taking you from Pulefen Farm if I did not."

He was still stiff, sore, grim. Last night's conversation had shaken us both.

"And I take it that you consider the Ice-crossing a better risk than waiting about till spring for a sea-crossing?"

He nodded. "Solitude," he explained, laconic.

I thought it over for a while. "I hope you've taken my inadequacies into account. I'm not as coldproof as you, nowhere near it. I'm no expert on skis. I'm not in good shape—though much improved from a few days ago."

Again he nodded. "I think we might make it," he said, with that complete simplicity I had so long taken for irony.

"All right."

He glanced at me, and drank down his cup of tea. Tea it might as well be called; brewed from roasted perm-grain, orsh is a brown, sweetsour drink, strong in vitamins A and C, sugar, and a pleasant stimulant related to lobeline. Where there is no beer on Winter there is orsh; where there is neither beer nor orsh, there are no people.

"It will be hard," he said, setting down his cup. "Very hard. Without luck, we will not make it."

"I'd rather die up on the Ice than in that cesspool you got me out of."

He cut off a chunk of dried breadapple, offered me a slice, and sat meditatively chewing. "We'll need more food," he said.

"What happens if we do make it to Karhide—to you, I mean? You're still proscribed."

He turned his dark, otter's glance on me. "Yes. I suppose I'd stay on this side."

"And when they found you'd helped their prisoner escape—?"

"They needn't find it." He smiled, bleak, and said, "First we have to cross the Ice."

I broke out, "Listen, Estraven, will you forgive what I said yesterday—"

"Nusuth." He stood up, still chewing, put on his hieb, coat, and boots, and slipped otterlike out the self-sealing valved door. From outside he stuck his head back in: "I may be late, or gone overnight. Can you manage here?"

"Yes."

"All right." With that he was off. I never knew a person who reacted so wholly and rapidly to a changed situation as Estraven. I was recovering, and willing to go; he was out of thangen; the instant that was all clear, he was off. He was never rash or hurried, but he was always ready. It was the secret, no doubt, of the extraordinary political career he threw away for my sake; it was also the explanation of his belief in me and devotion to my mission. When I came, he was ready. Nobody else on Winter was.

Yet he considered himself a slow man, poor in emergencies.

Once he told me that, being so slow-thinking, he had to guide his acts by a general intuition of which way his "luck" was running, and that this intuition rarely failed him. He said it seriously; it may have been true. The Foretellers of the Fastnesses are not the only people on Winter who can see ahead. They have tamed and trained the hunch, but not increased its certainty. In this matter the Yomeshta also have a point: the gift is perhaps not strictly or simply one of foretelling, but is rather the power of seeing (if only for a flash) *everything at once: seeing whole.*

I kept the little heater-stove at its hottest setting while Estraven was gone, and so got warm clear through for the first time in—how long? I thought it must be Thern by now, the first month of winter and of a new Year One, but I had lost count in Pulefen.

The stove was one of those excellent and economical devices perfected by the Gethenians in their millennial effort to outwit cold. Only the use of a fusion-pack as power source could improve it. Its bionic-powered battery was good for fourteen months' continuous use, its heat output was intense, it was stove, heater, and lantern all in one, and it weighed about four pounds. We would never have got fifty miles without it. It must have cost a good deal of Estraven's money, that money I had loftily handed over to him in Mishnory. The tent, which was made of plastics developed for weather-resistance and designed to cope with at least some of the inside water-condensation that is the plague of tents in cold weather; the pesthry-fur sleeping-bags; the clothes, skis, sledge, food-supplies, everything was of the finest make and kind, lightweight, durable, expensive. If he had gone to get more food, what was he going to get it with?

He did not return till nightfall next day. I had gone out several times on snowshoes, gathering strength and getting practice by waddling around the slopes of the snowy vale that hid our tent. I was competent on skis, but not much good on snowshoes. I dared not go far over the hilltops, lest I lose my backtrack; it was wild country, steep, full of creeks and ravines, rising fast to the cloud-haunted mountains eastward. I had time to wonder what I would do in this forsaken place if Estraven did not come back.

He came swooping over the dusky hill—he was a magnificent skier—and stopped beside me, dirty and tired and heavy-laden. He had on his back a huge sooty sack stuffed full of bundles: Father Christmas, who pops down the chimneys of old Earth. The bundles contained kadik-germ, dried breadapple, tea, and slabs of the hard, red, earthy-tasting sugar that Gethenians refine from one of their tubers.

"How did you get all this?"

"Stole it," said the onetime prime minister of Karhide,

holding his hands over the stove, which he had not yet turned down; he, even he, was cold. "In Turuf. Close thing." That was all I ever learned. He was not proud of his exploit, and not able to laugh at it. Stealing is a vile crime on Winter; indeed the only man more despised than the thief is the suicide.

"We'll use up this stuff first," he said, as I set a pan of snow on the stove to melt. "It's heavy." Most of the food he had laid in previously was "hyper-food" rations, a fortified, dehydrated, compressed, cubed mixture of high-energy foods—the Orgota name for it is gichy-michy, and that's what we called it, though of course we spoke Karhidish together. We had enough of it to last us sixty days at the minimal standard ration: a pound a day apiece. After he had washed up and eaten, Estraven sat a long time by the stove that night figuring out precisely what we had and how and when we must use it. We had no scales, and he had to estimate, using a pound box of gichy-michy as standard. He knew, as do many Gethenians, the caloric and nutritive value of each food; he knew his own requirements under various conditions, and how to estimate mine pretty closely. Such knowledge has high survival-value, on Winter.

When at last he had got our rations planned out, he rolled over onto his bag and went to sleep. During the night I heard him talking numbers out of his dreams: weights, days, distances. . . .

We had, very roughly, eight hundred miles to go. The first hundred would be north or northeast, going through the forest and across the northernmost spurs of the Sembensyen range to the great glacier, the ice-sheet that covers the double-lobed Great Continent everywhere north of the 45th parallel, and in places dips down almost to the 35th. One of these southward extensions is in the region of the Fire-Hills, the last peaks of the Sembensyens, and that region was our first goal. There among the mountains, Estraven reasoned, we should be able to get onto the surface of the ice-sheet, either descending onto it from a mountain-slope or climbing up to it on the slope of one of its effluent glaciers. Thereafter we would travel on the Ice itself, eastward, for some six hundred miles. Where its edge trends north again near the Bay of Guthen we would come down off it and cut southeast a last fifty or a hundred miles across the Shenshey Bogs, which by then should be ten or twenty feet deep in snow, to the Karhidish border.

This route kept us clear from start to finish of inhabited, or inhabitable, country. We would not be meeting any Inspectors. This was indubitably of the first importance. I had no papers, and Estraven said that his wouldn't hold up under any further forgeries. In any case, though I could pass for a Gethenian when no one expected anything else, I was not disguisable to an eye looking for me. In this respect, then, the way Estraven proposed for us was highly practical.

In all other respects it seemed perfectly insane.

I kept my opinion to myself, for I fully meant what I'd said about preferring to die escaping, if it came down to a choice of deaths. Estraven, however, was still exploring alternatives. Next day, which we spent in loading and packing the sledge very carefully, he said, "If you raised the Star Ship, when might it come?"

"Anywhere between eight days and a halfmonth, depending on where it is in its solar orbit relative to Gethen. It might be on the other side of the sun."

"No sooner?"

"No sooner. The NAFAL motive can't be used within a solar system. The ship can come in only on rocket drive, which puts her at least eight days away. Why?"

He tugged a cord tight and knotted it before he answered. "I was considering the wisdom of trying to ask aid from your world, as mine seems unhelpful. There's a radio beacon in Turuf."

"How powerful?"

"Not very. The nearest big transmitter would be in Kuhumey, about four hundred miles south of here."

"Kuhumey's a big town, isn't it?"

"A quarter of a million souls."

"We'd have to get the use of the radio transmitter somehow; then hide out for at least eight days, with the Sarf alerted. . . . Not much chance."

He nodded.

I lugged the last sack of kadik-germ out of the tent, fitted it into its niche in the sledge-load, and said, "If I had called the ship that night in Mishnory—the night you told me to—the night I was arrested. . . . But Obsle had my ansible; still has it, I suppose."

"Can he use it?"

"No. Not even by chance, fiddling about. The

coordinate-settings are extremely complex. But if only I'd used it!"

"If only I'd known the game was already over, that day," he said, and smiled. He was not one for regrets.

"You did, I think. But I didn't believe you."

When the sledge was loaded, he insisted that we spend the rest of the day doing nothing, storing energy. He lay in the tent, writing in a little notebook in his small, rapid, vertical-cursive Karhidish hand. He hadn't been able to keep up his journal during the past month, and that annoyed him; he was pretty methodical about that journal. Its writing was, I think, both an obligation to and a link with his family, the Hearth of Estre. I learned that later, however; at the time I didn't know what he was writing, and I sat waxing skis, or doing nothing. I whistled a dance-tune, and stopped myself in the middle. We only had one tent, and if we were going to share it without driving each other mad, a certain amount of self-restraint, of manners, was evidently required. . . . Estraven had looked up at my whistling, all right, but not with irritation. He looked at me rather dreamily, and said, "I wish I'd known about your Ship last year. . . . Why did they send you onto this world alone?"

"The First Envoy to a world always comes alone. One alien is a curiosity, two are an invasion."

"The First Envoy's life is held cheap."

"No; the Ekumen really doesn't hold anybody's life cheap. So it follows, better to put one life in danger than two, or twenty. It's also very expensive and time-consuming, you know, shipping people over the big jumps. Anyhow, I asked for the job."

"In danger, honor," he said, evidently a proverb, for he added mildly, "We'll be full of honor when we reach Karhide. . . ."

When he spoke, I found myself believing that we would in fact reach Karhide, across eight hundred miles of mountain, ravine, crevasse, volcano, glacier, ice-sheet, frozen bog or frozen bay, all desolate, shelterless, and lifeless, in the storms of midwinter in the middle of an Ice Age. He sat writing up his records with the same obdurate patient thoroughness I had seen in a mad king up on a scaffolding mortaring a joint, and said, "*When* we reach Karhide. . . ."

His *when* was no mere dateless hope, either. He intended to reach Karhide by the fourth day of the fourth month of winter, Arhad Anner. We were to start tomorrow, the thirteenth of the first month, Tormenbod Thern. Our rations, as well as he could calculate, might be stretched at farthest to three Gethenian months, 78 days; so we would go twelve miles a day for seventy days, and get to Karhide on Arhad Anner. That was all settled. No more to do now but get a good sleep.

We set off at dawn, on snowshoes, in a thin, windless snowfall. The surface over the hills was *bessa*, soft and still unpacked, what Terran skiers I think call "wild" snow. The sledge was heavy loaded; Estraven guessed the total weight to pull at something over 300 pounds. It was hard to pull in the fluffy snow, though it was as handy as a well-designed little boat; the runners were marvels, coated with a polymer that cut resistance almost to nothing, but of course that was no good when the whole thing was stuck in a drift. On such a surface, and going up and down slopes and gullies, we found it best to go one in harness pulling and one behind pushing. The snow fell, fine and mild, all day long. We stopped twice for a bite of food. In all the vast hilly country there was no sound. We went on, and all of a sudden it was twilight. We halted in a valley very like the one we had left that morning, a dell among white-humped hills. I was so tired I staggered, yet I could not believe the day was over. We had covered, by the sledge-meter, almost fifteen miles.

If we could go that well in soft snow, fully loaded, through a steep country whose hills and valleys all ran athwart our way, then surely we could do better up on the Ice, with hard snow, a level way, and a load always lighter. My trust in Estraven had been more willed than spontaneous; now I believed him completely. We would be in Karhide in seventy days.

"You've traveled like this before?" I asked him.

"Sledged? Often."

"Long hauls?"

"I went a couple of hundred miles on the Kerm Ice one autumn, years ago."

The lower end of Kerm Land, the mountainous southernmost peninsula of the Karhide semi-continent, is, like the north, glaciated. Humanity on the Great Continent of Gethen lives in a strip of land between two white walls. A further decrease of 8% in solar radiation, they calculate, would bring the walls creeping together; there would be no men, no land; only ice.

"What for?"

"Curiosity, adventure." He hesitated and smiled slightly. "The augmentation of the complexity and intensity of the field of intelligent life," he said, quoting one of my Ekumenical quotations.

"Ah, you were consciously extending the evolutionary tendency inherent in Being; one manifestation of which is exploration." We were both well pleased with ourselves, sitting in the warm tent, drinking hot tea and waiting for the kadik-germ porridge to boil.

"That's it," he said. "Six of us. All very young. My brother and I from Estre, four of our friends from Stok. There was no purpose for the journey. We wanted to see Teremander, a mountain that stands up out of the Ice, down there. Not many people have seen it from the land."

The porridge was ready, a different matter from the stiff bran mush of Pulefen Farm; it tasted like the roast chestnuts of Terra, and burned the mouth splendidly. Warm through, benevolent, I said, "The best food I've eaten on Gethen has always been in your company, Estraven."

"Not at that banquet in Mishnory."

"No, that's true. . . . You hate Orgoreyn, don't you?"

"Very few Orgota know how to cook. Hate Orgoreyn? No, how should I? How does one hate a country, or love one? Tibe talks about it; I lack the trick of it. I know people, I know towns, farms, hills and rivers and rocks, I know how the sun at sunset in autumn falls on the side of a certain plowland in the hills; but what is the sense of giving a boundary to all that, of giving it a name and ceasing to love where the name ceases to apply? What is love of one's country; is it hate of one's uncountry? Then it's not a good thing. Is it simply self-love? That's a good thing, but one mustn't make a virtue of it, or a profession. . . . Insofar as I love life, I love the hills of the Domain of Estre, but that sort of love does not have a boundary-line of hate. And beyond that, I am ignorant, I hope."

Ignorant, in the Handdara sense: to ignore the abstraction, to hold fast to the thing. There was in this attitude something feminine, a refusal of the abstract, the ideal, a submissiveness to the given, which rather displeased me.

Yet he added, scrupulous, "A man who doesn't detest a bad government is a fool. And if there were such a thing as a good government on earth, it would be a great joy to serve it."

There we understood each other. "I know something of that joy," I said.

"Yes; so I judged."

I rinsed our bowls with hot water and dumped the rinsings out the valve-door of the tent. It was blind dark outside; snow fell fine and thin, just visible in the oval dim shaft of light from the valve. Sealed again in the dry warmth of the tent, we laid out our bags. He said something, "Give the bowls to me, Mr. Ai," or some such remark, and I said, "Is it going to be 'Mr.' clear across the Gobrin Ice?"

He looked up and laughed. "I don't know what to call you."

"My name is Genly Ai."

"I know. You use my landname."

"I don't know what to call you either."

"Harth."

"Then I'm Ai. —Who uses first names?"

"Hearth-brothers, or friends," he said, and saying it was remote, out of reach, two feet from me in a tent eight feet across. No answer to that. What is more arrogant than honesty? Cooled, I climbed into my fur bag. "Good night, Ai," said the alien, and the other alien said, "Good night, Harth."

A friend. What is a friend, in a world where any friend may be a lover at a new phase of the moon? Not I, locked in my virility: no friend to Therem Harth, or any other of his race. Neither man nor woman, neither and both, cyclic, lunar, metamorphosing under the hand's touch, changelings in the human cradle, they were no flesh of mine, no friends; no love between us.

We slept. I woke once and heard the snow ticking thick and soft on the tent.

Estraven was up at dawn getting breakfast. The day broke bright. We loaded up and were off as the sun gilded the tops of the scrubby bushes rimming the dell, Estraven pulling in harness and I as pusher and rudder at the stern. The snow was beginning to get a crust on it; on clear downslopes we went like a dog-team, at a run.

That day we skirted and then entered the forest that borders Pulefen Farm, the forest of dwarfs, thickset, gnurl-limbed, ice-bearded thore-trees. We dared not use the main road north, but logging-roads lent their direction to us sometimes for a while, and as the forest was kept clear of fallen trees and undergrowth we got on well. Once we were in Tarrenpeth there were fewer ravines or steep ridges. The sledge-meter at evening said twenty miles for the day's run, and we were less tired than the night before.

One palliative of winter on Winter is that the days stay light. The planet has a few degrees of tilt to the plane of the ecliptic, not enough to make an appreciable seasonal difference in low latitudes. Season is not a hemispheric effect but a global one, a result of the ellipsoid orbit. At the far and slow-moving end of the orbit, approaching and departing from aphelion, there is just enough loss of solar radiation to disturb the already uneasy weather patterns, to chill down what is cold already, and turn the wet gray summer into white violent winter. Dryer than the rest of the year, winter might be pleasanter, if it were not for the cold. The sun, when you see it, shines high; there is no slow bleeding away of light into the darkness, as on the polar slopes of Earth where cold and night come on together. Gethen has a bright winter, bitter, terrible, and bright.

We were three days getting through Tarrenpeth Forest. On the last, Estraven stopped and made camp early, in order to set traps. He wanted to catch some pesthry. They are one of the larger land-animals of Winter, about the size of a fox, oviparous vegetarians with a splendid coat of gray or white fur. He was after the meat, for pesthry are edible. They were migrating south in vast numbers; they are so light-footed and solitary that we saw only two or three as we hauled, but the snow was thick-starred in every glade of the thore-forest with countless little snowshoe tracks, all heading south. Estraven's snares were full in an hour or two. He cleaned and cut up the six beasts, hung some of the meat to freeze, stewed some for our meal that night. Gethenians are not a hunting people, because there is very little to hunt—no large herbivores, thus no large carnivores, except in the teeming seas. They fish, and farm. I had never before seen a Gethenian with blood on his hands.

Estraven looked at the white pelts. "There's a week's room and board for a pesthry-hunter," he said. "Gone to waste." He held out one for me to touch. The fur was so soft and deep that you could not be certain when your hand began to feel it. Our sleeping-bags, coats, and hoods were lined with that same fur, an unsurpassed insulator and very beautiful to see. "Hardly seems worth it," I said, "for a stew."

Estraven gave me his brief dark stare and said, "We need protein." And tossed away the pelts, where overnight the *russy,* the fierce little rat-snakes, would devour them and the entrails and the bones, and lick clean the bloody snow.

He was right; he was generally right. There was a pound or two of edible meat on a pesthry. I ate my half of the stew that night and could have eaten his without noticing. Next morning, when we started up into the mountains, I was twice the sledge-engine I had been.

We went up that day. The beneficent snowfall and *kroxet*—windless weather 0°F and 20°—that had seen us through Tarrenpeth and out of range of probable pursuit, now dissolved wretchedly into above-freezing temperatures and rain. Now I began to understand why Gethenians complain when the temperature rises in winter, and cheer up when it falls. In the city, rain is an inconvenience; to a traveler it is a catastrophe. We hauled that sledge up the flanks of the Sembensyens all morning through a deep, cold porridge of rain-sodden snow. By afternoon on steep slopes the snow was mostly gone. Torrents of rain, miles of mud and gravel. We cased the runners, put the wheels on the sledge, and hauled on up. As a wheeled cart it was a bitch, sticking and tipping every moment. Dark fell before we found any shelter of cliff or cave to set up the tent in, so that despite all our care things got wet. Estraven had said that a tent such as ours would house us pretty comfortably in any weather at all, so long as we kept it dry inside. "Once you can't dry out your bags, you lose too much body-heat all night, and you don't sleep well. Our food-ration's too short to allow us to afford that. We can't count on any sunlight to dry things out, so we must not get them wet." I had listened, and had been as scrupulous as he about keeping snow and wet out of the tent, so that there was only the unavoidable moisture from our cooking, and our lungs and pores, to be evaporated. But this night everything was wet through before we could get the tent up. We huddled steaming over the Chabe stove, and presently had a stew of pesthry meat to eat, hot and solid, good enough almost to compensate for everything else. The sledge-meter, ignoring the hard uphill work we had done all day, said we had come only nine miles.

"First day we've done less than our stint," I said.

Estraven nodded, and neatly cracked a legbone for the marrow. He had stripped off his wet outer clothes and sat in shirt and breeches, barefoot, collar open. I was still too cold to take off my coat and hieb and boots. There he sat cracking marrowbones, neat, tough, durable, his sleek furlike hair shedding the water like a bird's feathers: he dripped a little onto his shoulders, like house-eaves dripping, and never noticed it. He was not discouraged. He belonged here.

The first meat-ration had given me some intestinal cramps, and that night they got severe. I lay awake in the soggy darkness loud with rain.

At breakfast he said, "You had a bad night."

"How did you know?" For he slept very deeply, scarcely moving, even when I left the tent.

He gave me that look again. "What's wrong?"

"Diarrhea."

He winced and said savagely, "It's the meat."

"I suppose so."

"My fault. I should—"

"It's all right."

"Can you travel?"

"Yes."

Rain fell and fell. A west wind off the sea kept the

temperature in the thirties, even here at three or four thousand feet of altitude. We never saw more than a quarter-mile ahead through the gray mist and mass of rain. What slopes rose on above us I never looked up to see: nothing to see but rain falling. We went by compass, keeping as much to northward as the cut and veer of the great slopes allowed.

The glacier had been over these mountainsides, in the hundreds of thousands of years it had been grinding back and forth across the North. There were tracks scored along granite slopes, long and straight as if cut with a great U-gouge. We could pull the sledge along those scratches sometimes as if along a road.

I did best pulling; I could lean into the harness, and the work kept me warm. When we stopped for a bite of food at midday, I felt sick and cold, and could not eat. We went on, climbing again now. Rain fell, and fell, and fell. Estraven stopped us under a great overhang of black rock, along in mid-afternoon. He had the tent up almost before I was out of harness. He ordered me to go in and lie down.

"I'm all right," I said.

"You're not," he said. "Go on."

I obeyed, but I resented his tone. When he came into the tent with our night's needs, I sat up to cook, it being my turn. He told me in the same peremptory tone to lie still.

"You needn't order me about," I said.

"I'm sorry," he said inflexibly, his back turned.

"I'm not sick, you know."

"No, I didn't know. If you won't say frankly, I must go by your looks. You haven't recovered your strength, and the going has been hard. I don't know where your limits lie."

"I'll tell you when I reach them."

I was galled by his patronizing. He was a head shorter than I, and built more like a woman than a man, more fat than muscle; when we hauled together I had to shorten my pace to his, hold in my strength so as not to out-pull him: a stallion in harness with a mule—

"You're no longer ill, then?"

"No. Of course I'm tired. So are you."

"Yes, I am," he said. "I was anxious about you. We have a long way to go."

He had not meant to patronize. He had thought me sick, and sick men take orders. He was frank, and expected a reciprocal frankness that I might not be able to supply. He, after all, had no standards of manliness, of virility, to complicate his pride.

On the other hand, if he could lower all his standards of shifgrethor, as I realized he had done with me, perhaps I could dispense with the more competitive elements of my masculine self-respect, which he certainly understood as little as I understood shifgrethor. . . .

"How much of it did we cover today?"

He looked around and smiled a little, gently. "Six miles," he said.

The next day we did seven miles, the next day twelve, and the day after that we came out of the rain, and out of the clouds, and out of the regions of mankind. It was the ninth day of our journey. We were five to six thousand feet above sea level now, on a high plateau full of the evidences of recent mountain-building and vulcanism; we were in the Fire-Hills of the Sembensyen Range. The plateau narrowed gradually to a valley and the valley to a pass between long ridges. As we approached the end of the pass the rain-clouds were thinning and rending. A cold north wind dispersed them utterly, laying bare the peaks above the ridges to our right and left, basalt and snow, piebald and patchwork of black and white brilliant under the sudden sun in a dazzling sky. Ahead of us, cleared and revealed by the same vast sweep of the wind, lay twisted valleys, hundreds of feet below, full of ice and boulders. Across those valleys a great wall stood, a wall of ice, and raising our eyes up and still up to the rim of the wall we saw the Ice itself, the Gobrin Glacier, blinding and horizonless to the utmost north, a white, a white the eyes could not look on.

Here and there out of the valleys full of rubble and out of the cliffs and bends and masses of the great ice-field's edge, black ridges rose; one great mass loomed up out of the plateau to the height of the gateway peaks we stood between, and from its side drifted heavily a mile-long wisp of smoke. Farther off there were others: peaks, pinnacles, black cindercones on the glacier. Smoke panted from fiery mouths that opened out of the ice.

Estraven stood there in harness beside me looking at that magnificent and unspeakable desolation. "I'm glad I have lived to see this," he said.

I felt as he did. It is good to have an end to journey towards; but it is the journey that matters, in the end.

It had not rained, here on these north-facing slopes. Snow-fields stretched down from the pass into the valleys of moraine. We stowed the wheels, uncapped the sledge-runners, put on our skis, and took off—down, north, onward, into that silent vastness of fire and ice that said in enormous letters of black and white DEATH, DEATH, written right across a continent. The sledge pulled like a feather, and we laughed with joy.

16

BETWEEN DRUMNER AND DREMEGOLE

Odyrny Thern. A<small>I ASKS FROM HIS SLEEPING-BAG,</small> "W<small>HAT</small> is it you're writing, Harth?"

"A record."

He laughs a little. "I ought to be keeping a journal for the Ekumenical files; but I never could stick to it without a voice-writer."

I explain that my notes are intended for my people at Estre, who will incorporate them as they see fit into the Records of the Domain; this turning my thoughts to my Hearth and my son, I seek to turn them away again, and ask, "Your parent—your parents, that is—are they alive?"

"No," says Ai. "Seventy years dead."

I puzzled at it. Ai was not thirty years old. "You're counting years of a different length than ours?"

"No. Oh, I see. I've timejumped. Twenty years from

Earth to Hain-Davenant, from fifty to Ellul, from Ellul to here seventeen. I've only lived off-Earth seven years, but I was born there a hundred and twenty years ago."

Long since in Erhenrang he had explained to me how time is shortened inside the ships that go almost as fast as starlight between the stars, but I had not laid this fact down against the length of a man's life, or the lives he leaves behind him on his own world. While he lived a few hours in one of those unimaginable ships going from one planet to another, everyone he had left behind him at home grew old and died, and their children grew old. . . . I said at last, "I thought myself an exile."

"You for my sake—I for yours," he said, and laughed again, a slight cheerful sound in the heavy silence. These three days since we came down from the pass have been much hard work for no gain, but Ai is no longer downcast, nor overhopeful; and he has more patience with me. Maybe the drugs are sweated out of him. Maybe we have learned to pull together.

We spent this day coming down from the basaltic spur that we spent yesterday climbing. From the valley it looked a good road up onto the Ice, but the higher we went the more scree and slick rock-face we met, and a grade ever steeper, till even without the sledge we could not have climbed it. Tonight we are back down at the foot of it in the moraine, the valley of stones. Nothing grows here. Rock, pebble-dump, boulder-fields, clay, mud. An arm of the glacier has withdrawn from this slope within the last fifty or hundred years, leaving the planet's bones raw to the air; no flesh of earth, of grass.

Here and there fumaroles cast a heavy yellowish fog over the ground, low and creeping. The air smells of sulphur. It is 12°, still, overcast. I hope no heavy snow falls until we have got over the evil ground between this place and the glacier-arm we saw some miles to the west from the ridge. It seems to be a wide ice-river running down from the plateau between two mountains, volcanoes, both capped with steam and smoke. If we can get onto it from the slopes of the nearer volcano, it may provide us a road up onto the plateau of ice. To our east a smaller glacier comes down to a frozen lake, but it runs curving and even from here the great crevasses in it can be seen; it is impassable to us, equipped as we are. We agreed to try the glacier between the volcanoes, though by going west to it we lose at least two days' mileage towards our goal, one in going west and one in regaining the distance.

Opposthe Thern. Snowing *neserem.** No travel in this. We both slept all day. We have been hauling nearly a halfmonth; the sleep does us good.

Ottormenbod Thern. Snowing *neserem.* Enough sleep. Ai taught me a Terran game played on squares with little stones, called *go,* an excellent difficult game. As he remarked, there are plenty of stones here to play *go* with.

He endures the cold pretty well, and if courage were enough, would stand it like a snow-worm. It is odd to see him bundled up in hieb and overcoat with the hood up, when the temperature is above zero; but when we sledge,

---

* *neserem*: fine snow on a moderate gale: a light blizzard.

if the sun is out or the wind not too bitter, he takes off the coat soon and sweats like one of us. We must compromise as to the heating of the tent. He would keep it hot, I cold, and either's comfort is the other's pneumonia. We strike a medium, and he shivers outside his bag, while I swelter in mine; but considering from what distances we have come together to share this tent a while, we do well enough.

Getheny Thanern. Clear after the blizzard, wind down, the thermometer around 15° all day. We are camped on the lower western slope of the nearer volcano: Mount Dremegole, on my map of Orgoreyn. Its companion across the ice-river is called Drumner. The map is poorly made; there is a great peak visible to the west not shown on it at all, and it is all out of proportion. The Orgota evidently do not often come into their Fire-Hills. Indeed there is not much to come for, except grandeur. We hauled eleven miles today, difficult work: all rock. Ai is asleep already. I bruised the tendon of my heel, wrenching it like a fool when my foot was caught between two boulders, and limped out the afternoon. The night's rest should heal it. Tomorrow we should get down onto the glacier.

Our food-supplies seem to have sunk alarmingly, but it is because we have been eating the bulky stuff. We had between ninety and a hundred pounds of coarse foodstuffs, half of it the load I stole in Turuf; sixty pounds of this are gone, after fifteen days' journey. I have started on the gichy-michy at a pound a day, saving two sacks of kadik-germ, some sugar, and a chest of dried fishcakes for variety later. I am glad to be rid of that heavy stuff from Turuf. The sledge pulls lighter.

Sordny Thanern. In the 20s; frozen rain, wind pouring down the ice-river like the draft in a tunnel. Camped a quarter mile in from the edge, on a long flat streak of firn. The way down from Dremegole was rough and steep, on bare rock and rock-fields, the glacier's edge heavily crevassed, and so foul with gravel and rocks caught in the ice that we tried the sledge on wheels there too. Before we had got a hundred yards a wheel wedged fast and the axle bent. We use runners henceforth. We made only four miles today, still in the wrong direction. The effluent glacier seems to run on a long curve westerly up to the Gobrin plateau. Here between the volcanoes it is about four miles wide, and should not be hard going farther in towards the center, though it is more crevassed than I had hoped, and the surface rotten.

Drumner is in eruption. The sleet on one's lips tastes of smoke and sulphur. A darkness loured all day in the west even under the rain-clouds. From time to time all things, clouds, icy rain, ice, air, would turn a dull red, then fade slowly back to gray. The glacier shakes a little under our feet.

Eskichwe rem ir Her hypothesized that the volcanic activity in N.W. Orgoreyn and the Archipelago has been increasing during the last ten or twenty millennia, and presages the end of the Ice, or at least a recession of it and an interglacial period. CO_2 released by the volcanoes into the atmosphere will in time serve as an insulator, holding in the long-wave heat-energy reflected from the earth, while permitting direct solar heat to enter undiminished. The average world temperature, he says, would in the end be raised some thirty degrees, till it attains 72°. I am glad I shall not be present. Ai says that similar theories have been propounded by Terran scholars to explain the still incomplete recession of their last Age of Ice. All such theories remain largely irrefutable and unprovable; no one knows certainly why the ice comes, why it goes. The Snow of Ignorance remains untrodden.

Over Drumner in the dark now a great table of dull fire burns.

Eps Thanern. The meter reads sixteen miles hauled today, but we are not more than eight miles in a straight line from last night's camp. We are still in the ice-pass between the two volcanoes. Drumner is in eruption. Worms of fire crawl down its black sides, seen when wind clears off the roil and seethe of ash-cloud and smoke-cloud and white steam. Continuously, with no pause, a hissing mutter fills the air, so huge and so long a sound that one cannot hear it when one stops to listen; yet it fills all the interstices of one's being. The glacier trembles perpetually, snaps and crashes, jitters under our feet. All the snow-bridges that the blizzard may have laid across crevasses are gone, shaken down, knocked in by this drumming and jumping of the ice and the earth beneath the ice. We go back and forth, seeking the end of a slit in the ice that would swallow the sledge whole, then seeking the end of the next, trying to go north and forced always to go west or east. Above us Dremegole, in sympathy with Drumner's labor, grumbles and farts foul smoke.

Ai's face was badly frostbitten this morning, nose, ears, chin all dead gray when I chanced to look at him. Kneaded him back to life and no damage done, but we must be more careful. The wind that blows down off the Ice is, in simple truth, deadly; and we have to face it as we haul.

I shall be glad to get off this slit and wrinkled ice-arm between two growling monsters. Mountains should be seen, not heard.

Arhad Thanern. Some sove-snow, between 15 and 20°. We went twelve miles today, about five of them profitable, and the rim of the Gobrin is visibly nearer, north, above us. We now see the ice-river to be miles wide: the "arm" between Drumner and Dremegole is only one finger, and we now are on the back of the hand. Turning and looking down from this camp one sees the glacier-flow split, divided, torn and churned by the black steaming peaks that thwart it. Looking ahead one sees it broaden, rising and curving slowly, dwarfing the dark ridges of earth, meeting the ice-wall far above under veils of cloud and smoke and snow. Cinders and ash now fall with the snow, and the ice is thick with clinkers on it or sunk in it: a good walking surface but rather rough for hauling, and the runners need recoating already. Two or three times volcanic projectiles hit the ice quite near us. They hiss loudly as they strike, and burn themselves a socket in the ice. Cinders patter, falling with the snow.

We creep infinitesimally northward through the dirty chaos of a world in the process of making itself.

Praise then Creation unfinished!

Netherhad Thanern. No snow since morning; overcast and windy, at about 15°. The great multiple glacier we are on feeds down into the valley from the west, and we are on its extreme eastern edge. Dremegole and Drumner are now somewhat behind us, though a sharp ridge of Dremegole still rises east of us, almost at eye level. We have crept and crawled up to a point where we must choose between following the glacier on its long sweep westward and so up gradually onto the plateau of ice, or climbing the ice-cliffs a mile north of tonight's camp, and so saving twenty or thirty miles of hauling, at the cost of risk.

Ai favors the risk.

There is a frailty about him. He is all unprotected, exposed, vulnerable, even to his sexual organ, which he must carry always outside himself; but he is strong, unbelievably strong. I am not sure he can keep hauling any longer than I can, but he can haul harder and faster than I—twice as hard. He can lift the sledge at front or rear to ease it over an obstacle. I could not lift and hold that weight, unless I was in dothe. To match his frailty and strength, he has a spirit easy to despair and quick to defiance: a fierce impatient courage. This slow, hard, crawling work we have been doing these days wears him out in body and will, so that if he were one of my race I should think him a coward, but he is anything but that; he has a ready bravery I have never seen the like of. He is ready, eager, to stake life on the cruel quick test of the precipice.

"Fire and fear, good servants, bad lords." He makes fear serve him. I would have let fear lead me around by the long way. Courage and reason are with him. What good seeking the safe course, on a journey such as this? There are senseless courses, which I shall not take; but there is no safe one.

Streth Thanern. No luck. No way to get the sledge up, though we spent the day at it.

Sove-snow in flurries, thick ash mixed with it. It was dark all day, as the wind veering around from the west again blew the pall of Drumner's smoke on us. Up here the ice shakes less, but there came a great quake while we tried to climb a shelving cliff; it shook free the sledge where we had wedged it and I was pulled down five or six feet with a bump, but Ai had a good handhold and his strength saved us from all careering down to the foot of the cliff, twenty feet or more. If one of us breaks a leg or shoulder in these exploits, that is probably the end of both of us; there, precisely, is the risk—rather an ugly one when looked at closely. The lower valley of the glaciers behind us is white with steam: lava touches ice, down there. We certainly cannot go back. Tomorrow we shall try the ascent farther west.

Beren Thanern. No luck. We must go farther west. Dark as late twilight all day. Our lungs are raw, not from cold (it remains well above zero even at night, with this west wind) but from breathing the ash and fumes of the eruption. By the end of this second day of wasted effort, scrabbling and squirming over pressure-blocks and up ice-cliffs always to be stopped by a sheer face or overhang, trying farther on and failing again, Ai was exhausted and enraged. He looked ready to cry, but did not. I believe he considers crying either evil or shameful. Even when he was very ill and weak, the first days of our escape, he hid his face from me when he wept. Reasons personal, racial, social, sexual—how can I guess why Ai must not weep? Yet his name is a cry of pain. For that I first sought him out in Erhenrang, a long time ago it seems now; hearing talk of "an Alien" I asked his name, and heard for answer a cry of pain from a human throat across the night. Now he sleeps. His arms tremble and twitch, muscular fatigue. The world around us, ice and rock, ash and snow, fire and dark, trembles and twitches and mutters. Looking out a minute ago I saw the glow of the volcano as a dull red bloom on the belly of vast clouds overhanging the darkness.

Orny Thanern. No luck. This is the twenty-second day of our journey, and since the tenth day we have made no progress eastward, indeed have lost twenty or twenty-five miles by going west; since the eighteenth day we have made no progress of any kind, and might as well have sat still. If we ever do get up on the Ice, will we have food enough left to take us across it? This thought is hard to dismiss. Fog and murk of the eruption cut seeing very close, so that we cannot choose our path well. Ai wants to attack each ascent, however steep, that shows any sign of shelving. He is impatient with my caution. We have got to watch our tempers. I will be in kemmer in a day or so, and all strains will increase. Meanwhile we butt our heads on cliffs of ice in a cold dusk full of ashes. If I wrote a new Yomesh Canon I should send thieves here after death. Thieves who steal sacks of food by night in Turuf. Thieves who steal a man's Hearth and name from him and send him out ashamed and exiled. My head is thick, I must cross out all this stuff later, too tired to reread it now.

Harhahad Thanern. On the Gobrin. The twenty-third day of our journey. We are on the Gobrin Ice. As soon as we set out this morning we saw, only a few hundred yards beyond last night's camp, a pathway open up to the Ice, a highway curving broad and cinder-paved from the rubble and chasms of the glacier right up through the cliffs of ice. We walked up it as if strolling along the Sess Embankment. We are on the Ice. We are headed east again, homeward.

I am infected by Ai's pure pleasure in our achievement. Looked at soberly it is as bad as ever, up here. We are on the plateau's rim. Crevasses—some wide enough to sink villages in, not house by house but all at once— run inland, northward, right out of sight. Most of them cut across our way, so we too must go north, not east. The surface is bad. We screw the sledge along amongst great lumps and chunks of ice, immense debris pushed up by the straining of the great plastic sheet of ice against and among the Fire-Hills. The broken pressure-ridges take queer shapes, overturned towers, legless giants, catapults. A mile thick to start with, the Ice here rises and thickens, trying to flow over the mountains and choke the fire-mouths with silence. Some miles to the north a peak rises up out of the Ice, the sharp graceful barren cone of a young volcano: younger by thousands of years than the ice-sheet that grinds and shoves, all shattered into chasms and jammed up into great blocks and ridges, over the six thousand feet of lower slopes we cannot see.

During the day, turning, we saw the smoke of Drumner's eruption hang behind us like a gray-brown extension of the surface of the Ice. A steady wind blows along at ground level from the northeast, clearing this higher air of the soot and stink of the planet's bowels, which we have breathed for days, flattening out the smoke behind us to cover, like a dark lid, the glaciers, the lower mountains, the valleys of stones, the rest of the earth. There is nothing, the Ice says, but Ice. But the young volcano there to northward has another word it thinks of saying.

No snowfall, a thin, high overcast. −4° on the plateau at dusk. A jumble of firn, new ice, and old ice underfoot. The new ice is tricky, slick blue stuff just hidden by a white glaze. We have both been down a good deal. I slid fifteen feet on my belly across one such slick. Ai, in harness, doubled up laughing. He apologized and explained he had thought himself the only person on Gethen who ever slipped on ice.

Thirteen miles today; but if we try to keep up such a pace among these cut, heaped, crevassed pressure-ridges we shall wear ourselves out or come to worse grief than a bellyslide.

The waxing moon is low, dull as dry blood; a great brownish, iridescent halo surrounds it.

Guyrny Thanern. Some snow, rising wind and falling temperature. Thirteen miles again today, which brings our distance logged since we left our first camp to 254 miles. We have averaged about ten and a half miles a day; eleven and a half omitting the two days spent waiting out the blizzard. 75 to 100 of those miles of hauling gave us no onward gain. We are not much nearer Karhide than we were when we set out. But we stand a better chance, I think, of getting there.

Since we came up out of the volcano-murk our spirit is not all spent in work and worry, and we talk again in the tent after our dinner. As I am in kemmer I would find it easier to ignore Ai's presence, but this is difficult in a two-man tent. The trouble is of course that he is, in his curious fashion, also in kemmer: always in kemmer. A strange low-grade sort of desire it must be, to be spread out over every day of the year and never to know the choice of sex, but there it is; and here am I. Tonight my extreme physical awareness of him was rather hard to ignore, and I was too tired to divert it into untrance or any other channel of the discipline. Finally he asked, had he offended me? I explained my silence, with some embarrassment. I was afraid he would laugh at me. After all he is no more an oddity, a sexual freak, than I am; up here on the Ice each of us is singular, isolate, I as cut off from those like me, from my society and its rules, as he from his. There is no world full of other Gethenians here to explain and support my existence. We are equals at last, equal, alien, alone. He did not laugh, of course. Rather he spoke with a gentleness that I did not know was in him. After a while he too came to speak of isolation, of loneliness.

"Your race is appallingly alone in its world. No other mammalian species. No other ambisexual species. No animal intelligent enough even to domesticate as pets. It must color your thinking, this uniqueness. I don't mean scientific thinking only, though you are extraordinary hypothesizers—it's extraordinary that you arrived at any concept of evolution, faced with that unbridgeable gap between yourselves and the lower animals. But philosophically, emotionally: to be so solitary, in so hostile a world: it must affect your entire outlook."

"The Yomeshta would say that man's singularity is his divinity."

"Lords of the Earth, yes. Other cults on other worlds have come to the same conclusion. They tend to be the cults of dynamic, aggressive, ecology-breaking cultures. Orgoreyn is in the pattern, in its way; at least they seem bent on pushing things around. What do the Handdarata say?"

"Well, in the Handdara . . . you know, there's no theory, no dogma. . . . Maybe they are less aware of the gap between men and beasts, being more occupied with the likenesses, the links, the whole of which living things are a part." Tormer's Lay had been all day in my mind, and I said the words,

Light is the left hand of darkness
and darkness the right hand of light.
Two are one, life and death, lying
together like lovers in kemmer,
like hands joined together,
like the end and the way.

My voice shook as I said the lines, for I remembered as I said them that in the letter my brother wrote me before his death he had quoted the same words.

Ai brooded, and after some time he said, "You're isolated, and undivided. Perhaps you are as obsessed with wholeness as we are with dualism."

"We are dualists too. Duality is an essential, isn't it? So long as there is *myself* and *the other*."

"I and Thou," he said. "Yes, it does, after all, go even wider than sex. . . ."

"Tell me, how does the other sex of your race differ from yours?"

He looked startled and in fact my question rather startled me; kemmer brings out these spontaneities in one. We were both self-conscious. "I never thought of that," he said. "You've never seen a woman." He used his Terran-language word, which I knew.

"I saw your pictures of them. The women looked like pregnant Gethenians, but with larger breasts. Do they differ much from your sex in mind behavior? Are they like a different species?"

"No. Yes. No, of course not, not really. But the difference is very important. I suppose the most important thing, the heaviest single factor in one's life, is whether one's born male or female. In most societies it determines one's expectations, activities, outlook, ethics, manners— almost everything. Vocabulary. Semiotic usages. Clothing. Even food. Women . . . women tend to eat less. . . . It's extremely hard to separate the innate differences from the learned ones. Even where women participate equally with men in the society, they still after all do all the childbearing, and so most of the child-rearing. . . ."

"Equality is not the general rule, then? Are they mentally inferior?"

"I don't know. They don't often seem to turn up mathematicians, or composers of music, or inventors, or abstract thinkers. But it isn't that they're stupid. Physically they're less muscular, but a little more durable than men. Psychologically—"

After he had stared a long time at the glowing stove, he shook his head. "Harth," he said, "I can't tell you what women are like. I never thought about it much in the abstract, you know, and—God!—by now I've practically forgotten. I've been here two years. . . . You don't know. In a sense, women are more alien to me than you are. With you I share one sex, anyhow. . . ." He looked away and laughed, rueful and uneasy. My own feelings were complex, and we let the matter drop.

Yrny Thanern. Eighteen miles today, east-northeast by compass, on skis. We got clear of the pressure-ridges and crevasses in the first hour of pulling. Both got in harness, I ahead at first with the probe, but no more need for testing: the firn is a couple of feet thick over solid ice, and on the firn lie several inches of sound new snow from the last fall, with a good surface. Neither we nor the sledge broke through at all, and the sledge pulled so light that it was hard to believe we are still hauling about a hundred pounds apiece. During the afternoon we took turns hauling, as one can do it easily on this splendid surface. It is a pity that all the hard work uphill and over rock came while the load was heavy. Now we go light. Too light: I find myself thinking about food a good deal. We eat, Ai says, ethereally. All day we went light and fast over the level ice-plain, dead white under a gray-blue sky, unbroken except for the few black nunatak-peaks now far behind us, and a smudge of darkness, Drumner's breath, behind them. Nothing else: the veiled sun, the ice.

17

AN ORGOTA CREATION MYTH

The origins of this myth are prehistorical; it has been recorded in many forms. This very primitive version is from a pre-Yomesh written text found in the Isenpeth Cave Shrine of the Gobrin Hinterlands.

In the beginning there was nothing but ice and the sun.

Over many years the sun shining melted a great crevasse in the ice. In the sides of this crevasse were great shapes of ice, and there was no bottom to it. Drops of water melted from the ice-shapes in the sides of the chasm and fell down and down. One of the ice-shapes said, "I bleed." Another of the ice-shapes said, "I weep." A third one said, "I sweat."

The ice-shapes climbed up out of the abyss and stood on the plain of ice. He that said "I bleed," he reached up to the sun and pulled out handfuls of excrement from the bowels of the sun, and with that dung made the hills and valleys of the earth. He that said "I weep," he breathed on the ice and melting it made the seas and the rivers. He that said "I sweat," he gathered up soil and seawater and with them made trees, plants, herbs and grains of the field, animals, and men. The plants grew in the soil and the sea, the beasts ran on the land and swam in the sea, but the men did not wake. Thirty-nine of them there were. They slept on the ice and would not move.

Then the three ice-shapes stooped down and sat with their knees drawn up and let the sun melt them. As milk they melted, and the milk ran into the mouths of the sleepers, and the sleepers woke. That milk is drunk by the children of men alone and without it they will not wake to life.

The first to wake up was Edondurath. So tall was he that when he stood up his head split the sky, and snow fell down. He saw the others stirring and awakening, and was afraid of them when they moved, so he killed one after another with a blow of his fist. Thirty-six of them he killed. But one of them, the next to last one, ran away. Haharath he was called. Far he ran over the plain of ice and over the lands of Earth. Edondurath ran behind him and caught up with him at last and smote him. Haharath died. Then Edondurath returned to the Birthplace on the Gobrin Ice where the bodies of the others lay, but the last one was gone: he had escaped while Edondurath pursued Haharath.

Edondurath built a house of the frozen bodies of his brothers, and waited there inside that house for that last one to come back. Each day one of the corpses would speak, saying, "Does he burn? Does he burn?" All the other corpses would say with frozen tongues, "No, no." Then Edondurath entered kemmer as he slept, and moved and spoke aloud in dreams, and when he woke the corpses were all saying, "He burns! He burns!" And the last brother, the youngest one, heard them saying that, and came into the house of bodies and there coupled with Edondurath. Of these two were the nations of men born, out of the flesh of Edondurath, out of Edondurath's womb. The name of the other, the younger brother, the father, his name is not known.

Each of the children born to them had a piece of darkness that followed him about wherever he went by daylight. Edondurath said, "Why are my sons followed thus by darkness?" His kemmering said, "Because they were born in the house of flesh, therefore death follows at their heels. They are in the middle of time. In the beginning there was the sun and the ice, and there was no shadow. In the end when we are done, the sun will devour itself and shadow will eat light, and there will be nothing left but the ice and the darkness."

18

ON THE ICE

Sometimes as I am falling asleep in a dark, quiet room I have for a moment a great and treasurable illusion of the past. The wall of a tent leans up over my face, not visible but audible, a slanting plane of faint sound: the susurrus of blown snow. Nothing can be seen. The light-emission of the Chabe stove is cut off, and it exists only as a sphere of heat, a heart of warmth. The faint dampness and confining cling of my sleeping-bag; the sound of the snow; barely audible, Estraven's breathing as he sleeps; darkness. Nothing else. We are inside, the two of us, in shelter, at rest, at the center of all things. Outside, as always, lies the great darkness, the cold, death's solitude.

In such fortunate moments as I fall asleep I know beyond doubt what the real center of my own life is, that time that is past and lost and yet is permanent, the enduring moment, the heart of warmth.

I am not trying to say that I was happy, during those weeks of hauling a sledge across an ice-sheet in the dead of winter. I was hungry, overstrained, and often anxious, and it all got worse the longer it went on. I certainly wasn't happy. Happiness has to do with reason, and only reason earns it. What I was given was the thing you can't earn, and can't keep, and often don't even recognize at the time; I mean joy.

I always woke up first, usually before daylight. My metabolic rate is slightly over the Gethenian norm, as are my height and weight; Estraven had figured these differences into the food-ration calculations, in his scrupulous way, which one could see as either house-wifely or scientific, and from the start I had had a couple of ounces more food per day than he. Protests of injustice fell silent before the self-evident justice of this unequal division. However divided, the share was small. I was hungry, constantly hungry, daily hungrier. I woke up because I was hungry.

If it was still dark I turned up the light of the Chabe stove, and put a pan of ice brought in the night before, now thawed, on the stove to boil. Estraven meanwhile engaged in his customary fierce and silent struggle with sleep, as if he wrestled with an angel. Winning, he sat up, stared at me vaguely, shook his head, and woke. By the time we were dressed and booted and had the bags rolled up, breakfast was ready: a mug of boiling hot orsh, and one cube of gichy-michy expanded by hot water into a sort of small, doughy bun. We chewed slowly, solemnly, retrieving all dropped crumbs. The stove cooled as we ate. We packed it up with the pan and mugs, pulled on our hooded overcoats and our mittens, and crawled out into the open air. The coldness of it was perpetually incredible. Every morning I had to believe it all over again. If one had been outside to relieve oneself already, the second exit was only harder.

Sometimes it was snowing; sometimes the long light of early day lay wonderfully gold and blue across the miles of ice; most often it was gray.

We brought the thermometer into the tent with us, nights, and when we took it outside it was interesting to watch the pointer swing to the right (Gethenian dials read counterclockwise) almost too fast to follow, registering a drop of twenty, fifty, eighty degrees, till it stopped somewhere between zero and -60°.

One of us collapsed the tent and folded it while the other loaded stove, bags, etc., onto the sledge; the tent was strapped over all, and we were ready for skis and harness. Little metal was used in our straps and fittings, but the harnesses had buckles of aluminum alloy, too fine to fasten with mittens on, which burned in that cold exactly as if they were red-hot. I had to be very careful of my fingers when the temperature was below minus twenty, especially if the wind blew, for I could pick up a frostbite amazingly fast. My feet never suffered—and that is a factor of major importance, in a winter-journey where an hour's exposure can, after all, cripple one for a week or for life. Estraven had had to guess my size and the snow-boots he got me were a little large, but extra socks filled the discrepancy. We put on our skis, got into harness as quick as possible, bucked and pried and jolted the sledge free if its runners were frozen in, and set off.

Mornings after heavy snowfall we might have to spend some while digging out the tent and sledge before we could set off. The new snow was not hard to shovel away, though it made great impressive drifts around us, who were, after all, the only impediment for hundreds of miles, the only thing sticking out above the ice.

We pulled eastward by the compass. The usual direction of the wind was north to south, off the glacier. Day after day it blew from our left as we went. The hood did not suffice against that wind, and I wore a facial mask to protect my nose and left cheek. Even so my left eye froze shut one day, and I thought I had lost the use of it: even when Estraven thawed it open with breath and tongue, I could not see with it for some while, so probably more had been frozen than the lashes. In sunlight both of us wore the Gethenian slit-screen eyeshields, and neither of us suffered any snow-blindness. We had small opportunity. The Ice, as Estraven had said, tends to hold a high-pressure zone above its central area, where thousands of square miles of white reflect the sunlight. We were not in this central zone, however, but at best on the edge of it, between it and the zone of turbulent, deflected, precipitation-laden storms that it sends continually to torment the subglacial lands. Wind from due north brought bare, bright weather, but from northeast or northwest it brought snow, or harrowed up dry fallen snow into blinding, biting clouds like sand or dust-storms, or else, sinking almost to nothing, crept in sinu-ous trails along the surface, leaving the sky white, the air white, no visible sun, no shadow: and the snow itself, the Ice, disappeared from under our feet.

Around midday we would halt, and cut and set up a few blocks of ice for a protective wall if the wind was strong. We heated water to soak a cube of gichy-michy in, and drank the water hot, sometimes with a bit of sugar melted in it; harnessed up again and went on.

We seldom talked while on the march or at lunch, for our lips were sore, and when one's mouth was open the cold got inside, hurting teeth and throat and lungs; it was necessary to keep the mouth closed and breathe through the nose, at least when the air was forty or fifty degrees below freezing. When it went on lower than that, the whole breathing process was further complicated by the rapid freezing of one's exhaled breath; if you didn't look out your nostrils might freeze shut, and then to keep from suffocating you would gasp in a lungful of razors.

Under certain conditions our exhalations freezing instantly made a tiny cracking noise, like distant fire-crackers, and a shower of crystals: each breath a snow-storm.

We pulled till we were tired out or till it began to grow dark, halted, set up the tent, pegged down the sledge if there was threat of high wind, and settled in for the night. On a usual day we would have pulled for eleven or twelve hours, and made between twelve and eighteen miles.

It does not seem a very good rate, but then conditions were a bit adverse. The crust of the snow was seldom right for both skis and sledge-runners. When it was light and new the sledge ran through rather than over it; when it was partly hardened, the sledge would stick but we on skis would not, which meant that we were perpetually being pulled up backward with a jolt; and when it was hard it was often heaped up in long wind-waves, *sastrugi*, that in some places ran up to four feet high. We had to haul the sledge up and over each knife-edged or fantastically corniced top, then slide her down, and up over the next one: for they never seemed to run parallel to our course. I had imagined the Gobrin Ice Plateau to be all one sheet like a frozen pond, but there were hundreds of miles of it that were rather like an abruptly frozen, storm-raised sea.

The business of setting up camp, making everything secure, getting all the clinging snow off one's outer clothing, and so on, was trying. Sometimes it did not seem worthwhile. It was so late, so cold, one was so tired, that it would be much easier to lie down in a sleeping-bag in the lee of the sledge and not bother with the tent. I remember how clear this was to me on certain evenings, and how bitterly I resented my companion's methodical, tyrannical insistence that we do everything and do it correctly and thoroughly. I hated him at such times, with a hatred that rose straight up out of the death that lay within my spirit. I hated the harsh, intricate, obstinate demands that he made on me in the name of life.

When all was done we could enter the tent, and almost at once the heat of the Chabe stove could be felt as an enveloping, protecting ambiance. A marvelous thing surrounded us: warmth. Death and cold were elsewhere, outside.

Hatred was also left outside. We ate and drank. After we ate, we talked. When the cold was extreme, even the excellent insulation of the tent could not keep it out, and we lay in our bags as close to the stove as possible. A little fur of frost gathered on the inner surface of the tent. To open the valve was to let in a draft of cold that instantly condensed, filling the tent with a swirling mist of fine snow. When there was a blizzard, needles of icy air blew in through the vents, elaborately protected as they were, and an impalpable dust of snow-motes fogged the air. On those nights the storm made an incredible noise, and we could not converse by voice, unless we shouted with our heads together. On other nights it was still, with such a stillness as one imagines as existing before the stars began to form, or after everything has perished.

Within an hour after our evening meal Estraven turned the stove down, if it was feasible to do so, and turned the light-emission off. As he did so he murmured a short and charming grace of invocation, the only ritual words I had ever learned of the Handdara: "Praise then darkness and Creation unfinished," he said, and there was darkness. We slept. In the morning it was all to do over.

We did it over for fifty days.

Estraven kept up his journal, though during the weeks on the Ice he seldom wrote more than a note of the weather and the distance we had come that day. Among these notes there is occasional mention of his own thoughts or of some of our conversation, but not a word concerning the profounder conversation between us that occupied our rest between dinner and sleep on many nights of the first month on the Ice, while we still had enough energy to talk, and on certain days that we spent storm-bound in the tent. I told him that I was not forbidden, but not expected, to use paraverbal speech on a non-Ally planet, and asked him to keep what he learned from his own people, at least until I could discuss what I had done with my colleagues on the ship. He assented, and kept his word. He never said or wrote anything concerning our silent conversations.

Mindspeech was the only thing I had to give Estraven, out of all my civilization, my alien reality in which he was so profoundly interested. I could talk and describe endlessly; but that was all I had to give. Indeed it may be the only important thing we have to give to Winter. But I can't say that gratitude was my motive for infringing on the Law of Cultural Embargo. I was not paying my debt to him. Such debts remain owing. Estraven and I had simply arrived at the point where we shared whatever we had that was worth sharing.

I expect it will turn out that sexual intercourse is possible between Gethenian double-sexed and Hain-ishnorm one-sexed human beings, though such intercourse will inevitably be sterile. It remains to be proved; Estraven and I proved nothing except perhaps a rather subtler point. The nearest to crisis that our sexual desires brought us was on a night early in the journey, our second night up on the Ice. We had spent all day struggling and backtracking in the cut-up, crevassed area east of the Fire-Hills. We were tired that evening but elated, sure that a clear course would soon open out ahead. But after dinner Estraven grew taciturn, and cut my talk off short. I said at last after a direct rebuff, "Harth, I've said something wrong again, please tell me what it is."

He was silent.

"I've made some mistake in shifgrethor. I'm sorry; I can't learn. I've never even really understood the meaning of the word."

"Shifgrethor? It comes from an old word for *shadow*."

We were both silent for a little, and then he looked at me with a direct, gentle gaze. His face in the reddish light was as soft, as vulnerable, as remote as the face of a woman who looks at you out of her thoughts and does not speak.

And I saw then again, and for good, what I had always been afraid to see, and had pretended not to see in him: that he was a woman as well as a man. Any need to explain the sources of that fear vanished with the fear; what I was left with was, at last, acceptance of him as he was. Until then I had rejected him, refused him his own reality. He had been quite right to say that he, the only person on Gethen who trusted me, was the only Gethenian I distrusted. For he was the only one who had entirely accepted me as a human being: who had liked me personally and given me entire personal loyalty, and who therefore had demanded of me an equal degree of recognition, of acceptance. I had not been willing to give it. I had been afraid to give it. I had not wanted to give my trust, my friendship to a man who was a woman, a woman who was a man.

He explained, stiffly and simply, that he was in kemmer and had been trying to avoid me, insofar as one of us could avoid the other. "I must not touch you," he said, with extreme constraint; saying that he looked away.

I said, "I understand. I agree completely."

For it seemed to me, and I think to him, that it was from that sexual tension between us, admitted now and understood, but not assuaged, that the great and sudden assurance of friendship between us rose: a friendship so much needed by us both in our exile, and already so well proved in the days and nights of our bitter journey, that it might as well be called, now as later, love. But it was from the difference between us, not from the affinities and likenesses, but from the difference, that that love came: and it was itself the bridge, the only bridge, across what divided us. For us to meet sexually would be for us to meet once more as aliens. We had touched, in the only way we could touch. We left it at that. I do not know if we were right.

We talked some more that night, and I recall being very hard put to it to answer coherently when he asked me what women were like. We were both rather stiff and cautious with each other for the next couple of days.

A profound love between two people involves, after all, the power and chance of doing profound hurt. It would never have occurred to me before that night that I could hurt Estraven.

Now that the barriers were down, the limitation, in my terms, of our converse and understanding seemed intolerable to me. Quite soon, two or three nights later, I said to my companion as we finished our dinner—a special treat, sugared kadik-porridge, to celebrate a twenty-mile run—"Last spring, that night in the Corner Red Dwelling, you said you wished I'd tell you more about paraverbal speech."

"Yes, I did."

"Do you want to see if I can teach you how to speak it?"

He laughed. "You want to catch me lying."

"If you ever lied to me, it was long ago, and in another country."

He was an honest person, but rarely a direct one. That tickled him, and he said, "In another country I may tell you other lies. But I thought you were forbidden to teach your mind-science to . . . the natives, until we join the Ekumen."

"Not forbidden. It's not done. I'll do it, though, if you like. And if I can. I'm no Educer."

"There are special teachers of the skill?"

"Yes. Not on Alterra, where there's a high occurrence of natural sensitivity, and—they say—mothers mind-speak to their unborn babies. I don't know what the babies answer. But most of us have to be taught, as if it were a foreign language. Or rather as if it were our native language, but learned very late."

I think he understood my motive in offering to teach him the skill, and he wanted very much to learn it. We had a go at it. I recalled what I could of how I had been educed, at age twelve. I told him to clear his mind, let it be dark. This he did, no doubt, more promptly and thoroughly than I ever had done: he was an adept of the Handdara, after all. Then I mindspoke to him as clearly as I could. No result. We tried it again. Since one cannot bespeak until one has been bespoken, until the telepathic potentiality has been sensitized by one clear reception, I had to get through to him first. I tried for half an hour, till I felt hoarse of brain. He looked crestfallen. "I thought it would be easy for me," he confessed. We were both tired out, and called the attempt off for the night.

Our next efforts were no more successful. I tried sending to Estraven while he slept, recalling what my Educer had told me about the occurrence of "dream-messages" among pre-telepathic peoples, but it did not work.

"Perhaps my species lacks the capacity," he said. "We have enough rumors and hints to have made up a word for the power, but I don't know of any proven instances of telepathy among us."

"So it was with my people for thousands of years. A few natural Sensitives, not comprehending their gift, and lacking anyone to receive from or send to. All the rest latent, if that. You know I told you that except in the case of the born Sensitive, the capacity, though it has a physiological basis, is a psychological one, a product of culture, a side-effect of the use of the mind. Young children, and defectives, and members of unevolved or regressed societies, can't mindspeak. The mind must exist on a certain plane of complexity first. You can't build up amino acids out of hydrogen atoms; a good deal of complexifying has to take place first: the same situation. Abstract thought, varied social interaction, intricate cultural adjustments, esthetic and ethical perception, all of it has to reach a certain level before the connections can be made—before the potentiality can be touched at all."

"Perhaps we Gethenians haven't attained that level."

"You're far beyond it. But luck is involved. As in the creation of amino acids. . . . Or to take analogies on the cultural plane—only analogies, but they illuminate— the scientific method, for instance, the use of concrete, experimental techniques in science. There are peoples of the Ekumen who possess a high culture, a complex society, philosophies, arts, ethics, a high style and a great achievement in all those fields; and yet they have never learned to weigh a stone accurately. They can learn how, of course. Only for half a million years they never did. . . . There are peoples who have no higher mathematics at all, nothing beyond the simplest applied arithmetic. Every one of them is capable of understanding the calculus, but not one of them does or ever has. As a matter of fact, my own people, the Terrans, were ignorant until about three thousand years ago of the uses of zero." That made Estraven blink. "As for Gethen, what

I'm curious about is whether the rest of us may find ourselves to have the capacity for Foretelling—whether this too is a part of the evolution of the mind—if you'll teach us the techniques."

"You think it a useful accomplishment?"

"Accurate prophecy? Well, of course!—"

"You might have to come to believe that it's a useless one, in order to practice it."

"Your Handdara fascinates me, Harth, but now and then I wonder if it isn't simply paradox developed into a way of life. . . ."

We tried mindspeech again. I had never before sent repeatedly to a total non-receiver. The experience was disagreeable. I began to feel like an atheist praying. Presently Estraven yawned and said, "I am deaf, deaf as a rock. We'd better sleep." I assented. He turned out the light, murmuring his brief praise of darkness; we burrowed down into our bags, and within a minute or two he was sliding into sleep as a swimmer slides into dark water. I felt his sleep as if it were my own: the emphatic bond was there, and once more I bespoke him, sleepily, by his name—*"Therem!"*

He sat bolt upright, for his voice rang out above me in the blackness, loud. "Arek! is that you?"

"No: Genly Ai: I am bespeaking you."

His breath caught. Silence. He fumbled with the Chabe stove, turned up the light, stared at me with his dark eyes full of fear. "I dreamed," he said, "I thought I was at home—"

"You heard me mindspeak."

"You called me— It was my brother. It was his voice I heard. He's dead. You called me—you called me Therem? I. . . . This is more terrible than I had thought." He shook his head, as a man will do to shake off a nightmare, and then put his face in his hands.

"Harth, I'm very sorry—"

"No, call me by name. If you can speak inside my skull with a dead man's voice then you can call me by my name! Would *he* have called me 'Harth'? Oh, I see why there's no lying in this mindspeech. It is a terrible thing. . . . All right. All right, speak to me again."

"Wait."

"No. Go on."

With his fierce, frightened gaze on me I bespoke him: *"Therem, my friend, there's nothing to fear between us."*

He kept on staring at me, so that I thought he had not understood; but he had. "Ah, but there is," he said.

After a while, controlling himself, he said calmly, "You spoke in my language."

"Well, you don't know mine."

"You said there would be words, I know. . . . Yet I imagined it as—an understanding—"

"Empathy's another game, though not unconnected. It gave us the connection tonight. But in mindspeech proper, the speech centers of the brain are activated, as well as—"

"No, no, no. Tell me that later. Why do you speak in my brother's voice?" His voice was strained.

"That I can't answer. I don't know. Tell me about him."

"*Nusuth.* . . . My full brother, Arek Harth rem ir Estraven. He was a year older than I. He would have been Lord of Estre. We . . . I left home, you know, for his sake. He has been dead fourteen years."

We were both silent for some time. I could not know, or ask, what lay behind his words: it had cost him too much to say the little he had said.

I said at last, "Bespeak me, Therem. Call me by my name." I knew he could: the rapport was there, or as the experts have it, the phases were consonant, and of course he had as yet no idea of how to raise the barrier voluntarily. Had I been a Listener, I could have heard him think.

"No," he said. "Never. Not yet. . . ."

But no amount of shock, awe, terror could restrain that insatiable, outreaching mind for long. After he had cut out the light again I suddenly heard his stammer in my inward hearing—"*Genry*—" Even mindspeaking he never could say "l" properly.

I replied at once. In the dark he made an inarticulate sound of fear that had in it a slight edge of satisfaction. "No more, no more," he said aloud. After a while we got to sleep at last.

It never came easy to him. Not that he lacked the gift or could not develop the skill, but it disturbed him profoundly, and he could not take it for granted. He quickly learned to set up the barriers, but I'm not sure he felt he could count on them. Perhaps all of us were so, when the first Educers came back centuries ago from Rokanon's World teaching the "Last Art" to us. Perhaps a Gethenian, being singularly complete, feels telepathic speech as a violation of completeness, a breach of integrity hard for him to tolerate. Perhaps it was Estraven's own character, in which candor and reserve were both strong: every word he said rose out of a deeper silence. He heard my voice bespeaking him as a dead man's, his brother's voice. I did not know what, besides love and death, lay between him and that brother, but I knew that whenever I bespoke him something in him winced away as if I touched a wound. So that intimacy of mind established between us was a bond, indeed, but an obscure and austere one, not so much admitting further light (as I had expected it to) as showing the extent of the darkness.

And day after day we crept on eastward over the plain of ice. The midpoint in time of our journey as planned, the thirty-fifth day, Odorny Anner, found us far short of our halfway point in space. By the sledgemeter we had indeed traveled about four hundred miles, but probably only three-quarters of that was real forward gain, and we could estimate only very roughly how far still remained to go. We had spent days, miles, rations in our long struggle to get up onto the Ice. Estraven was not so worried as I by the hundreds of miles that still lay ahead of us. "The sledge is lighter," he said. "Towards the end it will be still lighter; and we can cut rations, if necessary. We have been eating very well, you know."

I thought he was being ironic, but I should have known better.

On the fortieth day and the two succeeding we were snowed in by a blizzard. During these long hours of lying blotto in the tent Estraven slept almost continuously, and ate nothing, though he drank orsh or sugar-water at mealtimes. He insisted that I eat, though only half-rations. "You have no experience in starvation," he said.

I was humiliated. "How much have you—Lord of a Domain, and prime minister—?"

"Genry, we practice privation until we're experts at it. I was taught how to starve as a child at home in Estre, and by the Handdarata in Rotherer Fastness. I got out of practice in Erhenrang, true enough, but I began making up for it in Mishnory. . . . Please do as I say, my friend; I know what I'm doing."

He did, and I did.

We went on for four more days of very bitter cold, never above −25°, and then came another blizzard whooping up in our faces from the east on a gale wind. Within two minutes of the first strong gusts the snow blew so thick that I could not see Estraven six feet away. I had turned my back on him and the sledge and the plastering, blinding, suffocating snow in order to get my breath, and when a minute later I turned around he was gone. The sledge was gone. Nothing was there. I took a few steps to where they had been and felt about. I shouted, and could not hear my own voice. I was deaf and alone in a universe filled solid with small stinging gray streaks. I panicked and began to blunder forward, mindcalling frantically, *"Therem!"*

Right under my hand, kneeling, he said, "Come on, give me a hand with the tent."

I did so, and never mentioned my minute of panic. No need to.

This blizzard lasted two days; there were five days lost, and there would be more. Nimmer and Anner are the months of the great storms.

"We're beginning to cut it rather fine, aren't we?" I said one night as I measured out our gichy-michy ration and put it to soak in hot water.

He looked at me. His firm, broad face showed weight-loss in deep shadows under the cheekbones, his eyes were sunken and his mouth sorely chapped and cracked. God knows what I looked like, when he looked like that. He smiled. "With luck we shall make it, and without luck we shall not."

It was what he had said from the start. With all my anxieties, my sense of taking a last desperate gamble, and so on, I had not been realistic enough to believe him. Even now I thought, Surely when we've worked so hard—

But the Ice did not know how hard we worked. Why should it? Proportion is kept.

"How is your luck running, Therem?" I said at last.

He did not smile at that. Nor did he answer. Only after a while he said, "I've been thinking about them all, down there." *Down there*, for us, had come to mean the south, the world below the plateau of ice, the region of earth, men, roads, cities, all of which had become hard to imagine as really existing. "You know that I sent word to the king concerning you, the day I left Mish-nory. I told him what Shusgis told me, that you were going to be sent to Pulefen Farm. At the time I wasn't clear as to my intent, but merely followed my impulse. I have thought the impulse through, since. Something like this may happen: the king will see a chance to play shifgrethor. Tibe will advise against it, but Argaven should be growing a little tired of Tibe by now, and may ignore his counsel. He will inquire. Where is the Envoy, the guest of Karhide?—Mishnory will lie. He died of horm-fever this autumn, most lamentable.—Then how does it happen that we are informed by our own Embassy that he's in Pulefen Farm?—He's not there, look for yourselves.—No, no, of course not, we accept the word of the Commensals of Orgoreyn. . . . But a few weeks after these exchanges, the Envoy appears in North Karhide, having escaped from Pulefen Farm. Consternation in Mishnory, indignation in Erhenrang. Loss of face for the Commensals, caught lying. You will be a treasure, a long-lost hearthbrother, to King Argaven, Genry. For a while. You must send for your Star Ship at once, at the first chance you get. Bring your people to Karhide and accomplish your mission, at once, before Argaven has had time to see the possible enemy in you, before Tibe or some other councillor frightens him once more, playing on his madness. If he makes the bargain with you, he will keep it. To break it would be to break his own shifgrethor. The Harge kings keep their promises. But you must act fast, and bring the Ship down soon."

"I will, if I receive the slightest sign of welcome."

"No: forgive my advising you, but you must not wait for welcome. You will be welcomed, I think. So will the Ship.

Karhide has been sorely humbled this past half-year. You will give Argaven the chance to turn the tables. I think he will take the chance."

"Very well. But you, meanwhile—"

"I am Estraven the Traitor. I have nothing whatever to do with you."

"At first."

"At first," he agreed.

"You'll be able to hide out, if there is danger at first?"

"Oh yes, certainly."

Our food was ready, and we fell to. Eating was so important and engrossing a business that we never talked anymore while we ate; the taboo was now in its complete, perhaps its original form, not a word said till the last crumb was gone. When it was, he said, "Well, I hope I've guessed well. You will . . . you do forgive . . ."

"You're giving me direct advice?" I said, for there were certain things I had finally come to understand. "Of course I do, Therem. Really, how can you doubt it? You know I have no shifgrethor to waive." That amused him, but he was still brooding.

"Why," he said at last, "why did you come alone— why were you sent alone? Everything, still, will depend upon that ship coming. Why was it made so difficult for you, and for us?"

"It's the Ekumen's custom, and there are reasons for it. Though in fact I begin to wonder if I've ever understood the reasons. I thought it was for your sake that I came alone, so obviously alone, so vulnerable, that I could in myself post no threat, change no balance: not an invasion, but a mere messenger-boy. But there's more to it than that. Alone, I cannot change your world. But I can be changed by it. Alone, I must listen, as well as speak. Alone, the relationship I finally make, if I make one, is not impersonal and not only political: it is individual, it is personal, it is both more and less than political. Not We and They; not I and It; but I and Thou. Not political, not pragmatic, but mystical. In a certain sense the Ekumen is not a body politic, but a body mystic. It considers beginnings to be extremely important. Beginnings, and means. Its doctrine is just the reverse of the doctrine that the end justifies the means. It proceeds, therefore, by subtle ways, and slow ones, and queer, risky ones; rather as evolution does, which is in certain senses its model. . . . So I was sent alone, for your sake? Or for my own? I don't know. Yes, it has made things difficult. But I might ask you as profitably why you've never seen fit to invent airborne vehicles? One small stolen airplane would have spared you and me a great deal of difficulty!"

"How would it ever occur to a sane man that he could fly?" Estraven said sternly. It was a fair response, on a world where no living thing is winged, and the very angels of the Yomesh Hierarchy of the Holy do not fly but only drift, wingless, down to earth like a soft snow falling, like the windborne seeds of that flowerless world.

Towards the middle of Nimmer, after much wind and bitter cold, we came into a quiet weather for many days. If there was storm it was far south of us, *down there*, and we inside the blizzard had only an all but windless overcast. At first the overcast was thin, so that the air was vaguely radiant with an even, sourceless sunlight reflected from both clouds and snow, from above and below. Overnight the weather thickened somewhat. All brightness was gone, leaving nothing. We stepped out of the tent onto nothing. Sledge and tent were there, Estraven stood beside me, but neither he nor I cast any shadow. There was dull light all around, everywhere. When we walked on the crisp snow no shadow showed the footprint. We left no track. Sledge, tent, himself, myself: nothing else at all. No sun, no sky, no horizon, no world. A whitish-gray void, in which we appeared to hang. The illusion was so complete that I had trouble keeping my balance. My inner ears were used to confirmation from my eyes as to how I stood; they got none; I might as well be blind. It was all right while we loaded up, but hauling, with nothing ahead, nothing to look at, nothing for the eye to touch, as it were, it was at first disagreeable and then exhausting. We were on skis, on a good surface of firn, without sastrugi, and solid—that was certain— for five or six thousand feet down. We should have been making good time. But we kept slowing down, groping our way across the totally unobstructed plain, and it took a strong effort of will to speed up to a normal pace. Every slight variation in the surface came as a jolt—as in climbing stairs, the unexpected stair or the expected but absent stair—for we could not see it ahead: there was no shadow to show it. We skied blind with our eyes open. Day after day was like this, and we began to shorten our hauls, for by midafternoon both of us would be sweating and shaking with strain and fatigue. I came to long for snow, for blizzard, for anything: but morning after morning we came out of the tent into the void, the white weather, what Estraven called the Unshadow.

One day about noon, Odorny Nimmer, the sixty-first day of the journey that bland blind nothingness about us began to flow and writhe. I thought my eyes were fooling me, as they had been doing often, and paid scant attention to the dim meaningless commotion of the air until, suddenly, I caught a glimpse of a small, wan, dead sun overhead. And looking down from the sun, straight ahead, I saw a huge black shape come hulking out of the void towards us. Black tentacles writhed upwards, groping out. I stopped dead in my tracks, slewing Estraven around on his skis, for we were both in harness hauling. "What is it?"

He stared at the dark monstrous forms hidden in the fog, and said at last, "The crags. . . . It must be Esherhoth Crags." And pulled on. We were miles from the things, which I had taken to be almost within arm's reach. As the white weather turned to a thick low mist and then cleared off, we saw them plainly before sunset: nunataks, great scored and ravaged pinnacles of rock jutting up out of the ice, no more of them showing than shows of an iceberg above the sea: cold drowned mountains, dead for eons.

They showed us to be somewhat north of our shortest course, if we could trust the ill-drawn map that was all we had. The next day we turned for the first time a little south of east.

19

HOMECOMING

In a dark windy weather we slogged along, trying to find encouragement in the sighting of Esherhoth Crags, the first thing not ice or snow or sky that we had seen for seven weeks. On the map they were marked as not far from the Shenshey Bogs to the south, and from Guthen Bay to the east. But it was not a trustworthy map of the Gobrin area. And we were getting very tired.

We were nearer the southern edge of the Gobrin Glacier than the map indicated, for we began to meet pressure-ice and crevasses on the second day of our turn southward. The Ice was not so upheaved and tormented as in the Fire-Hills region, but it was rotten. There were sunken pits acres across, probably lakes in summer; false floors of snow that might subside with a huge gasp all around you into the air-pocket a foot deep beneath;

areas all slit and pocked with little holes and crevasses; and, more and more often, there were big crevasses, old canyons in the Ice, some wide as mountain gorges and others only two or three feet across, but deep. On Odyrny Nimmer (by Estraven's journal, for I kept none) the sun shone clear with a strong north wind. As we ran the sledge across the snow-bridges over narrow crevasses we could look down to left or right into blue shafts and abysses, in which bits of ice dislodged by the runners fell with a vast, faint, delicate music, as if silver wires touched thin crystal planes, falling. I remember the racy, dreamy, light-headed pleasure of that morning's haul in the sunlight over the abysses. But the sky began to whiten, the air to grow thick; shadows faded, blue drained out of the sky and snow. We were not alert to the danger of white weather on such a surface. As the ice was heavily corrugated, I was pushing while Estraven pulled; I had my eyes on the sledge and was shoving away, mind on nothing but how best to shove, when all at once the bar was nearly wrenched out of my grip as the sledge shot forward in a sudden lunge. I held on by instinct and shouted "Hey!" to Estraven to slow him down, thinking he had speeded up on a smooth patch. But the sledge stopped dead, tilted nose-down, and Estraven was not there.

I almost let go the sledge-bar to go look for him. It was pure luck that I did not. I held on, while I stared stupidly about for him, and so I saw the lip of the crevasse, made visible by the shifting and dropping of another section of the broken snow-bridge. He had gone right

down feetfirst, and nothing kept the sledge from following him but my weight, which held the rear third of the
runners still on solid ice. It kept tipping a little farther
nose-downward, pulled by his weight as he hung in harness in the pit.

I brought my weight down on the rear-bar and pulled
and rocked and levered the sledge back away from the
edge of the crevasse. It did not come easy. But I threw
my weight hard on the bar and tugged until it began
grudgingly to move, and then slid abruptly right away
from the crevasse. Estraven had got his hands onto the
edge, and his weight now aided me. Scrambling, dragged
by the harness, he came up over the edge and collapsed
face- down on the ice.

I knelt by him trying to unbuckle his harness, alarmed
by the way he sprawled there, passive except for the great
gasping rise and fall of his chest. His lips were cyanotic,
one side of his face was bruised and scraped.

He sat up unsteadily and said in a whistling whisper,
"Blue—all blue—Towers in the depths—"

"What?"

"In the crevasse. All blue—full of light."

"Are you all right?"

He started rebuckling his harness.

"You go ahead—on the rope—with the stick," he
gasped. "Pick the route."

For hours one of us hauled while the other guided,
mincing along like a cat on eggshells, sounding every
step in advance with the stick. In the white weather one
could not see a crevasse until one could look down into

it—a little late, for the edges overhung, and were not always solid. Every footfall was a surprise, a drop or a jolt. No shadows. An even, white, soundless sphere: we moved along inside a huge frosted-glass ball. There was nothing inside the ball, and nothing was outside it. But there were cracks in the glass. Probe and step, probe and step. Probe for the invisible cracks through which one might fall out of the white glass ball, and fall, and fall, and fall. . . . An unrelaxable tension little by little took hold of all my muscles. It became exceedingly difficult to take even one more step.

"What's up, Genry?"

I stood there in the middle of nothing. Tears came out and froze my eyelids together. I said, "I'm afraid of falling."

"But you're on the rope," he said. Then, coming up and seeing that there was no crevasse anywhere visible, he saw what was up and said, "Pitch camp."

"It's not time yet, we ought to go on."

He was already unlashing the tent.

Later on, after we had eaten, he said, "It was time to stop. I don't think we can go this way. The Ice seems to drop off slowly, and will be rotten and crevassed all the way. If we could see, we could make it: but not in unshadow."

"But then how do we get down onto the Shenshey Bogs?"

"Well, if we keep east again instead of trending south, we might be on sound ice clear to Guthen Bay. I saw the Ice once from a boat on the Bay in summer. It comes up against the Red Hills, and feeds down in ice-rivers to the Bay. If we came down one of those glaciers we could run due south on the sea-ice to Karhide, and so enter at the coast rather than the border, which might be better. It will add some miles to our way, though—something between twenty and fifty, I should think. What's your opinion, Genry?"

"My opinion is that I can't go twenty more feet so long as the white weather lasts."

"But if we get out of the crevassed area . . ."

"Oh, if we get out of the crevasses I'll be fine. And if the sun ever comes out again, you get on the sledge and I'll give you a free ride to Karhide." That was typical of our attempts at humor, at this stage of the journey; they were always very stupid, but sometimes they made the other fellow smile. "There's nothing wrong with me," I went on, "except acute chronic fear."

"Fear's very useful. Like darkness; like shadows." Estraven's smile was an ugly split in a peeling, cracked brown mask, thatched with black fur and set with two flecks of black rock. "It's queer that daylight's not enough. We need the shadows, in order to walk."

"Give me your notebook a moment."

He had just noted down our day's journey and done some calculation of mileage and rations. He pushed the little tablet and carbon-pencil around the Chabe stove to me. On the blank leaf glued to the inner back cover I drew the double curve within the circle, and blacked the yin half of the symbol, then pushed it back to my companion. "Do you know that sign?"

He looked at it a long time with a strange look, but he said, "No."

"It's found on Earth, and on Hain-Davenant, and on Chiffewar. It is yin and yang. *Light is the left hand of darkness* . . . how did it go? Light, dark. Fear, courage. Cold, warmth. Female, male. It is yourself, Therem. Both and one. A shadow on snow."

The next day we trudged northeast through the white absence of everything until there were no longer any cracks in the floor of nothing: a day's haul. We were on ⅔ ration, hoping to keep the longer route from running us right out of food. It seemed to me that it would not matter much if it did, as the difference between little and nothing seemed a rather fine one. Estraven, however, was on the track of his luck, following what appeared to be hunch or intuition, but may have been applied experience and reasoning. We went east for four days, four of the longest hauls we had made, eighteen to twenty miles a day, and then the quiet zero weather broke and went to pieces, turning into a whirl, whirl, whirl of tiny snow-particles ahead, behind, to the side, in the eyes, a storm beginning as the light died. We lay in the tent for three days while the blizzard yelled at us, a three-day-long, wordless, hateful yell from the unbreathing lungs.

"It'll drive me to screaming back," I said to Estraven in mindspeech, and he, with the hesitant formality that marked his rapport: *"No use. It will not listen."*

We slept hour after hour, ate a little, tended our frostbites, inflammations, and bruises, mindspoke, slept again. The three-day shriek died down into a gabbling, then a sobbing, then a silence. Day broke. Through the opened door-valve the sky's brightness shone. It lightened the heart, though we were too rundown to be able to show our relief in alacrity or zest of movement. We broke camp—it took nearly two hours, for we crept about like two old men—and set off. The way was downhill, an unmistakable slight grade; the crust was perfect for skis. The sun shone. The thermometer at midmorning showed −10°. We seemed to get strength from going, and we went fast and easy. We went that day till the stars came out.

For dinner Estraven served out full rations. At that rate, we had enough for only seven days more.

"The wheel turns," he said with serenity. "To make a good run, we've got to eat."

"Eat, drink, and be merry," said I. The food had got me high. I laughed inordinately at my own words. "All one—eating-drinking-merrymaking. Can't have merry without eats, can you?" This seemed to me a mystery quite on a par with that of the yin-yang circle, but it did not last. Something in Estraven's expression dispelled it. Then I felt like crying, but refrained. Estraven was not as strong as I was, and it would not be fair, it might make him cry too. He was already asleep: he had fallen asleep sitting up, his bowl on his lap. It was not like him to be so unmethodical. But it was not a bad idea, sleep.

We woke rather late next morning, had a double

breakfast, and then got in harness and pulled our light sledge right off the edge of the world.

Below the world's edge, which was a steep rubbly slope of white and red in a pallid noon light, lay the frozen sea: the Bay of Guthen, frozen from shore to shore and from Karhide clear to the North Pole.

To get down onto the sea-ice through the broken edges and shelves and trenches of the Ice jammed up amongst the Red Hills took that afternoon and the next day. On that second day we abandoned our sledge. We made up backpacks; with the tent as the main bulk of one and the bags of the other, and our food equally distributed, we had less than twenty-five pounds apiece to carry; I added the Chabe stove to my pack and still had under thirty. It was good to be released from forever pulling and pushing and hauling and prying that sledge, and I said so to Estraven as we went on. He glanced back at the sledge, a bit of refuse in the vast torment of ice and reddish rock. "It did well," he said. His loyalty extended without disproportion to things, the patient, obstinate, reliable things that we use and get used to, the things we live by. He missed the sledge.

That evening, the seventy-fifth of our journey, our fifty-first day on the plateau, Harhahad Anner, we came down off the Gobrin Ice onto the sea-ice of Guthen Bay. Again we traveled long and late, till dark. The air was very cold, but clear and still, and the clean ice-surface, with no sledge to pull, invited our skis. When we camped that night it was strange to think, lying down, that under us there was no longer a mile of ice, but a few feet of it, and then salt water. But we did not spend much time thinking. We ate, and slept.

At dawn, again a clear day though terribly cold, below −40° at daybreak, we could look southward and see the coastline, bulged out here and there with protruding tongues of glacier, fall away southward almost in a straight line. We followed it close inshore at first. A north wind helped us along till we skied up abreast a valley-mouth between two high orange hills; out of that gorge howled a gale that knocked us both off our feet. We scuttled farther east, out on the level sea-plain, where we could at least stand up and keep going. "The Gobrin Ice has spewed us out of its mouth," I said.

The next day, the eastward curve of the coastline was plain, straight ahead of us. To our right was Orgoreyn, but that blue curve ahead was Karhide.

On that day we used up the last grains of orsh, and the last few ounces of kadik-germ; we had left now two pounds apiece of gichy-michy, and six ounces of sugar.

I cannot describe these last days of our journey very well. I find, because I cannot really remember them. Hunger can heighten perception, but not when combined with extreme fatigue; I suppose all my senses were very much deadened. I remember having hunger-cramps, but I don't remember suffering from them. I had, if anything, a vague feeling all the time of liberation, of having got beyond something, of joy; also of being terribly sleepy. We reached land on the twelfth, Posthe Amer, and clambered over a frozen beach and into the rocky, snowy desolation of the Guthen Coast.

We were in Karhide. We had achieved our goal. It came near being an empty achievement, for our packs were empty. We had a feast of hot water to celebrate our arrival. The next morning we got up and set off to find a road, a settlement. It is a desolate region, and we had no map of it. What roads there might be were under five or ten feet of snow, and we may have crossed several without knowing it. There was no sign of cultivation. We strayed south and west that day, and the next, and on the evening of the next, seeing a light shine on a distant hillside through the dusk and thin falling snow, neither of us said anything for some time. We stood and stared. Finally my companion croaked, "Is that a light?"

It was long after dark when we came shambling into a Karhidish village, one street between high-roofed dark houses, the snow packed and banked up to their winter-doors. We stopped at the hot-shop, through the narrow shutters of which flowed, in cracks and rays and arrows, the yellow light we had seen across the hills of winter. We opened the door and went in.

It was Odsordny Anner, the eighty-first day of our journey; we were eleven days over Estraven's proposed schedule. He had estimated our food supply exactly: seventy-eight days' worth at the outside. We had come 840 miles, by the sledge-meter plus a guess for the last few days. Many of those miles had been wasted in back-tracking, and if we had really had eight hundred miles to cover we should never have made it; when we got a good map we figured that the distance between Pulefen Farm and this village was less than 730 miles. All those miles and days had been across a houseless, speechless desolation: rock, ice, sky, and silence: nothing else, for eighty-one days, except each other.

We entered into a big steaming-hot bright-lit room full of food and the smells of food, and people and the voices of people. I caught hold of Estraven's shoulder. Strange faces turned to us, strange eyes. I had forgotten there was anyone alive who did not look like Estraven. I was terrified.

In fact it was rather a small room, and the crowd of strangers in it was seven or eight people, all of whom were certainly as taken aback as I was for a while. Nobody comes to Kurkurast Domain in midwinter from the north at night. They stared, and peered, and all the voices had fallen silent.

Estraven spoke, a barely audible whisper. "We ask the hospitality of the Domain."

Noise, buzz, confusion, alarm, welcome.

"We came over the Gobrin Ice."

More noise, more voices, questions; they crowded in on us.

"Will you look to my friend?"

I thought I had said it, but Estraven had. Somebody was making me sit down. They brought us food; they looked after us, took us in, welcomed us home.

Benighted, contentious, passionate, ignorant souls, countryfolk of a poor land, their generosity gave a noble ending to that hard journey. They gave with both hands. No doling out, no counting up. And so Estraven received what they gave us, as a lord among lords or a beggar among beggars, a man among his own people.

To those fishermen-villagers who live on the edge of the edge, on the extreme habitable limit of a barely habitable continent, honesty is as essential as food. They must play fair with one another; there's not enough to cheat with. Estraven knew this, and when after a day or two they got around to asking, discreetly and indirectly, with due regard to shifgrethor, why we had chosen to spend a winter rambling on the Gobrin Ice, he replied at once, "Silence is not what I should choose, yet it suits me better than a lie."

"It's well known that honorable men come to be outlawed, yet their shadow does not shrink," said the hot-shop cook, who ranked next to the village chief in consequence, and whose shop was a sort of living-room for the whole Domain in winter.

"One person may be outlawed in Karhide, another in Orgoreyn," said Estraven.

"True; and one by his clan, another by the king in Erhenrang."

"The king shortens no man's shadow, though he may try," Estraven remarked, and the cook looked satisfied. If Estraven's own clan had cast him out he would be a suspect character, but the king's strictures were unimportant. As for me, evidently a foreigner and so the one outlawed by Orgoreyn, that was if anything to my credit.

We never told our names to our hosts in Kurkurast. Estraven was very reluctant to use a false name, and our true ones could not be avowed. It was, after all, a crime to speak to Estraven, let alone to feed and clothe and house him, as they did. Even a remote village of the Guthen Coast has radio, and they could not have pleaded ignorance of the Order of Exile; only real ignorance of their guest's identity might give them some excuse. Their vulnerability weighed on Estraven's mind, before I had even thought of it. On our third night there he came into my room to discuss our next move.

A Karhidish village is like an ancient castle of Earth in having few or no separate, private dwellings. Yet in the high, rambling old buildings of the Hearth, the Commerce, the Co-Domain (there was no Lord of Kurkurast) and the Outer-House, each of the five hundred villagers could have privacy, even seclusion, in rooms off those ancient corridors with walls three feet thick. We had been given a room apiece, on the top floor of the Hearth. I was sitting in mine beside the fire, a small, hot, heavy-scented fire of peat from the Shenshey Bogs, when Estraven came in. He said, "We must soon be going on from here, Genry."

I remember him standing there in the shadows of the firelit room barefoot and wearing nothing but the loose fur breeches the chief had given him. In the privacy and what they consider the warmth of their houses Karhiders often go half-clothed or naked. On our journey Estraven had lost all the smooth, compact solidity that marks the Gethenian physique; he was gaunt and scarred, and his face was burned by cold almost as by fire. He was a dark, hard, and yet elusive figure in the quick, restless light.

"Where to?"

"South and west, I think. Towards the border. Our first job is to find you a radio transmitter strong enough to reach your ship. After that, I must find a hiding place, or else go back into Orgoreyn for a while, to avoid bringing punishment on those who help us here."

"How will you get back into Orgoreyn?"

"As I did before—cross the border. The Orgota have nothing against me."

"Where will we find a transmitter?"

"No nearer than Sassinoth."

I winced. He grinned.

"Nothing closer?"

"A hundred and fifty miles or so; we've come farther over worse ground. There are roads all the way; people will take us in; we may get a lift on a power-sledge."

I assented, but I was depressed by the prospect of still another stage of our winter-journey, and this one not towards haven but back to that damned border where Estraven might go back into exile, leaving me alone.

I brooded over it and finally said, "There'll be one condition that Karhide must fulfill before it can join the Ekumen. Argaven must revoke your banishment."

He said nothing, but stood gazing at the fire.

"I mean it," I insisted. "First things first."

"I thank you, Genry," he said. His voice, when he spoke very softly as now, did have much the timbre of a woman's voice, husky and unresonant. He looked at me, gently, not smiling. "But I haven't expected to see my home again for a long time now. I've been in exile for twenty years, you know. This is not so much different, this banishment. I'll look after myself; and you look after yourself, and your Ekumen. That you must do alone. But all this is said too soon. Tell your ship to come down! When that's done, then I'll think beyond it."

We stayed two more days in Kurkurast, getting well fed and rested, waiting for a road-packer that was due in from the south and would give us a lift when it went back again. Our hosts got Estraven to tell them the whole tale of our crossing of the Ice. He told it as only a person of an oral-literature tradition can tell a story, so that it became a saga, full of traditional locutions and even episodes, yet exact and vivid, from the sulphurous fire and dark of the pass between Drumner and Dremegole to the screaming gusts from mountain-gaps that swept the Bay of Guthen; with comic interludes, such as his fall into the crevasse, and mystical ones, when he spoke of the sounds and silences of the Ice, of the shadowless weather, of the night's darkness. I listened as fascinated as all the rest, my gaze on my friend's dark face.

We left Kurkurast riding elbow-jammed in the cab of a road-packer, one of the big powered vehicles that rolls and packs down the snow on Karhidish roads, the main means of keeping roads open in winter, since to try to keep them plowed clear would take half the kingdom's time and money, and all traffic is on runners in the winter anyway. The packer ground along at two miles an hour, and brought us into the next village south of Kurkurast long after nightfall. There, as always, we were welcomed, fed, and housed for the night; the next day we went on afoot. We were now landward of the coastal hills that take the brunt of the north wind off the Bay of Guthen, in a more heavily settled region, and so went not from camp to camp but from Hearth to Hearth. A couple of times we did get a lift on a power-sledge, once for thirty miles. The roads, despite frequent heavy snowfall, were hard-packed and well-marked. There was always food in our packs, put there by the last night's hosts; there was always a roof and a fire at the end of the day's going.

Yet those eight or nine days of easy hiking and skiing through a hospitable land were the hardest and dreariest part of all our journey, worse than the ascent of the glacier, worse than the last days of hunger. The saga was over; it belonged to the Ice. We were very tired. We were going the wrong direction. There was no more joy in us.

"Sometimes you must go against the wheel's turn," Estraven said. He was as steady as ever, but in his walk, his voice, his bearing, vigor had been replaced by patience, and certainty by stubborn resolve. He was very silent, nor would he mindspeak with me much.

We came to Sassinoth. A town of several thousand, perched up on hills above the frozen Ey: roofs white, walls gray, hills spotted black with forest and rock outcropping, fields and river white; across the river the disputed Sinoth Valley, all white. . . .

We came there all but empty-handed. Most of what remained of our travel-equipment we had given away to various kindly hosts, and by now we had nothing but the Chabe stove, our skis, and the clothes we wore. Thus unburdened we made our way, asking directions a couple of times, not into the town but to an outlying farm. It was a meager place, not part of a Domain but a single-farm under the Sinoth Valley Administration. When Estraven was a young secretary in that Administration he had been a friend of the owner, and in fact had bought this farm for him, a year or two ago, when he was helping people resettle east of the Ey in hopes of obviating dispute over the ownership of the Sinoth Valley. The farmer himself opened his door to us, a stocky soft-spoken man of about Estraven's age. His name was Thessicher.

Estraven had come through this region with hood pulled up and forward to hide his face. He feared recognition, here. He hardly needed to; it took a keen eye to see Harth rem ir Estraven in the thin weatherworn tramp. Thessicher kept staring at him covertly, unable to believe that he was who he said he was.

Thessicher took us in, and his hospitality was up to standard though his means were small. But he was uncomfortable with us, he would rather not have had us. It was understandable; he risked the confiscation of his property by sheltering us. Since he owed that property to Estraven, and might by now have been as destitute as we if Estraven had not provided for him, it seemed not unjust to ask him to run some risk in return. My friend, however, asked his help not in repayment but as a matter of friendship, counting not on Thessicher's obligation but on his affection. And indeed Thessicher thawed after his first alarm was past, and with Karhidish volatility became demonstrative and nostalgic, recalling old days and old acquaintances with Estraven beside the fire half the night. When Estraven asked him if he had any idea as to a hiding place, some deserted or isolated farm where a banished man might lie low for a month or two in hopes of a revocation of his exile, Thessicher at once said, "Stay with me."

Estraven's eyes lit up at that, but he demurred; and agreeing that he might not be safe so near Sassinoth, Thessicher promised to find him a hideout. It wouldn't be hard, he said, if Estraven would take a false name and hire out as a cook or farmhand, which would not be pleasant, perhaps, but certainly better than returning to Orgoreyn. "What the devil would you do in Orgoreyn? What would you live on, eh?"

"On the Commensality," said my friend, with a trace of his otter's smile. "They provide all Units with jobs, you know. No trouble. But I'd rather be in Karhide . . . if you really think it could be managed. . . ."

We had kept the Chabe stove, the only thing of value left to us. It served us, one way or another, right to the end of our journey. The morning after our arrival at Thessicher's farm, I took the stove and skied into town. Estraven of course did not come with me, but he had explained to me what to do, and it all went well. I sold the stove at the Town Commerce, then took the solid sum of money it had fetched up the hill to the little College of the Trades, where the radio station was housed, and bought ten minutes of "private transmission to private reception." All stations set aside a daily period of time for such shortwave transmissions; as most of them are sent by merchants to their overseas agents or customers in the Archipelago, Sith, or Perunter, the cost is rather high, but not unreasonable. Less, anyway, than the cost of a secondhand Chabe stove. My ten minutes were to be early in Third Hour, late afternoon. I did not want to be skiing back and forth from Thessicher's farm all day long, so I hung around Sassinoth, and bought a large, good, cheap lunch at one of the hot-shops. No doubt that Karhidish cooking was better than Orgota. As I ate, I remembered Estraven's comment on that, when I had asked him if he hated Orgoreyn; I remembered his voice last night, saying with all mildness, "I'd rather be in Karhide. . . ." And I wondered, not for the first time, what patriotism is, what the love of country truly consists of, how that yearning loyalty that had shaken my friend's voice arises, and how so real a love can become, too often, so foolish and vile a bigotry. Where does it go wrong?

After lunch I wandered about Sassinoth. The business of the town, the shops and markets and streets, lively despite snow-flurries and zero temperature, seemed like a play, unreal, bewildering. I had not yet come altogether out of the solitude of the Ice. I was uneasy among strangers, and constantly missed Estraven's presence beside me.

I climbed the steep snow-packed street in dusk to the College and was admitted and shown how to operate the public-use transmitter. At the time appointed I sent the *wake* signal to the relay satellite, which was in stationary orbit about 300 miles over South Karhide. It was there as insurance for just a situation as this, when my ansible was gone so that I could not ask Ollul to signal the ship, and I had not time or equipment to make direct contact with the ship in solar orbit. The Sassinoth transmitter was more than adequate, but as the satellite was not equipped to respond except by sending to the ship, there was nothing to do but signal it and let it go at that. I could not know if the message had been received and relayed to the ship. I did not know if I had done right to send it. I had come to accept such uncertainties with a quiet heart.

It had come on to snow hard, and I had to spend the night in town, not knowing the roads well enough to want to set off on them in the snow and dark. Having a bit of money still, I inquired for an inn, at which they insisted that I put up at the College; I had dinner with a lot of cheerful students, and slept in one of the dormitories. I fell asleep with a pleasant sense of security, an assurance of Karhide's extraordinary and unfailing kindness to the stranger. I had landed in the right country in the first place, and now I was back. So I fell asleep; but I woke up very early and set off for Thessicher's farm before breakfast, having spent an uneasy night full of dreams and wakenings.

The rising sun, small and cold in a bright sky, sent shadows westward from every break and hummock in the snow. The road lay all streaked with dark and bright. No one moved in all the snowy fields, but away off on the road a small figure came towards me with the flying, gliding gait of the skier. Long before I could see the face I knew it for Estraven.

"What's up, Therem?"

"I've got to get to the border," he said, not even stopping as we met. He was already out of breath. I turned and we both went west, I hard put to keep up with him. Where the road turned to enter Sassinoth he left it, skiing out across the unfenced fields. We crossed the frozen Ey a mile or so north of town. The banks were steep, and at the end of the climb we both had to stop and rest. We were not in condition for this kind of race.

"What happened? Thessicher—?"

"Yes. Heard him on his wireless set. At daybreak." Estraven's chest rose and fell in gasps as it had when he lay on the ice beside the blue crevasse. "Tibe must have a price on my head."

"The damned ungrateful traitor!" I said stammering, not meaning Tibe but Thessicher, whose betrayal was of a friend.

"He is that," said Estraven, "but I asked too much of him, strained a small spirit too far. Listen, Genry. Go back to Sassinoth."

"I'll at least see you over the border, Therem."

"There may be Orgota guards there."

"I'll stay on this side. For God's sake—"

He smiled. Still breathing very hard, he got up and went on, and I went with him.

We skied through small frosty woods and over the hillocks and fields of the disputed valley. There was no hiding, no skulking. A sunlit sky, a white world, and we two strokes of shadow on it, fleeing. Uneven ground hid the border from us till we were less than an eighth of

a mile from it; then we suddenly saw it plain, marked
with a fence, only a couple of feet of the poles showing
above the snow, the pole-tops painted red. There were
no guards to be seen on the Orgota side. On the near
side there were ski-tracks, and, southward, several small
figures moving.

"There are guards on this side. You'll have to wait till
dark, Therem."

"Tibe's Inspectors," he gasped bitterly, and swung
aside.

We shot back over the little rise we had just topped,
and took the nearest cover. There we spent the whole
long day, in a dell among the thick-growing hemmen-
trees, their reddish boughs bent low around us by loads of
snow. We debated many plans of moving north or south
along the border to get out of this particularly troubled
zone, of trying to get up into the hills east of Sassinoth,
even of going back up north into the empty country, but
each plan had to be vetoed. Estraven's presence had been
betrayed, and we could not travel in Karhide openly as
we had been doing. Nor could we travel secretly for any
distance at all: we had no tent, no food, and not much
strength. There was nothing for it but the straight dash
over the border, no way was open but one.

We huddled in the dark hollow under dark trees, in the
snow. We lay right together for warmth. Around midday
Estraven dozed off for a while, but I was too hungry and
too cold for sleep; I lay there beside my friend in a sort of
stupor, trying to remember the words he had quoted to
me once: *Two are one, life and death, lying together. . . .* It

was a little like being inside the tent up on the Ice, but without shelter, without food, without rest: nothing left but our companionship, and that soon to end.

The sky hazed over during the afternoon, and the temperature began to drop. Even in the windless hollow it became too cold to sit motionless. We had to move about, and still around sunset I was taken by fits of shuddering like those I had experienced in the prison-truck crossing Orgoreyn. The darkness seemed to take forever coming on. In the late blue twilight we left the dell and went creeping behind trees and bushes over the hill till we could make out the line of the border-fence, a few dim dots along the pallid snow. No lights, nothing moving, no sound. Away off in the southwest shone the yellow glimmer of a small town, some tiny Commensal Village of Orgoreyn, where Estraven could go with his unacceptable identification papers and be assured at least of a night's lodging in the Commensal Jail or perhaps on the nearest Commensal Voluntary Farm. All at once—there, at that last moment, no sooner—I realized what my selfishness and Estraven's silence had kept from me, where he was going and what he was getting into. I said, "Therem—wait—"

But he was off, downhill: a magnificent fast skier, and this time not holding back for me. He shot away on a long quick curving descent through the shadows over the snow. He ran from me, and straight into the guns of the border-guards. I think they shouted warnings or orders to halt, and a light sprang up somewhere, but I am not sure; in any case he did not stop, but flashed on towards the fence, and they shot him down before he reached it. They did not use the sonic stunners but the foray gun, the ancient weapon that fires a set of metal fragments in a burst. They shot to kill him. He was dying when I got to him, sprawled and twisted away from his skis that stuck up out of the snow, his chest half shot away. I took his head in my arms and spoke to him, but he never answered me; only in a way he answered my love for him, crying out through the silent wreck and tumult of his mind as consciousness lapsed, in the unspoken tongue, once, clearly, *"Arek!"* Then no more. I held him, crouching there in the snow, while he died. They let me do that. Then they made me get up, and took me off one way and him another, I going to prison and he into the dark.

20

A FOOL'S ERRAND

Somewhere in the notes Estraven wrote during our trek across the Gobrin Ice he wonders why his companion is ashamed to cry. I could have told him even then that it was not shame so much as fear. Now I went on through the Sinoth Valley, through the evening of his death, into the cold country that lies beyond fear. There I found you can weep all you like, but there's no good in it.

I was taken back to Sassinoth and imprisoned, because I had been in the company of an outlaw, and probably because they did not know what else to do with me. From the start, even before official orders came from Erhenrang, they treated me well. My Karhidish jail was a furnished room in the Tower of the Lords-Elect in Sassinoth; I had a fireplace, a radio, and five large meals daily. It was not comfortable. The bed was hard, the covers thin, the floor bare, the air cold—like any room in Karhide. But they sent in a physician, in whose hands and voice was a more enduring, a more profitable comfort than any I ever found in Orgoreyn. After he came, I think the door was left unlocked. I recall it standing open, and myself wishing it were shut, because of the chill draft of air from the hall. But I had not the strength, the courage, to get off my bed and shut my prison door.

The physician, a grave, maternal young fellow, told me with an air of peaceable certainty, "You have been underfed and overtaxed for five or six months. You have spent yourself. There's nothing more to spend. Lie down, rest. Lie down like the rivers frozen in the valleys in winter. Lie still. Wait."

But when I slept I was always in the truck, huddling together with the others, all of us stinking, shivering, naked, squeezed together for warmth, all but one. One lay by himself against the barred door, the cold one, with a mouth full of clotted blood. He was the traitor. He had gone on by himself, deserting us, deserting me. I would wake up full of rage, a feeble shaky rage that turned into feeble tears.

I must have been rather ill, for I remember some of the effects of high fever, and the physician stayed with me one night or perhaps more. I can't recall those nights, but do remember saying to him, and hearing the querulous keening note in my own voice, "He could have stopped. He saw the guards. He ran right into the guns."

The young physician said nothing for a while. "You're not saying that he killed himself?"

"Perhaps—"

"That's a bitter thing to say of a friend. And I will not believe it of Harth rem ir Estraven."

I had not had in mind when I spoke the contemptibility of suicide to these people. It is not to them, as to us, an option. It is the abdication from option, the act of betrayal itself. To a Karhider reading our canons, the crime of Judas lies not in his betrayal of Christ but in the act that, sealing despair, denies the chance of forgiveness, change, life: his suicide.

"Then you don't call him Estraven the Traitor?"

"Nor ever did. There are many who never heeded the accusations against him, Mr. Ai."

But I was unable to see any solace in that, and only cried out in the same torment, "Then why did they shoot him? Why is he dead?"

To this he made no answer, there being none.

I was never formally interrogated. They asked how I had got out of Pulefen Farm and into Karhide, and they asked the destination and intent of the code message I had sent on their radio. I told them. That information went straight to Erhenrang, to the king. The matter of the ship was apparently held secret, but the news of my escape from an Orgota prison, my journey over the Ice in winter, my presence in Sassinoth, was freely reported and discussed. Estraven's part in this was not mentioned on the radio, nor was his death. Yet it was known. Secrecy in Karhide is to an extraordinary extent a matter of discretion, of an agreed, understood silence—an omission of questions, yet not an omission of answers. The Bulletins spoke only of the Envoy Mr. Ai, but everybody knew that it was Harth rem ir Estraven who had stolen me from the hands of the Orgota and come with me over the Ice to Karhide to give the staring lie to the Commensals' tale of my sudden death from horm-fever in Mishnory last autumn. . . . Estraven had predicted the effects of my return fairly accurately; he had erred mainly in underestimating them. Because of the alien who lay ill, not acting, not caring, in a room in Sassinoth, two governments fell within ten days.

To say that an Orgota government fell means, of course, only that one group of Commensals replaced another group of Commensals in the controlling offices of the Thirty-Three. Some shadows got shorter and some longer, as they say in Karhide. The Sarf faction that had sent me off to Pulefen hung on, despite the not unprecedented embarrassment of being caught lying, until Argaven's public announcement of the imminent arrival of the Star Ship in Karhide. That day Obsle's party, the Open Trade faction, took over the presiding offices of the Thirty-Three. So I was of some service to them after all.

In Karhide the fall of a government is most likely to mean the disgrace and replacement of a prime minister along with a reshuffling of the kyorremy; although assassination, abdication, and insurrection are all frequent alternatives. Tibe made no effort to hang on. My current value in the game of international shifgrethor, plus my vindication (by implication) of Estraven, gave me as it were a prestige-weight so clearly surpassing his, that he resigned, as I later learned, even before the Erhenrang Government knew that I had radioed to my ship. He acted on the tip-off from Thessicher, waited only until he got word of Estraven's death, and then resigned. He had his defeat and his revenge for it all in one.

Once Argaven was fully informed, he sent me a summons, a request to come at once to Erhenrang, and along with it a liberal allowance for expenses. The City of Sassinoth with equal liberality sent their young physician along with me, for I was not in very good shape yet. We made the trip in power-sledges. I remember only parts of it; it was smooth and unhurried, with long halts waiting for packers to clear the road, and long nights spent at inns. It could only have taken two or three days, but it seemed a long trip and I can't recall much of it till the moment when we came through the Northern Gates of Erhenrang into the deep streets full of snow and shadow.

I felt then that my heart hardened somewhat and my mind cleared. I had been all in pieces, disintegrated. Now, though tired from the easy journey, I found some strength left whole in me. Strength of habit, most likely, for here at last was a place I knew, a city I had lived in, worked in, for over a year. I knew the streets, the towers, the somber courts and ways and façades of the Palace. I knew my job here. Therefore for the first time it came plainly to me that, my friend being dead, I must accomplish the thing he died for. I must set the keystone in the arch.

At the Palace gates the order was for me to proceed to one of the guest-houses within the Palace walls. It was the Round-Tower Dwelling, which signaled a high degree of shifgrethor in the court: not so much the king's favor, as his recognition of a status already high. Ambassadors from friendly powers were usually lodged there. It was a good sign. To get to it, however, we had to pass by the Corner Red Dwelling, and I looked in the narrow arched gateway at the bare tree over the pool, gray with ice, and the house that still stood empty.

At the door of the Round-Tower I was met by a person in white hieb and crimson shirt, with a silver chain over his shoulders: Faxe, the Foreteller of Otherhord Fastness. At sight of his kind and handsome face, the first known face that I had seen for many days, a rush of relief softened my mood of strained resolution. When Faxe took my hands in the rare Karhidish greeting and welcomed me as his friend, I could make some response to his warmth.

He had been sent to the kyorremy from his district, South Rer, early in the autumn. Election of council-members from the Indwellers of Handdara Fastnesses is not uncommon; it is however not common for a Weaver to accept office, and I believe Faxe would have refused if he had not been much concerned by Tibe's government and the direction in which it was leading the country. So he had taken off the Weaver's gold chain and put on the councillor's silver one; and he had not spent long in making his mark, for he had been since Thern a member of the Hes-kyorremy or Inner Council, which serves as counterweight to the prime minister, and it was the king who had named him to that position.

He was perhaps on his way up to the eminence from which Estraven, less than a year ago, had fallen. Political careers in Karhide are abrupt, precipitous.

In the Round-Tower, a cold pompous little house, Faxe and I talked at some length before I had to see anyone else or make any formal statement or appearance. He asked with his clear gaze on me, "There is a ship coming, then, coming down to earth: a larger ship than the one you came to Horden Island on, three years ago. Is that right?"

"Yes. That is, I sent a message that should prepare it to come."

"When will it come?"

When I realized that I did not even know what day of the month it was, I began to realize how badly off I had in fact been, lately. I had to count back to the day before Estraven's death. When I found that the ship, if it had been at minimum distance, would already be in planetary orbit awaiting some word from me, I had another shock.

"I must communicate with the ship. They'll want instructions. Where does the king want them to come down? It should be an uninhabited area, fairly large. I must get to a transmitter—"

Everything was arranged expeditiously, with ease. The endless convolutions and frustrations of my previous dealings with the Erhenrang Government were melted away like an ice-pack in a flooding river. The wheel turned. . . . Next day I was to have an audience with the king.

It had taken Estraven six months to arrange my first

audience. It had taken the rest of his life to arrange this second one.

I was too tired to be apprehensive, this time, and there were things on my mind that outweighed self-consciousness. I went down the long red hall under the dusty banners and stood before the dais with its three great hearths, where three bright fires cracked and sparkled. The king sat by the central fireplace, hunched up on a carven stool by the table.

"Sit down, Mr. Ai."

I sat down across the hearth from Argaven, and saw his face in the light of the flames. He looked unwell, and old. He looked like a woman who has lost her baby, like a man who has lost his son.

"Well, Mr. Ai, so your ship's going to land."

"It will land in Athten Fen, as you requested, sir. They should bring it down this evening at the beginning of Third Hour."

"What if they miss the place? Will they burn everything up?"

"They'll follow a radio-beam straight in; that's all been arranged. They won't miss."

"And how many of *them* are there—eleven? Is that right?"

"Yes. Not enough to be afraid of, my lord."

Argaven's hands twitched in an unfinished gesture. "I am no longer afraid of you, Mr. Ai."

"I'm glad of that."

"You've served me well."

"But I am not your servant."

"I know it," he said indifferently. He stared at the fire, chewing the inside of his lip.

"My ansible transmitter is in the hands of the Sarf in Mishnory, presumably. However, when the ship comes down it will have an ansible aboard. I will have thenceforth, if acceptable to you, the position of Envoy Plenipotentiary of the Ekumen, and will be empowered to discuss, and sign, a treaty of alliance with Karhide. All this can be confirmed with Hain and the various Stabilities by ansible."

"Very well."

I said no more, for he was not giving me his whole attention. He moved a log in the fire with his boot-toe, so that a few red sparks crackled up from it. "Why the devil did he cheat me?" he demanded in his high strident voice, and for the first time looked straight at me.

"Who?" I said, sending back his stare.

"Estraven."

"He saw to it that you didn't cheat yourself. He got me out of sight when you began to favor a faction unfriendly to me. He brought me back to you when my return would in itself persuade you to receive the Mission of the Ekumen, and the credit for it."

"Why did he never say anything about this larger ship to me?"

"Because he didn't know about it: I never spoke to anyone of it until I went to Orgoreyn."

"And a fine lot you chose to blab to there, you two. He tried to get the Orgota to receive your Mission. He was working with their Open Traders all along. You'll tell me that was not betrayal?"

"It was not. He knew that, whichever nation first made alliance with the Ekumen, the other would follow soon: as it will: as Sith and Perunter and the Archipelago will also follow, until you find unity. He loved his country very dearly, sir, but he did not serve it, or you. He served the master I serve."

"The Ekumen?" said Argaven, startled.

"No. Mankind."

As I spoke I did not know if what I said was true. True in part; an aspect of the truth. It would be no less true to say that Estraven's acts had risen out of pure personal loyalty, a sense of responsibility and friendship towards one single human being, myself. Nor would that be the whole truth.

The king made no reply. His somber, pouched, furrowed face was turned again to the fire.

"Why did you call to this ship of yours before you notified me of your return to Karhide?"

"To force your hand, sir. A message to you would also have reached Lord Tibe, who might have handed me over to the Orgota. Or had me shot. As he had my friend shot."

The king said nothing.

"My own survival doesn't matter all that much, but I have and had then a duty towards Gethen and the Ekumen, a task to fulfill. I signaled the ship first, to ensure myself some chance of fulfilling it. That was Estraven's counsel, and it was right."

"Well, it was not wrong. At any rate they'll land here; we shall be the first. . . . And they're all like you, eh? All perverts, always in kemmer? A queer lot to vie for the honor of receiving. . . . Tell Lord Gorchern, the chamberlain, how they expect to be received. See to it that there's no offense or omission. They'll be lodged in the Palace, wherever you think suitable. I wish to show them honor. You've done me a couple of good turns, Mr. Ai. Made liars of the Commensals, and then fools."

"And presently allies, my lord."

"I know!" he said shrilly. "But Karhide first—Karhide first!"

I nodded.

After some silence, he said, "How was it, that pull across the Ice?"

"Not easy."

"Estraven would be a good man to pull with, on a crazy trek like that. He was tough as iron. And never lost his temper. I'm sorry he's dead."

I found no reply.

"I'll receive your . . . countrymen in audience tomorrow afternoon at Second Hour. Is there more needs saying now?"

"My lord, will you revoke the Order of Exile on Estraven, to clear his name?"

"Not yet, Mr. Ai. Don't rush it. Anything more?"

"No more."

"Go on, then."

Even I betrayed him. I had said I would not bring the ship down till his banishment was ended, his name cleared. I could not throw away what he had died for, by insisting on the condition. It would not bring him out of this exile.

The rest of that day went in arranging with Lord Gorchern and others for the reception and lodging of the ship's company. At Second Hour we set out by powersledge to Athten Fen, about thirty miles northeast of Erhenrang. The landing site was at the near edge of the great desolate region, a peat-marsh too boggy to be farmed or settled, and now in mid-Irrem a flat frozen waste many feet deep in snow. The radio beacon had been functioning all day, and they had received confirmation signals from the ship.

On the screens, coming in, the crew must have seen the terminator lying clear across the Great Continent along the border, from Guthen Bay to the Gulf of Charisune, and the peaks of the Kargav still in sunlight, a chain of stars; for it was twilight when we, looking up, saw the one star descending.

She came down in a roar and glory, and steam went roaring up white as her stabilizers went down in the great lake of water and mud created by the retro; down underneath the bog there was permafrost like granite, and she came to rest balanced neatly, and sat cooling over the quickly refreezing lake, a great, delicate fish balanced on its tail, dark silver in the twilight of Winter.

Beside me Faxe of Otherhord spoke for the first time since the sound and splendor of the ship's descent. "I'm glad I have lived to see this," he said. So Estraven had said when he looked at the Ice, at death; so he should have said this night. To get away from the bitter regret that beset me I started to walk forward over the snow towards the ship. She was frosted already by the interhull coolants, and as I approached the high port slid open and the exitway was extruded, a graceful curve down onto the ice. The first off was Lang Heo Hew, unchanged, of course, precisely as I had last seen her, three years ago in my life and a couple of weeks in hers. She looked at me, and at Faxe, and at the others of the escort who had followed me, and stopped at the foot of the ramp. She said solemnly in Karhidish, "I have come in friendship." To her eyes we were all aliens. I let Faxe greet her first.

He indicated me to her, and she came and took my right hand in the fashion of my people, looking into my face. "Oh, Genly," she said, "I didn't know you!" It was strange to hear a woman's voice, after so long. The others came out of the ship, on my advice: evidence of any mistrust at this point would humiliate the Karhidish escort, impugning their shifgrethor. Out they came, and met the Karhiders with a beautiful curtsey. But they all looked strange to me, men and women, well as I knew them. Their voices sounded strange: too deep, too shrill. They were like a troupe of great, strange animals, of two different species; great apes with intelligent eyes, all of them in rut, in kemmer. . . . They took my hand, touched me, held me.

I managed to keep myself in control, and to tell Heo Hew and Tulier what they most urgently needed to know about the situation they had entered, during the sledge-ride back to Erhenrang. When we got to the Palace, however, I had to get to my room at once.

The physician from Sassinoth came in. His quiet voice and his face, a young, serious face, not a man's face and not a woman's, a human face, these were a relief to me, familiar, right. . . . But he said, after ordering me to get to bed and dosing me with some mild tranquilizer, "I've seen your fellow-Envoys. This is a marvelous thing, the coming of men from the stars. And in my lifetime!"

There again was the delight, the courage, that is most admirable in the Karhidish spirit—and in the human spirit—and though I could not share it with him, to deny it would be a detestable act. I said, without sincerity, but with absolute truth, "It is a marvelous thing indeed for them as well, the coming to a new world, a new mankind."

At the end of that spring, late in Tuwa when the Thaw-floods were going down and travel was possible again, I took a vacation from my little Embassy in Erhenrang, and went east. My people were spread out by now all over the planet. Since we had been authorized to use the aircars, Heo Hew and three others had taken one and flown over to Sith and the Archipelago, nations of the Sea Hemisphere, which I had entirely neglected. Others were in Orgoreyn, and two, reluctant, in Perunter, where the Thaws do not even begin until Tuwa and everything refreezes (they say) a week later. Tulier and Ke'sta were getting on very well in Erhenrang, and could handle what might come up. Nothing was urgent. After all, a ship setting out at once from the closest of Winter's new allies could not arrive before seventeen years, planetary time, had passed. It is a marginal world, on the edge. Out beyond it towards the South Orion Arm no world has been found where men live. And it is a long way back from Winter to the prime worlds of the Ekumen, the hearth-worlds of our race: fifty years to Hain-Davenant, a man's lifetime to Earth. No hurry.

I crossed the Kargav, this time on lower passes, on a road that winds along above the coast of the southern sea. I paid a visit to the first village I had stayed in, when the fishermen brought me in from Horden Island three years ago; the folk of that Hearth received me, now as then, without the least surprise. I spent a week in the big port city Thather at the mouth of the River Ench, and then in early summer started on foot into Kerm Land.

I walked east and south into the steep harsh country full of crags and green hills and great rivers and lonely houses, till I came to Icefoot Lake. From the lakeshore looking up southward at the hills I saw a light I knew: the blink, the white suffusion of the sky, the glare of the glacier lying high beyond. The Ice was there.

Estre was a very old place. Its Hearth and outbuildings were all of gray stone cut from the steep mountainside to which it clung. It was bleak, full of the sound of wind.

I knocked and the door was opened. I said, "I ask the hospitality of the Domain. I was a friend of Therem of Estre."

The one who opened to me, a slight, grave-looking fellow of nineteen or twenty, accepted my words in silence and silently admitted me to the Hearth. He took me to the wash-house, the tiring-rooms, the great kitchen, and when he had seen to it that the stranger was clean, clothed, and fed, he left me to myself in a bedroom that looked down out of deep slit-windows over the gray lake and the gray thore-forests that lie between Estre and Stok. It was a bleak land, a bleak house. Fire roared in the deep hearth, giving as always more warmth for the eye and spirit than for the flesh, for the stone floor and walls, the wind outside blowing down off the mountains and the Ice, drank up most of the heat of the flames. But I did not feel the cold as I used to, my first two years on Winter; I had lived long in a cold land, now.

In an hour or so the boy (he had a girl's quick delicacy in his looks and movements, but no girl could keep so grim a silence as he did) came to tell me that the Lord of Estre would receive me if it pleased me to come. I followed him downstairs, through long corridors where some kind of game of hide-and-seek was going on. Children shot by us, darted around us, little ones shrieking with excitement, adolescents slipping like shadows from door to door, hands over their mouths to keep laughter still. One fat little thing of five or six caromed into my legs, then plunged and grabbed my escort's hand for protection. "Sorve!" he squeaked, staring up wide-eyed at me all the time, "Sorve, I'm going to hide in the brewery—!" Off he went like a round pebble from a sling. The young man Sorve, not at all discomposed, led me on and brought me into the Inner Hearth to the Lord of Estre.

Esvans Harth rem ir Estraven was an old man, past seventy, crippled by an arthritic disease of the hips. He sat erect in a rolling-chair by the fire. His face was broad, much blunted and worn down by time, like a rock in a torrent: a calm face, terribly calm.

"You are the Envoy, Genry Ai?"

"I am."

He looked at me, and I at him. Therem had been the son, child of the flesh, of this old lord. Therem the younger son; Arek the elder, that brother whose voice he had heard in mine bespeaking him; both dead now. I could not see anything of my friend in that worn, calm, hard old face that met my gaze. I found nothing there but the certainty, the sure fact of Therem's death.

I had come on a fool's errand to Estre, hoping for solace. There was no solace; and why should a pilgrimage to the place of my friend's childhood make any difference, fill any absence, soothe any remorse? Nothing could be changed now. My coming to Estre had, however, another purpose, and this I could accomplish.

"I was with your son in the months before his death. I was with him when he died. I've brought you the journals he kept. And if there's anything I can tell you of those days—"

No particular expression showed on the old man's face. That calmness was not to be altered. But the young one with a sudden movement came out of the shadows into the light between the window and the fire, a bleak uneasy light, and he spoke harshly: "In Erhenrang they still call him Estraven the Traitor."

The old lord looked at the boy, then at me.

"This is Sorve Harth," he said, "heir of Estre, my son's son."

There is no ban on incest there, I knew it well enough. Only the strangeness of it, to me a Terran, and the strangeness of seeing the flash of my friend's spirit in this grim, fierce, provincial boy, made me dumb for a while. When I spoke my voice was unsteady. "The king will recant. Therem was no traitor. What does it matter what fools call him?"

The old lord nodded slowly, smoothly. "It matters," he said.

"You crossed the Gobrin Ice together," Sorve demanded, "you and he?"

"We did."

"I should like to hear that tale, my Lord Envoy," said old Esvans, very calm. But the boy, Therem's son, said stammering, "Will you tell us how he died?—Will you tell us about the other worlds out among the stars—the other kinds of men, the other lives?"

THE
GETHENIAN CALENDAR
AND CLOCK

THE YEAR

Gethen's period of revolution is 8401 Terran Standard Hours, or .96 of the Terran Standard Year.

The period of rotation is 23.08 Terran Standard Hours: the Gethenian year contains 364 days.

In Karhide/Orgoreyn years are not numbered consecutively from a base year forward to the present; the base year is the current year. Every New Year's Day (Getheny Thern) the year just past becomes the year "one-ago," and every past date is increased by one. The future is similarly counted, next year being the year "one-to-come," until it in turn becomes the Year One.

The inconvenience of this system in record-keeping is palliated by various devices, for instance reference to well-known events, reigns of kings, dynasties, local lords, etc. The Yomeshta count in 144-year cycles for the Birth of Mesthe (2022 years-ago, in Ekumenical Year 1492), and keep ritual celebrations every twelfth year, but this system is strictly cultic and is not officially employed even by the government of Orgoreyn, which sponsors the Yomesh religion.

THE MONTH

The period of revolution of Gethen's moon is 26 Gethenian days; the rotation is captured, so that the moon presents the same face to the planet always. There are 14 months in the year, and as solar and lunar calendars concur so closely that adjustment is required only about once in 200 years, the days of the month are invariable, as are the days of the phases of the moon. The Karhidish names of the months:

WINTER:

1. Thern
2. Thanern
3. Nimmer
4. Anner

SUMMER:

8. Osme
9. Ockre
10. Kus
11. Hakanna

SPRING:

5. Irrem
6. Moth
7. Tuwa

AUTUMN:

12. Gor
13. Susmy
14. Grende

The 26-day month is divided into two *halfmonths* of 13 days.

THE DAY

The day (23.08 T.S.H.) is divided into 10 hours (see next page); being invariable, the days of the month are generally referred to by name, like our days of the week, not by number. (Many of the names refer to the phase of the moon, *e.g.* Getheny, "darkness," Arhad, "first crescent," etc. The prefix *od-* used in the second halfmonth is a reversive, giving a contrary meaning, so that Odgetheny might be translated as "undarkness.") The Karhidish names of the days of the month:

1.	Getheny	14.	Odgetheny
2.	Sordny	15.	Odsordny
3.	Eps	16.	Odeps
4.	Arhad	17.	Odarhad
5.	Netherhad	18.	Onnetherhad
6.	Streth	19.	Odstreth
7.	Berny	20.	Obberny
8.	Orny	21.	Odorny
9.	Harhahad	22.	Odharhahad
10.	Guyrny	23.	Odguyrny
11.	Yrny	24.	Odyrny
12.	Posthe	25.	Opposthe
13.	Tormenbod	26.	Ottormenbod

THE HOUR

The decimal clock used in all Gethenian cultures converts as follows, very roughly, to the Terran double-twelve-hour clock. (Note: This is a mere guide to the time of day implied by a Gethenian "Hour"; the complexities of an exact conversion, given the fact that the Gethenian day contains only 23.08 Terran Standard Hours, are irrelevant to my purpose.):

First Hour	*noon to 2:30 p.m.*
Second Hour	*2:30 to 5:00 p.m.*
Third Hour	*5:00 to 7:00 p.m.*
Fourth Hour	*7:00 to 9:30 p.m.*
Fifth Hour	*9:30 to midnight*
Sixth Hour	*midnight to 2:30 a.m.*
Seventh Hour	*2:30 to 5:00 a.m.*
Eighth Hour	*5:00 to 7:00 a.m.*
Ninth Hour	*7:00 to 9:30 a.m.*
Tenth Hour	*9:30 to noon*

AFTERWORD

BY CHARLIE JANE ANDERS

When I first read *The Left Hand of Darkness*, it struck me as a guidebook to a place that I desperately wanted to visit but had never known how to reach. This novel showed me a reality where storytelling could help me question the ideas about gender and sexuality that had been handed down to all of us, take-it-or-leave-it style, from childhood. But also, Ursula K. Le Guin's classic novel felt like an invitation to a different kind of storytelling, one based on understanding the inner workings of societies as well as individual people.

Of course, *The Left Hand of Darkness* is literally a guidebook to the fictional world of Gethen, also known as Winter. This book takes the form of a travelogue, roaming around the nations of Karhide and Orgoreyn. And by the time you finish reading, you might actually feel like you've been to these places, to the point where you kind of know what their food tastes like and how the people act. But for me, and for a lot of other people, *The Left Hand of Darkness* also left us with a piece of map that leads to another way of telling stories.

I've read *The Left Hand of Darkness* a few times, and each time I come away with a new piece of that map. Le Guin's writing still surprises me every time I read it. In particular, I'm startled over and over by all the strange details and beautiful quirks that she packs into her descriptions of her made-up world.

I'm also startled by the warmth and generosity of *The Left Hand of Darkness*, considering how bleak and brutal the actual story is. Somehow, in the midst of a horrifying ordeal, Le Guin finds an incredible sweetness.

Genly Ai faces many challenges in his mission to the frigid world of Gethen, but the biggest is his struggle to understand a society of people who are gender neutral most of the time, except for once a month when they go into kemmer and become either male or female.

In the hands of an ordinary writer, this "ambisexual" approach to gender would be an interesting "what-if." But Le Guin goes much further, building an entire world that feels so rich and undeniable that kemmer, and everything that goes with it, come to seem like an actual feature of a society that exists. She does this with a million lovely details and a lively, chatty tone, but also by including lots of Gethenian folklore and sayings, which weave together into something that feels bigger than just one novel.

* * *

*T*he *Left Hand of Darkness* was published fifty years ago, but still packs as much power as it did in 1969. Maybe even more so, because now more than ever we need its core story of two people learning to understand each other in spite of cultural barriers and sexual stereotypes.

Genly Ai doesn't trust his main ally on Gethen, a native named Therem Harth rem ir Estraven, and the two of them keep failing to communicate, even as things get worse and worse for both of them. Le Guin captures perfectly the pitfalls of communicating across cultures: the way people talk past each other and pick up on meanings that the other person didn't intend.

Genly and Estraven's shared journey is what gives this book its emotional arc, and also that brightness in spite of all the misery in the actual story. The novel's title comes from a Gethenian proverb about light and dark existing together, which Genly relates back to the yin-yang symbol of Daoism. And it's really true that the darker the events in this book turn, the brighter its spark of hope and friendship becomes.

Even beyond the uplifting story of Genly and Estraven building a friendship, this book is suffused with an optimism that feels especially brave in 2019. We're never given cause to doubt that the Ekumen is an enlightened society. Or that everyone can make the rough, messy journey from ignorance to awareness. Or that sharing knowledge among different cultures will lead to the advancement of science. Or that spirituality and scientific curiosity can go hand in hand.

While Genly Ai spends the novel learning to see past his own prejudices, Estraven's story is all about just how far someone will go to create a better future for their people. All of Estraven's sacrifices are driven by his determination to bring progress and enlightenment to Gethen.

But the highest praise I can give *The Left Hand of Darkness* is that Le Guin captures some of the texture of life. This book is full of little moments, bits of sensation and emotion that show what it feels like to be alive, day after day. Something about the kindness and curiosity in her voice gives substance to all the breadapples and roast blackfish and hot showers and frozen trucks in this book: all the little pleasures and discomforts, the endless struggle and occasional relief of living.

And this is especially true during the long sequence where Genly and Estraven trek across the Gobrin Ice, the frozen waste to the north of Orgoreyn and Karhide. Every inch of their journey is beautifully described, with phrases like "mincing along like a cat on eggshells," and "cinders patter, falling with the snow." These little moments of poetry go hand in hand with the unrelenting grind of hauling a sled, pitching a tent, eating gichy-michy.

Le Guin gets a lot of the vivid details of an ice journey from the first-hand accounts of Antarctic explorers that she studied. Two of her previous novels, *Rocannon's World* and *City of Illusions*, also include lengthy sequences in which the hero travels across a frozen wasteland along with one companion—but in both those books, the trek feels somewhat sketched-in. Here, she packs in so much indelible imagery that you feel like you're risking frostbite right alongside Genly.

Le Guin never lets go of that connection to the low-level stuff, the tiny physical details and emotional shifts that make up so much of our awareness of the world. And that makes the book, in turn, feel brilliantly alive. I think that's a big part of why this story feels so hopeful and heartfelt, even at its most dismal.

Becoming so immersed in a society without men and women can be a liberating experience for those of us who still live in a world of labels.

The biggest lie that society tells us about gender is that the identities we're assigned at birth are "natural," and that anyone who flouts the boy-girl industrial complex is a pervert. Which is the same thing that the Gethenians believe about their mostly gender-free existence—even down to calling people who have a fixed gender identity "perverts."

A huge part of the value of a science fiction story like *The Left Hand of Darkness* is that it allows you to imagine that things could be very different. And then, when you come back to the "real" world, you bring with you that sense that we can choose our own reality, and the world is ours to reshape.

Gethen's vastly different genderscape feels real enough

that it casts a reflection on all the fixed ideas in our own world. Maybe our rigid gender binary is just as made-up as their neutral-except-once-a-month gender is. Maybe our government-issued pronouns and official stereotypes don't have to define us always. Especially for my fellow trans and nonbinary people, a story that undermines the assumptions behind coercive labels feels magical.

When Le Guin wrote this novel, there were plenty of trans people around, but most people only knew about a handful of famous examples, like Christine Jorgensen or Michael Dillon. Nonbinary people didn't have a widely accepted gender-neutral pronoun (even though some people did use "they" colloquially for this purpose). There was a hugely popular and controversial musical called *Hair*, trading on the shock value of men having long hair!

The Left Hand of Darkness draws on a tradition in science fiction of questioning gender norms, the same way science fiction questions everything else. There have been many novels and stories about all-female or female-dominated societies, going back to 1905's *Sultana's Dream* by Rokeya Sakhawat Hossain and 1915's *Herland* by Charlotte Perkins Gilman. And in 1960, Theodore Sturgeon had published *Venus Plus X*, in which the descendants of humanity have become non-gendered, with both male and female reproductive organs (and two uteruses per person).

But what makes Gethen's ambisexual world so striking and memorable is the care Le Guin takes to show how the existence of kemmer changes every other part of the society. We read folktales about star-crossed kemmering, hear about the public kemmerhouses where people can mate freely, and also learn that people must live in big enough communities that there are enough possible pairings for people who are kemmering.

Unresolved sexual tension is a huge motif in *The Left Hand of Darkness*—it can be a source of power and human closeness. It can also lead to despair. When we witness the foretellers of the Handdara answering Genly Ai's question, in the book's strangest and most delirious scene, a big part of the process turns out to involve a Pervert (someone who's always male) and one foreteller who happens to be in kemmer. But elsewhere in the book, we witness attempted seductions and unrequited longing, torment and frustration.

In many ways, *The Left Hand of Darkness* disrupts gender as well as it ever did. But there are some issues, too. Le Guin chooses to use "he" as a gender-neutral pronoun for the Gethenians, which undercuts the idea that they're supposed to be neither male nor female. Even when the book was brand-new, many feminists complained about this pronoun choice, and Le Guin later wrote that she "couldn't help but feel that justice was on their side." In 1975, when Le Guin reprinted a short story that takes place on Gethen called "Winter's King," she changed all the pronouns from "he" to "she." But she felt that "they" was too confusing as a gender-neutral pronoun.

At the same time, some feminists, including *The Female Man* author Joanna Russ, complained about the fact that we never see child-rearing or other stereotypically female pursuits in this novel, even though every Gethenian is potentially a mother as well as a father. Le Guin made up for this, years later, by writing another short story about Gethenian domestic life, "Coming of Age in Karhide."

Le Guin's thought experiment about gender is still rooted in essentialism. Everything about the Gethenians' gender identities is driven by their biology, and even the Perverts are different only because of a biological happenstance. Even as this book drives you to question all of our assumptions about male and female bodies, it never raises any questions about how gender shapes us independently of our biological sex (the way a lot of science fiction has, in the decades since). If anything, *The Left Hand of Darkness* reaffirms the idea that biology always determines your gender and sexuality.

But these weaknesses in the book's approach to gender are also strengths—because they help us to understand what's wrong with the book's severely flawed narrator, Genly Ai.

Genly Ai is a misogynist. This becomes more apparent to me every time I reread *The Left Hand of Darkness*, and it's the main reason why Genly is bad at his job.

Le Guin makes this very apparent early on in the book, and keeps giving us little hints thereafter. Anytime Genly notices any traits that he considers feminine in the Gethenians, he's disgusted. Especially when he talks to Estraven, who's actually trying to open up to him, Genly sees these attempts to communicate as "womanly" and thus lacking in substance. The only person in the book who gets a female job title is Genly's "landlady," who's mocked for her overly feminine "prying" and for having a fat ass.

Even King Argaven, who comes across as high-strung and paranoid, is described as having a shrill laugh. (*Shrill* is one of those words that's always used to describe women who speak up too much.)

Much later in the novel, Genly informs Estraven that in the Ekumen, women seldom seem to become mathematicians, composers of music, inventors, or abstract thinkers. "But it isn't that they're stupid," Genly adds, digging himself in deeper. (He doesn't include "science fiction writers" in that list, but in 1969, most people would have. That same year, Le Guin herself was forced to use the byline U. K. Le Guin for a story published in *Playboy*, so readers wouldn't know that she was a woman.)

It's not just that Genly Ai is incapable of seeing Estraven as both man and woman—it's that any hint of femaleness revolts him, especially in people who are supposed to be powerful. Genly can't respect anyone whom he sees as having female qualities, and thus he recoils from Estraven, the one person who tries to be real with him. And Genly's character arc is about getting over his hang-ups about women and his macho pride, every bit as much as learning to understand his friend.

It's fascinating, and very realistic, that Genly Ai is an

enlightened representative of an advanced, harmonious culture—while also being a deeply messed-up individual who cannot see past his own limited ideas about gender and sexuality. He's curious and open-minded about everything, except for the huge areas where his mind has been long since closed. He doesn't even glimpse all the things that his privilege has allowed him to avoid looking at.

In this context, the use of the male pronoun for the Gethenians feels like an extension of Genly Ai's own issues. And his slow progress towards opening his mind is part of one of the main overarching preoccupations of *The Left Hand of Darkness*: the attainment of wisdom.

The Left Hand of Darkness is full of those beautiful observations of snow and food and daily life, as well as stories and sayings and little touches that illuminate the societies of Karhide and Orgoreyn. But another reason this novel shines so brilliantly is all of the philosophical and mystical dialogues that are embedded within it.

So many of the discussions in this book are endlessly quotable, like the explanation of why "to oppose something is to maintain it."

You can't separate the politics of this novel from its spirituality. People are constantly grappling with big questions about what makes a group of people into a nation, and the meaning of patriotism, alongside discussions of the balance of light and darkness (borrowed liberally from Daoism) and Gethenian cultural concepts like *shifgrethor*.

Gethen is a world without war—which may be due to its harsh climate, or to its lack of men—but it's also just beginning to develop the concept of the nation-state. Orgoreyn, with its oppressive bureaucracy and lethal secret police, is closer to nationhood than Karhide, but a territorial dispute is pushing both countries closer to patriotic fervor. (And we're reminded, over and over, that patriotism is based on fear more than love.)

Part of what Genly Ai offers to the people of Gethen is the hope that they could leapfrog over this drive toward nationalism, by joining the Ekumen and becoming one unified world among many.

One of the most striking moments in the story comes early on, when Genly shows King Argaven his ansible (a device that can communicate instantaneously across the galaxy). For a moment this petty ruler of one kingdom is connected to a huge cosmic backdrop. And of course, their attempt to communicate is largely a failure. The Ekumen remains in the background, something we glimpse in the distance even as the story stays small and local. (And the story of a "more civilized" person visiting a less advanced society manages to be less problematic than it could have been, because Genly tries to learn from the Gethenians, and doesn't bring more people or technology to them until they are ready to receive it.)

And the Ekumen is just one of the things in the book that we glimpse, which feels important but too big to see clearly. The nature of prophecy in this book is the same way—we visit the foretellers and see them at work, but we don't really understand how it works, and the future remains huge and unknowable even after they speak. And of course, when prophecy falters, it's always due to communication failure, because someone asked the wrong question or misunderstood the answer.

Also tantalizing: the story of Meshe, who was a Weaver in a foretelling where someone asked for the meaning of life, and it all went horribly wrong. Afterward, Meshe became a mystical figure who could see all of time, who still has worshippers over two thousand years later.

The Gethenian concept of *shifgrethor*, too, feels huge and difficult to understand, even after we get an explanation. It's got elements of status, or prestige, but it's more than that, and our best hints about it come from some of those fables that are sprinkled throughout the text, including the story of Getheren of Shath. This, along with other linguistic concepts like the untranslatable *nusuth*, feels like a nod to the famous Sapir-Whorf hypothesis that language shapes the way we think. (Edward Sapir, who helped develop that theory, worked with Le Guin's father, anthropologist Alfred Kroeber, and also helped translate for Ishi, the lone survivor of the Yahi tribe whom Kroeber befriended and studied.)

So this book is full of contrasts between the intimate, human-sized world, and the unseeable hugeness in the distance. (Much like the enormity of the Gobrin Ice, with the Esherhoth Crags looming on the horizon.) In fact, you could almost say that the people in this novel are operating in the shadows of these massive background objects, in keeping with this book's preoccupation with shadows.

The Left Hand of Darkness surprises me again, every time I reread it. There are so many wonderful ideas and stark emotional moments, and Le Guin's language always startles with its sheer power and wonder. And every detail in the book has little stories embedded inside it, and these stories keep intersecting and building on each other every time I revisit them—until you start to realize that everything is made of stories. As Genly Ai says on the very first page, "Truth is a matter of the imagination."

Gender, sex, romance, desire, power, nationalism, oppression . . . they're all just stories we tell ourselves. And we can tell different stories if we choose.

Ready to find
your next great read?

Let us help.

Visit prh.com/nextread

Penguin
Random
House